SIBERIAN LIGHT

ROBIN WHITE

Delacorte  Press

Published by
Delacorte Press
Bantam Doubleday Dell Publishing Group, Inc.
1540 Broadway
New York, New York 10036

Library of Congress Cataloging in Publication Data

White, Robin A.
Siberian light / by Robin A. White.
p.   cm.
ISBN 0-385-31688-7
I. Title.
PS3573.H47476S56   1997
813'.54—dc 20   96-38243
CIP

Manufactured in the United States of America
Published simultaneously in Canada

September 1997

10 9 8 7 6 5 4 3 2 1

BVG

To Anna, Sasha, Viktor, and Yelena, for giving names and faces to an unknown land; to Lisa, for everything else.

The line separating good and evil passes not through states nor between political parties either, but straight through the human heart.

—Alexander Solzhenitsyn

Hope is a species of happiness, and perhaps the chief happiness which this world affords.

—Samuel Johnson

Markovo, Irkutsk Oblast

CHAPTER
1

IT'S THE NIGHT of April twenty-eighth and the temperature
hovers near the freezing mark. In Moscow it might as well be
summer, but seven time zones to the east it's the first warm
night of the year. Icicles weep, crack, and fall into heaps of wet
snow. A flickering aurora drapes a web of violent energy over
Markovo, casting cold light across dark streets.

Markovo emerges from its winter armor slowly, like a developing photograph; first the walls, next the roofs, the streets.
Finally the tangle of water, steam, and sewer pipes that run
exposed along the sidewalks appear like artifacts from a lost
civilization. The buildings hold the heat of the day, but it's
colder down by the river.

The *Mat Lena,* the Mother Lena, flows through town between high concrete embankments. It rises in the ring of
mountains that surround Lake Baikal. Its mouth opens to the
Arctic. Tonight, the ice that has stood so firm and reliable since
last September is breaking. Tonight it's a heaving sludge of ice
under fog, where air blurs to water, liquid to solid, where solids
dissolve and the sky shifts in patterns of light and dark.

A mustard-yellow militia jeep sputtered and fumed as it sat
parked in front of Medical Sobering Facility #3. It was a *bobyk,*
or terrier. Its engine gagged on a rough blend of gasoline and
unrefined by-products. Dawn was still an hour and a half away.

Inside the jeep, Militiaman Gorits waited for his partner to return. Gorits had once been a sergeant in the town militia. He'd also been a notorious drunk. In a town where everyone drinks, notoriety was an achievement, but that was not the entire story.

For months, his fellow officers had treated him like someone with an incurable disease, not for his drinking, not for his Chechen last name though that hardly helped. Gorits had committed an offense that was at once more subtle and less excusable: Gorits had fallen.

When the Ministerial Anticorruption Task Force swept into Markovo following the shooting death of the militia's commanding general, Gorits had answered their questions eagerly and, worst of all, with a fair degree of honesty. For this he was demoted from the rank of sergeant, appointed the rescuer of drunks, sent to the muddy bottom of the midnight shift. Honesty was his flaw, his disease. It marked him as someone to be careful around because in Russia, sinking is more contagious than even cholera.

The jeep's radio crackled in lockstep to the aurora overhead, blizzarding transmissions with static. Gorits didn't mind. In the silent moments that filled the midnight shift, he found time to wonder that a magnetic hurricane on the sun was giving him a night of peace here on earth.

With his link to the dispatcher rendered unreliable, Gorits couldn't know about gang wars, about bar fights, about burglars shot by Markovo's increasingly well-armed citizenry. Just pliant drunks freezing to death on wet snow.

He looked up at the sound of a door slamming. His partner lumbered in his direction, a bottle in hand. He was short and overweight. His shoes sank in the snow, emerging like breaching whales, all spume and ice water. The car door squealed open and he got in. The jeep listed, an overloaded dinghy. He held the bottle up and said, "For later."

Gorits shook his head. "You keep it."

"What are you now, some kind of monk?" His eyebrows bridged solidly across his brow.

"Not yet. But I'm thinking about it."

The two could have been brothers in their matching sheepskin coats and *ushanka* caps, two boulders sitting shoulder to shoulder, steaming white breath against cold glass. They even shared the first name of Alexander.

But inside their sweaty coats, Gorits was as thin and dark as his partner was fat and blond. His hair was a cap of black Chechen knots, his partner's the wheat-yellow of a pure Slav. Gorits wore polished boots and he carried a Makarov 9mm. His partner's shoes were smashed to ovals and, except for a flashlight, he was unarmed.

Gorits clutched into gear and made for the river. Much of Markovo's informal commerce took place in the alleys that fringed it; a district of brick communal flats and empty warehouses known as the Black Lung.

In summer, soot-belching diesel barges came south from the inland port city of Yakutsk loaded with food, medicines, fuel, the occasional Japanese automobile. Their exhaust coated the embankments, the walls, giving the Black Lung its name. The barges returned with unprocessed lumber, asbestos boards, and bales of *anasha,* locally grown marijuana. In winter trucks used the thick river ice for a highway. In spring Markovo's only connection with the outside world was by helicopter and plane. In bad weather Markovo was not merely isolated; it was removed to a different planet.

Whatever the season, the embankments were a popular place to drink. That also made them a popular place to die. Through some unexplained force, drunks were drawn down to the swift water. In winter they would freeze to it. In summer they would drown. But now with spring so near, they would stumble out and find themselves suddenly surrounded by veins of oozing black water, marooned on platters of spinning ice. The Lena took them north to where the ravens, the magpies, would find them and pick them to the bone.

Markovo once was uniformly gray. A river town, a way station for trappers and loggers under the czars, a small moon orbiting the Planet Stalin under the gulag. Then oil was discov-

ered at Tunguska a hundred kilometers north. Not just a scent
of petroleum, a trickle, but what was known as an "elephant"
field.

The elephant brought Markovo's thirty-eight thousand citi-
zens a television station, a daily newspaper, a vodka distillery, a
modern clinic. A big metallurgical mill was built to run off
mazut, the thickest, filthiest sort of fuel oil no overseas buyer
would bother with. The mill swallowed raw silicate ores and
spewed out pressed asbestos sheets and drifts of fibrous gray
waste. There was even a condom factory that produced thick,
durable products built to survive whole seasons of love.

People worked. Paychecks were honored. Bread trucks made
their rounds. Squint, and Markovo looked prosperous. Squint
harder and it even looked fair.

Now with the empire dead, poverty and wealth were no
longer illegal. Markovo had better districts and worse. An
American company was trying to revive the Tunguska oil fields.
Their dollars had fertilized parts of Markovo. The town divided
into two, into four, into eight. Poverty increased in direct pro-
portion to the distance from the old Intourist Hotel, renamed
the Siber. The Lena was a kind of economic demilitarized
zone: one side rich with dollars, the other with envy. In between, swelling and collapsing in parallel with the town's for-
tunes, the Black Lung.

The militia patrol drove by a silver oil derrick that stood
behind a chain-link fence. A monument to the hero workers
who had opened up Tunguska, it had been faithfully painted
each year for May Day. Now, after five years of neglect, it wept
dull brown rust.

The jeep turned a corner and slowed. In the headlights, a
figure emerged from an alley and danced across the street, half
walking, half skating. The spotlight came on in time to catch a
bottle flying at the jeep in a glittering arc, tumbling end for
end. It struck a fender and shattered.

They skidded to a stop. Gorits grabbed his truncheon. "See
who has room." He got out and tasted the soft wetness in the

air, as feminine and seductive as deep cold was blunt and masculine. The drunk had lost his shoes.

Hair wild and with his shirt undone, the man held a hand up against the spotlight. He didn't try to run away. It was a well-rehearsed routine with a beginning, a middle, an end. "Where's Jesus? Where is that bastard? I want him *now*."

Gorits cautiously approached, slapping his nightstick against the palm of his hand. Leather-wrapped truncheons had been part of an economic development grant from the United States. They were called *demokratizers*. The empire was lost, the old rules demolished, but who said humor was dead?

"I want Jesus!"

"Scream all you want. It's healthy." Gorits walked up close enough to smell the vodka. He hadn't touched liquor in a month, but he still had a finely calibrated nose. One whiff and he knew it was dirt-cheap German stuff. A distillery right here in Markovo, and German vodka was still cheaper. Like the aurora overhead, like the line that divided businessmen from thieves, it was one more mystery. "So where are your shoes?"

When the drunk looked down, Gorits pushed with his truncheon and the man toppled to the snow. He dragged him back to the jeep, leaving two bloody grooves. Ice had shredded the drunk's feet, not that he could feel it.

"I made contact," his partner said proudly. There was spittle on the microphone as though he'd given it a tentative lick. "Number Two has a cell."

"Wonderful. Give me a hand."

Together, they maneuvered the drunk into position at the back of the jeep. The hatch was open and ready.

Medical Sobering Facility #2 was in the nice part of town across the river. Close to the Hotel Siber, the wide plaza still called the Square of the Soviets, the mayor's office, and the old KGB building. Land of restaurants with food, stores with goods, where foreign oil businessmen stayed, where dollar whores slept warm and *mafiya*s ruled.

They tossed the drunk like cordwood into the back and slammed the hatch shut. The *bobyk* had a simple box bolted to its frame. The cage had no windows, one lockable door, its skin reinforced by heavy wire mesh. The door was pounded once, twice, then went silent.

The jeep belched oil smoke as they drove away. Good motor fuel was getting hard to find. Here was another mystery: the Tunguska oil fields once supplied a large fraction of the Soviet Union's petroleum. A new pipeline made from good Japanese steel went right through town on its way south to the refineries at Irkutsk, intended for the anticipated tons of Siberian Light Sweet crude lifted by the American joint-venture company, AmerRus.

So far it managed to pump trickles, not tons, and good gasoline could be found only with the right connections or hard currency, which in any event were one and the same. True, the militia could requisition fuel from the refinery. They could also roll the forms into a bottle and throw them in the Lena. The result would be the same.

The big criminals, the ones called *vory v zakone*—thieves in law—used their dollars to buy gasoline directly from the refinery. It came north in barges in the summer, tanker trucks in winter, even by the drum in helicopters. The *vory*'s black BMWs, their Jeep Cherokees, never went hungry for petrol. *Mafiya* lieutenants, the *brodyagi,* resold what was left on the black market. They hired young men known as *byki:* pit bulls. The bulls kept the wheels of commerce rolling. The militia had to ambush the *vory* tank trucks and confiscate the fuel to keep their patrols on the street.

It was a dangerous game. The police had *demokratizers* and pistols; the *mafiya*s had Glocks and Uzis. The head of the Markovo militia, an ambitious general named Skhurat, had been killed on just such an ambush. The reports called Skhurat a hero in the war against crime. The whispers said he'd been betrayed by his own men who, after all, had families to feed. A new general was due up from Irkutsk to take command. So far there was no sign of him.

As the little jeep rattled in the direction of the river, the hiss and crackle of the radio resolved into a squeal, the squeal into

the garbled voice of the dispatcher. Gorits picked up the microphone. "Angara Three." Their radio call sign. "Repeat."

The speaker crashed with static, all pounding surf and
swirling elemental particles.

". . . Three, report . . . dog . . . howling . . . without . . . muzzle . . . bit two . . ." a longer break, a flare of
pale red light from the sky, then a surge of noise. ". . . the
owner . . ." The signal dissolved as the sky shimmered pink.

"Who is he? The owner?"

The seas calmed, the particles cooperated. "Ryzkhov, A. V.
. . . Number Eight . . . Rossinka . . . an Alsatian . . ."
The signal dissolved. ". . . Three?"

Both officers looked at each other.

"Andrei Valentinovich?" his partner said with a reverential
whisper.

Gorits picked up the microphone. "Angara Three, on our
way." He flipped the blue flasher on and turned toward Rossinka, the fancy, western-designed town house complex across
the river.

Andrei Valentinovich Ryzkhov was well known to the
whole town, to all of the wild frontier that was Siberia. Son of a
Moscow bigshot from the old days, Ryzkhov was a *biznisman,*
one of the new breed, and aside from the gangsters, or perhaps
because of them, he was one of the richest men in all Irkutsk
Oblast.

Andrei Ryzkhov was an arranger, an interpreter. For a foreign business seeking to tap Siberia's considerable natural
wealth, Ryzkhov was insurance against misstep in a landscape
studded with bureaucratic mines. He was well paid for his inside knowledge. His pockets overflowed with dollars. His piss
was golden. Stand close and some could splash the way of two
militiamen.

Gorits pressed the gas pedal to the floor. With a cough and a
surge, the jeep picked up speed. Crossing the old bridge spanning the Lena, they could feel it shudder as prisms of ice splintered around the footings. The scenery changed quickly on the
far side.

Don't misunderstand. The good part of Markovo isn't New York. It isn't even Mombasa. But there was a hotel with hot water all year, a few cafes, and in the stores, all carefully shuttered, there were goods worth buying and stealing. A few lights still burned at this hour. The little Armenian cafe was open, hard currency only. A Cherokee sat parked in front, its engine idling. A sign buzzed above the entrance: THE ALAMO. Men in leather coats lounged in the pool of light.

Its blue strobe flashing, the jeep shot through the streets like a lit-up pinball through a blacked-out maze. In the back, through the thin metal divider, the drunk moaned, cursed, and retched.

They entered the big open Square of the Soviets, clattered by the old KGB building, next the town offices, under the old billboard that proclaimed *Mui Stroyem Kommunism!,* by the brightly lit Hotel Siber. The jeep plunged into a road that narrowed once, and again. The road became a street, the street became an alley, the alley ended at an iron security fence. The gate was open. A nicely lettered sign arched overhead. ROSSINKA. A guard booth stood next to it. The blue flasher glittered against dark glass. Overhead the heavens sizzled with energy. The booth was empty.

The town houses would be unremarkable anywhere but here. Two-story boxes, each with a garage in back, a fancy arched door in front with a glazed transom above. They were arrayed around a circular drive. The entire complex was surrounded by three-meter-tall iron fencing. Building materials lay buried by drifts of snow at one end next to an unfinished row of units.

A legal dispute between the American contractor and the Russian landowners had halted the project. The Americans claimed they were underpaid. The Russians disagreed. The case was mired in court where it would likely stay forever.

Gorits switched off the blue flasher as he pulled up to Number Eight. Ryzkhov's flat. The windows upstairs pulsed with a blue glow. "Spotlight."

"I don't hear any howling." His partner switched on the

rooftop light and swiveled the beam onto the front door of Ryzkhov's town house, nervously hunting for the unmuzzled dog. "I hope he isn't hungry."

"Ryzkhov's dog eats better than you."

Tire tracks scored the snow. Not from some rattletrap Moskvitch or a Lada. No, at Rossinka, at least a Volvo. Security grates. Lightbulbs in the fixtures. Puffs of steam rising from chimneys. Gorits took it all in. Things worked. There was money here. You didn't need a nose to smell it.

"What kind of dog?"

"An Alsatian," said Gorits. "Eighty kilos. Teeth this big." He held two fingers far apart.

"That's a wolf. You're sure? Eighty kilos?"

Gorits left the spotlight centered on the front door to Number Eight. He reached into his tunic and pulled out the Makarov automatic. "Plus nine grams." The weight of a bullet. "Bring your light and remember, don't grab. Wait for an offer."

The town hadn't paid them their regular salary in over a month, though the mayor had arranged for them to receive credit at the local shops. A contribution of, say, twenty dollars equaled their pay for one week and was infinitely more spendable. Honor was one thing. Hunger something else.

They got out and slogged through wet snow up to the front door of Number Eight. The northern horizon frosted white, the sun's warm breath on a windowpane of sky.

His partner swept the flashlight over the ground. "It *is* a wolf."

The snow by the front door was a moonscape of pawmarks. Big ones. Alsatians were guard dogs, and sometimes they were trained to attack without warning, without sound. They listened. There was no howling, but something else: rock music. Heavy bass notes played loud enough to travel through the insulated walls, the triple-pane windows, the steel door.

The spotlight made their shadows huge as they walked to the door. Gorits pressed the bell button. The music upstairs thumped. He waited, then flipped the Makarov and used its grip as a knocker. Once, twice, three times, spaced carefully between the beats of the music. Then, in the time-honored manner known to policemen everywhere, he called out.

"Militia! Open the door!"

The music continued to throb. He tried the doorknob. It turned. He pushed it partly open. The door came to a soft stop. The *bobyk*'s spotlight flooded in.

A paw.

They both leaped backward. The pistol swung level with the door, finger around the spit-curl trigger.

The paw didn't move.

Still aiming the Makarov, Gorits walked forward and gave the door a push. The music was very loud now. The blue flicker from upstairs filled the stairwell. The door swung against something heavy, something soft.

Something dead.

"Mother of God."

The entry vestibule was awash in blood. A black Alsatian lay sprawled just inside the front door. The animal's throat had been cut, just below the jawline. White tissue feathered out from the wound, already puckering. Its pointed ears were flat against a massive, wedge-shaped skull.

The blood trail went upstairs.

Gorits ignored the short corridor leading back to the garage and pounded up the stairs two at a time. At the top, he found a light switch.

The aquarium glow of an enormous television became lost in the warm yellow of a sparkling chandelier. A computer sat with its cursor symbol endlessly flashing on a screen filled with gibberish. Data disks lay scattered on the floor, bent, crushed.

"Fuck. Look at—"

"Don't touch anything!" Gorits commanded.

The room was one open living space with doors leading to other more private quarters. The walls were white, the floors deep in plush maroon carpet. A kitchen gleamed with Japanese stainless steel. A big refrigerator occupied an arched alcove like an oversized icon. A Toshiba, top of the line.

Gorits held the 9mm in both hands now. He shouted, "Citizen Ryzkhov!" He let the weapon sweep the perimeter of the room, just like in training. Slow, steady.

The music boomed from the television. On the screen, men wearing flapping rags stood under hot lights as women wearing almost nothing slithered on the dance floor like glistening snakes. The stage backdrop was a renaissance Madonna figure cradling an infant devil with spiked horns. Three small glasses stood on a low coffee table, one was full, the other two empty, a bottle of cognac next to them. There was a wall safe behind the television. It was open.

His partner said, "Robbers."

"What thief would leave all this behind?" His own words made the hairs on his neck rise. "Go turn that noise off." The automatic leading the way, Gorits went to a closed door.

A large area of wetness spread across the thick pile carpet. He reached down and when his fingers came back they were red. He turned his attention to a series of photos on the wall beside the bedroom door. Most were black and white. Only one was color. The old ones showed men posing stiffly in that old-fashioned way.

Militiaman Gorits stepped around the blood and tried the knob. Like the front door, it turned easily.

He flattened himself against the photos and threw it open. The music died away. The silence was heavy as velvet draped over his ears. His head was pounding as he stepped in.

A gust of overheated air came out, carrying with it the stink of feces, the dark, coppery smell of blood, and the unmistakable tang of gunpowder. All the bedroom lights were on. He looked for a moment, then backed away. "Sasha."

Militiamen were the guardian angels of drunks, muzzlers of howling dogs. Collectors of bribes, diggers of ditches, and catchers of shit. This was beyond them. "Sasha?" He started to turn.

A hand grabbed a fistful of his black hair and yanked. His neck bones crackled in protest. His mouth opened in surprise. A sting, no more than the draw of a blade of grass across his neck. He spun, off-balance, in time to see silver smeared with red. Reflex jerked his finger. The Makarov boomed. A hole appeared in the far wall.

Falling. Gorits was falling. Sergeant, angel to drunks, his partner an imbecile. Down to this soft red carpet. His head was flat to the floor but still he fell. He choked on blood, heavy and warm. Memories, sights, sounds, and smells. Falling, falling like a meteor against a winter sky. At the end of a long incandescent trail, a white flare, then red, evaporating into the color that conquers all others.

CHAPTER
2

HERE IT COMES. There. Now. Hold it.

Gregori Nowek felt the violin take over and sing with its own voice as the last notes of the Khachaturian adagio radiated from his fingers and melted into the kitchen walls. Water trembled in a glass as he drew the bow. Look up and see Nina's photograph on the wall. Admit it: it wasn't just a picture. It was a shrine.

Half the bow is gone. The E flat note is endless. He's not even sure he's making it. The sound creates itself. It resonates everywhere. It fills his ears. But not his eyes.

The photo. Nina sits surrounded by sunflowers, their radiant heads bowed low with late summer fullness. They seem interested in what she's about to say. She smiles, one hand to sweep back an unruly lock of hair. Nina, his wife, so he ought to know. *Wait! Let me straighten this first!* But there's nothing.

The note nears its end. It's 1997 and Nina's three years dead. Nowek closed his eyes and pressed the violin to his cheek. The polished wood tickles his sparse beard. There. Ready? End it. Now.

The E flat echoed through him for a few seconds and then faded. The adagio from the great *Gayne* ballet had been Nina's favorite short piece. He'd played it well. Not perfectly.

Long ago his teacher cautioned that striving for perfection

was the surest way to kill beauty. In real beauty there is always something wrong. Thus, he used to say to Nowek, it can be proven that life in Russia is more beautiful than any other place.

His father had a different view. He'd said that life is different, but the violin never betrays you. The more you give to it, the more it gives back. He also told Nowek that making your living grinding horsehair on stretched gut demanded an excellent ear and a highly developed sense of the absurd.

It wasn't so different being mayor of Markovo.

As he snapped the velvet-lined case on the instrument, the telephone hanging on the kitchen wall jangled.

He picked it up. *"Ya sluchayu."*

"Grisha!" It was Arkady Volsky, the presidential representative down in Irkutsk. He'd once been a coal miner. He still shouted as though yelling "FIRE IN THE HOLE!" down an open shaft. As Moscow's official watchdog for the state of Irkutsk, a loud voice still came in handy. "I'm interrupting you?"

"No." He looked at his watch. Nearly eight. "Not now. What is it, Arkasha? My driver will be here any second."

"That's good because I need you to go somewhere this morning. You've heard about Andrei Ryzkhov?"

"What about him?"

"He's dead. Murdered. It happened last night. There's still some confusion."

"Over whether he's dead?" *Mafiyas*, thought Nowek.

"Funny. Two of your militia were also killed."

Two more. He didn't have any militia to spare. Finding men willing to work for rubles was hard. Finding men willing to risk their lives for them was impossible. "What happened?"

"I'm working from a very sketchy report. Last night sometime. You can find out yourself when you go."

"Go where?"

"He lived in Rossinka. Understand, with a name like Ryzkhov there will be demands for a thorough investigation. His father was one of Stalin's aides. People still know the name and I mean in Moscow, not Markovo. It can't be dealt with in the conventional manner."

"My two men. Do they also have names?"

"Gorits was one. I don't know the other. Imagine, a *chornye* on the militia," said Volsky. It meant "black," the name used for all Chechens.

Nowek knew Gorits. He had a family with young children.

"You know what they say, scratch a *chornye* and find a thief. Why else would he be at Ryzkhov's flat? Anyway, you can make your own determinations. We want you to take on the investigation. You know why."

"Actually, I don't." Actually, he did. The general of the Markovo militia had been killed in a recent *mafiya* shootout. General Skhurat had never been replaced. "Send me a new general for my militia," said Nowek. "I'll put him to work."

"I can't. That's Gromov's job. All I can give you is a good reason. AMR. Do these letters mean something?"

"AmerRus." The joint venture operation drilling the Tunguska oil fields. "Ryzkhov was connected with them? How?"

"The way a tick is connected with a vein. The Americans are very important to our economy. To Markovo's even more. We can't afford to scare them off. Ryzkhov's murder could have broad effects."

"It's probably a *mafiya* matter."

"Maybe, maybe not. AMR's made a lot of promises to Moscow. I'm speaking now of hard currency promises. We can't allow something like this to get in the way."

"Of course."

"And there's the question of your two men. You'll want this matter resolved for their sakes. You'll want to know the truth, won't you?"

"I'm not so sure."

"Don't play games. You're asking for a bribe?"

"I'm asking for a reason. I don't know Ryzkhov. Just his reputation. He lived in Rossinka. It's expensive. You say he worked with AmerRus?"

"Excellent! You'll keep me informed?"

"Arkasha, there's nothing to inform you about."

"That's where you come in." Volsky hung up.

Nowek stood there as the wood stove clicked, the iron crystals changing from one phase state to another, contracting along their geometric fault planes as the metal cooled.

He hung the phone back up.

Three murders. The *Gayne* adagio had been a good choice for his morning's practice. Tchaikovsky was for life, Mendelssohn for hope, Sibelius for madness, and Elgar for despair. But dark, oriental Khachaturian of the flashing sabers and pounding tempos was made to order when it came to killing.

Andrei Ryzkhov. An entrepreneur. Live by the dollar, die by the dollar. But his two men, that was a different situation entirely. Unless, of course, it wasn't. More than a few of his militia had taken jobs in private security. Jobs that paid. Maybe these two had done it with their uniforms still on. Or tried to. A disagreement over a bribe? Possibly.

He glanced at his watch. Seven-fifty.

Nowek gave a quick, disapproving look at the dead cigarette sitting on the edge of the scarred table. His daughter had already left for school, leaving a dirty coffee cup, a half pack of Yavas, and an American fashion magazine. *Cosmopolitan.* A woman with flaming red hair was on the cover. She wore a scornful expression and some kind of cloth tied over her impossible breasts. The coffee cup had left a ring around the model's head, turning her into a kind of icon, a saint.

Galena. Who was it this time? A visiting official? An American Baptist missionary? An oil worker with cowboy boots? It had to be someone big to make her forget her cigarettes and her *Cosmopolitan.* When had he last seen her without a curl of smoke rising from her slender fingers?

He stuffed the box of Yavas in his pocket and grabbed his jacket. It was a peculiar shade of green that nearly matched his pants. He wore a dark shirt and a darker tie. With the thin beard he'd grown it was almost gangsterish. But then, looking like *mafiya* was protective coloration these days.

He walked to the front door. Passing a small alcove, he gave a quick, guilty look at his set of weights. Dusty. He had plenty of time for exercise, and no interest. The results were evident: the

roll of flab at his waist, his thin arms, the slack way his suit hung
like sails on an airless day.

The weights were from another, better time. Nowek made
them from short lengths of eight-centimeter pipe with massive
oil-well drill bits threaded onto each end. The bits weighed
twenty kilos each and looked like electron photographs of a
worm's mouth; gaping jaw, flared throat, and prominent rasp-
ing teeth, though these teeth were worn badly. Drilling into
Siberia's granite shield up at Samotlor was hell on bits. It had
been the same for the crews.

He stopped at the front hall and looked through the small,
triple-glazed window. Outside, the sun had burned its way
through the white horizon. A steady drip of meltwater came
from the eaves, bright diamonds in the sun. Nowek scored it to
Vivaldi. The *Quattro Stagione*. Springtime. Season of hope?

Maybe three years ago. Illusions were more real back then.

There was a mirror. Nowek faced the glass, squared the padded shoulders of his jacket, and straightened his tie.

Gregori Nowek was as Russian as any Siberian, but he'd
always been called the Pole. He had a thin, intelligent face
framed by brown hair that was cut close to his head all around
except in front; there it spilled over his forehead like water over
a rock. His prominent ears and dark blue eyes belonged on
different faces. Without the beard he looked twenty. With it he
looked ridiculous.

The muscles he'd built as a geologist at Samotlor had melted
away. He pulled the knot of his tie tighter. The dark shirt
belled out around his chest. He wasn't losing weight so much as
evaporating.

A few years back he wouldn't have been caught dead wearing a tie. Nobody cared what a geologist looked like. At
Samotlor, the only men who wore them were troublemakers
fresh off the morning flight from Moscow. But Nowek was no
longer a petroleum geologist. He was no longer a great many
things. He was no longer a rising young violin soloist from the
wilds of Siberia. He was no longer married; an Aeroflot crash
had seen to that. When his birthday arrived with the summer

solstice, he'd no longer be thirty-seven. It was a downward trend, true, but with points for consistency.

He began to jot down instructions for his housecleaner, leaning on the mineral display case that stood by the front door. Two days from today his father would celebrate his seventy-fifth birthday. Three quarters of a century; a ridiculously long life, but then, musicians tended to linger.

Unlike entrepreneurs. Unlike officers of the Markovo militia. Unlike mayors.

A wall clock, an old windup model his father had brought back from a concert tour of occupied Austria, softly ticked away the time.

Could Volsky just order him to lead a criminal investigation? Probably. And probably not. It all depended on the time of day, the phase of the moon, and who picked the telephone up in Moscow, in Irkutsk. There was no such thing as law in Russia. Law was merely the jumping-off point for further negotiations. Especially here.

Irkutsk was an autonomous province as big as all of western Europe. It was more than just a state and not yet a country. Its governor was more than a governor and not yet a czar. He was a virtual president ruling a virtual nation. He had a sheriff in the form of Chief Prosecutor Nikolai Gromov who was anything but virtual. Gromov patrolled the borders of the governor's preserve to make sure nothing was taken, nothing touched, nothing so much as moved without his lord's approval.

Against all of this was Arkady Volsky, the man Moscow appointed to watch far-off Irkutsk; to stop anything that might harm Moscow's interests, any redirection of taxes, license fees, or "facilitating payments" from overseas investors. What the world knew better as a bribe. Volsky was one of those jolly men who smiled, as the saying went, with "iron teeth." Not even the governor and his henchman Gromov could quite afford to ignore him.

Volsky and the governor. Could one exist without the other? Together with the elected *Duma,* they pretended to run Irkutsk. On a rare day, they might speak to each other. Usually they issued contradictory decrees, lobbing laws at each other from dug-in trenches like mortar shells. It was a deeply political system that was all politics and no system.

The scratchy beep of a car horn sounded from the street. Two impatient jabs. Outside, a stark white Toyota Land Cruiser sat idling.

He checked the thermostat by his front door. A Korean company had given an electric heating system to Nowek as a "demonstration." It worked very well, too well. At full power it reliably blacked out the neighborhood.

Andrei Ryzkhov and two of his militiamen. No. Too cumbersome. Better the Ryzkhov Murders, as though it might be a famous case written up in a legal text. Nowek knew it wouldn't. Who would care that it was open season on the police in a small town in the middle of nowhere? In Siberia, death had always been the one commodity that met its quota.

Still, Gorits, his partner, and Ryzkhov. Three men from different universes. A rich, well-connected businessman. A militia officer with a Chechen last name, a partner who didn't even have that much. One somebody and two nobodies. Somehow their universes had connected, collided, ended. Why?

He buttoned his green jacket, opened the front door, and breathed in the crisp morning air. Spring was not his favorite season. The mud rose in a sucking tide to cover everything. Forgotten things that stayed buried under the snow became visible. The slow tumble to fall, to elegy, to deep bowing strings and minor keys, notes flying like red and golden leaves, that was Nowek's time. In between there were only mosquitos so dense it took an act of will to go out.

The white Land Cruiser fumed in a cloud of steam and cigarette smoke.

Gregori Nowek. The Pole. His great-grandfather Wojzek had helped plot the Warsaw revolt against Russian rule in 1863. The czar returned the favor by packing the entire district onto cattle trains that rolled east until the tracks ran out. There, beyond the Urals, with Europe at their backs and wild, forested country ahead, they were marched to exile and forgotten.

The unlucky Nowek cut trees until the frost took him, but not before he'd fathered a son, Sergei. Sergei begat Tadeus, Nowek's father. Tadeus was a concert soloist in the old manner. He was also a builder of achingly sweet, fragile violins. They were always coming apart.

The glue was inferior, the wood not dried long enough in the kiln, or too long. It was always something. Nowek's father never found anything to his liking. Especially his son.

The Toyota driver saw him standing there in the doorway and leaned on the horn button in earnest. An impatient puff of smoke rose from the driver's window.

Nowek ducked under the dripping icicles.

The white Land Cruiser was a gift from a Japanese trade delegation hoping to swap cars for timber, especially the valuable Korean pine that carpeted much of Irkutsk. Barely a year old, the Toyota looked like the survivor of some great tank battle fought in mud.

Cars had arrived late in Markovo. The first two went, naturally, to district Party men. That was how the system worked. The next day, the only two passenger vehicles in a thousand square kilometers collided head-on. That too was how the system worked.

He opened the passenger's door and out spilled a dense, poisonous cloud of incinerated tobacco. He took a last clean breath and got in.

"We're stopping off at . . ."

"Rossinka?" Chuchin grinned from behind a pair of obsidian black sunglasses. "Good morning, Mr. Mayor."

"How did you know?"

"I do my job. Remember when I ask for a raise."

Nowek scowled at the cigarette dangling from his driver's lip. A *papirosa*. A cardboard tube stuffed with the very worst kind of tobacco. "Keep smoking. You'll spend your raise on a hospital bed."

"I'm an honest Russian," said Chuchin. "I'm too poor to be sick."

Chuchin's face was leathery and lined. He wore sunglasses whenever the light was stronger than dusk or dawn. It wasn't an affectation; he'd developed severe light sensitivity from his time in the camps. When he took them off you saw a hint of a fold at the corners of his eyes: not all of Chuchin's genes had been marched to Siberia. His face was European enough to show he was up to something, but Asian enough to keep you guessing what it was.

Chuchin had survived two "ten ruble notes"—twenty years—in the camps. He wore an old padded jacket, heavy gloves, and insulated boots. Like the dark glasses, it was another artifact; once the cold got into you, not even the second warm day of spring could make it go. He would turn sixty this year.

"I'm not even sure they'll let me into Rossinka," said Chuchin. "It's too fancy for me. Only thieves can live there. I have a reliable method for determining honesty, Mayor."

"Oh?"

"If the house is more than one story, there're thieves inside." He eyed Nowek's stubble disapprovingly. "You lost your razor this morning?"

"I thought a beard would help me look more trustworthy."

"It makes you look more like a gangster."

"You see? I was right." Nowek sat back. "It's getting late. Don't you think we'd better go?"

"No." Chuchin put the car in gear, took another drag, then spoke between a jet of foul smoke. "You should smoke. Then people would trust you more."

Nowek tried to avoid breathing. "Smoking is slow suicide. Here." He gave him his daughter's box of Yavas. "Your coffin will smell better."

"I don't worry about coffins." Chuchin slipped out a virgin Yava and snuffed out the stub he'd been smoking with a hiss of a wet thumb. He pocketed the box in a flash of reflex born in the camps. "Science has proven that everyone dies of some-thing."

They left the dead-end street and turned onto a slightly larger road. The sun dazzled from banks of rotting snow.

Everyone dies of something, thought the Pole. The lucky die their own deaths. But some, like Ryzkhov, like Gorits, like his Nina, were not so lucky.

"Though when it comes to dying," Chuchin said with a shrug, "some people are in a big rush."

Chuchin had been his driver since the election, some three years now, and he knew enough to sit back and wait for the inevitable. "I'm listening."

"A man finds his wife screwing someone, he kills them both." Chuchin shifted up. "You find out someone has written an *anonymka* denouncing you, you cut the little shit and feed his heart to the pigs. These things make sense." He held the Yava between two yellow-stained fingers and waved it under Nowek's nose. "But suicide? Suicide makes no sense."

"Gorits didn't commit suicide. From what I hear neither did Ryzkhov."

"I'm talking about you."

So that was it. "Someone killed two of my officers. Three if you add General Skhurat. I can't pretend it didn't happen. It's my job."

"Your officers? You hardly even pay them. Anyway, Skhurat thought that arresting *mafiya*s was his job. Those two farm boys with shit between their toes thought Ryzkhov's business was their job, too. Where did it get them?"

Dead. But there was no reason to say so. Ice water splashed in over the doorsill. Soon, mushrooms would sprout from the carpet. He looked at his face in the cracked rearview mirror and scowled. "Anyway, someone has to be in charge until they send us another militia general."

"Pah. Someone. Why you?"

"To enhance my popularity with the voters."

Chuchin swung his head and saw Nowek's expression. "Go ahead and make jokes. The truth is, you won't get reelected next year if you start raising the dead."

"Chuchin."

The Land Cruiser nosed down an empty street, headed for Rossinka.

"It's true. It was one thing to be poor when you were building something." Chuchin waved the Yava like a baton. "It's another thing to be poor so that some rich thief can get richer." Puff, another cloud, a long exhale. "Everything used to be shit. Now it's also insulting. Who's in charge?"

"No one is in charge."

"No, Mr. Mayor," said Chuchin. "You are."

Was he? Not really. And in any event, not for long. Next year there would be an election. Then what? Russia had become a shadowland. A caricature, a heap of wreckage suitable only for scavengers and thieves. Capitalism had arrived wrapped in hope and glory. It hadn't come to save Russia, but to finish it off.

There was a nascent market, but no laws to govern it. An elected parliament, but made up of the same old Party hacks. There were prominent rich and the desperate poor, and only fools or foreigners paid taxes. Government intrusion was the norm. So was secrecy. Decrees were signed but not published. Decisions were shrouded in rumor. You could buy a cellular phone on any street corner, but a phone book? Utter fantasy.

Russia was a place where ownership meant nothing, control everything, and everything, absolutely everything, was up for grabs.

"Say what you will." Chuchin spat a ring of smoke that curled over and over on itself before smashing into the windshield. "It took these democrats just three years to do what the Party couldn't manage in eighty."

"I know. To 'make Russians love communism.'"

Another drag, another ring of smoke folding, twisting, bursting. "Everything is different, but *kto kogo* is still the only theory that matters." It meant, who beats whom?

"Maybe it's time for some new theories."

Chuchin brightened. "Actually, I have one. I call it the bald and hairy view."

When he turned to face Nowek, the Pole saw two perfect reflections in his sunglasses. "Bald and hairy?"

"Think, Mayor. Lenin was bald as a potato. Who took over when he died?"

"Stalin."

"Hairy as a hedgerow. And afterward?"

"Khrushchev."

"Another cannonball. Brezhnev was furry as an ape and even his wife said he was almost as smart. Then Mikhail Sergeivich with his beauty mark and his big ideas. Where was his hair? On poor, pickled Yeltsin. Now some general rides in on a white horse and expects us to sweep up the shit."

He meant General Lebed, the former paratrooper out to recast himself as savior of the nation, a new Pinochet, a new Franco, wrapped in the flag like a birthday present to the motherland. "Lebed's hair is thick."

"You've never heard of a wig?"

Nowek watched the empty streets go by. The water pipes, steam lines, and power cables were emerging from the snow. The accumulated trash, the broken glass, the garbage, the bodies, would soon appear. "Snow flowers" was the slang expression for all things buried by winter and revealed in spring. Ryzkhov and his two officers had just sprouted a little early. "What am I going to miss this morning?"

"An American at nine-thirty. He wants to save tigers. If they had them running loose in New York, would they want to save them?"

In Russia, environmentalists swarmed like mayflies and missionaries. They wanted to protect the taiga, to keep Baikal pure, to save the Amur tigers, the snow cranes. They brought all kinds of fancy gear and none of them had so much as a dollar or an ampule of vaccine. "What else?"

"A housing dispute. Someone bought up the vouchers for an apartment building. Now he's trying to evict the tenants."

"A ventilator." It was the label for an entrepreneur who took money and delivered air.

"Also, the director of the district heating system wants to shut down early this year to save oil."

"You mean he wants to sell what's left to the black market."

Chuchin regarded the comment as too naive to warrant a reply. "Excuse me, but these murders." Another pull on the glowing cigarette, another cloud of smoke. "Fucking Rossinka. Thieves killing thieves. Is that even a crime?"

"It takes a genius to know what's against the law, Chuchin."

"In the old days, one step out of line and the hammer came down. A little of that wouldn't be so bad."

"True, but there's a problem."

"What?"

"It never stops with just a little."

They drove into the wide Square of the Soviets. A huge billboard atop the old KGB building announced MORE TUN-GUSKA OIL FOR THE MOTHERLAND! The red letters were faded to a dusty pink. There was talk of turning it into a history museum, as if tourists might pay money to view showcased dioramas of all the old horrors. For now the building remained locked. A history museum, thought Nowek, closed for rewrit-ing.

Another sign, bright and fresh, sat atop the Hotel Siber. Its message had been changed to fit the times: it once read FOR LENIN: LIVE! WORK! FIGHT! Now the bright letters proclaimed VSEGDA COCA-COLA! Always Coca-Cola.

"A rich businessman murdered," Chuchin muttered, but loud enough to be sure Nowek heard. "What else can it be but the *mafiya*? What do you think they'll do to you? Hang a medal from your ears?"

"Relax. I'm just the mayor. The *mafiya's* dangerous only when they take you seriously."

Chuchin whistled. "Over by the Intourist." He insisted on calling the hotel by its old name. "The meat market is open for business."

A line of girls stood outside the Siber's lobby, a palisade of dark-stockinged legs, heavy coats, and high heels teetering in snow. A guard stood between them and the heated lobby, his own long coat concealing more than just his torso.

A ripple went through the line as Nowek's car approached. One of the girls leaped out of line and ran to the front. The guard blocked her. She slammed against his chest. He fended her off. He seemed to find it amusing.

Nowek saw something in those legs, those flailing arms, the dark hair. Something. "Stop."

The Land Cruiser skidded on a patch of wet ice and came to a halt. Nowek rolled down his window. "Hey!"

The guard looked up. The girl took the opportunity to rear back and kick a sharp toe into his shin.

Mayor or no, this was no longer amusing. He threw a punch to her breast, hard enough to hurt, hard enough to show he was now serious. It knocked her back. She slipped out of her heels and fell.

Nowek threw open the door and shouted again.

The girls all turned. The guard had a cut-barrel shotgun out, pointing down at the one who'd fallen.

"Mayor! Don't!"

But Nowek wasn't listening. He ran to the front of the line, slipping and sliding in the wet snow. Inside the lobby, people watched, amused at the show. "It's all right! Put the gun away! Put it down!"

The shotgun swiveled a few degrees.

The fallen girl sat crying, legs sprawled out, a naked toe poked through a hole in her ruined stockings. One shoe in her hand, the other half-buried in slush. She looked up, her mascara smudged.

He tried to help her up, but she wouldn't take his hand. "Galena."

"Leave me alone!" His daughter put her shoes back on with as much dignity as she could muster and stood, wobbly with fright and shock from the guard's blow. Her coat fell open to reveal a thin black dress cut low enough to show a red bruise.

"Are you all right?"

Her expression hardened. "Sure. Don't I look all right?" She brushed loose snow off her coat. "Just leave, okay? You're ruining everything."

"I won't just leave. What are you doing here?" said Nowek. She was all of sixteen. He noticed a smudge of lipstick on her cheek. Sixteen! "You should be at school. What is this, career day? A class trip to the whorehouse?"

"They're my friends, and who are you to ask anyway?" Her chin was set, determined, but her teeth chattered. Dark hair the color of sable, blue eyes like Baikal, his own eyes, so clear and pure you could toss a coin and see it tumble a hundred meters down. "They're interviewing and we wanted to be first. You're such an expert. Is that against the law?"

"Law?" He paused. "Who's interviewing?"

"Fucking Chinese," muttered Chuchin. He'd come up behind them both. He glared at the guard from behind his dark glasses. It was amazing how threatening he could look, especially with a short silver barrel extending from his fist. The ancient Nagant pistol compensated for its age by firing a very big bullet. It didn't hurt that Chuchin looked crazy enough to pull the trigger. The shotgun wavered, then disappeared under the guard's coat.

She pursed her lips at Chuchin, then flipped a dark bang away from her face. "I'm going to be a hostess and make lots of money in Hong Kong. But I have to get into the interview first." She turned and glared at the guard. "Tell that ape who you are. Maybe he'll let me in."

"When did Hong Kong come up? What about the university next year?"

"The university costs. The Chinese pay." She rebuttoned her coat.

"Bez compleksov," muttered Chuchin. Without inhibitions. It was a code word used in advertisements to advise the applicant that services of a more intimate nature would be required. The old Nagant pistol was out of sight now.

"So what?" she said with a casual shrug. "Working in Hong Kong is better than living in this dump. You think I should try to be a belly dancer in Cairo instead? At least the Chinese have real money."

Dump? Markovo? "I can't believe you would come here for this. Your mother—"

"Is dead. I would have gone with her but I've never been lucky."

It was as if a bright light had suddenly gone out. Black. He stood there, not knowing what to say. He'd seen her turn into a woman in the last few years. A beauty. And what for? So that she could sit in some Chinaman's lap? So she could feed him drinks while . . . he grabbed a fistful of her heavy coat and yanked her toward the Land Cruiser. "You aren't going anywhere. We're going to talk about this privately."

"No we aren't." She twisted away. "Leave me alone. I'm staying here with my friends. Go play politics and pretend you're doing something useful. In case you didn't know, I'm no politician. I have to work for a living."

They faced each other, glaring.

Pretend you're doing something useful? "You can't go anywhere unless I sign the papers."

"Oh, really?" She had that insolent look she knew would drive her father crazy. "Thank you for that information."

"Your grandfather's coming to dinner in two days. He's waited seventy-five years for this. You can't wait a week?"

"He's your father, not mine." She walked back to the line of watching girls, pulling her ripped stockings around so the tear wouldn't be so obvious.

"Galena!"

Chuchin put his hand on his shoulder. "Mr. Mayor?" he said. "Talk to her later. Away from her friends. She'll be more sensible then. And now that everyone knows who her father is, they won't hire her. Trust me."

Nowek blinked again. What was it like to live in Russia after the collapse? After three years of his term as mayor? He thought of the day Nina told him she was pregnant. They weren't married yet but so what? They had most of what mattered, and with Galena, everything. He thought of her then, and now.

Galena's made-up face, the smudged lipstick, her bright eyes, her legs. She was slender, girlishly so, not the starved, ravenous look a Russian woman gets when she diets to stay slim. He saw her as the Hong Kong businessmen would see her.

He saw Markovo as she saw it, too.

"Let's go. There's still Rossinka." Chuchin led Nowek back to the Land Cruiser and stuffed him inside.

The car moved away from the hotel. "When Galena thinks something up, nothing can stop her. Not sense, not logic."

Chuchin nodded. "She's impulsive?"

"Very."

"Determined? Not always so logical? Even when it's dangerous?"

"That's her."

"Well," said Chuchin. "Think. Who is her father?"

The morning was caving in around him. The phone call. The dark Khachaturian piece invading his soul. Now this. "What have we created? Do you ever ask yourself that?"

"Never."

"I mean, we threw out the bastards, didn't we?"

"Not far enough," said Chuchin.

Not far enough. Sometimes it seemed to Nowek that he was riding an enormous barge down a swift river with a very small rudder under his command. Turn it left with all your strength, turn it right, the barge went where it wanted. The rocks loom. There is no way to avoid them, to avoid making the same old mistakes. History wasn't the dialectical science of people plus politics, of Marxism plus electrification. History was hydraulics.

Chuchin took a narrow side street made even slimmer by piles of wet snow plowed to each side.

"You know so much," said Nowek. "What do you know about Ryzkhov?"

"He was a *biznisman*." Chuchin's tone was the same as a man might use to describe a child molester. "A real *demokrad*." The word had grown two meanings: the first was obvious. The second was *thief*. "You know how much it costs to live at Rossinka? Two thousand a month. And that's not rubles, either. How does a man have so much money?"

"Making money isn't against the law anymore."

"Maybe it should be." He turned onto a slightly wider road. "Just look around." Chuchin lit another Yava from Galena's box. "The foreigners think we're Africans with rockets. You know? They trade us beads and we hand them our balls. They should remember, one phone call and those rockets can still fly."

"The phones aren't very reliable. Count on two calls," said Nowek. "What do you know about Ryzkhov's business?"

But Chuchin was not to be deterred. "One million rich shits and a hundred and fifty million in chains. You want the truth? It's worse than under Stalin. With Stalin, at least you knew where you stood."

"Absolutely. Bring back the Party. In the camps everyone farted through silk."

Chuchin snorted. "Fucking Stalin," he said. He hated the communists as much as Nowek, and he had better personal reasons for it, too. But the taste of Stalin's name in his mouth reminded him of Nowek's question. "Ryzkhov's father must be a hundred. He was Stalin's personal interpreter all during the war. He lives in America. His son is just rich."

"Not anymore. What about his business?"

"Informal banking. Imports. Oil. He was a *tolkach* for AMR."

Tolkach meant arranger, a hustler who knew how to get things. An arranger for AMR. That Ryzkhov was involved with AmerRus wasn't shocking. In Markovo, it was one way to get your hands on dollars and Ryzkhov probably hadn't so much as touched a ruble in years.

AmerRus, thought Nowek. Siberian light oil from Tunguska was where it hoped to win big. The oil was there, oceans of it. The market for crude was exploding in developing China. A billion motorbikes. A new power plant every week. It was money waiting to be made.

On paper, the prospects for AmerRus looked excellent. Why

hadn't they brought Tunguska back by now? The pipeline running through Markovo ran dry most of the time. Had the fields been left in so bad a state? Nowek thought, Yes. Probably.

The Soviets paid their oil workers to drill holes, not to produce oil. So many meters drilled, so many rubles. Not surprisingly, the result was a great many holes. At Tunguska, the natural pressure that forced up the crude was quickly depleted by pincushion drilling, rendering most of the oil unrecoverable without advanced, expensive technologies. Fracture hydraulics. Fire flooding. Tertiary recovery. All these made perfect sense everywhere else in the world. But then, Russia was always a little bit different.

Now this. Andrei Ryzkhov had played some role in the enterprise. But what? Nowek sat back. No wonder Volsky had called. An AmerRus connection. A political complication, as if a killing at Rossinka wasn't already studded with them.

An ambulance suddenly appeared, hurtling in the opposite direction. It nearly sideswiped them as it went by.

Chuchin turned into a short drive, then came to an iron security gate. A guard stepped out of a glass booth and waved them to a stop. "Who are you here to see?"

Chuchin hawked, then spit a gob of saliva a centimeter from the guard's fancy snowboots. "Excuse me, but who are you to ask? This is Mayor Nowek sitting next to me. Open the gate." The guard retreated and hit the gate button. They drove in.

Nowek said, "I wonder how the murderer got by him last night?"

"How? In his limousine."

There were no limousines in sight, but there was a lot of activity in the courtyard. It was filled with yellow militia jeeps and one private car, a white Volvo sedan. One police *bobyk* stood apart from the rest, its doors open. Chuchin stalled the Land Cruiser against a snowbank and parked.

Officers milled around in the sunshine, standing in circles, smoking, talking. A short, stocky man stood at the focus of one of the circles. He wore a glossy brown leather coat, double-breasted, that went below his knees. He wore no hat, and his face was hidden behind dark aviator sunglasses that reflected the low sun in brilliant flashes.

"Fuck," said Chuchin. "You see who's here? The Fisherman."

The Fisherman. Ex-KGB Major Oleg Kaznin, now a private security consultant. As State Security's *rezident* in Markovo, he'd been an expert at infiltrating the budding oil workers' union. Kaznin the Fisherman got his name one spring when the ice-dammed Lena spilled from its bed across a marsh. The water cut a new bank in a forgotten mass grave that wept bodies for months.

The dead were perfectly preserved by the frost, tanned by the acidic soil, hollow as dolls. They floated down the Lena high and light, their faces still young and horribly identifiable. Mothers saw long-dead sons. Husbands found first wives. All frozen in youth, all with the same two trademark holes in the head: one small at the back, one gaping, ragged crater in the front. Kaznin organized the expedition to net the impertinent corpses and return them to the land of the forgotten.

"I better find out what he's up to," said Nowek.

"It's still not too late, you know," said Chuchin. "Call in sick. Play your violin. Tomorrow it's Gromov's worry."

Chief Prosecutor Gromov in Irkutsk would probably want nothing to do with a murder in Markovo, especially one that would remind him that he still had not sent a new general to command the town militia.

"No. I want to see what Kaznin is up to first."

"Nachal' stvu luchshe vidno," said Chuchin. The boss always knows best. He pointed the smoldering cigarette at the ex-KGB man. "Kaznin's a snake. You want help?"

"Don't worry," said Nowek. He composed himself. He was the mayor of Markovo. He was the rule of law, even if there were no rules, no laws, other than those for sale to the highest bidder. "I can handle him."

Chuchin licked his fingers, snuffed out the glowing Yava, and placed it in his jacket pocket for later. "Well," he said, "that's definitely one way to look at it."

CHAPTER
3

THE FISHERMAN was talking loud enough to hear from a distance, loud enough so that his voice echoed from the walls of the fancy town houses. The brilliant red lapel pin of the new Russian Communist Party blazed from his chest; the party that promised fairness and equality not when True Communism arrived, but in time for the next election. It reminded Nowek of an old zoology professor who said that in nature, small, brightly colored, and loud usually meant dangerous.

". . . earned what? Three hundred rubles each month and not only could you live you could save forty. Now you can make *four hundred thousand* and be poor as some African in his mud hut. But that's all going to change. You have my word."

The officers leaned in, listening.

"There's a war coming, comrades. A war of what is right against what is wrong, and in such a war there can be no neutral parties. They say that Communists want to destroy everything these democrats have built. I say, what have they built? They've only *destroyed*." Kaznin's eyes flicked to Nowek. "Well, this must really be an important matter to get a politician out of his warm bed." The officers all turned, their red shoulder boards flashing like a flock of blackbirds taking flight. "I didn't expect to see you here, Mayor."

"Life is full of surprises."

Kaznin barked a quick laugh. His scalp peeked through thin strands of brown hair. In his mid-forties, he was a squat cannonball with a bull's neck and thick, wide hands. Fisherman's hands.

"I see you're keeping your hand in politics."

"This?" He fingered the pin proudly. "It's a way of declaring that not everything in the past was so bad. Our history is nothing to be ashamed of. What other history do we have?"

"It's difficult to say. Russian history can be unpredictable."

"Maybe to you, Mayor. But most people are fed up with watching American movies and having an inferiority complex. What we want is to be respected."

"You mean feared. Anyway, your party didn't do so well last time."

"We're patient. History is on our side. You'll see."

"What I see is you. What are you doing here? Isn't it a little early for speeches?"

"I'm not here for politics. That I leave to you." He winked at the gathered militiamen. "I'm here because I have extensive experience in criminal matters. Three men have been murdered." Kaznin puffed himself up a bit. "Crime has never broken through these gates before."

Ah, Rossinka, thought Nowek. Two thousand a month, dollars only. Crime had no need to break in when it was already living here so happily. "I respect the depth of your personal experience when it comes to crime, Major."

Kaznin gave another bark. "Funny. Maybe you'll laugh even harder when you see what's in there." He shook his head with exaggerated sadness. "Since you have asked me a question, I'll return the favor. What brings you out this morning?"

"Two of my officers are dead. Until your friend the prosecutor sends us a new general, I'm responsible for them. I've been asked to take charge."

"Who asked?"

"Irkutsk," said Nowek, deliberately vague. Let Kaznin guess. It might slow him down.

It didn't.

"You mean that Moscow politician Volsky." Kaznin raised his voice to be sure the officers all heard. "Isn't there enough to steal in Moscow? Why do they have to come and interfere in our affairs? Aren't we suffering enough?"

"You don't look like you're suffering." Nowek moved in closer. "And Arkady Volsky was a coal miner from Magadan, not a Moscow politician. But then, as KGB you would know this."

"I'm a retired officer." Retired or not, nobody liked the KGB. Kaznin changed the subject. "Well, no matter. We all must obey Irkutsk. For now, you can learn from my work." Kaznin gently grasped the elbow of one of the militiamen and drew him close. "Question the neighbors. Find out who saw what and when. Cars coming and going. And find the one who phoned in the complaint about the dog. Anyone who resists, take them to a drunk tank, forget them for an hour, then seek their cooperation." He reached into his pocket and withdrew a twenty-dollar bill. "For the one who finds the most."

Nowek watched. Twenty dollars. More than one hundred thousand rubles. A quarter of their monthly salary, if he'd been able to actually pay them their monthly salary. The militia officers sprang to work. "That was very effective."

"Modern methods have their advantages."

"What's modern about bribery?"

Kaznin started to answer, but then he said, "Follow me."

Nowek trailed him toward Number Eight. "How long have you been here?"

"I came immediately. There's no time to waste when it comes to murder. We call it the golden hour. The evidence is still fresh. And no matter how good they think they are, to a trained eye, criminals always leave something."

Unlike a squad of hungry militia officers. They would leave nothing. "What does your trained eye see?"

Kaznin didn't stop or turn. "Angara Three, the militia patrol, responded at four-thirty to a call from a neighbor. Ryzkhov's dog was loose and barking. Unfortunately, the militia showed up before the killers were finished. One of the officers fired his weapon, but his aim was off. When they didn't check back in to the dispatcher, another patrol investigated. Frankly," Kaznin's voice lowered, "they probably thought they were having a good time and wanted to be sure it was spread around."

"Probably."

"The second patrol arrived at five-fifteen and found both officers, the dog, and Ryzkhov. All dead. A real mess."

A real opportunity, given all that a man like Ryzkhov would have in his home. "Was Ryzkhov dead when the first patrol arrived?"

"Grossman's working on it now."

Grossman. The chief of the town clinic had a stubborn, independent streak; it explained why he was in Markovo.

Their feet crunched the rotten snow. Nowek saw the dead dog dragged to one side of Ryzkhov's door. The air had a peculiar feel to it, a damp, undecided chill that penetrated Nowek's light jacket and lodged straight in his ribs like a cough. Ah, spring.

Kaznin suddenly stopped and took hold of Nowek's elbow. He drew him in just as he had the officer, gently, not aggressively, but with no concern that Nowek might find such an act objectionable. There was something minty and antiseptic on the major's breath.

"Think," said Kaznin. "Ryzkhov is no ordinary man. I don't have to tell you he was a symbol, and don't forget the father, the family. Their name still means something in Moscow. To be frank, a murder investigation is no place for amateurs. You could do worse than to give it to a professional. Someone with experience."

"Someone like you?"

"Absolutely." His fingers measured the thinness of Nowek's jacket.

Nowek pulled free. "There's no budget for consultants."

"I'm not looking for pay. It would be a service to my town. What do you think?"

"Very generous," he said. "Let's continue."

Even in death, Nowek could tell that the dog had been

magnificent. Black coat sleek as sable. Heavy muscles and powerful limbs. Plainly well fed. It reminded him of a story a professor at the university had told of his trip to America; they had not just *one* type of dog food available on the shelves, but dozens. Entire *aisles* of them. Naturally, he'd been arrested for spreading anti–Soviet rumors.

Both the incident and the image of ranks of gleaming cans stayed with Nowek as a kind of ultimate indictment against both countries, both systems; one for monumental waste, the other for monumental stupidity.

The blood trail showed that the dog had been dragged out of the vestibule.

"The Alsatian was killed with a knife," said Kaznin, his tone lecturing, bored. "Even the neck bones were scored. The blade was very sharp. Like a pelt knife."

It didn't take an experienced criminal detective to realize this wasn't much of a clue. With wild sable in the taiga forests outside town and good skins bringing a hundred dollars each, every family in Markovo had one member quick with a trap and a blade. "What about my men?"

"Also cut. One worse than the other. They've already gone to the morgue. Believe me, Ryzkhov is bad enough. You wouldn't care to see them."

"What about Ryzkhov?"

"Cut. But fortunately he also was shot."

"What's so fortunate about that?"

"A knife is anonymous," said Kaznin, his tone that of a schoolteacher before a dull classroom. "A gun leaves its fingerprints. You'll see what I mean."

Nowek looked at the dead beast. Ears flat, eyes clouded, throat cut, black fur coated with a crust of stiff, dried blood. What was that in its mouth? Orange peel? He was about to look more closely at its mouth when Kaznin spoke.

"Mayor?"

The vestibule was slippery with half-melted slush swirling with dark maroon. The stairs had seen an army of feet. A geologist pays attention to color first, then texture, and finally the mineralogy. Nowek's eye automatically turned the gritty splotches of tans, browns, and grays into eolian sand, powdered Aldan siltstone, and decomposed Katanga and Nepa granites; what the less experienced, but more economical viewer might call mud. The blood was different.

Blood was everywhere. On the carpets, the walls, even a spray up near the ceiling. As though men were balloons ready to burst at the prick of a needle. Nowek forced his eyes away from it. The killer must have walked out of here looking like a butcher. A door at the back of a short hallway was open to an empty garage. The hallway was filthy with mud. Ryzkhov would have a car. A good one, not that there was anyplace to drive it once the Lena broke free of its ice.

Kaznin read his expression. "A new Japanese sedan was brought in for examination. A neighbor has already filed a claim against it for money Ryzkhov owed him. The matter will be decided on the strength of the documents."

"Good luck." The militia didn't have it for examination, thought Nowek. They had it for sale. Ryzkhov's car would bring a lot on the market.

"You know that Ryzkhov's father is famous," said Kaznin. "He was Stalin's interpreter during the war. Now he's in America writing books. Ryzkhov's wife lives there with him. Vika's her name. She's pretty and smart. Andrei sends them money to live on. The father keeps his eye on her for the son. The brother is with the Foreign Ministry in Moscow. I leave it to you to tell them all what happened. As you said, Volsky has put you in charge."

"I didn't. How do you know so much about the family?"

"Spend a life in intelligence and knowing becomes a habit."

Kaznin had spent a lot of time fishing corpses out of the Lena, too. Burying the past was also a habit. "I understand Ryzkhov worked for AmerRus. What did he do?"

"Andrei's responsibilities were broad." He went to the top of the stairs and paused. He gazed down at Nowek. His dark glasses were still on. "Remember. You asked to see this."

Nowek joined him at the top.

The main room was stripped bare of furnishings except for a low table that held three glasses, some framed photographs on one wall, and a wall safe, its mouth hanging wide open. The computer was gone, and so were all the crumpled disks. A refrigerator stood in the middle of the kitchen, its door hanging wide like the safe's. Two dark stains marred the carpet. One wall had a black circle marking a small hole.

"Well?" said Kaznin. "What do you think?"

"I think the killer must have brought a truck."

"Granted, at first look, it seems like robbery. Your two men walked in on them expecting a barking dog and a bribe, and instead, they fell into a trap. Gorits shoots, but what does he hit?" Kaznin nodded at the marked wall. "But is it simple robbery? I doubt it. The killing," he shook his head, not in distaste but in puzzlement, "the killing was savage, but there were methodical elements to it as well."

Savage and methodical. Nowek couldn't think of two better words to describe Kaznin's former employer, back in the days when methodical murder was another state monopoly. It didn't take much imagination to hear admiration in Kaznin's tone. "You're thinking *mafiya*?"

Kaznin took his dark glasses off. His eyes were small and pinkish. "Ryzkhov was a likely target. But which *mafiya*? And what for? Scare him, hurt him, maybe blow up his car. Kill the dog even. But killing *him* makes no sense. And the other two? Forgive me, but it's cheaper to buy the militia than waste a bullet." Kaznin paused at the bedroom door. "My offer stands. The middle of a lake is not a good place to learn to swim. How's your father?"

"Alive." Nowek's tongue tasted acid. The rooms were very warm, and the blowing air carried the coppery smell of blood. He remembered walking into a dormitory up at the Samotlor oil fields and smelling the same thing. A Buryat work brigade lived there. He found a butchered reindeer hanging upside down in the white-tiled common kitchen, its blood flowing across the floor to a drain.

Black worms tangled and knotted in Nowek's stomach. He

stopped, pretending to look at the photos on the wall. There was Stalin, his eyes like two bullet holes in the print, infinitely deep. Men in uniform flanked him. One face had been erased to a blur. "What happened to him?"

"Maybe too many people looked and the face wore off. It's difficult to say."

Wore off? Kaznin seemed serious. Amazing. He took a fast look at the other photos and nearly turned away when something stopped him. There was one color enlargement: a family shot taken here at Rossinka, the sky looking like dawn or dusk. Nearly dark. The town houses in the background, the father, both sons, and standing between them Ryzkhov's wife, Vika.

"Mayor?"

Only it wasn't Vika. It was Nina. Or someone very much like her. Not the Nina he knew after Galena and after half a life of struggle. But Nina when they had just met at Irkutsk University. Striking. Smart and beautiful. The same long, glossy dark hair pulled back behind her ears. Even the same unruly strand that fell over her smooth forehead and across her left eye. A strong face, high cheekbones and a narrow chin. He looked more closely, drawn to it.

Like Nina, this young woman's face wore the unmistakable mark of intelligence. The eyes were invisible, though, covered by the reflected flash of the camera, turned yellow. Hot eyes. Cat eyes.

He calmed himself. It was Ryzkhov's wife, not his. Vika wasn't mingled with charred aluminum and plastic, bulldozed into a common grave and hastily covered with dirt. Beautiful Vika was in America. A beautiful widow, now. No wonder the father had to keep his eye on her for the son.

"Mayor?"

Nowek took a deep breath and stepped inside the bedroom.

Dr. Grossman leaned over the bloody bed. He was a gaunt, dark-haired man in stained hospital whites. He held up a long hypodermic needle and tapped it. Then, with a quick jab, he slid it deep into the corpse's abdomen, further, further, until the glass cylinder came to a stop at skin. He looked at his watch. At the end of a silent count, Grossman withdrew the needle and examined the glass, then put it down and picked up a pen and clipboard. His hands shook as he tried to write. His feet were clad in disposable paper slippers. Like everything else in the room they were painted in blood.

"Dr. Grossman."

He looked up. "Oh."

Nowek's eyes kept straying back to the bed. A palette of genes, diet, and long dark winters turned Russian skin the color of a fish belly. Not Ryzkhov.

He was ruddy, his chest tanned, even a bit sunburned. The redness grew more pronounced the closer it came to the dark slash in his neck. Beneath the red was a gray pallor. His head was back, mouth open, as though complaining to Grossman about the prick of the needle. One eye was open, the other shut. A sly wink from hell. There was the distinct odor of shit.

"Thank you for coming so quickly."

"Kaznin called."

Grossman had been a surgeon down in Irkutsk. Now he worked as head of the Markovo Polyclinic, doubling as the district medical examiner. He was well liked. In Russia, fallen Jews are more popular than successful ones.

"I finished the other two first. They were simpler. One with his back open to the bone. Butchered. The other just the throat. But Ryzkhov? He's a little different."

Nowek hesitated. He put his hand out onto a chest of drawers. The room seemed to be a kaleidoscope, swirling, shifting in patterns of red on red. Blood everywhere. He looked. It was already on his shoes.

"Forensics is all in the details, Mayor. Come. You can't appreciate them from so far away."

Nowek approached the bed, breathing through his mouth as he came, as though murder were something you might catch like a cold, a virus. The carpet was sodden as bread soaked in meat juice. There were boot marks in it.

"With homicide, identification is our first concern. Here that isn't necessary. Everyone knows Ryzkhov."

"I never met him before."

"You're not meeting him now." Grossman turned to gaze down at the ruddy corpse. "The body presents with four gunshot wounds, one in each elbow, one in each knee. None of them fatal. The deep laceration to the throat was fatal. Ryzkhov suffered an acute hemorrhage, followed by hypovolemic shock, circulatory failure, and finally brain death. Of course, this means absolutely nothing."

Nowek looked up. Nothing? "Excuse me?"

"In the end we all die of oxygen deprivation. Cancer, a knife, a tree falls on our heads, a bullet in the brain. Oxygen deprivation. I could write that as the cause of death on any certificate. You might as well say he drowned."

"Ryzkhov wasn't swimming." Nowek's face flushed hot, cold.

"That's where you're wrong. Let me show you." Grossman pointed with his pen. "The laceration at the neck is profound, well defined, and deep. The tissue is parted, not sawed. See the incision in the platysma?" Grossman touched a sheath of whitish muscle just beneath the flayed skin of Ryzkhov's neck. "The blade was very sharp." He appraised the body with a hint of admiration, as though rating a competitor's work on the operating table.

Nowek looked away. To the ceiling. To the window. The chest of drawers. Fuck Volsky. This was not worth any favor the presidential representative might trade him for. Nothing. Give it to Prosecutor Gromov. To Kaznin. Anyone. Nowek swallowed, then again. "This doesn't affect you?"

"A cancer ward is worse," said Grossman. "They're still alive." He pushed a rigid arm aside. "All the gunshots were fired from very close range. The wounds are surrounded by burns. The gray tattoo, we call it. It's more typical in suicides." He let the arm fall. "The exit wounds are much less dramatic than you'd expect. Kaznin thinks he knows why, so you can ask him. In any event," he looked at his clipboard, "death occurred between two and three o'clock this morning."

Two and three? But the dog was alive, running loose and

howling at four-thirty. That was when a neighbor called to complain about the noise. Both officers had taken some time to arrive. And then they too were murdered. But Ryzkhov was already dead. What were the killers doing all that time? "Are you sure about the time?"

Grossman picked up the hypodermic. The long needle was smudged and dark, crusted with old blood. It wasn't made for injection at all, but rather, the glass cylinder held a thermometer. "Liver temperature. In a stable, indoor environment, it's an infallible indicator. The calculations are simple, actually." Grossman's teeth showed in a self-satisfied smile. They were stained brown by tea.

Nowek forced himself to look at the shattered white flakes of bone, spread out from each kneecap, each elbow, in a circular pattern, bursting up like a white flower through the skin. A naked businessman. A gun thrust against his limbs. The trigger is pulled once, twice, four times. His throat is split to the bone. Why didn't he try to escape? Was he incapacitated already? Drugged? Who would do such a thing?

Grossman used his pen to separate the loose tissue at Ryzkhov's throat. "Look here."

Nowek forced himself. Grossman had the pen stuck *into* Ryzkhov's throat. Two limp tubes, blind worms, emerged from the slit.

"Two carotids in front, two vertebrals in the back. Cut one of them and you're on your way to eternity. Life hangs from a slender rope, Mayor, don't you think? A string, actually."

Nowek nodded, then looked up at the ceiling.

"With both carotids open, blood drains into the esophagus and then to the stomach. The victim literally drowns in his own blood, so you see I was right. From start to end it takes as little as a minute. Maybe two. How long can you hold your breath?"

Nowek looked at him.

"How long can you hold your breath under water? Speaking generally, that was how long the victim lived once the carotids were severed. Gorits was the same, by the way. From ear to ear." Grossman slipped the pen into his jacket pocket. It left a dark smear.

"But you just said it wasn't a quick death."

"Remarkable. You actually pay attention? So few people bother these days. The gunshot wounds bled. Obviously, they occurred while the heart was still beating. The four bullets preceded the wound at the throat. The gunshots were serious, but not primary. They're more designed . . ." he stopped himself and looked out at the doorway. "Designed . . ."

"Designed for what?" Nowek asked.

"They're designed to inflict pain," said Kaznin. "Isn't that what you were going to say, Doctor?"

"Pain. Yes. Most probably so. Whoever they were, they wanted something. As a professional in the area of health, I would have advised Citizen Ryzkhov to give it to them."

Nowek turned away, his head spinning. He looked down. One push, like a slowing top, and everything would empty, everything would spill out. His eye came to rest on a peculiarly decorative design; a black imprint of a boot with a fleur-de-lis tread.

"Mayor? Are you feeling all right?" asked Kaznin.

He bent down. There were more smudged copies of the print all across the carpet. This one was intact. And near the center, where it had fallen from the lugged sole, a stone.

"Do you need some air, Mayor?" asked Kaznin.

"No," said Nowek. He picked up the stone. It was small, a piece of gravel, really. Nothing more than common, granitic gravel. The glaciers had paved much of Siberia with just such rocks. Clean mica faces flashed from its whites and feldspar reds with hints of darker tourmaline.

Common enough. Yet sitting there in the mud, the carpet soaked in Ryzkhov's blood, it seemed very out of place. As far from home as Nowek felt himself. He was about to examine it more closely when he spotted something else.

It was underneath the chest of drawers. Something yellow-white like a rolled-up pair of dirty socks. He pocketed the gravel and bent down.

"Mayor!"

Kaznin rushed in to catch him, but Nowek wasn't falling.

"I'm all right." He reached under the chest and pulled it out. It *was* a bone, thick as his wrist and knobbed at one end. A curious tunnel ran down its length, outside the core of marrow. It was very heavy and smooth. Like a fossil. Unlike a fossil, it exuded a rank, animal odor.

Grossman saw what he was holding. "The dog's?"

Nowek nodded. A bone like this would be a fitting toy for a rich man's dog. Forget the Alsatian. People would stand in line at the butcher's shop to put it in their soup, smell and all.

"I'll have the preliminary report ready this afternoon," said Grossman. "But I can tell you now the same knife cut both officers and Ryzkhov."

Nowek looked up from the unmarked bone in his hand. "Kaznin said a knife was anonymous. How can you tell?"

"I used to be a surgeon at Irkutsk Main Surgical Facility. I can still recognize the hand behind the cut."

Nowek's face was hot, his armpits cold. He needed fresh air. He walked out through the doorway. He forced himself not to look at the picture of Ryzkhov's wife. He didn't stop until he was at the head of the stairway. A cold breeze flowed up from the open front door.

"Well?" said Kaznin. He had his dark glasses on again. "You see what I mean? Four shots. Torture. Then the neck. Two militiamen show up. They're let in and killed without much struggle. Were they involved? Was it a falling out of thieves? All that can be said with certainty is that it's a real tangled knot." Kaznin noticed that Nowek was still holding the bone. "The room will have to be inventoried, photographed, dusted for fingerprints. You should probably put the dog's bone back where you found it. The room should remain intact."

Intact? He thought of all the missing items, the food, the furniture, the car, the money, the crowd of unpaid militiamen outside. He thought of the chunk of common gravel in his pocket, the fleur-de-lis boot print. Not Grossman's to be sure. He'd been wearing paper slippers. And not Kaznin's shoes either. They had the common chain-link tread pattern. A militiaman? The killer? He turned to the Fisherman. "What could they have wanted from him?"

The heater switched on, sending a gust from the vents.

"Ryzkhov had many things worth stealing." He glanced once more at the bone in Nowek's hand. "Remember the open safe. There's hard currency in this house. Perhaps they forced him to give the combination. Then things got out of hand. The bone," he said, looking at it again. "You have a dog?"

"You keep saying murderers."

"The second patrol found three glasses and a bottle of cognac on the coffee table, all empty. Perhaps Ryzkhov had a quick drink with the two militia. And perhaps he knew his killers. It's too soon to rule anything out."

With fancy lugged sole boots. Imported, surely. Or maybe worn by someone other than a Russian. "I asked before, what business did Ryzkhov have with AmerRus?"

One shoulder rose, then Kaznin stretched his neck in a curious, rolling motion. "I suppose it's no secret." Kaznin shifted on his feet. "He was a leasing agent. He knew what deals were pending, what oil and gas properties were available and which *krugovye poruki* controlled them." It meant family circle, though it had nothing to do with family and everything to do with networks of influence and corruption. "He had a lot of valuable information inside his head. You could say he was a kind of commercial espionage agent."

"For AmerRus." Nowek looked hard into those dark aviator sunglasses perched on Kaznin's nose. "You work for them, too. Did they ask you to be here?"

"A good consultant doesn't wait to be asked. A good consultant anticipates."

"What about before?" asked Nowek. "Did the security organs have dealings with Ryzkhov?"

"Please, I'll show you my uniform," said Kaznin, "but don't ask me to take off my shirt. Besides, that's all history now." Kaznin peered closely at Nowek. "Are you feeling well?"

Nowek steadied himself. He took a deep breath. His fist was closed hard around the bone. So solid and smooth. So unlike those shattered pieces in the other room. "What about the gunshots? The bullets?"

Kaznin reached into the slash pocket of his leather jacket and pulled out a heavy, misshapen drop of gray lead flecked with shards of blue plastic. "The laboratory in Irkutsk will charge a fortune, but I can tell you right now for free it's an American-made, Black Talon round. Nine millimeters. Definitely not militia issue."

"An American bullet?"

"A very special American bullet. They're designed to be used against hijackers on board passenger aircraft. They make the tips from plastic, so it penetrates, then explodes. No ricochets, no holes in the airplane to worry about. There's not much of an exit wound, and they're very expensive."

American bullets. American boots. "Well, only the best for Rossinka."

Kaznin barked a small laugh. "I'm glad murder has not affected your famous sense of humor. But let me remind you, an important member of the business community is tortured in his bed. You've lost two more officers though whether that's much of a loss is an open question."

"To you."

"That's why I'm ready to devote all my energy to see them caught. You'd be smart to let me do what I know how to do. You take care of the politics. You keep your friend Volsky happy. Let me track these fat bastards down."

He's right, but Nowek wondered, why fat? He heard a commotion from the bottom of the stairs, then the clump of heavy footfall. He leaned over the banister, his head light enough to float away. It was Chuchin heading up the stairs, and the sight of him made Nowek feel better.

Chuchin deliberately ignored the ex–KGB major. He looked at the bone in Nowek's hand, then reached into his pocket and pulled out a swatch of tattered orange cloth. "I found this in the dog's mouth."

Nowek had seen it before, too. It wasn't orange peel at all. It was bloodstained fabric, red and mottled orange.

"That's evidence," warned Kaznin.

"You're as quick as they say, Major." Chuchin turned his back to Kaznin and said, "I kept thinking, the color is familiar."

So it was. "AmerRus orange," said Nowek. It was the color of their uniforms, their jeeps, their helicopters. To "stand out better against the snow." A piece of AmerRus uniform in the guard dog's teeth was added to the list.

Why would a foreigner kill Ryzkhov?

But if they did, it gave reason to Kaznin showing up. He worked for them, and a good consultant doesn't wait to be asked. A good consultant anticipates.

"Cloth like that could have come from anywhere." Kaznin took a plastic bag from his pocket. "But just the same, it will have to be exhaustively tested. I'll see to it."

Nowek snatched the plastic bag instead and folded the bloody cloth into it. "That won't be necessary."

Kaznin glowered. "Make sure the clinic gets it fast. The blood will have to be preserved or it will be useless. Gromov will not be happy if inexperience costs us our first clue."

"Thank you for that information." He recalled Galena's use of the same phrase not very long ago. He admonished himself for acting petty. Kaznin was a liar. It didn't mean he wasn't truthful about some things. "Let's find out what the militiamen have learned."

Outside, an elegantly dressed woman of about fifty stood surrounded by militia officers. The sun was warm enough to force the sheepskin greatcoats off their backs, revealing a bewildering assortment of patched uniforms. They reminded Nowek of Trishka, a Russian folk character who mended holes in his shirt by tearing off pieces from his pants.

The woman was perfectly assembled. She wore a fur coat long enough to reveal only the silver-capped toes of her leather boots. Her unnaturally golden hair was drawn back and held by a clip studded with pearl. Sunglasses so black they might have been cut from basalt. Her face was puffy. The group parted to admit Kaznin. He two-fingered a twenty-dollar bill to the militiaman standing next to her.

"This is Citizen Geraskina," said the officer. He was speaking to Kaznin, not Nowek. "She lives in Number Ten."

"*Two* houses away," she said quickly and firmly. "I phoned the militia about the dog." She looked at Kaznin, then at Nowek. "I've already told everything I know." She pulled back the draping sable sleeve and looked at her watch. Gold and platinum flashed in the sun. "Nobody's safe. Not even the militia. I could be murdered in my bed just like Andrei."

How does she know it was in bed? Nowek had to shoulder his way next to her. "Excuse me. My name is Nowek."

She cocked her head. "Wasn't that the mayor's name?"

"It still is." Up close, he could smell the powder on her face. "When did you call exactly?"

"Four, maybe a little later. Czar was loose."

"Czar?"

"Andrei's dog. I called zero two, and the militia finally came. If they'd been quicker, you'd have the killer in his cell."

"If they'd been slower, they might still be alive."

She reached under her dark lens to wipe away a tear. "Andrei was a good man. Always helpful. He would even lend money to strangers."

"To you?"

"Sometimes. Why not?"

"Are you the one who filed a claim on his car?"

Her expression hardened. "Fair is fair."

"Did you notice a strange car last night?" asked Kaznin. "Anything out of the ordinary? Voices? An argument?"

"He was playing very loud music. I could hear it in my sleep." She lowered her voice. "He did have a special friend. Not his wife. I hope you'll keep this in confidence. A dead husband is bad enough for the wife."

Nowek thought of the photo upstairs, the young, beautiful woman in America with flashbulb eyes.

"A man with a wife so far away leads his own life," she

continued, "but this girl was strange. She always came after sunset and left early. Sometimes before sunrise. Like a vampire except it wasn't his blood she was after."

Nowek said, "What do you do for your money, Citizen Geraskina, other than borrow it?"

Kaznin broke in. "He never mentioned her name? This woman?"

"To me?"

Kaznin slipped her a business card. "Call if you think of anything else, no matter how trivial it seems."

"I'll say now what I think. When you catch them," she said, "I hope you cut off their balls."

A thump and a muffled shout came from the dead officer's patrol jeep. From inside the cage. Another shout, this one a distinct curse.

A key was found, it didn't fit. Another was tried. The third did the trick.

The door swung open and the reek of vomit and urine spilled out. A wild-eyed man stood at the lip, swaying, one hand up against the brilliant sun. Shoeless, stained shirt and pants, he squinted at the officers, the drunk Gorits had saved from freezing the night before.

"Who are you?" Kaznin called to him. "What's your name, citizen?"

The drunk sank to his knees. "Jesus," he said.

"Missionaries," muttered Kaznin.

Nowek turned away, and Kaznin followed him to his car. Chuchin was already inside, the engine started. "The offer stands, Mayor," he said. "I'll find these killers."

Chuchin opened the door for him, signaling with his eyebrows that he thought it wouldn't be such a bad idea.

Nowek tossed the heavy bone into the backseat, then climbed in up front. "Thank you for your interest in this matter, Major. I'll be in touch." The car door slammed. The Land Cruiser left a trail of oily exhaust behind.

★ ★ ★

The sun grew hot inside the car. Nowek opened his window. An American uniform. American bullets. A print of a boot with fancy patterns. It reminded him of the stone. He pulled it from his pocket.

"What's that?" asked Chuchin.

He turned it over in his hand, holding it up to the sunlight. It showed off the pretty crystals, the bright whites and deep reds better than the soft lighting in Ryzkhov's flat. Odd. One face glittered like an insect's eye in tiny, almost subliminal facets. It gave the surface a kind of oily, liquid sheen.

The piece showed little signs of wear and tear. That meant it wasn't far, or long, from its outcrop. Most probably it came from a gravel pit mined for laying roadbeds or foundation pads and not exposed by the grinding wall of a glacier. But that wasn't the feature that caught his attention.

"Are you all right?" Chuchin asked again when Nowek didn't answer.

He pocketed it. There was something odd about this chunk of gravel. The oily sheen didn't belong to a common stone. And the color, like Ryzkhov's flat, was too red.

CHAPTER
4

"IT'S JUST A STONE."

"So is a diamond," said Nowek.

"That's no diamond, Mr. Mayor."

"It's granite, probably from the Nepa formation, I'm not sure. I am sure that it's too red."

"Red?"

"Siberia's tough even on rocks. With all the freezing and thawing, minerals weather out of granite fast. Most rock we see is very pale. It's been bulldozed by glaciers. Washed down by rivers. Broken into dust. But not this one. This one," said Nowek, "is not far from its home in terms of time. That means it *is* far from its home in terms of space. There are no outcrops around Markovo. It came from someplace else. Someplace specific."

"I can show you tons of stones just like it."

"A whole continent of it. But you'll have to dig five, six hundred meters underground at least." He turned the stone in the light. "Those pretty crystals? They're mica. The pink is feldspar and there's some kind of a coating on one face. Like spray lacquer." Nowek held the stone between his fingers and looked at it closely. Murder was one thing. Rocks he knew.

"The stone could come from anywhere, Mayor."

He put it away again. "Maybe Kaznin was right. He said criminals always leave something."

"Kaznin." Chuchin looked like he was ready to spit. "You know, as much as I hate him, he's the man for this job."

"Kaznin's a vulture," said Nowek.

"Vultures have their place."

The Hotel Siber's driveway was deserted. The girls were gone, inside to their interviews, thrown back out on the streets, elevated to heaven in Hong Kong. Who knew anymore?

They passed a shop with a sign that read KHLEB. The bakery exuded the rich aroma of fresh bread.

"What about breakfast?"

"No." Nowek had left his stomach back in Rossinka. "I should buy some things for tomorrow night. My father's expecting to eat."

"Don't bother stopping there," said Chuchin with a look back at the shop. A sheet of paper was taped up inside the steamy windows: a green dollar sign. It was a less insulting way to say, *rubles not accepted.* Dollars were the stars, rubles were meteorites. "I'll find something. You'll see."

Nowek knew there was no better scrounger in Markovo.

Chuchin turned down the street that paralleled the river. High concrete embankments rose to the left; a warren of low brick buildings, warehouses, communal flats, and ice-choked alleys hemmed them in from the right. At an anonymous alley, Chuchin slowed, then stopped.

"What are you doing?"

Before Chuchin could answer, a face appeared at the side window. It was a strange, almost rubbery face. Long, thin, and nervous, it was an amalgam of both traditional thespian masks, one crying, one laughing, all at once.

"Hello, Nikki," said Chuchin. "What do you have for me?"

Nikki Malyshev smiled at Chuchin, frowned at Nowek, flickering, moving from one foot to the other. Like those strange elemental particles that existed only so long as they vibrated, that died when they were forced to remain still.

His heavy coat was unbuttoned at the neck in deference to

the new season. A glint of gold chain showed through tufts of black hair. "Videos," he said. *"Basic Instinct.* Sharon Stone. Nice legs. No underwear. *Verrry* sexy."

Chuchin touched his lips. "Nothing to eat?"

"Try later. What about cigarettes?"

Chuchin smiled. "You know."

The face disappeared.

"How do you know him?" asked Nowek as the man scurried back into the alley.

"Everyone knows Nikki. And Nikki knows everything."

"Why am I the only one in the dark?"

"You're the mayor."

Malyshev reappeared with a box.

"Just one." Chuchin held out a thick wad of one thousand ruble notes held together with a rubber band. "It's all I can pay for."

Malyshev shook his head so fast it looked like a bird drinking water. He pushed the box of cheap Russian smokes through the window. "Take it. Nobody else buys this shit but you. I have Hungarian Marlboros. You want a taste?"

"Too rich. I might become addicted." Chuchin was about to raise the window when Nowek stopped him.

Nikki's face froze in a frown. He looked ready to jump straight up, to fly away, to disappear.

Nowek leaned over. "I understand you're a man who knows things."

"Buy and sell. That's what I know. Who has, who wants. How much. That's it. You want some perfume? Real German perfume. So good you can drink it." He didn't laugh. It wasn't a joke.

"Did you know Andrei Ryzkhov?"

"Andrei. Who would want to kill *him?* Nice guy. Always paid. *Big* spender. In his own bed." Nikki looked up, scanning the street, then back down. "And the father. *Verrry* big guy."

Information was like sound; the colder the air, the higher the speed of transmission. But this seemed awfully fast, even for Markovo. "Who would want to kill him? Any ideas?"

"Who?" Nikki's eyes seemed to vibrate at a higher frequency. They almost hummed.

Chuchin held up a wad of rolled rubles.

Nikki's face broke like ice on the Lena into a grin big enough to see from a distance. He didn't touch the money. "Videos. I have the latest Disney. You have a kid? *Lion King.* She'll love it. Everybody loves *Lion King.*"

Where was Galena? "No videos. What about Ryzkhov?"

Malyshev looked beyond the Land Cruiser, watching the embankment. "Batteries?" he said without looking back into the car. "Cigarettes? I have Turkish tobacco. The best. No? Maybe another time." He turned and scurried back into the alley.

When they left the alley behind, Nowek said, "He's drunk."

"No, Mr. Mayor," said Chuchin. He pointed out two men standing on the levee. They weren't drunk. They weren't moving. They were watching. "He's scared."

As they drove off, Nowek said, "You know what they say? Communism is fear mixed with greed."

"So?"

"Capitalism is exactly the opposite."

The snow turned to slush under the intense spring sun.

"Think about it," Chuchin said. "Analyzed correctly, Kaznin is perfect for the job."

"Too perfect."

"Who made you an investigator? You know rocks. You think a rock came in and killed Ryzkhov with a knife? Please."

He thought of the piece of gravel in his pocket. "There are similarities," said Nowek. "A geologist is always working in the dark. You can never work in a straight line. You sit there staring at geologic sections, bedding sequences, maps, electric logs, and nothing makes any sense. Nothing at all. But if you keep staring long enough at nothing, all of a sudden it becomes something."

"That's what you think will happen with Ryzkhov?"

"Hope is a funny thing. What do you know about Gorits?"

"He's a dead Chechen. They're not so rare. Also, he used to be a sergeant but he fucked up." Chuchin looked at Nowek with those two dark, polished lenses. "Can you imagine how badly you have to fuck up to be demoted in the Markovo militia?"

It would take a lot. "What did he do?"

"The Skhurat business. He got involved in areas that were none of his concern. You wouldn't understand."

But he did. The Skhurat probe. Had the general of the Markovo militia been killed by *mafiya,* his own men, or some combination? "He cooperated with the Interior Ministry? How?"

"By telling them what honest officers his fellow militiamen were. They thanked him with the midnight shift. You're sure about breakfast?"

"Drive." The worms coiled and tangled again. He hunted the streets for Galena. Would she come home tonight?

Already a few pedestrians were out hoping to fill their "what if" shopping bags with something. Everyone had a string bag ready in case a store had something to sell. Most had their heavy coats off. Another five degrees and they'd revert to pagan sun-worship, men stripped to their undershirts and women not so far behind.

Reversion was everywhere. Russia had replaced Marxism with magic crystals, swapped Party cadres promising true communism for evangelists offering eternal life. The two most popular shows on television? *Santa Barbara* and a faith healer who induced orgasm in pretty young women by channeling his energy through "focusing crystals." The crystals sold by the trainload.

Russians were nothing if not adaptable, but the most adaptable of all were the *mafiyas.*

The *urki* flourished under the czars. They did even better under the Bolsheviks. Stalin called them innocents driven to crime by class conflict. Condemn the poet, let the devious doctors and wrecker engineers feed the fat Kolyma mosquitos with their blood, but don't mistreat the poor thief.

The *urki, mafiyas,* were like weeds: the worse things got, the more they thrived. And look around; when had things ever been so bad as now?

The *urki* left their imprint on Siberia, just as the romantic Decembrists exiled by the czars had before them. Where their predecessors had written poetry, started art institutes, ballets, and debating societies, the children of the gulag had left an altogether different legacy: people who could make shoes from rags, solder up vodka stills from tin cans, fashion playing cards from pieces of paper glued together with potato starch, and devour the weak.

Like any well-run organization, the Markovo *mafiya*s were divided into zones of specialization. The Black Lung district was staked out with a surveyor's precision: one group here, another there. My alley. Yours. Border crossings were rare. Repeat offenders even rarer.

One gang bought and sold fuel, food, alcohol, and medicines. It was led by Semyon Yufa, a middle-aged Ukrainian with an office twice the size of Nowek's, dominated inside by an oversize roulette wheel and outside by oversize men with bulges under their jackets.

Yufa was a "black" Ukrainian, more Turk than Slav. His headquarters was in the old Mercury Condom Factory. The old MERCURY CONDOMS sign still was lit up at night in bright red, and the corporate motto, THE BEST PROTECTION AGAINST INFLATION, was repainted each year on the perimeter wall.

Service industries constituted the next layer: drugs, money changing, and prostitution. A hundred-dollar bill bought an evening with a pretty young Buryat girl; twenty thousand rubles rented a woman nearing pension age in an alley for five minutes. But then, it was usually too cold to linger.

An exiled Armenian named Mulkunyan ruled this kingdom of desire. One of his many brothers operated a gaudy all-night cafe, hard currency only, called The Alamo. A favorite of American oil workers, it was Siberia's only Tex-Mex bar.

Finally, there were the bottom feeders specializing in car

theft and burglary, eager to join a *bratsky krug,* the brotherhood of thieves, available for a price. And who set the price?

The same prosecutors, officials, and judges who used to protect the Party's interests now looked after their own. The *nomenklatura* had once ruled the USSR. Now they ruled Russia.

True, there were differences. Instead of the KGB, the new *nomenklatura* used the *mafiyas* to maintain their authority.

The governor, his legal enforcers, their illegal comrades, the *mafiyas.* Top to bottom, a balanced criminal ecology. If Nowek's town government worked half so well he'd never recognize it.

"Well, Mr. Mayor. Here we are."

The town offices occupied a modern brick building that had once housed the headquarters of a wood fiber cooperative. Nowek inherited the director's suite upstairs. Chuchin parked beneath a huge, heroic mural. On it two men and a woman stood, leaning into an invisible wind, hair and clothes streaming, under the words MUI STROYIM KOMMUNISM!; We're Building Communism! One of the men held a satellite in his hand, the other a compass; the woman, what else? A sheaf of wheat. Someone had drawn a fat *apparatchik* on his knees before the trio, with blast waves emanating from his upraised ass; a fart that gave new meaning to the invisible wind the three were leaning into.

Chuchin turned. "A rich thief is dead. If Kaznin is willing to take responsibility, I say let him. You saw Malyshev. Even he knew when to keep his mouth shut."

"I thought you said Kaznin was a snake."

"He is." Chuchin switched off the engine. "It's not every day a snake offers to bite himself for the public good."

"If AmerRus is involved, Kaznin will bury it."

Chuchin nodded. "Burying things is what Kaznin is best at."

"Skhurat, now two more officers. Forget Ryzkhov. If the *mafiya* now feels invulnerable, if they can kill without being punished, no one is safe. Don't you think we should catch this killer?"

"This is Siberia. Murder is what we breathe. If you caught him, you'd have to throw him in a cell. You can't keep *mafiya* in a cell for one hour. You know that's true."

"Maybe they're not *mafiya*. Maybe they're foreigners."

"Even worse. Think. If it's some American, what will you do? Two, maybe three days and they'd put them on a plane. You couldn't hold them. People would say that foreigners murder us and nothing happens. AmerRus would say fuck Markovo. We'll spend our money elsewhere. You'd be like a whore with two soldiers. Screwed from both sides."

"The law . . ."

"Don't talk to me about laws." Chuchin's face darkened. A red tinge crept up his leathery neck. "We had seventy years of laws. How did the czars rule? *Bolshaya krov*." Bloodshed. "And the Bolsheviks? *Bolshaya krov*. You think one election changes anything? Pah. It's *Bolshaya krov* again. What's new? Nothing. This is Russia. We don't change. So don't talk about laws. Laws have killed more Russians than a madman with a knife."

"Killing thieves is still a crime, Chuchin."

"Maybe it shouldn't be. You think you live in a real country? Forget Russia. Forget laws. It's *Vorovskoi Mir*. That's what it always was. That's what it still is."

Nowek got out and slammed the door. He took out the plastic evidence bag and tossed it at Chuchin. "Take this to the clinic. Make sure they look at the blood right away."

"Fine. Don't forget your rocks and your bones."

He reached through the car window and grabbed them and left. As he walked into the municipal building, an icicle broke free from the eaves and plunged into the snow at his feet. All Nowek could see was the hard clear eye of its stump, staring up at him. *Vorovskoi Mir*. Thieves' World.

The lobby was rank with the sour smell of old boiled cabbage. Like backed-up toilets, sweat, and cigarettes, it was an unnoticeable part of the environment. Except that Nowek noticed it. His stomach rolled in on itself again. He went upstairs.

Outside his office, two old women and an even older man sat on a wooden bench.

"Mayor!"

They rose up, a flock of crows kicked by a gunshot, their dark coats beating wings. The man's chest was plated with cheap, tinkling military medals. It was how you knew they were real; the fakes were made from better metal.

"Mayor! We need your help!"

". . . a hero of the War! How can they do this?"

"They'll have us die on the street for a single ruble!"

One ruble? There was nostalgia for you. Nowek tried to dodge them, but the old man got a handful of his green sleeve and yanked. A rip came from under his arm. He disentangled himself and made a dash for his door, keeping it between him and them. "Please! One moment. Your turn will come. Be patient!" He half-hoped to find Galena waiting inside. He went in.

Empty. But one of the five black phones on his desk was ringing. He pulled off his jacket. The strained seam was pulled open but the threads had not quite ripped. He picked up the phone. "Nowek."

"This is the prosecutor's office calling. From Irkutsk."

As if he didn't know where Gromov's office was. "I'm pleased they haven't moved it. Who's this?"

"First Deputy Prosecutor Kvint." A thin-lipped reply.

Kvint. The name didn't ring any bells. There was no surprise in that. You could fit a dozen first deputy prosecutors in Nikolai Gromov's spacious new offices; in a land where the prosecutor decided what was legal and what was not, deputy prosecutors bred like mice in straw. "What can I do for you, Deputy Prosecutor?"

"We're calling regarding the murder at Rossinka."

"Actually, it's murders."

There was a pause, an annoyed click of a tongue. "The prosecutor wants you to know that he appreciates the time and effort you've spent on the investigation."

"When are we getting our new militia commander?"

"Sadly, Prosecutor Gromov won't be able to assign a new militia general to Markovo as quickly as we all might hope."

It had already been half a year. "I'm shocked to hear that." Nowek leafed through the messages that had accumulated so far this morning. "Was there something more?"

"Yes. We believe there's no reason to expect you to assume duties that are not your responsibility."

Nowek stopped. All sarcasm left his voice. "Until you send me a general, those two officers are my responsibility."

Kvint spoke louder to let Nowek know there was no deviation from the script. "We believe the Ryzkhov matter could become sensitive. The governor himself has expressed concern. Ryzkhov was not just anyone. This is a criminal matter. It should not be tainted by politics."

"Oddly enough, I agree." But there was something coming at him. He could hear the clank of tank treads even if he couldn't quite see the turret swing in his direction. "So?"

"We can't risk this investigation getting delayed or led in unproductive directions."

"Which directions worry you, First Deputy Prosecutor?"

Kvint ignored the bait. "We thank you for your help, and ask that you give your fullest cooperation to our designated representative. He will take charge of the investigation and see it through to a professional conclusion."

Nowek knew, but he asked anyway. "Who?"

"Major Oleg Kaznin."

Nowek felt his face flush red. How long since he'd left Rossinka? Long enough. "You know he works for AmerRus."

"Kaznin is a specialist."

"In making things disappear. Look," said Nowek, "Ryzkhov worked for AmerRus. There's some physical evidence that his killing may be connected with them, too. Now Kaznin. Where does he earn his money? AmerRus." Nowek's voice was rising. He was losing control. "Now I'm just a geologist, not a lawyer, not even a First Deputy Prosecutor . . ."

"Mayor . . ."

"But even I can feel the pinch when a conflict of interest

bites me on the ass. How about you, First Deputy Prosecutor? Or have you been sitting in your chair too long?"

"There's no conflict in asking an experienced man to do a difficult job. It's not necessary for you to be concerned."

"Well, that's a relief."

Kvint was a bureaucrat, but he wasn't quite stupid. "Mayor, discord between government elements is one of the unproductive directions that concerns us the most." Another pause. This Kvint was a master of the rest, the discontinued phrase. The unnerving syncopation. "A mayor is not a murder investigator."

"And a consultant who earns his dollars from a possible suspect shouldn't be one either."

"AmerRus is a joint venture corporation, not a suspect. I shouldn't have to tell you how vital they are to your town's economy. If there's some *individual* associated with them that you feel merits close examination, you will inform Major Kaznin." There was finality in Kvint's tone. Nowek was a minor irritant who had reached the limit of Kvint's already taxed indulgence. "Any further questions should be addressed to Prosecutor Gromov."

"Put him on."

"That won't be possible. He's flying to Markovo to personally oversee the investigation. Is there anything else we can do for you?"

"To be honest, it seems you have things well in hand." Nowek hung up. That was that. Volsky. The presidential representative should know that Gromov was handing everything to Kaznin.

Nowek had met Prosecutor Gromov twice, and each time there was the same wariness that comes when a man sees in another a natural enemy. Not that Gromov had any reaction; Nowek was just a mayor. Gromov functioned on a different level.

The prosecutor general was a powerful figure in modern Russia. Like the criminal class, his influence expanded as the empire and its laws crumbled. Under the direction of the governor, Gromov placed legal obstacles in the path of anything, and anyone, who didn't see the wisdom of sharing. In a way, Andrei Ryzkhov's work had been to help clients avoid men like Gromov. It made for hazardous duty. How hazardous? Ryzkhov was dead.

Nowek glanced at the dog's chew bone he'd found at Ryzkhov's flat.

A geologic "Great Death," a period where species had died off by the thousands, had given the world petroleum. It had created oceans of Siberian light, sweet crude. More recently, twenty million inconvenient men and women had died to make Siberia the OPEC of bones. A feast of bones. Someday, some future geologist would sink a hole and strike the distilled horror of all that. A heavy, bitter black liquid made from congealed blood and rotted hope. *Vorovskoi Mir*. Thieves' World. Maybe Chuchin was right. He got up and walked to a rust-stained sink.

Nowek's office was simply furnished. A chair, a desk, a battered sofa he sometimes slept on when it was too late to go home. Sometimes, when he knew Galena would be out, when the weight of the empty house became too crushing, it got late very early. Add *father* to his list of failed careers.

There was a plate window with rusting frames. The bookshelves groaned under the dead weight of a thousand conflicting rules, most of them unenforceable. Too many laws and too few had the same effect, which is to say, no laws at all.

Enter Prosecutor Gromov. Enter, and exit, Andrei Ryzkhov. What had he known that was worth killing him to get? Some secret path through Gromov's legal maze? Or more likely, around it? AmerRus would surely prize information like that. And just as surely Gromov would not. He looked up.

A copy of Nowek's campaign poster hung on the wall. On it, his image gazed down in a wry, amused way at a row of heads, each a former mayor of Markovo, each cast from a mold of loose jowls, bulging eyes, and neckless necks. Defenders of the People. Stalwarts of the Party. Gray clones very much like the ones trying to recapture the nation.

Beneath it all was Nowek's campaign slogan of 1993:

BE HONEST: CAN I DO ANY WORSE?

The poster was a success, capitalizing on his one main strength: he wasn't one of *them*. Can I do any worse? The early 1990s were heady times, and a geologist's political career could rise on flimsy wings.

That was then. Now it reminded him every day of the old Gorbachev joke. You remember it? Gorbachev walks by his official Kremlin portrait and says, "Some day they'll take us both down." The portrait replies, "Don't be a fool, Misha. *Me* they'll take down. *You* they will hang."

Nowek looked across an alley at the old KGB station. Kaznin's former office. His stomach twisted. He turned away and opened the cold water tap. The faucet hissed as the air inside the pipe escaped, then it spat water the color of blood. A squeamish ghost stirred in his belly. He looked away. When the water cleared, he filled a small teapot and then plugged it into a wall socket. The outlet was open, unprotected by a cover plate, the wires visible.

He went to his desk to go through the pile of papers.

Public health warnings over cholera; new tax collection deadlines; cutbacks in federal subsidies to town governments, yet another date for the resumption of full airline service in Siberia. If it meant Aeroflot, Nowek could wait forever. A dark green bill appeared. What was this? Money?

No. A cleverly printed brochure, its cover a nice reproduction of the new hundred–dollar bill. Ben Franklin seemed a bit unstable, printed as he was off-center. He unfolded it and saw inside a listing of money-making opportunities in Irkutsk Oblast. The brochure bore the official stamp of the state government.

REF A1: Mercury Mine. Potential to produce 10% of world demand, plus antimony . . . radically downsized workforce and capable of additional cost improvements . . .

REF A2 was an electric lamp factory. Next a brickworks that bragged its staff had been *reengineered from 5,500 to 2,900.* Nowek thought, if only they could reengineer the workers to live on snow they'd really have something.

Coal mines, vitreous silica crucibles, commercial gases, a diamond sorting plant, even a reindeer meat packing facility. Siberia wasn't so much flirting with the world as inviting rape. He crumpled the brochure and threw it at the wastebasket.

Next to the pile of papers was a note from the switchboard saying that a call had come in this morning from America. His stomach tightened. Ryzkhov's famous father, or his beautiful wife Vika.

Nowek thought, for a father to outlive his son was tragedy; for a wife to outlive her husband's dollars, that was serious. But that photograph. Was it such a remarkable likeness? Vika, Nina. Or was he just becoming desperate?

He caught himself fingering his ring like a worry bead. He pushed the note aside.

Beneath it was a glossy color brochure with a business card clipped to it. There was a message on the card.

Sorry to miss you. I had to catch my flight back to Vladivostok. Maybe next time through?—Dr. P. Gabriel.

The tiger man. The environmental activist. One side of the card was printed in English: *Dr. Peter Gabriel, Delegate, World Tiger Trust,* with addresses in California and in Vladivostok.

Saving tigers. Amazing. The Americans have it so easy they have to comb the world for problems to solve. Here, problems came looking for you. Nowek looked up and remembered the three pensioners waiting out in the hall. He pulled open a desk drawer and took out three cafeteria chits.

He opened his door. They rose again, calmer this time than

last. Or weaker. He held up the coupons. "Don't worry," he told them. "Have something to eat downstairs. Go home. No one will throw you onto the street. You have my word. Make sure they give you ice cream. It just arrived yesterday."

"We're counting on you to do what's right," said the old man as he snatched the tickets. He left with a faint jingle of his military decorations.

Well, thought Nowek as he watched them go, right was never simple. It was enough to know what was possible.

It was time to call Volsky.

He picked up the phone and listened for a dial tone. Miracles! He dialed the presidential representative's number in Irkutsk. The line was busy. He hung up and tried again. This time it rang and rang as though he'd dialed a number on the moon. Once more. He looked at the brochure left behind on his desk as the line popped and wheezed.

The cover had two photographs placed side by side. One showed a snarling tiger, green eyes, white teeth, and red mouth. The other, a bloody corpse being skinned by a poacher. The words at the bottom said, in Russian,

The Amur Tiger on the Brink of Extinction: A Special Report by the World Tiger Trust.

He looked at the photo. Not Siberia. The poacher was dressed for the tropics, and tiger hunting here took place when there was snow on the ground. It made for easier tracking.

The pops in the telephone resolved to a faint ring. It clicked. The teapot steamed.

"Allo."

"It's Nowek."

"Grisha!" Volsky's voice filled the phone with a hearty, good-natured boom. "So what do you have?"

"A lot. Your friend Gromov just called, my daughter is going to be a Chinese whore, and the day's still young."

Politicians were like the very old; they grew selective ears. "Gromov's no friend. If I met him at night, I'd squeeze him

like a boil. How is your daughter anyway? She's coming to
Irkutsk this fall for school?"

"It depends. Gromov ordered me to hand over the Ryzkhov
murders to an ex-Committee major named Kaznin. Just to be
sure it happens, he's flying up here today. I thought you'd like
to know."

"KGB," said Volsky with new respect. The KGB had
changed its name a dozen times since the empire's demise.
Federal Security Service. The Russian National Intelligence
Directorate. It was easier to call it by its old name and more
accurate, too. "So now the wolves are guarding the sheep.
What kind of wolf is this Kaznin?"

"A watchdog. He runs a private security firm here in town.
He's hired a lot of my militiamen. He pays in dollars. Maybe I
should apply."

"A watchdog with money."

"AmerRus is his main client."

A whistle. "Real money."

"You know, Arkasha, they say that once everything is stolen,
there will be no more thieves. What do you think?"

"It's a long time to wait."

"That's what I think, too. Look. I need a favor. You said that
you'd do something if I poked my nose into the Ryzkhov
mess? I need to make sure the families of my two officers are
protected."

"What about Ryzkhov?"

He remembered the stripped apartment, the missing car.
"Too late."

"I'll see what I can do. I have a friend at Interior."

"That's Moscow. Don't you have any closer friends?"

"You and me. We're all that's left. Of course, there's always
the future."

"Which future?"

"The Communists could sweep the next regional elections.
If they do, neither one of us will have anything to worry about.
But this Kaznin. What did you find out that scared Gromov
into moving so fast?"

"Nothing. That's what's strange. I went to Rossinka and looked around. Kaznin was already there. He did all of the finding, not me." Then he remembered the strip of orange cloth, the bullets, the chunk of red gravel. "There's some evidence. Ryzkhov was shot with unusual bullets. I'm told that they only come from America. There's also some cloth with blood on it. Ryzkhov had a guard dog that may have bitten one of the killers. The cloth was in his teeth. And a rock but I don't know enough yet about it."

"A rock?"

"It was tracked in by someone. Caught in the tread of his boot." He thought of that odd, red stone. As though the granite had taken on some of Ryzkhov's blood. "Nothing is certain, but it looks to me like the cloth came from an AmerRus uniform. You know the color?"

"The same as money. But it explains one thing: if AMR is really involved, Gromov had to move. He and the governor have a lot to lose."

"You mean their bribes."

"Sure. AMR is Markovo's number-one source of dollars. Who do you think is the governor's number-one source? Did you know bribes can now be put on MasterCard?" said Volsky. "There is a direct deposit agreement between SiberBank and Credit Suisse. It never even has to change into rubles. They aren't even bothering to be subtle."

"Tunguska oil is a national asset. It doesn't belong to Irkutsk any more than it belongs to AmerRus. Doesn't Moscow have a say in what happens?"

"Moscow is like the moon, Grisha. It goes from light to dark, and it's far away. Gromov is right here. You can't fart without him deciding whether or not you have to pay a gas tax. Who is this Kaznin anyway? I don't know the name."

"Someone who will make sure AmerRus stays protected."

"Obviously." There was a pause. "Unless we find out that AMR is really connected with Ryzkhov's death."

"I'm inclined to suspect Gromov before I worry about AMR. Ryzkhov helped the Americans avoid the prosecutor."

"Even better if we take that smug bastard down a peg. You see, people still remember Ryzkhov's father. He lives abroad now, which is something you and I should consider while there's still some time."

"What if evidence points at Gromov? How do we proceed?"

"You know who would prosecute the case."

"Yes." Gromov.

"Then you see what I mean. Attacking from the front won't work. If you found some connection, maybe we can nail them from behind."

"I won't find out much with Kaznin in charge."

"True," Volsky admitted. "Still, the fact that Gromov is coming up to Markovo is a good sign."

"Of what?"

"He's worried. We could squeeze him. Threaten to make some noise. Everyone knows these new bastards are just as corrupt as the Communists. They *were* the Communists."

"I don't care about noises."

But Volsky wasn't listening any more closely than Deputy Prosecutor Kvint. "In fact, the more I think of it, the better it sounds. We could send you up to Tunguska for a fact-finding trip. Moscow is unhappy about not making money off Tunguska oil. I told you?"

Nowek remembered the deal, a sweet arrangement between the Oil and Gas Ministry, AmerRus, and sprinkled with holy water by the prime minister himself: a five-year moratorium on export fees on all Tunguska oil. "They gave away too much."

"Everything is Moscow's fault. You and me. We're the only innocent ones left. Still, a scandal with AMR could be useful. You're an old oil man so you'd have credibility. If you found something good, Gromov would shit in his pants. I can arrange to get you on a flight. If we found some way to grab Gromov's prick, we could be heroes."

"Or dead."

"What?"

"I said, AmerRus puts a lot of dollars into Markovo even if they don't send any to Moscow. If they're guilty of something, then they should be made to pay. But I don't see any good coming from harassing them. Frankly, my concerns are simpler. I think it would be nice to know who killed my two men. I want a trial. I want them put into a cell. I want things to work as they should just *once* before I'm unelected."

"That's all?"

"Not quite. I think we should launch rockets against Hong Kong. Do you think that's still possible?"

There was a static-riddled pause; the sound of bacon frying. "Sometimes I worry about your state of mind."

"So do I. What do you want me to do?"

"It would be best if you could keep your thumb on the investigation. Buzz around it like a mosquito, but . . ."

"Don't get slapped?"

"Exactly. I know you aren't a professional investigator. But you're a troublemaker. That's better. We have to help one another. It's you and me against them. Maybe I can get someone in Moscow interested. As I said, there's already grumbling about the deal that was cut with the Americans. It would be different if AMR was paying off."

"The Tunguska fields are the biggest in Siberia. There should be plenty of oil to steal. What's happening up there?"

"I think the Americans got caught in a war between the clans," said Volsky. "You have the Gas and Oil clan fighting the clan that advocates westernization. You have the agricultural *apparatchiki* ready to stick pitchforks into the bankers who are squeezing everyone's nuts. The bankers are fighting the military industrial combines and the army, and the army's ready to march behind General Lebed all the way to the Kremlin. Who knows why AmerRus isn't paying off. You go and find that out and we'll both be—"

"I'm mayor, not a hero," said Nowek. Russian politics, he thought, made better opera than government. "The answer is no."

"No? What do you mean?"

"If you want to find out who killed Ryzhkov and my two

men, maybe I can help. If you want to dig up dirt to throw at Gromov, hire a farmer.''

''Listen. Don't make up your mind. Think about it. We'll talk tonight. Meanwhile I'll see what Moscow wants done and call you back. Maybe we can do something for the families.''

''Thank you.''

''You know, AMR flies to Tunguska from the Markovo airport. I can make a deal. You could go visit Tunguska and make some useful noises.''

''For useful noise call a pianist. I play violin.''

''We'll talk tonight. Don't decide until you think it over.'' The line clicked off. Nowek pushed aside a clear space on his desk. He found his little pocket loupe, switched on the lamp and let its light fall on the chunk of gravel.

The lens magnified it to a boulder. Definitely granitic origin; the source bedrock for much of the central Siberian plateau. The same rock was all over Markovo in the form of decomposed granite dust. Mud stripped by age and weather of its magnesium and iron.

But here it was new, fresh, and the color. The reds looked brilliant enough to have been cooked inside the rising loaf of molten rock the day before yesterday.

He looked closely at the oddly brilliant face. The lens wasn't powerful enough to see where all the glitter was coming from. Something painted on it? A spilled chemical? That would be a real break if it were so, not that spilled chemicals were so unusual in Siberia. Safely contained toxics, they were rare.

Whatever the cause, the gravel was too fresh, too red to have come from anywhere around here. It came from someplace newer. Someplace north. A gravel pit. A fresh outcrop. But definitely north. What boot had picked it up and dropped it in Ryzkhov's bloody flat? He put the lens down. He had a binocular microscope at home. The glittery face would have to wait.

Rigorous chemical analysis could pinpoint the rock to a specific formation. A place where a boot might have picked it up and carried it all the way to Number Eight Rossinka. But he had as large a budget for that as he had for consultants. He was staring at nothing. It had yet to transform itself into something. Instead, he opened the brochure and began to read.

The Amur tiger, largest of all the world's great cats, seems to materialize out of the taiga shadows, a striped vision of might and mystery that has captured the imaginations of human beings for untold generations . . .

Nowek flipped the page. A map showed the tiger's range at the turn of the century and now. There was a pocket down near Vladivostok in the Primorsky Mountains. A few isolated dots, and a large area up north, the Tunguska Biosphere Preserve.

The teapot shrieked. He stopped and got up to pour himself some tea. He chose a jar of Yugoslavian plum preserves and swirled some into the cup. Yugoslavian preserves were like Markovo condoms; sturdy enough to outlast their own country. Like the governor. Like Prosecutor Gromov. Unlike Andrei Ryzkhov. He sat down and scanned the brochure.

The world called them Siberian tigers and to science they were *Panthera tigris Altaica,* but in Russian the tiger was just *Amba.* It meant, Great Sovereign. They were enormous; the world's biggest cat, sometimes five meters from nose to tail. A tiger the size of a bureaucrat's limousine. He turned the page again.

Tiger skins sell for as much as $15,000, but tiger bones are worth far more, and are easier to smuggle.

A photo showed the various products tiger parts were used to create. Bones for arthritis medicine. The tail for skin disease. The nose for epilepsy. Elixirs for flagging libidos, soups for keener eyesight. The brain cured acne. Wines, powders, balms of all descriptions.

Unusually dense, tiger bone sells for $500 per gram.

That told the whole story, didn't it? With a handful of tigers and a billion Chinese, it could only go one way. A hundred and fifty million lived right over the border. Compared to that, Siberians were just another vanishing species.

Nowek stopped and looked at the yellow knob of bone on his desk, so solid, so unmarked. He picked it up. It weighed a kilo, maybe more. A dog's toy, or something else? A price of five hundred hard dollars a gram would surely interest a hungry entrepreneur.

A man like Ryzkhov.

He sat back and sipped the sweetened tea. The bone. What if Ryzkhov was involved in smuggling? There was enough money in it. But why was this bone left under a dresser? At five hundred dollars a gram it belonged in a safe. Of course, his safe was found open. Why would the murderers leave behind something so valuable?

He turned the bone over in his hand, examining the odd tunnel that burrowed down its length. Drilled? It looked natural. What thief would leave a fortune under a dresser? One who didn't know it was valuable. That would mean it wasn't a falling-out of tiger poachers.

With new interest, he flipped to the next page.

> *The Amur tiger census operation now underway at the Tunguska Biosphere Preserve suggests as few as 200 tigers survive. Some were native to the remote area, but most once roamed the more ecologically vulnerable habitats near the porous border with China. There they were trapped, tranquilized, and reintroduced to Tunguska. Nevertheless, breeding pairs have fallen under the critical . . .*

But Nowek stopped reading.

At the bottom of the page were three more photographs. The first was of V. I. Danilov, the "Minister for the Protection of the Environment and Natural Resources." His puffy cheeks, bald head, and tiny black eyes gave him the look of an offended frog. The second photo was of the American, Dr. Peter Gabriel. He was smiling, but then all Americans smiled.

It was the last picture that stopped him cold.

The picture breathed with life. It was of a beautiful young woman, thick dark hair framing a delicate face, a single lock of hair curling down to partially cover one cheek. She sat in a field of tall grass, spring wildflowers.

This time he could see her eyes.

Dr. Anna Vereskaya, PhD, Tunguska Field Station

Andrei Ryzkhov was married to a woman named Vika. According to Kaznin she was in America, basking in the California sun.

But Dr. Anna Vereskaya was the woman he'd seen that morning in the photograph on the dead man's wall. And she was not in America. This woman was counting tigers up at Tunguska, not a hundred kilometers away.

CHAPTER

5

CALL IT INTRIGUE. Call it chemistry. Call it falling through Chandrasekhar's Limit, the astronomical horizon that surrounds a black hole. Go through it and not even a ghostly photon, never mind the mayor of Markovo, can escape the pull.

Or just call Nowek a troublemaker. When a cat crosses paths with a dog, it doesn't matter that the dog knows there's little hope of catching it. Or if he does, he may well wish he hadn't. It's hope, and hope is like love. Who could ever explain either one?

Nowek left Anna Vereskaya's picture open as he called V. I. Danilov, the Minister for the Protection of the Environment and Natural Resources. But Danilov was at a scientific symposium in Hawaii. Nowek didn't blame him. From Irkutsk, it was better than an invitation to heaven. After all, you didn't have to die to get there.

Five calls, four of them ending with an abrupt hang up and dial tone, yielded an assistant zoology professor from his own alma mater: Irkutsk State University.

"Tiger trade? What is it you wish to know? And who did you say you are?" Professor Yulya Fedorovna sounded like a librarian asking for the latest technique in burning books.

"I'm the mayor of Markovo and what I want to know is, how do you identify a bone from a tiger?"

"You have the carcass. You have the bone. Is there something else?"

"The bone is all I have." Nowek picked up the fragment and turned it in his hand. "It's fifteen centimeters long, eight centimeters thick. Dense and . . ." He put it to his nose and took a quick whiff. "There's a smell."

"Color?"

"Yellow. And there's a kind of a tunnel bored through its length."

"So. The supracondylar foramen. It's indicative of a cat's skeletal structure. At the size you mentioned, a big cat."

"Big as a tiger?"

"There are plenty of dealers who would drill the hole you described in a cow bone in order to sell it as tiger."

Nowek put it down. It had an odd, percussive ring to it when it struck his desktop, like some primitive wooden xylophone. "Then there's no sure way to know."

"Without the skull or claws it's not easy," said Fedorovna. "In Taiwan they bring the whole skeleton to the pharmacy and put it back together piece by piece like a puzzle to prove it's a tiger and not a goat. For amateurs it's the only reliable method."

"But you're a professional. Tell me more about the market in bones."

"It's hard to believe, but global trade in illegal wildlife is the second most lucrative crime after smuggling drugs. Even bigger than smuggling guns. It amounts to six, maybe seven billion a year. And I'm speaking of dollars."

Bigger than drugs? Bones? "I had no idea."

"It's all a matter of incentive. A native hunter who has never earned one honest ruble in all his life will get maybe six hundred dollars for a dead tiger. The smugglers in Vladivostok get ten times that, but they're Armenians."

Most people would say that an Armenian smuggler was a redundancy. "What happens from there?"

"The body is broken down into pieces at what is called a 'black pharmacy.' The pieces go to the highest bidder. The mainland Chinese usually. A whole unprocessed body, fetches thirty thousand dollars. By the time the animal is reduced to apothecary powders, it's worth as much as gold. Even more."

Thirty thousand dollars was a lot of money. Worth killing for, surely. He hefted the bone. "There's no way to stop the trade?"

"Once when we had borders that meant something, laws, police. But now? Tiger bones, gallbladders from black bears, goral goats. If it moves and there's a market willing to pay, you have a line of men with rifles ready to shoot."

From a half-billion starving peasants to a billion entrepreneurs. "To Grow Rich Is Glorious!" was their slogan. How had the Chinese done it? Nowek wondered. Maybe capitalism was in their genes, the way horror and tragedy and drunkenness spiraled through Russian DNA. "Where do the poachers find these tigers?"

"Once wherever there was taiga, you had tigers. Their natural range extended from the Pacific all through Siberia and northern China. In 1900 there were eight distinct species. Today three of them are gone and three more have for all practical purposes vanished."

"The Amur is surviving?"

"Barely. When the situation became tense with China in the sixties, the transborder range of tigers was split in two. The Chinese wiped their population out. Only on our side was there any chance of survival. Now it's more difficult. The irony is, tigers did better under the Communists."

"A lot of people feel the same way."

There was just the smallest hesitation to register the professor's surprise. "They sealed the borders against smugglers and prohibited hunting. Now, anything goes. A few tigers survive down near Vladivostok in the Primorsky Mountains, but not for long. The Koreans are logging it, so the boar and elk population will suffer. Tigers eat boar and elk, so you could say the die is cast. That's why a large number of Primorsky tigers were trapped and flown up to—"

"Tunguska?"

"Today it holds the largest wild population. Probably in excess of two hundred but nobody really knows."

Nowek did the math. Two hundred tigers, thirty thousand dollars each. Six million. Enough to interest Ryzhkov, though hardly what you would call an infinite resource. "The Americans are redrilling the Tunguska oil fields. That can't be so good for tigers from an environmental standpoint."

"Just the opposite. The Americans control access, in and out. They have rules that mean something. Poachers respect them. And Tunguska is hard to get to even if there were no Americans."

Nowek thought of Ryzhkov. A man with his connections could go there. "Do you know a tiger specialist named Vereskaya? She's at Tunguska."

"Vereskaya?" Another pause. "She's not of the Academy."

Scientists were worse snobs than even violinists. You were either of the Academy, or you were nothing. "But you've heard of her."

"Those people come and go. One day they're here, the next day who knows? They get their money overseas. It's all a great mystery. We have to work for our bread. That's what I know."

Those people? Worse snobs, and even more jealous. He looked at her picture in the tiger brochure. Nina. Anna. Counter of tigers, friend to the dead. Nothing fit. It made his head hurt. He tossed the paper aside. "Do you think the tigers are safe up at Tunguska?"

"For the moment. The rule is, where people can go, the tigers are doomed. Of course, the fewer tigers they kill, the more expensive they become. The more expensive they become, the longer the line of hunters with rifles. Did you know that a pair of gallbladders from a bear will buy a jeep? And now there's even hunting by helicopter. So you see, it's market forces. Supply and demand. What can you do?"

"Not much." No wonder they called economics the dismal science, he thought. "Tell me, without a carcass, without the entire skeleton to reassemble, how could a professional identify one bone?"

"Proceeding formally, there would have to be tests, DNA sampling, chemical analysis. There would be a lot of time and expense . . ." There was a pause.

"There are less formal approaches?"

"I work for the Natural Resources Ministry, Mayor Nowek," she said. But then, more softly, "On Mondays, Tuesdays, and Wednesdays. I assure you, the university lab is well equipped for identifying skeletal remains."

"You should be. When it comes to bones, Siberia leads the world. Thank you for your information. I'll let you know what I decide." He hung up, then lifted the phone again and dialed the clinic.

Dr. Grossman answered.

"Anything yet on that piece of orange cloth from the dog?"

"Yes and no. We extracted blood onto five sample slides, then used our typing kit to identify—"

"Please, Doctor. Just tell me what you know, not how."

"It's a puzzle. We got the same result from all five tests."

"What's so puzzling?"

"The blood type test kits are all from civil defense materials issued in the sixties. We're decades beyond the expiration dates stamped on them. It's amazing when they work at all, much less agree. *That's* what's strange. Anyway, the blood was type AB negative. That's rare. Ryzkhov's was type O. Of course, the dog is completely different. You understand? In Markovo there can't be more than twenty people with AB negative blood. One of them may have a hole in his backside for his troubles."

"So there's progress."

"If we knew who had type AB negative blood."

"We don't?"

"We're lucky if we know who is still alive. You might try army records or police files. But there's a faster way."

"I'm listening."

"Announce a shortage of AB negative with an offer to pay in dollars. You'd have your killer in an hour."

"If he's Russian."

"But who else could it be?"

Good question. Nowek was worrying his wedding band again. It was a terrible habit. "Thank you for your assistance. Please be sure there's some kind of written report." Nowek hung up, jotted down *Army/Police—blood type AB neg.* Maybe he could get someone in Irkutsk to look into that. He dialed Chuchin's extension in the commissary.

"What? What is it?" said Chuchin. He seemed annoyed at the interruption. There were voices in the background and the sound of metal pots clanging.

"Get the car ready."

"We just arrived. Where are we going now?"

Nowek looked at the heavy bone. "Fishing," he said.

CHAPTER

6

A SIGN SCALED for a skyscraper wrapped itself around Kaznin's two-floor office building, its letters picked out in fresh red paint: SECURITY ASSOCIATES OF MARKOVO.

Chuchin parked the Land Cruiser at a safe distance from Kaznin's white Volvo, as though he might catch diphtheria from it. "You'll be long?"

"I hope not."

Two Ladas, old Soviet-era Fiat clones, were parked next to a jet-black BMW, its engine puffing white exhaust; a millionaire with a cigar. The driver peered over a magazine, watching as Nowek got out, almost, but not quite, interested.

SAM's lobby contained a receptionist, a desk, and behind her a huge mirror that could only be one-way glass.

Just inside the entrance was a display cabinet filled with an assortment of western perfumes, cosmetics, toiletries, and colognes. What was the connection? In Markovo, security and shaving cream were both rare and valuable commodities.

The receptionist had just one phone, a modern type with multiple lines rather than the usual array of black units molded from some indestructible chemical. "Can I help you?" she asked cheerfully.

Cheerfulness was another rare commodity. She was blond, about twenty. Gold links disappeared down the neck of her blouse. Her face was a mask of powders and rouges. Her smile all paint and teeth. A button pinned to the pneumatic slope of her breast invited a closer look. It said HI! MY NAME IS SAM!

"I'm here to see Kaznin," said Nowek. He sniffed. What was that smell?

"Your name?"

"Mer," he said impatiently. The mayor.

She cocked her head. "First or last?"

"First. The last is Nowek. Is your name really Sam?"

"One moment." Long red nails played across the telephone keypad. She looked up. "Is he expecting you?"

"Probably."

"One—" Before she could speak, the door opened and a short man in a long black coat emerged, followed by two *byki,* pit bulls, who didn't need little tags to announce their job titles. Their jackets were buttoned, but the bulges showing through the navy blue fabric were more than just muscles. Both had close-cropped hair on top, worn long down the sides.

Their boss's hair was silver streaked with jet black, as though precious metals had been poured over a knob of basalt. His skin was deep olive and it glistened like some rare, polished wood. Semyon Yufa, the dark Ukrainian, the demi-Turk, was a deity in the pantheon of Markovo's underworld.

"Mayor," he said, his teeth even and white. His eyes didn't match the smile. "It's a pleasure to finally meet you. But after three years? Your term is almost over. You've stayed a stranger all this time. Why?" He seemed honestly curious.

"It's just a theory I've developed."

"Theory?"

"That government should keep its distance from business-men like you." There was a slight stiffening in the guards. "What could we do but get in your way?"

"Sure, sure." Yufa glanced at the two and they relaxed. "But we should work together. We're all Siberians. We all breathe the same air and piss the same water."

"And bleed the same blood."

Yufa seemed taken aback at the mention of blood, as though

someone had belched in the middle of a testimonial speech. "I heard all about young Andrei and your two men. Tell me, do you need some help?"

"What did you have in mind?"

Yufa clapped both of his pit bulls. "Borya, Vanya, you can take one on loan. I'll cover the costs. Life has been generous to me. Why not give something back?"

There were clear advantages, Nowek thought. They'll steal less than my officers. But he said, "No thanks."

"Well, come and visit if you change your mind."

"You're still at Mercury Condom?"

"Sure. The 'Best Protection Against Inflation.' " Yufa smiled benevolently and left, trailed by his two watchdogs, heading for the idling BMW.

"Mayor?"

Nowek turned.

Kaznin stood in the doorway next to the mirror. "You've surprised me twice in one day. You should have called. I have a busy afternoon."

"So I understand. When does Gromov show up?"

"When he arrives." Kaznin glanced at the secretary. "Come in. We'll talk for a moment."

Beyond the door was a kind of squad room with chairs, desks, and a buffet loaded with more food than Nowek had seen in one place for years. Despite himself, his stomach growled. His suit felt looser than it had even this morning, like the cartoon characters who evaporate, leaving only loose change and a pile of clothes behind. He didn't have any loose change. What had Galena said? Go pretend to do something useful? Eating would be very useful. But Kaznin's food?

Never.

There was no harm in looking. There was roast chicken, slabs of smoked fish, a train yard of sausage coiled round and round, a creamy mountain of cheese. A pile of cucumbers and tomatoes gave off a tart, vinegary smell. There were two samovars and steam rose from both of them. A staircase rose at the back of the room. In a small alcove beyond it, a Coca-Cola vending machine hummed.

"You put all this out for Gromov?" Nowek was impressed.

"This? No. It's all for my boys," said Kaznin. "What they don't eat by the end of the day we donate to the militia and to the poor. Actually, that's saying the same thing."

Nowek didn't rise to the Fisherman's bait.

"Anyway, we employ forty now. My boys guard warehouses, motor pools. We're branching into corporate security as our next big push. New applications come in every day. More than we can possibly hire, but we keep them on file just in case. It's only natural. Where else can they find a job that pays real wages and offers real benefits?"

"There's Yufa."

Kaznin barked a quick laugh. "I admire your ability to joke, but I know you also have your pride. You want something? Coffee? We have both decaf and regular. How about a Coke?"

Nowek saw that it was in fact an American soda machine, right down to the one-dollar cost. Who had a dollar to spend on fizzy brown water? Who had a dollar?

Kaznin could see what Nowek was thinking. "Come on, Mayor. For you it's free." Kaznin reached behind the machine and touched a control. The lights blinked, and a can thumped out the chute. "You just have to know where the buttons are hidden." Kaznin popped the can and poured it into a glass. He held it up.

Nowek didn't touch it. "What about Ryzkhov?"

"What about him?" Kaznin put the drink aside.

"Did he know where they were hidden?"

Kaznin's eyes seemed almost transparent, a hint of blue, a flash of green, the fleshy pink lids. "Ryzkhov was very well connected," he said. "A famous father, a brother in a power ministry. An arrangement with a big foreign company that paid enough to support both the father and a wife in America. An apartment at Rossinka. A house in California. Cars. Only . . ."

"He wasn't connected well enough?"

"Everyone must have his *kryusha*." It was slang for roof. Protection. "The more you have inside the house, the higher your *kryusha* must be. Ryzkhov had a good one, but in the end, it must be said that it leaked."

Nowek thought of the blood-soaked carpet. "An AmerRus roof shouldn't leak."

"Maybe he was involved with other matters than AMR. Not all of them so clear-cut."

Nowek was drawn to a platter of sliced cucumbers and dill. The smells were dizzying. He straightened. "You think Ryzkhov did business with *mafiyas*?"

"*Mafiyas*." Kaznin's entire face seemed to come into slightly sharper focus. "It's easy to suspect, but difficult to prove. Let me explain. Ivan imports a truckload of film. He pays duty tax. Sergei pays the custom official to look the other way. Sergei sells his film at half price and becomes rich. Ivan is left with unsold goods. He points a finger and cries *mafiya*. Is it *mafiya*, or is the other guy smarter? You see, it's a matter of view-point."

"What's your viewpoint?"

"Siberia is cold in the winter and hot in the summer. That a communist with a dollar is a happier man than a democrat with a ruble." Kaznin smiled. "You see, I'm only interested in facts."

Nowek noticed a small metal box on the buffet. It was dark brown and stamped in faded yellow lettering. A Red Army field ration? A beggar at a banquet, it was utterly out of place. Nowek picked it up. The label said it was cottage cheese and prune. "For your boys?"

Kaznin held out his hand, but Nowek flipped it over and read the reverse side:

DON'T EAT AFTER 1991

"It's probably fossilized," said Nowek. "What's it doing here?"

"Souvenirs from a bad time." Kaznin took the ancient ration

box away and pulled a cord to open the curtain shrouding the one-way glass.

The receptionist was mending some small tear in the hem of her skirt. The front of the desk had hidden how short it was. What was the new word for it? Handkerchief skirt. From here, Nowek saw it barely covered the tops of her thighs as she ran a needle and thread in and out, in and out, swiftly, mechanically, as though caught in the act of spinning her own dress from cobwebs.

He watched. In Moscow secretaries no longer looked like whores, or so he'd read. But in Markovo, everything comes later. He wondered, do they look like schoolgirls in Hong Kong?

Kaznin nodded at the receptionist. "Can you imagine?" he said as they both watched her work. "I found her in a special school." She leaned over and bit off a piece of thread, then carefully smoothed the skirt back down.

"For secretaries?"

"For witches. It's in Irkutsk right next to the university. They train them to accompany businessmen on big deals. The girls learn how to cast spells so the terms come out favorably. Or perhaps they divert the opposition in other ways. Now every businessman has to have his witch."

He thought of the photo of Anna Vereskaya. The tiger woman. Not his wife. Not even Andrei Ryzkhov's wife. "It's a shame Ryzkhov didn't have a witch."

Kaznin moved close. "Actually, I think he did."

"The woman his neighbor saw?"

"Coming and going at strange hours, 'like a vampire.' She must be a pretty vampire. A rich man like Ryzkhov would buy nothing less than the best. Is she a dancer at one of the clubs? Or someone more educated, more refined? More capable of amusing a cultured person? What's your opinion?"

"That a thief with a dollar is the same as a thief with a ruble. That you and Prosecutor Gromov are hanging noodles from my ears about finding Ryzkhov's murderer. That a consultant for AmerRus makes a poor investigator when it comes to pointing a finger at his employer. You see," said Nowek, "like you I'm only interested in facts."

"You always look for the dark side."

"In Siberia, they're easier to see."

"Maybe this woman will also be easy to see. I hope so. What if she isn't so innocent? What if she witnessed the murder?" Kaznin lowered his voice. "What if she herself is the killer? It's not impossible, you know."

The boot mark in blood. The stone, the bullets. The torture. It didn't feel like a woman's touch. "Ryzkhov could keep her fed, warm, happy. What could be her reason to kill him?"

"Ah," said Kaznin. "There's a question. Why would someone kill Ryzkhov? Politics? Money? Sex? Remember, no place in Russia is more dangerous than the bedroom."

"For the woman." Kaznin was painting an outline of the criminal without giving the outline a name. A name that Nowek was sure they both knew. Why? "You'll look for her?"

"I'll find her," said Kaznin. "Give me this person and I'll give you your case. Perhaps she wanted more of what Andrei had and decided to get it by any means necessary."

"With a knife and a gun?"

"And an accomplice."

"Wearing an AmerRus uniform?"

"Before you say a word, listen. AmerRus brings their uniforms into Markovo for cleaning. Sometimes they don't all return to Tunguska. You can find them for sale over in the Black Lung. Anyone can buy one. To wear a faded American jacket is considered fashionable."

Nowek had to admit that this was perfectly true. He'd seen some orange fabric in Galena's own closet, though it wasn't a whole uniform. Why hadn't he remembered this before now? "Those three bullets. The special, American-made one you found?"

"Yes?"

"You said they were designed to inflict damage but not penetrate the body. How did you find them?"

"An experienced investigator knows first of all how to dig."

Nowek looked at him.

"About the woman," Kaznin said. "Think. She had access to Ryzkhov. She knew he had money. Maybe she has a friend who says, let's kill the bastard and live well forever. You have a knife? I have a gun. We'll do it tonight."

"I don't—"

"Wait. She introduces him to Andrei. He takes them up-stairs. He pours his own killers a glass of cognac. Now we have three glasses, just what was found. The woman talks. Perhaps he has disappointed her in some way? Or worse," said Kaznin darkly, "betrayed her trust. They argue. He's confused. What has he done but help her? She diverts him long enough to allow—"

"The accomplice to do his dirty work."

"Absolutely." Kaznin smiled. "The first blow stuns Andrei. He wakes up in his bed to a nightmare."

Nowek had to agree.

"The music is turned up full to muffle their crime. These two want more than what they can grab. They want what's in the safe, too. He resists. The man holds him while the gun is brought next to a knee." Kaznin moved close to Nowek and thrust a finger against his leg. "The trigger is pulled. To be honest, there's even a name for this."

Nowek moved away. "A name?"

"Tickling the bone. An extreme measure practiced by members of State Security beyond the control of calmer heads. An ice pick is shoved into a vertebra, an elbow, a knee, and you scrape it along the bone. The effect was dramatic. A bullet would be even more dramatic."

"I can imagine."

"But poor Andrei doesn't have to imagine. It's happening to him. There's a fortune in hard currency in his safe. They want the combination. He refuses." Kaznin's finger touches the other knee. "The trigger is pulled again."

"Stop it."

Kaznin jabs him again in the elbow. "And a final time. He's paralyzed now. But not unconscious. A man in this condition has only one thing left, and that's hope. He gives them the combination. But there's a problem. The dog has acute hearing. The gunshots alarm him. He begins to bark. It draws the attention of a neighbor. The neighbor calls the militia. The militia arrive. Now the killers have a real problem. Ryzkhov isn't dead. Not yet. He's filled with pain, but he still isn't imagining his own death. You see, hope is the last to die."

"You paint such a detailed picture, Major. Are you sure you weren't there?"

"A professional sees things that others can't. They open the safe," Kaznin went on. "And they give him the blade. But now there's the militia. What to do? The killers ambush your two officers and make their escape." He slapped one hand against the other. "Simple."

Nowek looked up. "Too simple."

"Criminals have obvious minds. If she was there that night, we're almost ready to put this matter in a box and wrap a ribbon around it. But first we need to find her. That's what I will do." Kaznin pulled the curtain closed. "Let me show you my office."

Upstairs, Kaznin's office was aggressively furnished in Danish modern. A Fisher VCR fed a wide-screen Toshiba. There were no books in the shelves. Instead they were filled with hundreds of videotapes. Nowek walked over to look. Some were Swedish and German pornography, some were action movies, and some were unmarked. Blanks. Kaznin's desk was made from blond ash. It was neater than Nowek's but then, so was his life.

Kaznin installed himself behind his desk. He looked proud of it, but not too proud. A well-earned consideration for hard, difficult jobs professionally done. "You like the place?"

"Very sophisticated." The tinted window looked down on the fenced yards, piles of rusted machinery, and anonymous workshops that dominated the district.

As Nowek looked down, a car pulled into the parking lot below. It was dark and came to an abrupt, impatient stop as though any pause was an intolerable diversion from important matters. The driver got out and scurried to open the back door.

Prosecutor Gromov unfolded himself and stood, resplendent in a dark blue general's uniform. He wore no coat and no hat, as though weather was a minor irritant not to be taken seriously. His hair was cut close to his skull.

"He's here," said Nowek. "Perhaps I should go."

"Wait. This will only take a moment." Kaznin's leather swivel chair squealed as he turned. "Prosecutor Gromov is standing on my throat to catch these murderers quickly. Why? You think you're the only one who cares about law. But remember, Gromov is the number-one law enforcement official in Irkutsk. However, there's more to such a simple story."

"AmerRus."

"Exactly. Our number-one source of capital. A piece of orange cloth at the murder scene is suggestive. A handful of foreign bullets? Even more. Could they be involved in this dirty work? We know the victim worked with them."

"You tell me."

Kaznin scowled. "You think that evidence will be forgotten, but believe me, if it points firmly in their direction then I say, let's follow it with all powers at our command." He paused to gauge the impact of his words.

"But?"

"But if there are ambiguities that result in wild accusations, not only do we risk losing the true criminal, but we endanger an important part of our entire economy. Are we a safe place to invest? Robbery, gangs, policemen shot. False charges. You know, there's no line of people waiting to throw money at us anymore. Why would an American invest in such a dangerous place?"

"I have enough trouble understanding Russians."

"Plainly. You don't trust Prosecutor Gromov to do his job. You think he needs your help. But he thinks he needs *my* help. You can't put two bears in one den. Napoleon himself said that one bad general is better than two good ones."

"Napoleon had a lot of time to think about it at Elba."

"Elba?"

"It's like a resort on the Black Sea," said Nowek. "Only a little more basic. Suppose that AmerRus *is* involved. Your best client. The number-one source of dollars in all Irkutsk."

"Justice has only one flag." The telephone buzzed. Kaznin picked it up. "I'll be right down," he said without waiting. He hung it back up. "Prosecutor Gromov will not be pleased if he discovers that you're meddling in delicate matters against his wishes. And don't forget, where there's Gromov, there's the governor."

"And Visa, MasterCard, SiberBank, and Credit Suisse."

"Money is too dirty for you to touch? Think. If the Americans pull out of Irkutsk there will be anarchy, not justice. Then, when we're too busy fighting each other to notice, a hundred million Chinese will stream over the border and take what they've wanted from the beginning. Our oil, our timber, our gold . . ."

"Our tigers?"

"Tigers?" Was it a sports team? A new car? Kaznin seemed baffled. "What do you mean?"

"Amba. Big cats. Illegal smuggling of carcasses," Nowek explained. "The Chinese medicinal trade. Bones. I'm sure a professional like you would know of it."

"*Those* tigers. Why do you bring them up?"

"We both know there are some up at Tunguska."

"And?"

"They're very valuable on the black market. Valuable enough to interest an entrepreneur. Maybe a person engaged in less well-defined activities. As you say, it's not a matter of law so much as viewpoint." Nowek stood up.

"Mayor?"

"Yes?"

"Let this drop. Let a professional do what he knows how to do. And most of all, when a man dies, all black thoughts should die with him. Accusing Andrei Ryzkhov of smuggling tiger parts is a bad idea. He has an influential family and you don't need more enemies."

"I'm just the mayor," said Nowek. "I have no enemies."

"In that case, I'd like you to meet Prosecutor Gromov."

Prosecutor N. I. Gromov stood at the receptionist's desk
with her telephone to his ear. She stared up at him dreamily, as
though he were a famous rock star.

Gromov's dark blue uniform was decorated with a gold star
and a few tasteful medals. His bony face had the look that was
the trademark of entire generations of Russian bureaucrats: a
studiously empty expression that could be mistaken for anything, preferably a sense of high great purpose. You saw it in
the courts of the czars, you saw it on Lenin, Brezhnev. It was a
kind of badge.

His eyes flicked up as the door to the squad room opened
and Nowek appeared. He held up a hand before Nowek could
speak. "Wait."

Gromov was a Socialist Realist rendering of a prosecutor
general; his face was angular, his manner that of a man striding
resolutely into a bright and just future. His hair was shaved
down to an efficient pink fuzz. His black leather belt had luster,
not just shine. His shoes, too. Nowek wondered how he'd
managed to keep them pristine walking in from the car. Maybe
Gromov floated, impervious to gravity.

"Where did you find them? Kiev? How did they get so far?"
He listened. "Well. Now we know. Keep me informed if
there's any further progress." Gromov hung up without saying
anything else, took out a leather-bound notebook and a gold
pen. He jotted a few notes, snapped it shut, slipped it into his
breast pocket, and then, finally, looked at Nowek as though
he'd just entered the prosecutor's office with a tray of sweet
cakes. "Yes?"

Nowek ran a hand over the stubble of his beard, wishing
he'd shaved this morning. "I'm Nowek."

"This is the mayor," prompted Kaznin as he stepped from
behind. "How was the flight up from Irkutsk?"

"Bumpy," said Gromov. "You're the mayor?"

"Don't worry about bumps," said Kaznin. "Things will be

smooth from here on." He took Nowek's elbow again and with the slightest pinch said, "We've had a useful talk about the division of efforts in the matter of the Ryzkhov murder."

"Murders," Nowek corrected.

Gromov's eyes sharpened. His face nearly glowed with intensity. "I trust everything has been explained? Your role has been made clear? This matter is going to be resolved quickly and there's no time or energy to waste on unproductive measures. This is going to be a model investigation, a model prosecution, and a . . ."

"Excuse me," said Nowek, "but isn't a model a small imitation of the real thing?"

Gromov looked at Kaznin. "What did he say?"

"That we will have his full cooperation."

"Well, good then." Gromov cleared his throat. "I'm needed back in Irkutsk. We have Korean lumber workers running off and showing up all over the place. One made it to Kiev. Can you believe it? *Kiev*. Who would go there?"

The North Koreans maintained logging camps in Siberia. Labor camps, actually. It was a measure of how desperate things were in their own country that they would willingly escape, on foot, across Siberia instead of returning home.

"Personally, I'd try for Saudi Arabia," said Nowek. "It's warmer and they don't have trees."

Gromov glared. "Your briefing with Major Kaznin was thorough." It was not phrased as a question. A question had one possible answer too many.

Nowek came up with a third possibility. "Yes and no. So far I've heard a great deal about AmerRus. I haven't heard very much about justice, but it's early."

"Justice is my worry," said Gromov. "You do your job. Kaznin and I will do ours." His face flickered off, uninterested. The intense shine receded. He looked at Kaznin. "I want to hear what progress you've made."

"Don't worry. Please come upstairs," Kaznin said with an uneasy glance at Nowek.

Gromov walked up to Nowek expecting him to step aside. When he didn't, he stopped. "Is there something else, Mayor?"

"Since you mention it, yes. My job includes seeing to the families of men killed in the line of duty."

Gromov looked wary. "So?"

"Two militia died in Ryzkhov's flat. There's no pension for their families. I thought you might have some advice."

Gromov edged a bit closer, hoping to bump Nowek aside, but the mayor seemed rooted to the floor. "All right," he said, his jaw tense. "My office will call you later today to make the necessary arrangements. Thank you for bringing the matter to my personal attention. You'll be hearing from us."

Nowek stepped aside and the prosecutor steamed by like a battleship jostling a scow out of the way.

The night was sweet with promise, the air soft, the stars bright. The temperature's drop was arrested by a southwest wind that brought the first clouds of mosquitos drifting in from the marshes by the river and summoned the bald heads of spring mushrooms poking from the snow.

You're too soon, he thought. In Russia it didn't pay to be too early, too avid about doing your job. It was true whether you were out for blood, or out for justice. No matter how warm things seemed now, it was wise to remember that it would surely freeze again.

Nowek returned home to find the weights dusted, the stove ready to light with a match, even the mirror by his front door was polished. He walked in and shut the door. He listened. There was just the soft ticking of the windup clock. "Galena?"

Nothing.

The kitchen was cleared, the dirty dishes washed and stacked neatly by the basin. The wooden railing on the stairs leading up to the bedrooms was polished. But of his daughter there was no sign. He would give a lot for a filthy ashtray and a cold cup of coffee sitting on the table. He went to the picture of Nina. The shrine.

He heard a noise and looked up "Galena?"

It was just the mild wind picking at the bones of the old house. He looked back at Nina. Three years. He could feel the emptiness of the upstairs trailing down like a breeze from an open window.

He checked the time. Six. If it got to be eight, the militia would hear of it and, embarrassment or not, they'd drag her in.

If they could find her. If she wasn't halfway to Hong Kong. If the last honest member of the Markovo militia had not just gotten himself killed. You couldn't expect much certainty from life anymore. Life was filled with unknowns. Music was more dependable.

Nowek walked to the *Zvyezda* record player and switched it on. It hummed pleasantly as he found Beethoven's Violin Sonata in A, the *Kreutzer,* and set it spinning.

The tone arm dropped. There was a scratch, a hiss, and then God himself appeared in Nowek's kitchen in the guise of vibrating strings, flying fingers, and the kind of paranormal concentration that permits men to lift cars. It lifted his worry, his memory.

He opened the wooden microscope case and set it up on the kitchen table. The stage was etched for establishing grain size, but for the chunk of red granite that wasn't necessary. He wanted a good look. He moved the table lamp to shed light down, then put his eye to the binocular eyepieces, running the focus in and out until it was razor sharp.

The crystals were large nuggets under medium magnification. Big crystals meant a slow cooling process; slow-cooling granite from deep underground, deep within the rising pluton of magma that formed the basement rock of all Siberia.

Progress! He'd narrowed the sample's origin down to a subcontinent. He turned it over.

The feldspars looked like crumbling cubes of pink sugar, all fractured faces, shot through with white quartzite veining. The quartz had come much later, introduced through percolating groundwaters that seeped through the stress-fractured rock. He turned it one last time to the odd face, the glittery face.

What to the naked eye looked like glints of light appeared in the microscope as a landscape of tiny spheres. He increased the magnification.

Now he floated above a field of remarkably similar beads. The spheres were utterly transparent, and not at all round. More like teardrops, like beads of sweat.

He took an eyedropper of acid and squirted some onto the sample. No reaction. Not organic. With a probe he scraped along the surface. A bead broke free.

With the point of his probe he pressed down on it. It cracked with the classic, conchoidal fracture of glass.

Glass is nothing more than melted sand; calcium, sodium, silica, plus a near-infinite number of potential impurities. Add lime of soda and you had a windowpane. Add boron and you had heat-resistant glass suitable for a lightbulb. Lead-alkali impurities yielded fine crystal. Natural glass, obsidian, was a volcanic by-product. A material born of great heat.

What were these tiny teardrops?

Molten silica. Liquid sand. A glassworks? More like an explosion at a glassworks. A nuclear test sent material like this into the air as well. These tiny, delicate drops of frozen glass bespoke great forces. Violent forces.

An explosion. A volcano? An atomic blast?

He put his eyes to the microscope once more. He thought back to a photograph he'd once seen, one of the early ultrahigh-speed pictures. A boxer is hit in the jaw, his sweat flies out in a halo caught in the strobe's fire.

That's what he was looking at here. Molten silicates blasted into the air. As the globules cooled, they assumed the classic, streamlined, teardrop shape. A violent punch. An explosion. Who had thrown the punch, and where?

You could make a thin section of it. You could take a diamond saw and slice it to a thinness of three-hundredths of a millimeter, place it between microscope slides. Its components would flash their signature colors. If you were still unsure you could do chemical analysis, X-ray fluorescence spectrometry. You could look at the chemistry of each crystal; like snow, it was absolutely individual. With the right maps you could guess where the chunk of gravel carried by that boot had come from.

That was how they might approach such a problem in the civilized world. If Nowek had so much as suggested it here, they would throw him in the drunk tank.

He peered down at the field of glass. Stare at nothing long enough, it becomes something.

A violent explosion. A punch capable of fusing sand, blasting it into the sky, spraying exposed outcrops of Nepa granite. The moon was dusted with material just like this, ejected from craters. One crater in particular, Tycho, was surrounded by a brilliant white halo of glass so bright even the naked eye could see it when the angle was right.

He stood up as the record player worked its way through the *Kreutzer*. He went to a bookshelf and found a volume on astronomy. His father had always wanted him to take an interest in the stars, mainly to divert him from what he termed, "grubbing in the dirt."

He flipped by the chapters on the birth of stars, the organization of galaxies, their place in the universe. He came, at last, to the solar system, the planets, and finally to the detritus that was left over after the planets had formed.

Asteroids. Comets. The construction debris that littered the solar system. They hurtled through space at unimaginable speeds. When they struck the earth's atmosphere, the smaller ones made shooting stars. The bigger ones made craters. He was searching for a photomicrograph of pyroclastic ejecta— glass beads—when he found something else.

A photograph of charred, toppled trees. It looked a lot like a typical Soviet oil development in the Siberian taiga except that there were no rigs present.

The scene is Siberia, in the great taiga forests below the Arctic Circle; the date is June 30, 1908. There is no warning at 7:30 on this sunny morning when a column of fire descends from the east. A fireball bright as the sun speeds silently toward the deso-

late wilderness . . . it explodes with the force of a ten-megaton nuclear blast . . .

The photograph is captioned, *The Tunguska Event.*

He put the book down. The tiger brochure, Ryzkhov's vampire, a tiger researcher. Now this. It was as if he'd picked up a compass and found the needle pointing to a new pole; a pole named Tunguska.

Arkady Volsky was still at his office in Irkutsk when Nowek called. The *Kreutzer* was building to its climax.

"*Allo.*"

"I'm calling you back."

"Grisha! I made a bet with myself whether you would."

"Did you win or lose?"

"Funny. What have you decided?"

Nowek thought of the woman in the tiger brochure. The woman on Ryzkhov's wall. The woman on his own wall. Their faces flew into his mind, mingled, separated. A fireball descending silently from the east, exploding with the force of a hydrogen bomb. "I spoke with Gromov today. I'm afraid we didn't hit it off."

"That prick. He expects his turds to stand up and salute on the way out. What did he say?"

"That justice was his worry."

"He's got a real sense of humor, I'll give him that. What about Tunguska?"

The music died away to silence. The room seemed even more empty. Where was Galena? In some dingy basement? In a bar? She couldn't be in Hong Kong, could she? On a plane? How fast did they fly? "How soon can you get me on a flight to Tunguska?"

You could hear Volsky's smile through the telephone. "Tomorrow morning."

"Then do it. Also, who do you know with access to army records? The clinic here analyzed the cloth we found. The blood type is rare. Type AB negative. It's not Ryzkhov's blood. It's not the dog's, either. I think it may be from the killer."

"Sure. But what changed your mind about Tunguska?"

"Did you know that an asteroid struck it in 1908?"

"We catch shit from everyone. I'm glad you decided to go. What do you want from me?"

"Proshli mne kapustu." It meant send me a cabbage.

"What flavor?"

"You can run down those medical records for me. Blood type AB negative, okay?"

"Got it. Meet the helicopter at the Markovo airfield. By the way, it will be an AMR flight so . . ."

"I know. Behave."

"That would be something to see." Volsky hung up.

Nowek listened to the record player hiss. If he tried a little harder, he could even hear the soft ticking of the clock out by the front door. An empty, hollow sound that kept time with an echo from his heart.

He took hold of his wedding ring and pulled it off. His eyes went to Nina's picture on the wall. He set it down onto the table with a slap, like a man seeing the devil's bet, and raising it.

CHAPTER

7

IN SIBERIA, everything leaves a trail. In Siberia, even the most rugged things are alarmingly delicate. Break the steel-hard hide of the tundra with the tread of a snow tank and you create a phenomenon known as "thermokarst"; in one year the ruts become chasms. In two, they're geology. By the third winter they have a name on the map.

In a land designed to swallow whole nations without a trace, people also left trails. In deep cold the winds die, the sky empties, and each molecule of air hangs motionless in suspended animation. It gets so still that a breath so small it couldn't blow out a candle will send an avalanche of snow cascading down from the trees. Great cold scalds the face. People steam like dray horses pulling uphill, each breath a shower of live steel in the lungs; each exhalation an explosion of steam.

At sixty degrees of frost the steam has nowhere to go. It coalesces into a dense mist the locals call "people fog." The mist is as motionless as the air. Walk and you leave a tunnel swirling behind. The fog can last all day, and Markovo becomes a warren of tunnels marking a person's travel to work, to a shop, to an alley to drink. When it leads to a body congealing on the snow, the trail can outlast its maker.

But it's spring, and for now the great colds are gone. The trail left behind by Militiaman Gorits consists of a sealed jar of rice, a slice of bread, an official photograph, a half-drunk bottle of vodka, and an empty glass. These were assembled on a chipped wooden table covered by a silk Mudejar prayer rug. As a celebration for the dead, it was part Chechen, part Russian, part mystical. In short, Siberian.

His wife stood by the table accepting gifts of food brought by neighbors and relatives. She was a tiny dark-haired woman with red-rimmed eyes. Two young children clung to her skirt, both girls, both with their father's tightly curled helmet of hair. In another room, an uncle, a brother, an older woman cooking over a single-ring electric stove.

The smell of lamb made Nowek's mouth water. Where had they found lamb? He felt a flash of suspicion, the kind that any Russian naturally feels toward any Chechen. Of course they'd stolen it. Where else could they find meat fresh enough to bleed? But this was old thinking of the very worst kind. He covered the suspicion, though he could still feel the spike of it poking him in the side.

He walked over and handed the dead man's wife an envelope bearing the town's official seal.

She took the envelope and said, "It should have been you."

Nowek looked at her. Had she just said that?

She pushed the two young children away. As she stood she seemed to grow inward, to darken. "He stayed in the militia because he said you were different." She paused, then said, "Now he's dead and you're alive. That's different all right."

"I'm sorry."

He turned and left. He stopped outside the front door and heard a loud male voice call out, "How much?"

Another warm day and the snow was melting in earnest. The wind stirred by the Land Cruiser's passage made the pines shiver in heavy wet clumps.

Chuchin said, "In dollars?"

Nowek said, "Two thousand for Gorits, fifteen hundred for his partner."

"They'll celebrate for a month. What made Gromov do it?"

"The prosecutor did his job," said Nowek. "I did mine." He paused, then said, "I told the militia to start looking."

"She'll come back," said Chuchin. "Galena's just torturing you."

"It's working."

"You have other worries. This trip for example. What is it really for anyway? Gromov and Kaznin, they're in charge."

He'd shown him Vereskaya's picture and seen the look on Chuchin's face. "She may be able to identify the bone."

"Forget bones. She's not Nina, Mayor. You can't stare at her picture and make her into someone else."

Nowek kept silent. Not because Chuchin was wrong.

The Land Cruiser sent a bow wave of ice water flying as it sped toward Markovo's municipal airport. They hit wet ice and slewed around a corner, heading for the ditch. "Hold on!"

Nowek braced as the car fell into a hole, then bounced up the other side. "Chuchin!"

"You want to get there or not?"

"It's not my dying wish."

The sun blazed yellow out of a clear blue sky. Soon the River Road out to the airfield would be bare to the concrete and impassable. Chasms, breaks, and potholes large enough to bear the names of their discoverers would appear. The road would be unusable until the first heavy snows repaved it.

"About Ryzkhov. I still don't understand," said Chuchin. "What difference does it make if he was a thief or a bone smuggler? Who cares if the *mafiya* or Americans killed him?"

"I do." A small box was on Nowek's lap. In it was the bone he'd found beneath Andrei Ryzkhov's dresser. He thought of Anna Vereskaya, the tiger woman. "Kaznin and the prosecutor have their heads together. There must be a good reason. It may involve AmerRus. Volsky thinks it's worth knowing."

"That only means it's worth something to Volsky."

"AmerRus isn't producing much at Tunguska. That's worth knowing, too. I'm curious what happened."

When Chuchin turned, his dark glasses became two perfect black mirrors. "Maybe Tunguska oil is like Trishka's dog."

"Trishka?" Nowek looked at him. Trishka, the hero of the *glubinka,* the deep countryside. There were a million Trishka stories, each one cut to fit a different situation. But Trishka's dog?

"His dog, Mayor. Trishka would sell his dog to some fool. The fool would pay and then, that night, the dog would come trotting home to Trishka. The next day he'd do it again to some new fool."

"You think like a *muzhik.*" A peasant.

"Why do you think I'm still around? Maybe those toads in Irkutsk aren't so dumb as you think, Mayor."

"I never said they were stupid." But there was a lot to what Chuchin was saying. Trishka the wise fool. Playing AmerRus for their dollars. When the Americans gave up, when the dog came home, they'd sell Tunguska to someone new. "You know, sometimes it sounds like you miss the old days."

"Look around and answer your own question."

"You miss when the Party told you what to think and where to piss? When there was no food in the stores to buy?"

"There may have been nothing to buy," said Chuchin with an impish grin, "but at least we could afford it."

The River Road was built on the banks of the Lena River, connecting ever smaller villages as it wormed its way north. At the edge of town was the old abandoned metallurgical mill; it was the only place in Markovo where the ground stayed white all summer; not with snow, but with heaps of white asbestos. The winds sent silicate plumes into the sky.

The road itself had been built in classic Soviet style: ten-ton dominoes of concrete thrown onto unprepared mud end to end. Beyond the airport was a village named Shpalozovod, a former prison camp dedicated to transforming trees into railroad ties.

Beyond the village the forests grew poorer. The bones of the earth showed through, barely wrapped in green moss, yellow gravel, bleached deadwood, stitched together by a filigree of pewter streams sluggishly flowing north. The end of the road came at a cluster of fishermen's cabins called Seversk, or simply, North.

"Maybe Ryzkhov found out who was playing Trishka," said Chuchin. "Maybe he was going to spell it out to AmerRus and the organs got to him first."

"You mean Gromov. What about the bone?"

Chuchin shrugged, allowing the point. "Prosecutor Gromov will find out about your trip. He won't like it."

"When did you start worrying about what he thinks?"

"When it means I may have to find a new job. Gromov will step on you and not even stop to wonder why his shoe smells."

He thought of those gleaming black shoes. "Drive."

Forty minutes after leaving town, the roof of gloomy cypresses and larches gave way to the wide, sunlit clearing of the airport. The roadway continued straight across the center of the field. Indeed, the road had been expropriated and turned into a runway. The concrete surface was painted black, and it was nearly dry with the heat of the sun. An AmerRus orange wind sock hung from a pole, empty of air.

A few old log buildings clung to the forest edge, the largest had a broad arch of metal for a roof. Rusty fuel drums were strewn like beer cans built for the fist of a careless giant. On the far right, occupying the highest ground, the AmerRus compound kept a safe distance from the mess. A tall fence surrounded it. Behind it was a snow plow and a helicopter, both painted AmerRus orange.

Chuchin drove up to the fence, coming to a stop in front of a closed gate. A prefabricated metal building lay beyond, its steeply raked roof studded with swaying antennas. There were no windows and only one door. Two Jeep wagons with the red moon and oil rig logo were parked by the door.

A tall narrow guard booth stood beside the gate. Inside was a keypad, a light, and a telephone. Chuchin handed the receiver to Nowek.

It was already buzzing efficiently when he put it to his ear. It clicked. Nowek shifted his brain into a low gear, dredging up the English he'd taken at university. "Hello?"

"Dispatch. What can I do for you two gents?"

How does he know we're two? "I'm Gregori Nowek, the mayor of Markovo. I'm supposed to travel to Tunguska this morning."

There was a long pause. "Who says?"

"The presidential representative in Irkutsk called to make the arrangements. His name is Volsky. Arkady Volsky."

"When was this?"

Chuchin didn't understand English, but he could read Nowek's face. "Problems?"

"Problems." He spoke into the phone again. "Perhaps I could call Irkutsk?"

The phone line went ominously quiet.

"What does he want?" asked Chuchin. "A bribe?"

Nowek was about to speak when the dispatcher interrupted.

"Park by the front door and stay clear of the chopper. The helicopter. And no smoking once you're inside my gate."

Without warning, the gate began to beep. A few seconds later, it rolled open for them.

Nowek handed the phone back to Chuchin. "Don't go near the helicopter." He gave a pointed look at the smoldering cigarette. The last Yava from Galena's pack.

Chuchin slapped the phone back onto its hook and snuffed the cigarette out between his thumb and forefinger. He slipped it into his jacket pocket. "I hope they counted the rocks. I wouldn't want to be accused of stealing." He parked between the two AmerRus jeeps.

Nowek got out and closed the door quickly.

The metal building had been put together someplace else and dropped onto pilings jackhammered down into the permafrost. It stood a meter off the ground to keep the ice beneath it from melting. Anything kept warm in Siberia was in danger of foundering like a leaking ship.

Some buildings had more rooms under the earth than above it. The very oldest had haunted basements occupied by true monsters: the thawing corpses of ancient animals, mammoths, strange little horses, giant bears, all caught on the day when

Siberia first earned its reputation for climatic excess. Some with crisp green grass still in their teeth.

Things changed quickly, savagely here. Veering from excess to excess. Nowek wondered, would today's *biznismenyi* and entrepreneurs be found one day frozen in some melted mire of a basement, their pockets stuffed with crisp dollar bills?

The walls of the AmerRus operations building were corrugated sheets, bolted at the seams. A camera panned slowly back and forth. The thrum of a diesel generator came from behind the building. Nowek climbed three steps and went inside through an air-lock entry.

Inside there was a strange odor, or to be more precise, an absence of smells. No sweat, no cigarettes. Not even a Russian hospital smelled so aggressively clean. Rows of orange plastic chairs were arranged to face a wide counter. A chalkboard was filled with AmerRus flight schedules.

A tall man with sandy hair stood behind the desk, his expression so studiously blank it reminded Nowek of someone who'd farted at a Party meeting. He wore orange coveralls with the moon and rig logo of AmerRus on one breast pocket, and *Higgins,* in script on the other.

"I'm Nowek. I was supposed to fly to Tunguska."

"So you said. But you aren't on my mission printout. I just spoke to Irkutsk and they haven't heard of you. Who'd you say was supposed to make the arrangements?"

"The presidential representative. I can try to call him."

"Wouldn't help. I just sent the morning chopper out. The next one won't be for a while, and it's a resupply bird back to Irkutsk. You can ride that one if you'd like."

"I know Irkutsk. But no thank you."

"Thought not. Well, my morning flights go north, afternoon runs head for Irkutsk. You might as well head back home unless they're sending a VIP bird up just for you. And to be real honest, they aren't. Me, I'd say you're out of luck."

"I'm getting used to bad luck. Today, this. Yesterday, I missed Dr. Gabriel from the Tiger Trust. He stopped at my office but I was out. Was he also going to Irkutsk?"

"I don't get involved with VIP crap. I just hold my nose and fold them into my regular ops."

"What do you mean by regular?"

Higgins pointed to the blackboard. "I run a kind of airline here. Arrivals, departures. It all has to fit together. Then comes a special request, I have to juggle things. You could say that VIPs are a real pain."

"Everywhere." The harried minor bureaucrat was a species that transcended nations. Wrap one in a sari, a business suit, polar bear fur, they were all brothers. Add boredom, a remote site that made Markovo seem exciting, and even Nowek could sympathize. He looked at the blackboard. "It looks like an AmerRus crew was in Markovo the night before last."

"VIP crap." Higgins reached under the counter and pulled out a metal clipboard. A set of keys dangled from the jaws of the clip. He ran a finger down the list of entries. "Had a crew fly down from Tunguska with the 'ologists."

"Excuse me?"

"Your pal Gabriel and the tiger lady. Decker brassed out at four-thirty in the afternoon, due back the next morning for the northbound hop. Can't have them flyin' around at night. Too risky. Course, it ain't exactly safe in Markovo either."

"I know." He didn't know Decker and "brassed" was a mystery, but even a mayor could guess who the tiger lady was. "Did Dr. Vereskaya fly back north the next day?"

"Like I told you, I don't get involved with VIPs. You can talk to the office down in Irkutsk. They might help you out."

"But you wouldn't count on it?"

"Anything's possible."

"There's no way I can get to Tunguska?"

Higgins pointed at the wall behind Nowek. "Like I said, anything's possible. She's about eighty klicks that way. Just follow the pipeline and keep on goin'. You can't miss it."

"Well?" asked Chuchin when Nowek returned. The interior was a miasma of cheap tobacco. It did keep the mosquitos out. "Did you learn anything?"

Nowek stopped for a moment and thought. "Kaznin was right about one thing. I'm no policeman."

"That's something to be proud of."

"But I found something out."

"It's lunchtime, Mayor." But then he said, "What?"

"Ryzkhov's friend was in town the night he was murdered."

"Friend?"

"Vereskaya. The tiger specialist. She could have been with Ryzkhov the night he was killed." Nowek raised his eyebrows.

"Don't gloat. Gromov will still hand you your head. Then what will happen to me?"

"Gromov has a nicer car."

"Work for those bastards? Never." Chuchin started the engine and backed out. The rolling gate was already beeping as they approached it. He patted his pocket and retrieved a stub. As Chuchin got it relit, he suddenly stopped and squinted out ahead. "Who's this?"

On the other side of the fence, a tall, gawky young man stood with his face assembled into an eager smile. He was dressed in a leather jacket with a jaunty scarf knotted at the open neck. Foreign clothes, but he was Russian. His teeth were too badly stained to be anything else.

Chuchin rolled down his window.

"Gentlemen!" The young man grabbed the windowsill. He looked ready to ride the Toyota's running board back to Markovo. "Can I be of any service? My name is Yuri Durashenko. You've heard of White Bird Aviation, I'm sure."

"Never," said Chuchin.

"If you're looking for transport, any time, any place, freight, personnel, anything. I'm your man."

"It's lunchtime, Mayor," said Chuchin once again.

"Mayor?" Yuri's eyes flicked to Nowek. "What brings the mayor here?"

"I was supposed to fly with AmerRus up to Tunguska."

"Believe me, you're lucky. AmerRus would charge a fortune. Tunguska's not on our route, but it could be fitted in."

"Informally?"

"Formal, informal. It's all the same."

Now they were getting someplace, thought Nowek. "How much?"

"Normally, White Bird would charge five hundred."

"Mayor, your father's birthday is tonight. Remember? We're supposed to pick him up at—"

"Five hundred rubles?"

Yuri laughed. "I can see you have a sense of humor. Lucky for you, we are in the earliest stages of organization. If dollars are unavailable, something else can be arranged."

"Arranged?" Chuchin fumed. "Who does he think he is? Maybe he should think about how he'll arrange his cell."

Yuri jutted out his chin. "Times have changed since privatization."

"Privatization, pah. It's thievery in a fancy hat. You're worse than the communists. At least they left crumbs for the rest of us to eat."

"Maybe crumbs was all you were worth."

"We gave our blood so weasels like you could . . ."

"That's enough." Nowek put his arm on Chuchin and squeezed, not gently. "You say the name of your company is White Bird?"

Yuri nodded. "Right. I'm president and chief pilot. Also, I manage personnel."

In other words, he had an airplane, he flew it, and he found laborers to help him load and unload. "How is it that I never heard of you?"

"Advertising is expensive. Look at those bastards at *Rostok Rossiya*. They make a Russian company pay five, six times what they charge foreigners. It should be a crime."

"It probably is. Still, you would think a company operating from Markovo would be familiar. I should have seen the articles of incorporation. You filed them of course."

"Put our name on a city registry and the next day there are five *byki* demanding pay for protection. You know I'm right."

He was. The gangs had suborned or penetrated every layer of local government. In a real sense, they *were* the government. A list of businesses only made extortion easier, more efficient. "What about taxes?"

"My chief of accounts is very responsible."

"Actually, as president you are. A *mafiya*-run company, that I would understand. They operate off the books and nobody knows a thing. But that's a matter for the prosecutor general to investigate. His name is Gromov. Maybe you know him."

Yuri had the look of an animal who hears the first click of a spring trap. His eyebrows twitched. "To be honest, I try to avoid complications."

"That's a good plan." Nowek smiled. "But maybe Prosecutor Gromov has heard of you. I could check." In the old days, there was no better way to put someone on a black list than to ask whether he was already on it.

The young pilot knew it. "There's no need. Keep things simple. This is our corporate motto. You say you need to visit Tunguska? The oil colony?"

Colony? It was an odd expression. Though probably accurate. "I wouldn't want to cause a problem with your schedule."

"I can drop you there, make my stops, then pick you up coming back. You'll be home by sunset. No problem. Consider it an introduction. Next time, when the town needs transport, come to White Bird and forget AmerRus. What do you say?"

"What can I possibly say? Get in."

Yuri yanked the back door open. "Have your driver park over there." He pointed at a log structure with an arched roof.

"You heard him, driver," said Nowek. "Over there."

Chuchin growled and slipped the Land Cruiser into gear.

The walls of the log hangar were hidden by piles of rotten snow. The field behind it was overgrown with a jungle of rusted tubes, flapping fabric, and the blackened hulks of old engines. The front doors were open, and from them the snout of a wrecked airplane emerged like an eel from its crevice.

As they drew near, the eel became the nose of an AN-2 biplane freighter. Its huge radial engine and four-bladed prop were swaddled in blue tarps and ripped blankets. Metal cables and loose wires hung from it like whiskers.

"One day White Bird will serve every town that Aeroflot abandoned," said Yuri. "There's no competition yet, but by the time someone notices, we'll be too big to catch."

The name Aeroflot iced Nowek's insides. Of course, when his wife had bought tickets to Moscow, Aeroflot was the only real way to get there. The train took a certain kind of character and a lot of patience. Nina had plenty of one but none of the other. He looked at the young entrepreneur. "What about AmerRus? Do you fly freight for them?"

"In the beginning. Now they have their own fleet and I don't mean little planes, either. I've seen their jets come and go. I don't know how they can afford it. Steal the fuel and it still couldn't pay. It must cost them a fortune."

Nowek thought, steal the fuel. It wouldn't be so difficult with AmerRus running the oil fields. They wouldn't have to get their hands black. They could do it with the stroke of a pen, so many tons less of Siberian light sweet crude than the wells actually produced, the difference split between the refinery, the *mafiyas*, AMR. And who else? The governor? Gromov? It was possible. Was it worth killing Ryzkhov and his two men to keep hidden? More than the bones of a dead tiger.

". . . but even today when the weather gets too dirty or something in their fancy machines breaks," Yuri went on, "they say, where is White Bird? Then they hire us to do the dirty work."

Dirty work reminded him of Kaznin. Nowek glanced up. "Do they pay well?"

Yuri looked rueful. "To be honest, except for tourists, they're the only ones who pay at all. Other than AMR there's almost no money involved, just barter. Medicines for fish, gold dust for tins of crab. We see a few rough diamonds, but not so many now that the Israelis are up in Yakutsk. Mostly there's slabs of salmon or a scrawny sable for a barrel of kerosene. Buying fuel is our biggest challenge. *Those* bastards only take money."

"It's a problem for the town, too," said Nowek.

"I heard about the general. What was his name?"

"Skhurat," Chuchin broke in at last. "A man who put his nose where it didn't belong and got it chopped off. He's Mayor Nowek's hero."

"Quiet, driver. So you don't fly for AmerRus on a regular basis?"

"I wish I did."

"But your business is surviving even without them."

Yuri laughed. "Business? You know what a Russian business deal is? One man agrees to sell another a thousand kilos of sugar. They sign documents and they both run for the door. Why are they running? The one selling has to find sugar, and the one buying has to find money. *That's* a Russian business deal."

Nowek looked beyond the hangar. More piles of snow. "Where's your airplane?"

"We're there." He pointed at the biplane freighter.

"That?"

"Absolutely." The wind swung around the compass from north to northwest, strengthening. *"Annushka* is the biggest biplane in the world." Yuri said it without irony, as though it were something to be proud of. The world's biggest stone ax. "Strong and cheap. Perfect for Siberia. We can fly almost any-place a helicopter can go and we're a lot safer. White Bird has never had an accident."

Nowek thought, how could you tell?

Yuri got out and opened Nowek's door. "Please. You're in good hands. You have my complete guarantee."

Nowek glanced at the pig-nosed biplane, then at Yuri.

"Mayor," said Chuchin, "what will I tell your father if you leave with this pirate and don't come back? Tonight's his birth-day dinner. What will he say?"

"That I should have been a soloist." Nowek grabbed the box with its bone inside and turned to Chuchin. "I'll be back be-fore sunset. There's plenty of time before my father's due. Go back to your friend Malyshev and buy some food. If you can find any caviar, *Osetrovakh* is his favorite. And Chuchin?"

"What?"

"While you're there, ask him who's in the market for obsolete army rations."

"You'd feed your father army rations with caviar?"

"Kaznin had some at his office. I'd like to know why."

"Just wait. You'll be eating them in a cell by tomorrow.
Mayor, this is Kaznin's job. Let him go with this buzzard.
Maybe we'll be lucky and they'll both crash."

"I never crash, grandfather." Yuri reached into his flightsuit
pocket and pulled out a pack of Marlboros. He opened them.
"Care for one?"

Chuchin's nose twitched.

"Look, we're all going to be business partners, right? Have
the whole pack." Yuri stuffed the box into Chuchin's jacket,
then turned to Nowek. "Ready?"

"Why not?" Nowek followed Yuri to White Bird's hangar.

"You know, Mayor," Yuri said when they were out of
Chuchin's hearing, "I didn't want to mention this in front of
others, but in a way we already have a kind of relationship."

"I don't think so."

"Excuse me, but you're wrong. You see, I know your
daughter."

Nowek looked at Yuri. Him, too?

"She used to beg rides from us to the airport and make eyes
at the American pilots, the AMR cowboys. They're *nekulturny*." Uncultured. "Mostly they thought she was funny, but
an eighteen-year-old girl can get herself into trouble with men
like that. I had to step in once or twice."

"She's just sixteen."

"Even worse. She tried to talk them into taking her to Irkutsk. You know they sometimes take girls up north and keep
them? I didn't want to see that happen to her, so I made her
ride the truck into town. She wasn't very happy, but then, Plet
didn't exactly give her a choice."

"Plet?"

"My chief partner. He threw her into the truck and sat on
her."

"She never mentioned it," said Nowek. "She never men-

tioned you, either. But thank you." He wondered, how long
had Galena been avoiding school? Why hadn't he heard about
it? And what had she done to make friends with the cowboys
from AmerRus? "Tell me about AMR."

"What's to say? They could save a pile of money if they hired
us full-time. I can fly *Annushka* all month on what it costs to
run one of those fancy helicopters for an hour. But they won't.
They think if it's Russian, it's shit. As if western planes never
crash."

Another ten degrees fell inside Nowek.

"A single snowflake and they cover up their machines and
wait for it to pass. They . . ."

Nowek was thinking about another time. Another snow. A
flurry deepening, the sky congealing to the color of wet cement. A typical winter day in Siberia. Was Nina sure she
wanted to go? How important could a meeting in Moscow be?

*"Who cares? It's a chance to see someplace different for a week. I'll
be back. I promise."*

They called the waiting room a holding tank, which says all a
person with ears needs to know about Aeroflot. The jet taxied
up to the terminal. The doors were flung open to the wind and
the passengers herded out to a rolling stairs.

Aeroflot had just leased the Airbus. It was new and shiny and
the paint was unscratched. It made their usual Tupolevs and
Ilyushins look like dirty laundry. They assigned their most veteran crews to fly it. Crews with families. Pilots with teenage
sons who found the cockpit an irresistible temptation. Can I
try? Just once? The cockpit had a blizzard of dials and television
screens, better than any computer game. It also had a tape
recorder.

Can I try?

Those were his very words.

Just once?

Once was enough.

The jet went down in a potato field. The authorities didn't
even bother to recover the bodies. They were too mingled with

the wreckage. They found the flight data recorder, then lost it, then ordered the plane bulldozed into the ground.

Weather, the official investigation decided, had been the cause, and where was there worse weather than Siberia? But for so vast a place, Siberia is actually very small. Everybody knows everybody. And everything. It didn't take long for the truth to come out.

Can I try? Just once?

Yuri continued. "Just because something is foreign doesn't make it better. Don't you agree?"

"Yes." He looked up.

Up close, the AN-2 was a scabrous white boxcar with wings; a rhinoceros in a tattered tutu. The slab-sided contraption had a dragonfly's glassed-in nose at one end and a round, billboard of a tail at the other. In between it sprouted four fat wings. The old Aeroflot blue and red striping had been painted over, though here and there it bled through a ghostly gray.

The hangar was filled with crates, fuel drums, and pieces of airplane. Lounging men waited by the gaping cargo hatch aft of the wings. All six were armed with Skorpions, cheap, Czech-manufactured machine pistols that sprayed thirty rounds in several directions, though it sprayed them very quickly. No expensive American bullets here. They wore military uniforms with the insignias ripped out.

"Your boys?" Nowek asked.

"As you said, finding fuel is tough." He put his fingers to his lips and whistled. They all looked up. "Okay *yomchiks!*" he shouted. "Let's get the show on the road!"

The tallest of the six had a huge red drill pipe wrench in one hand and an AK-47 slung over a shoulder. As the others finished loading the plane, he did nothing but watch. His neck was roped with muscle, an anatomist's drawing, his black hair glossy.

"Plet!"

The one with the rifle and wrench turned. Half his head was naked to the scalp, the skin a geography lesson in scars. He ambled over as the others pulled wooden chocks away from the Antonov's wheels.

"Plet is my chief mechanic, my load master, my labor brigade leader. He keeps everything running."

"He looks like a murderer."

Yuri shrugged. "A killer makes a better business partner than a thief."

Plet loomed. He squinted at Nowek, taking him apart slice by slice. His eyes were pale and blue as ball bearings. The wrench was known in the oil world as a "tong." It weighed a good fifteen kilos. Nowek noticed the tattoos on his hands. Daggers and teardrops. The marks a career killer accumulates in prison.

Yuri turned to Plet. "We're stopping off at Tunguska."

"Why?" He kept staring at Nowek.

"The mayor here needs to go and AMR screwed up on the flight schedule."

"Mayor?"

Yuri winked, then scrutinized the empty sky, gauging it. "There's no weather yet, the sun will stay up late so we aren't short on time. How's the load?"

Plet said, "Just over two thousand kilos of mixed goods. Tins, some vegetables, dried fruits, oil, plus the T-shirts they asked for. Half to Kristoforovo, the rest to Kupskaya. There's warm water for trading if you run into anything good."

Warm water. Vodka. "What do we get?"

"The usual. Horn and *chir*," he said, meaning reindeer horn and frozen slabs of Siberian white salmon. The horn was headed for the Asian medicinals market. The fish to fancy restaurants in Tokyo and Seoul, even Moscow.

"What about the bird?"

"She'll fly. Listen. Forget Tunguska. You know what I'm saying? We don't need those problems. Mayor or not."

"What problems? Don't worry."

"Just watch yourself." He turned and left.

Watch yourself, thought Nowek. How dangerous could they

be for someone like Plet to worry? "What happened to his hair?"

"My advice is not to ask. Come on. We're going flying."

The crew tossed the last boxes of supplies into the wide cargo hatch while Plet stood back, his head swiveling like a tank turret, hair to scalp, black to angry welts and scars. Yuri motioned for Nowek to follow him into *Little Annie.*

Nowek looked one last time, then stepped up on an empty wooden crate and pulled himself in.

Inside, the AN-2 was like a general store struck by an earthquake. It was stuffed to the overhead with drums of lamp fuel, wooden crates bearing onions, potatoes. Cartons filled with cans of Kamchatka crab, sacks of flour. White T-shirts with the words USA UNIVERSITY hung from a wire rack. A single cardboard box with a big red star on it announced that trade in Red Army supplies was a worthwhile market for new entrepreneurs. Maybe Chuchin was right; maybe privatization was just crime dressed up in a new hat.

There was a deep, organic smell in the air, part sloshed fuel, part tobacco, part rancid fish oil. *Annushka* was not so much maintained as preserved.

"How do you know how much is safe to carry?" Nowek asked.

"It's very carefully calculated. We haul two kilos for every meter of runway available."

Nowek stopped. "Your friend with the wrench said the load was over two thousand kilos."

"More or less."

"This runway isn't a thousand meters long."

"It's just a calculation. Go, go." Yuri urged him on. "Forward. The best seats in the house."

The only seats in the house. Nowek made his way up a narrow aisle between carelessly stacked goods. Nothing was tied down. The deck angled up like a ramp. From behind, two of Yuri's guards jumped in and pulled the hatch shut with a muffled thud. Two thousand kilos plus two hundred more. The pilot pulled a rough curtain away, exposing the cockpit. The fabric was faded pink. "Where did you learn to fly?"

"Frontal Aviation."

It made Nowek feel a bit better. Frontal Aviation. The fighter pilots, the knights of the air who made silly girls like Galena swoon. Maybe this pirate really did know his business. "What did you fly there? MiGs?"

"A little of everything. Most often I flew a Maz."

"I believe a Maz is a truck."

"The biggest." Yuri nodded. "I ran the base motor pool. I traded boxes kicked off the tailgate for hours in the cockpit." He smiled. "You see? Even then I was thinking in new ways."

A truck driver was taking him up in the air. A truck driver good at kicking things out the back. "Is there any part of this operation that's actually legal?"

"Excuse me," said Yuri earnestly, "but everything good for business is legal. Something bad for business is against the law. That's how they run things in America and how has it harmed them? Most people would give an eye to have only half what they throw into the garbage."

"Your goal is to have half what Americans throw away?"

"For a start." Yuri flopped down into the front left seat and busied himself at the controls. "But I have bigger plans."

The cockpit smelled of old wet leather, hydraulic oil, and cigarette smoke. There was an undernote of mildew from the wooden floorboards. The glass canopy overhead was shaded with fabric faded by sunlight to a delicate shell pink. Something black and armored scuttled into the shadows beneath the instrument panel.

"I'm afraid to ask, but where did the airplane come from?" Nowek settled into the right seat. The springs sagged nearly to the floor.

"Surplus property. Now watch." Yuri pumped the primer handle. The odor of raw fuel filled the cockpit. "Air Baikal is buying up western airplanes, but when times get rough, the bankers will clap their hands and they'll fold. Meanwhile, *Annushka* will still be hard at work. The whole territory will belong to White Bird. Get in on the ground floor. That's rule number one."

Surplus property? Stolen was more like it. Or worse, abandoned. He hunted beneath the crushed leather seat. His hand closed around a rolled-up magazine. "No safety belts?"

"I never crash. That's rule number two." Yuri kept pumping. The air reeked of fuel.

Would he die in a crash like Nina, or just go up in a fireball here on the ground? It was too late to wonder, certainly too late to choose. Nowek unrolled the magazine. It was an old *Domovoi,* a sort of Russian *Town and Country,* catering to the newly wealthy, offering advice on how their newfound riches should be spent: which Swiss school was best. Was it possible to wear Armani without a tie? Was real Vuitton luggage worth the price or was a knockoff just as impressive? How a real Rolex ticked away the seconds in little bites, and a quartz imitation leaped stupidly one, two, three, like a frog from rock to rock.

The air was nine-tenths gasoline to one part oxygen. Snap a finger and the air would ignite.

"I smell fuel."

"A certain degree of seepage is absolutely normal." Yuri switched the magnetos to the one-plus-two position, then leaned out the open side window. "Starting propeller!"

Nobody moved.

It was a job for an octopus. Or at least two good men. Yuri managed to open the brake valves, pressurize the pneumatic system, then hit the starter more or less simultaneously. A whoosh of compressed air spun up the engine flywheel. Yuri counted to ten, then snapped the starter switch to the right. The fat propeller began to turn, slowly, then faster. The one-thousand-horse radial engine shook itself awake in a clatter of pistons and rods.

A dense cloud of blue oil smoke belched from the stacks. The cockpit seemed to be shaking itself loose rivet by rivet. The engine galloped, stumbled, caught, and popped.

Yuri leaned close to Nowek. "Your daughter really wants to leave Markovo. You should warn her to be more careful."

Nowek leaned over and spoke into Yuri's ear. "It won't do any good to warn her. Your partner was right. You have to sit on her."

"Maybe your wife should speak to her."

Nowek sat back and looked at him for a long moment.

"Okay. I'm just making conversation. You're the boss."

The engine bucked and snorted, smoothing as it warmed up.

Yuri leaned out the open side window and yelled, "Ready!"

Plet waved good-bye with that enormous pipe wrench. In his fist it looked light as a twig.

Yuri ran the black knobbed throttle forward and the heavy biplane shook with power, spewing oil smoke. *Little Annie* broke free, leaving deep grooves in the mud as it trundled to the strip, air brakes hissing and whooshing like some winged long-haul truck.

Yuri kept them going, not bothering to stop as they came to the old roadbed. He slewed around to face north into the wind and jammed the black knob to the stops. The engine's roar deepened to a bellow. The engine seemed to be all around them. They were inside it, riding the red-hot pistons and rods. "Here we go!"

At first, the only difference was the noise. There was no rush of acceleration. The scattered dials on the panel went berserk, needles dancing from stop to stop, bypassing their safe ranges coming and going. Paint flakes rained down from the cabin overhead. Nowek had to look down at the wheels to see that they were moving at all. A muddy snail's trail smeared back from the fat tire.

"Twenty!" With a push, Yuri set the overloaded freighter level with the ground, tail high.

Two kilos per meter of runway. How many meters did they have? Forget it. It was just a calculation. Nowek looked out toward the treeline. The ground crew watched like people drawn to a spectacular shipwreck. He could see Chuchin, the white Land Cruiser. What on earth was he doing here? The box on his lap shifted.

"Forty!" Yuri yelled over the sound of the engine.

Forty what? Seconds left to live? Meters to go before impact? No instrument seemed to contain the number. The acceleration was majestic; a ship sliding down the stays to an inevitable splash. The biplane was overloaded. They would never pull free. *Little Annie* bounced and rolled at a leisurely pace toward the end of the strip.

"Fifty!"

The end rushed them.

Yuri hit the flap lever. They crept shyly from the trailing edges of the wings. "UP!" He yanked back on the heavy wheel.

Nowek looked down and saw the surface of the Lena River streak by a few feet beneath the muddy wheels. Were they flying?

Possibly.

The biplane freighter banked, following a twist in the river's bed. Yuri looked over, his face split by a grin. "This is rule number three!" he shouted above the roar. "Never give up! It saved my life a hundred times."

Never give up? It was an ambiguous rule, thought Nowek as he sat in the nose of an old biplane freighter piloted by an ex-truck driver with a taste for informal dealings.

It was a rule that could save a life, or end one.

CHAPTER
8

THE AMERICAN CAMP at Tunguska was laid out with the same attention to rank and privilege a medieval architect would have used for a cathedral city.

The outer rim nearest the work-over rigs was for local contract labor. Here forty-two Russian men lived in recycled steel storage tanks tipped onto their sides and covered with an insulating layer of snow. What the tanks lacked in style they made up in privacy. The crews had access to a steam *banya,* a prefab "labor hall" containing a weight room, a commissary, and a social club. They were well used, and the crews had a surprising amount of free time. The Americans called the Russian zone Dogpatch.

The inner zone was for the Americans, the consultants, the drill supervisors, the helicopter pilots and mechanics. They lived in gleaming white boxes set atop wooden pilings. The boxes were equipped with electric heat, running water, even satellite telephones. Their social center had a wide-screen television, a game room, and a gym. A cafeteria was stocked with food flown in from Alaska. The Russians called the American circle heaven. Few hoped to get there in this life.

Beyond Dogpatch a power plant burned flare gas piped directly from three half-buried storage tanks. The tanks were actually more like lids; they had no bottoms, no sides. A sealed chamber was achieved by melting holes in the impermeable ice with a jet engine bolted to a metal frame. The hot exhaust burrowed through the permafrost quickly. The walls were allowed to refreeze, then a gastight lid fitted to seal the top.

Old crank balance pumping units dipped endlessly, hypnotically, drawing up the light, sweet crude that still managed to find its way into a production well. From there it was piped to a central storage tank, where it was heated and sent into the new line running south to Irkutsk. Enough arrived there to run the refinery twice each week, no more.

If oil seemed scarce, gas was abundant at Tunguska. Soviet drilling had depleted the natural pressure that drove the crude up from the ground, but plenty of ethane, butane, and propane remained to flood the old well bores. Gas fed the generating plant. It produced steam and hot water for the complex. It ran the new work-over rigs installed to redrill the old wells.

After all of this there was still plenty of gas left over; enough to blow Tunguska back to Markovo. For safety reasons the surplus was sent up three tall stacks and burned off. For want of a gas pipeline to a market, millions of dollars went up the flue each day; a sort of eternal flame dedicated to waste. The prevailing winds blew the fumes across Dogpatch.

An airstrip built up on a gravel pad bisected the inner circle. The heart of the colony. On one side was the communications center and attached to it, the site supervisor's cabin and the visiting VIP dormitory. The cafeteria was a short walk away. They were nothing more than huge refrigerator boxes built in reverse to keep the warm in and the cold out.

On the other side of the raised runway, a cluster of small metal cabins stood a respectful distance from one another. It was here the AMR helicopter pilots, brought over from the North Slope or up from the Gulf of Mexico, could find privacy in one of the most remote spots on earth.

It was here that Paul Decker had taken Galena.

She sprawled on the musty bed and flipped through his pile of magazines for the third time. They were a boring procession of naked women doing ridiculous things. The hunting magazines were filled with rifles, handguns, and fat men standing over dead animals. Even the animals looked bored.

A tiger skin was staked out across one of the walls, an orange, black, and white mass that nearly covered the end of the cabin. Its long tail lay coiled in the corner. The head was missing. The end of the tail was chewed to straggles.

A scrabble came from the corner. Without turning her head, she glanced over in time to see a red-brown streak disappear under the bed. Decker's pet ferret. There was a cage but it never seemed to be in it. Decker let the little beast ride his pockets, dive into the front of his shirt. Galena thought Harley was cute, even though it looked like a kind of small, poor sable. Everyone knew sables were vicious.

A head appeared over the edge of the bed one whisker at a time. Then an eye. Both eyes, black and glittering as glass beads. It had a piece of tiger fur in its teeth.

"Come on," she said. "I won't hurt you." She put out a hand but Harley flashed away so fast she might have imagined him.

Decker's cabin contained a bed, a chair, a metal desk, a dresser. The empty cage stood next to the door, its wire door permanently open. There was no window. Galena wore her prized Levi's 504 jeans and a big, loose flannel shirt and the kind of boots that made sense in a Siberian spring. Built to resist sucking mud and ice melt.

Off the small room was a bathroom cubicle that contained a shower, a toilet, a sink. The taps worked, both hot and cold. Luxury by Galena's standards. But the only door was locked from the outside and that made this little cabin a prison.

She looked at her watch and found that it had stopped. Like time itself. Waiting. She hated it. Where was he?

She'd met Paul Decker at the hotel bar after that disastrous scene out in the interview line. Remet, really, since she'd first been introduced to him that afternoon out at the airport. She remembered him. He remembered her. He was good-looking, though he seemed a little angry at something. Everything. Maybe it was just an attitude. Like Mick Jagger.

When Harley's face appeared from his pocket she'd shrieked. He laughed and let the ferret climb along his outstretched arm like a gangplank. He rested the flat of his hand on her shoulder, squeezing it a little like a buyer testing a cut of meat. Stroking the soft skin behind her ear.

The ferret tiptoed nearer, nearer, as she sat frozen. It stepped onto her shoulder. Its sharp claws penetrated the thin fabric of her dress like pins. Harley edged to her neck, sniffing the perfume she'd dabbed. She couldn't help it. She made an involuntary shiver and it was gone.

"Ol' Harley's a lover, not a fighter," he'd told her with a laugh. Decker smiled. Did she still want to travel? To leave Markovo?

What a question!

"I'm like Aladdin," he said. "I got a magic carpet all ready to ride. What you think about that, sweetness?"

He brought her to his helicopter, his magic carpet. Harley rode in his breast pocket but Galena sat in the back with the baggage. No matter. She was leaving Markovo. How was not so important. She would ride outside on the skids for a ticket to the world. She would ride anywhere.

Decker promised to take her to Irkutsk, and from there you could go places. There were planes, trains, even *roads* that went somewhere. From Irkutsk, you could just keep on going and never once look back. That was what he'd promised her. That was what she'd believed. How bad could he be to have a cute pet he carried in his shirt pocket?

The magic carpet brought her here, locked in for her own security. He'd told her how hungry some of the workers were for women. It was safer in than out.

She rolled over on her back and stared at the acoustic ceiling tiles. They were measled with random dots, some small, some bigger. She imagined the dots to be cities on a grand itinerary that was just beginning. She was waiting for her life to finally begin. There was no time to waste. A sound. She turned her head and barely caught sight of Harley's tail as it flashed around a corner and into the bathroom.

Sneaky little sable, she thought. Her stomach growled. She was hungry as well as impatient. It had been hours and where were her cigarettes? He'd taken all her things when he left. For safekeeping, he said. Why were her things so much safer with *him*?

If she could get out she could go find him. But it was late, and she wasn't dressed for wandering. Her Levi's jeans had "air" holes; that was part of their charm. She'd found them poking from a bale of recycled cloth shipped in from overseas like a pearl in a pile of cracked shells. They were a little small, but that made them fit better.

She sat up on the bed and faced the mirror bolted to the wall. Tight jeans, loose shirt that belled out at the carefully unbuttoned neck, not too much and not too little. And a smoldering look from behind the curling smoke of a cigarette. It was her favorite look. She'd seen it in a foreign magazine and immediately recognized herself. It was who she was meant to be. She put her fingers to her mouth. Cigarettes. She'd kill for just one.

The ferret was balanced now on the lip of the sink like a swimmer poised at a pool.

She got up and walked to the dresser. Harley didn't move. He watched.

Lined up were a brush, a shaving kit, and a bottle. She opened the bottle and sniffed, then closed it again. Terrible. Like hay soaked in urine. She went through his drawers one by one. They were oddly empty. Just some pens and pencils and a calendar marked off day by day. She reached into the back of the upper drawer and pushed aside some pads of paper. Her hand closed around a familiar shape.

Yes!

She pulled the Marlboros out. The box was oddly heavy and clanked. Not even Russian cigarettes did that. She looked inside, then quickly shook the contents out onto the top of the desk.

There was one cigarette and an old, ornate lighter.

She examined the engraved lighter. Colored by age and the

oil of many hands, it was hinged down its length. She tried to open it with a nail, unsuccessfully, and then she found the tiny stud. She pressed it and a clever little door popped open.

Inside was a small photograph, like a locket. But this was no loved one, no girlfriend, no wife. Not even Harley.

It was Stalin. Stalin and another man with their arms around one another.

Stalin?

She listened as the heat clicked on. Was Decker a spy? She used the old lighter to get the last cigarette burning, then slipped the lighter into her pocket and greedily sucked in the expensive, exotic smoke.

Never mind the antique lighter. This was a real Marlboro, not the Hungarian shit they sold back at the Black Lung market. She took a long suck and slowly let it out, posing in front of the mirror. This was how she would look. Bored, knowing, but also vulnerable, just a little flash, not too much, not too little.

Arms over her head, she stood stiff and let herself fall backward onto the bed like an Olympic diver off a board. The springs screeched and it made her laugh. She took another drag, then got up to do it again.

A screech, soft, almost questioning. Harley was by the door, up on his hind legs, tail out for balance.

"Be quiet," she told him. "You're trapped, too."

A click came from the door. It opened.

"Hey there, sweetness," said Decker. Cold air rushed into the overheated cabin. "Found my smokes." He wore orange AmerRus coveralls and he carried a bottle. He reached down and the ferret leaped up and scurried into his breast pocket. It turned and watched.

She stared at the bottle. It was dark brown. "When do we leave?"

"Be a little delay, but don't you worry." He kicked the door shut, ran the bolt across the lock, and snapped a metal clip to it to keep it from being opened too easily. His coveralls were seamed with a multitude of bright metal zippers. Two on the chest, two at the waist, one by each knee, and one long one that ran from his neck all the way down between his legs. A tuft of black hair sprouted from the open neck. "Chef Paul's got some medicine for what ails ya." Decker held out the bottle for her to take.

Harley's tongue went out, tasting the air like a snake.

Her eyes flicked between Decker and the door. "No."

"Might as well. Be good for you. Here." He unscrewed the cap and offered it again.

His face was very narrow. There was a sheen to his shaven cheek. His dark hair was cut thick and glossy. A pelt, not hair. Actually, why hadn't she noticed it before? He and his pet sable had a lot in common. Not sable. Ferret. There was a difference, remember?

Sables were vicious.

She took the bottle and sniffed it. It was better than the after-shave, but not much. "I'm not thirsty." She handed the bour-bon back to him. His eyes seemed to glitter, too. "When will we go to Irkutsk?"

"Sweet thing, I don't think we're communicating," he said as he walked up close enough for her to smell a rancid odor of stale sweat and old smoke from his jumpsuit.

Decker held the bottle near her mouth. "First you drink. Then we can talk."

She sat back and tried to look accommodating. "No thank you. But maybe later. In Irkutsk?"

"Actually, I don't believe that will do at all."

She started to move back but he grabbed a fistful of her hair and yanked her head back hard enough to make her neck bones crackle. Her mouth involuntarily opened wide. He poured the bourbon down her throat. She gagged and it spilled down her shirt. She struck out at him. He laughed, pulled her head back, her mouth open, and drained the fiery liquid into her.

Harley screeched in alarm, dove from Decker's pocket, and made a streak for its cage.

She reached up and raked his cheek with her nails.

"Fuck!" The bottle crashed to the floor.

She spit out the bourbon and glared at him. "I want to go now!"

One nail had scratched him. He spit on his thumb and rubbed the wound. It made his cheek look ruddy. "See, everybody wants something," he said. "You want to go to Irkutsk. Harley likes a piece of fresh meat now and then. I guess we all got to give a little something in order to get."

Her throat burned and she felt like vomiting but it wouldn't come. "I don't belong here."

Decker reached down and brushed his hand against his knee. Magically, he now held a long, thin knife. It caught the fluorescent lights and glinted silver. He let it balance between his fingers. "That's where you're wrong," he said as he used his other hand to unzip the front of his coveralls from the bottom. "Sweetness, I guarantee you. You're right where you belong."

She retreated across the bed as he came. Galena hit the imitation wood paneling of the wall and stopped. She felt the cold of it through her shirt.

Decker kept coming. The point of the knife was a silver compass needle that seemed drawn to her. It touched her forehead. He pushed, ever so slightly. A new trickle of blood seeped down her nose. The blade filled the world. It pinned her like a specimen to a card. She realized he could lean forward and drive it like a spike through her brain. She had no doubt that he would. She froze. She couldn't fight. She couldn't speak.

"Now you're gettin' with the program," Decker said as he reached down and fumbled himself free of his white underwear. He pushed her face to the wool blanket and pinned her neck down with one hand.

There was a small ripping sound, and her prized Levi's jeans parted at the rear seam.

She felt air, and the heat of his body. Sick. She was going to be sick. "Please."

Decker laughed when he saw her panties covered with a pattern of butterflies and flowers. He sliced them and yanked the pieces off her like dead skin.

"Please. Don't."

"Can't hear you, sweetness. Not with your mouth all buried in the bed." He flipped her over onto her back.

"Please?" She pulled the denim around her legs. He slapped her hands away. She felt drugged with fear. Slowed down. As though she were on the ceiling looking down at the both of them, watching, knowing what was going to happen. "My father is the mayor. He'll kill you if—"

"You think so?" Still wearing the orange suit, Decker jammed a knee to open her legs. "Tell you what. He can surely try."

He lowered himself. The orange fabric was rough as sandpaper on her skin. He put his face near her neck. She could smell bourbon, sweat, smoke, and after-shave. He was grabbing her, squeezing her, kneading her like cold bread dough, opening her.

Harley squeaked from the safety of his cage.

The bourbon was rising in her throat when a loud pounding came from the cabin's door.

"Decker! You in there?"

"*Shit!*"

"Paul!"

She was about to scream but he clamped down hard on her windpipe.

"Come on! You gotta come to Ops."

"Hell I do." His face was red. "Get the fuck out of here, Joff. I'm busy with something."

"DeKalb says to come now," called the voice on the other side of the door. "We got an inbound. He said to hurry."

DeKalb wasn't someone to play with. DeKalb was someone to obey. He sighed, let go and stood up, rezipping his jumpsuit. The knife disappeared. "Keep it warm," he said. "I'll be back just as quick as I can."

She was crying into the blanket, swallowing hard to keep back the bourbon, the acid. She slowly got up onto her elbows. She needed air.

Decker unclipped the bolt and threw it open angrily. He opened the door and a cold flood of air revived her.

A head, then a voice. "Jesus! What are you doin' to that little—"

"She ain't nothin' you need to be concerned about, asshole. Come on. Sooner we get there, sooner I come back."

The door slammed. She brought her knees up and wrapped the rough blanket around her shoulders. Thank you, she said to that voice. Thank you.

The ferret eased up onto the bed and looked at her.

Galena struck. She wasn't even close.

CHAPTER
9

"Almost there," said Yuri.

They kept to the river's course, the crowns of trees still above their wingtips. A tributary emptied into the main course in a flash of rock and white water. Skimming the water, Yuri turned them upstream to follow it.

The prop picked up spray and sent it rattling back against the windscreen. The treeline receded as they slowly clawed for altitude. At an unremarkable bend, Yuri banked left and set off cross-country. Out ahead there was nothing but gently rolling taiga forest all the way to the white horizon. The hills were worn round and low. A network of silver waterways flowed north to the Arctic Sea.

The AN-2's shadow swept over the undulating ground. Then suddenly, a field. A fence line. Rows of shallow ditches. A collapsed roof. It was gone almost before Nowek realized what it was. He twisted in his seat and looked back.

An abandoned camp.

"I didn't know about that one," he said.

"You see a lot of things flying around up here."

The camp conformed to a familiar pattern. What Siberian didn't know it? A kilometer-square clearing partly reforested now, outlined with rotted stakes and drooping barbed wire. One guard tower was still erect, the others salvaged for firewood. The barracks themselves were gone; all that remained were long, linear depressions that held a deeper layer of snow. They took longer to melt, and so were whiter than the surrounding fields.

Somewhere nearby there would be a field of wooden crosses. If they hadn't been salvaged for firewood, too.

The plane's shadow fell across marsh, then an isolated hummock crowned with a stand of trees, next a braided stream. The camp receded behind, melting into the landscape.

Nowek said, "Another decade and they'll all be gone."

"Don't count on it. They all don't look like this. Some are in pretty good shape. They still have their wires and towers, even lights."

Wires? Lights? "You mean the Korean lumber camps?"

"I didn't stop and ask for identity papers. Maybe the army is running a secret base. Or maybe the Chinese have invaded. Who knows? I mind my business. That's rule number one."

Nowek thought, who would bother to occupy old labor camps besides the Koreans? The military? The same Russian Army that couldn't feed itself? That couldn't find the boots and the hats and the guns to fight the Chechens? Who else could it be? Prospectors? Tiger poachers?

Yuri plucked a Marlboro from his pocket, offering one to Nowek.

"No thanks. How do you know where to fly?"

He touched his nose.

"Seriously."

"Seriously. But I have a backup system. Look down."

Nowek peered below. The stream was gone, but a stripe of bald marsh had suddenly appeared. Perfectly straight, it didn't bother to deviate. Relentless and stubborn, it was a power line right-of-way. You could see the remains of the concrete stanchions. Some were still upright, but most leaned at crazy angles, sinking into the permafrost. The copper wire had already been looted. At the edge of the cleared stripe, half-hidden beneath the canopy of trees, a silver thread flashed into sight, then was gone.

"The new oil pipeline," said Yuri, taking a drag. "It runs all the way up to Tunguska. Made in Japan. Look how good it is after two winters. It could be new."

"It should look new. AmerRus isn't pumping much oil through it."

"The communists ruined the fields. The Americans will have to drill a little deeper."

"The communists ruined Tunguska, but deeper won't work. The temperature rises the deeper you go. There's a critical horizon for oil. It's like cooking a stew. Too low a flame and nothing is done. Too high and you get carbon and gas."

"Well, I hope the pipe is still good when they really start pumping oil. They will, you know. After all, stick a finger into the ground up here and it comes up black. It's a sure thing."

"The only sure thing is if you stick a finger into the ground you'll break it." On ice. On Nepa granite. On a barrier even more durable than these: a conglomerate composed of red tape and official corruption. Nowek wondered how long AmerRus would pump dollars into Markovo without pumping much oil from Tunguska. "You're right about Tunguska," he said to Yuri, "it's good oil. Very light and very sweet. There's almost no sulphur. That makes it more valuable on the world market and it isn't so corrosive."

"You sound like you know about oil."

"I know more about corrosion."

His specialty. The destructive process by which everything man-made slowly consumed itself in the slow fire of rust. Oil rigs. Pumps. Pipelines. Hope.

The clearing sneered at landscape as it marched northward. Broken pylons, scavenged power cables. The empty pipeline. Look at them and you knew everything about the Soviet way of producing oil.

Lenin said the future would arrive borne on the wheels of Soviet power plus electrification. It was up to everyone else to make sure his pronouncement came true. By decree every Russian rig ran on electricity, no matter if the oil field was next to a power plant or a thousand kilometers away from one.

Thus, while the rest of the world produced oil the Soviets built power lines, rights of way, stanchions. Heroic work crews struggled through Siberian winters laying cable to a new drilling site. It didn't matter that in a good year nine holes out of ten came up dry. The plan was all, and anything that jostled it, even good sense, was the enemy.

Especially good sense. It was a Soviet trademark to take something sensible and raise it to the level of farce.

Nowek recalled the pipeline up at Samotlor. It was made from tin and spit. Unlike Tunguska crude, Samotlor oil was both heavy and foul, sulphurous and intensely corrosive. Even worse, where every sensible drilling operation separated oil from the waste liquids right at the well, at Samotlor they pumped everything: gases, salt water, drilling mud, a Buryat roughneck if he happened to fall into the pit. Anything the pumps could grind small enough. Anything.

Made of good material, the Samotlor pipelines might have lasted five years. Made Soviet-style, Nowek figured they'd be lucky to survive two. Given the trouble and cost of building an Arctic pipeline, the delicate environment of the huge, unique lake at Samotlor, he felt it was an invitation to disaster. An expensive invitation at that.

He pointed it out to the representatives from the Oil and Gas Ministry. Or as Volsky would call them, the Oil and Gas Clan.

He calculated the costs of building a separation plant at the wellhead versus the cost of a new pipeline every three years. The plant wasn't cheap, but it produced valuable by-products that could be sold profitably. He didn't even bother to add in the cost of a hundred thousand square kilometers of contaminated land. Of oil choking the pristine Arctic rivers, clogging Samotlor Lake, killing the char, the white salmon, the reindeer, and, more slowly, the people who lived on them. A separation plant made sense without any of those.

His views were not well received.

Who was he, a geologist or an engineer? A facility planning expert? The engineers protested his intrusion onto their sacred ground. The Ministry bureaucrats bridled at the implied criticism. Oil flowed, export quotas were made, even exceeded. Samotlor oil filled the tanks of the Red Army. It poured hard export currency into the Kremlin's coffers. Tons, tons, and more tons for the Motherland! The Soviet Union was the greatest oil producer in the world: more than America and Saudi Arabia combined. There were so many failures to keep hidden; why tinker with success?

They ignored him.

The second winter, the pipeline ruptured.

Before it might have been kept secret. But by then Russia was open to the world, and suddenly the world was standing at Moscow's shoulder, looking on with horror as hot oil spurted from the burst pipe, freezing into shallow black lakes. Nowek knew they wouldn't stay frozen forever. Come spring, that oil was going to move.

He resubmitted his report, proving that a high quality, and more expensive, pipeline plus a separation plant would pay. It was worth putting the matter to open bid. It was worth allowing even foreign companies with Arctic construction experience in on the job. He sent a summary to the Minister for the Protection of Natural Resources, who leaked it to a western environmental organization under the strictest of confidences.

It made the front pages of *The New York Times*.

Nowek was summoned to Moscow and made to wait three days. Finally, he was admitted into a conference room at Oil and Gas. It was a gathering of the Clan.

Ten chairs surrounded a table. Ten men sat in them, some in uniform. There was no place for Nowek to sit, nor was he invited to find one. Oil was more than just a natural resource. It was the main source of foreign capital. Anything that endangered its rapid exploitation was heresy. Anyone who suggested such a step was a wrecker, a criminal, or at best a neophyte unused to the realities of fieldwork.

Didn't Nowek understand that the world waited for unfortunate accidents like this to heap criticism on Russia? Look what those bastards did with Chernobyl! And he, Nowek, was helping them. Perhaps, it was muttered darkly, Nowek hoped to gain international recognition, and dollars, in exchange for his help?

The black lakes melted in the spring. The tundra was buried under rivers of high-sulphur oil as the spill oozed north to the Arctic which, if you asked the Minister of Oil and Gas, was too white anyway.

Nowek gazed down. The right-of-way bored through a stand of stunted spruce, then emerged again. "What do you do in snow?" he asked. "Or after dark? How can you see to navigate?"

"If there's cargo, we fly. AMR has satellite navigation, inertial reference machines. Everything that money can buy. And they still let a few snowflakes ground them. Me? I start at Markovo, fly an exact heading and use my watch to time the flight. When the time is up, there I am."

"Where?"

"Where I'm going. It's called dead reckoning. You know why? An error of just one degree at Markovo, a bad wind, and by the time you should be over Tunguska you aren't. You're dead. But so far, so good."

So far, so good. Nowek thought, life works the same way. Dead reckoning. One deviation, one degree, and five years later, who knows where you are? If he hadn't seen Galena standing in that line, where would she be? If he hadn't found the yellow knot of bone, the piece of granite on Ryzkhov's bloody carpet, would he be here?

The AN-2 buzzed like an overloaded bee above an ocean of scrubby trees, broken ice ponds, and swamp. The right-of-way grew more indistinct, the concrete stanchions less frequent. Streams meandered like worms boring through soft, rotten wood.

Nowek reached under the seat for the old copy of *Domovoi*.

Yuri suddenly looked reverential. "You know who owns that? Vladimir Gusinsky. He's forty-four and a hundred times a millionaire already. His office is right in Moscow City Hall."

"I think the *gus* flew the coop," said Nowek, punning on Gusinsky's name. "He lives in London now."

"You see what I mean? He's *really* made it."

Made it, and taken it away for safekeeping. "How far to Tunguska?"

"Soon." Yuri took an enormous drag on the cigarette, reducing half its length to ash. "There are what? Ten, maybe fifteen Americans and forty Russians. The Americans live in little cabins, almost dachas. They have food flown in each week from the States. Steaks. Lobsters. Have you ever seen a lobster?"

"No, but I know where they spend the winter."

Yuri smiled. To a Russian, "where lobsters spend the winter" is a cold, dark place. "AmerRus has hot water and electricity twenty-four hours. They have VCRs. Telephones that work. You pick up, dial, and somebody answers."

"Very impressive." Yuri might be some South Sea islander talking about planes raining manna. "And the crews?"

"Steel storage tanks. You tip them over and throw snow on to keep out the cold. They say they're not so bad, but nobody cries with their mouth full."

Nowek had seen oil tank dwellings up at Samotlor. They were actually considered better than the hastily built concrete dormitories; they were warmer and more private. "Do you know the tiger researcher? Dr. Vereskaya?"

Yuri nodded. "She's good-looking." But then he said, "What business do you have with her?"

Nowek held up the box. He didn't open it to show the pilot what was inside. "I need her to identify some evidence for an investigation."

"It sounds like something the militia should do."

"So everyone tells me."

Yuri smiled. "Then it can't be such a good idea. I can see you're the kind to make his own way. That's good. It's time we stopped following orders. But still," said Yuri, "it must be a good crime to get the mayor involved."

"It's the best," said Nowek. "Murder."

Yuri's eyes opened slightly. "Who?"

"Two of my militia and Andrei Ryzkhov. Maybe you knew him."

"Ryzkhov." Yuri seemed genuinely alarmed. "Don't misunderstand, I had no dealings with him. He operates on a different level. But if they got to him, nobody is safe."

"He's safe now."

The ground below was getting wetter, flatter. Yet it was a region of sparse rainfall. The whole of Siberia was a huge sponge that locked up water in ice for most of the year, releasing enough of it to feed the low, stunted trees, the sedges, the rich rolling waves of green moss during the frantic hot summer. Fire and ice, a place of extremes. A very Russian sort of terrain.

"Ryzkhov," said Yuri. "I can still hardly believe it. He had connections. Good ones, too. Frankly, it's worrying." It was as though Yuri had found some expensive piece of equipment unreliable. He shrugged. "But there's no cause for you to be concerned. The Tunguska colony is the one place where the *mafiya*s won't go. It may be surrounded by Russia, but AMR runs it like their own country. They control access. You can't so much as put a toe onto the ground without their permission. Tunguska is their town."

"These murders were in Markovo," said Nowek with a feeling that surprised him. Dead reckoning. The initial perturbation that sent his life careening. "Markovo is my town."

The engine roar seemed a bit more endurable. Either that or it was deafening him. Nowek looked outside and saw the right-of-way climb a gentle rise, a long, sinuous hump in the landscape that trended southwest to northeast.

Nowek knew it was a terminal moraine, the southernmost limit of a glacier's travel. All the rock it bulldozed along the way was dumped right here. It would be full of boulders, gravel, alluvial gold, even diamonds. Beyond it, the ground was different. Flattened.

Siberia had been assembled like a cheap Zhiguli auto under the torch of a drunken welder facing his monthly production quota; bits and pieces were smashed together, made to fit. The bare geologic frame to which everything was attached was the solid, granite shield known as the Siberian Craton.

Pre-Cambrian in origin, it was an uninteresting zone for a geologist. All the promising places occurred at the welded, smashed margins where the Craton had cracked open. It was there that interesting liquids and vapors appeared. Gold and silver. Rare earths and diamond pipes.

After a while the welded zones sagged, then filled in with permeable rocks: the sandstones, siltstones, and ancient lake beds that were porous enough to hold oil like a sponge. Lake Baikal was an example of a new rift; Tunguska, dating from the Upper Jurassic, was a very old one.

Buried, compressed, and deformed over millions of years, Tunguska was blessed with two-thirds of the classic three-dimensional oil trap that makes an oilman drool. When the climate suddenly turned frigid, permafrost added the final dimension, sealing the oil beneath a lid of ice.

You couldn't tell by flying over it any more than you could see the contents of a vault by flying over the roof of a bank, but the earth below hid an ocean of oil. So much that even Soviet practices couldn't quite destroy it.

Then why couldn't AmerRus pump it to market?

Yuri gripped the big yoke with the fingertips of one hand, letting *Little Annie* find her own way north. He took a final drag, snuffed out the smoke, then reached down and switched fuel tanks. The engine stumbled, then caught.

The right-of-way was almost indistinguishable from the open marsh now. The land was stubbled in thin reeds and sun-rotted snow. Go down here and they'd never find you. Of course, who would look? Nothing more substantial than wind filled the wings. Disaster held in check by puffs of air, by the slimmest of margins, the most ephemeral of forces.

Fifteen minutes later, Yuri tapped him on the shoulder. "Take a look. Right on time."

Nowek saw three tall trees spike the horizon. Around them, lower, was a forest of less imposing growth. A bright yellow beacon burned from the tops of the three trees. The beacons became more orange, then red, then yellow again.

Flare gas, he thought. A lot of it, too. And the forest at their bases? Oil rigs. Hundreds of black crank balance pump units gathered at their skirts like crowding chicks.

The stacks grew taller as they approached. It looked like every other Siberian oil settlement Nowek had seen from the air: a drop of poison set out onto an enormous frozen petri dish. Life retreated from the poison in concentric circles that measured its toleration to death.

The runway ran southeast to northwest. A spiderweb of raised gravel roads connected the various districts of the alien settlement. Settling ponds, evaporation pits, gas storage tanks, and diked catchment basins for spilled oil.

Capped production wells. Christmas tree stacks. Crank balance pumps dipping, dipping, dipping. It looked very neat, very orderly. Still closer, Nowek saw a bright orange helicopter parked in a fenced-off square near the runway. Off to one side was another helicopter, even larger.

Yuri bored straight in. The gravel runway appeared dead ahead, tilted up at a strange angle. He pulled the throttle back. The heavy biplane dropped like a crate tossed from a bridge, the engine chuffing and backfiring.

The runway rushed up to meet them. They swooped over the end and settled. One bone-jarring bounce, another, then a steady machine-gun rattle of gravel against metal, slowing, slowing as the wheels spun down. Yuri pinned the tail wheel to the ground with a yank on the yoke. He kicked rudder and brake, slowing the big plane as he steered it off the strip and toward the prefab building.

"Get ready! I'll meet you back here in two hours. Go!"

"What about . . ."

"*Go!* I'll be back in two hours!"

Nowek stood up as *Little Annie* wheeled and came to a stop, its nose pointed back to the runway again. He hurried back to the cargo door. It was open, the two armed crewmen standing by, waiting for him to jump to the gravel. He hesitated for an instant, then felt a hard shove from behind.

He landed well, considering, though the bone box fell to the gravel. He scooped it up and looked back, but the cargo door was already closed, the engine turning up. The Antonov was rolling. He had to duck as the tail swept by him. In a moment, *Little Annie* was rumbling down the strip, tail up, wheels up, then with a mighty heave, she was airborne, her wings banked away, the roar of her engine receding into the infinite, empty sky.

He moved his head and a thousand hot sparkles reflected off the gravel airstrip. From a distance it had seemed dark, almost like basalt. But he saw that the darkness was an illusion; the gravel was wet.

He pushed away the wet surface stones and came to an un-disturbed layer just below. He picked up a sample. Fresh, clean, and richly hued. It sparkled.

The airstrip sat atop a long, deep bed of Nepa granite.

CHAPTER
10

TWO MEN IN ORANGE coveralls stood on a deck projecting from the operations building. The door behind them opened and they were joined by a third. He was taller than the first two, and when he turned to look at Nowek, sunlight flashed from a polished silver hard hat.

A breeze stirred and the red wind sock swiveled to scoop it into its mouth. The air was a witch's brew of sulphur dioxide, wet marsh, the sugary perfume of jet fuel, and the darker note of burned diesel. The scream of metal on metal came from a drill rig. It was the only one with any activity.

Nowek could see at a glance they were tripping; coming up out of the hole for a new bit, for analysis, for some reason. Crews hated tripping. The pace was faster, the work harder and in a deep well it could go on for days. But why were all the other rigs silent? They weren't producing. The Christmas tree valving was all screwed down shut. They were just sitting on Tunguska. Why?

As he watched, a steaming string of pipe rose from the active well, slick and wet with lubricating mud. It stopped and two men attacked it with pipe tongs, wrenches the size of a man, suspended on heavy chains from steel girders overhead. Wrenches like the one Yuri's partner carried so casually over his shoulder.

The tongs bit into the slick pipe and held. Then, standing at opposite sides, the two roughnecks threw their weight against the handles. The pipe came apart at a threaded joint. A fountain of black mud boiled out of its mouth as the two Russians guided it to rest against a storage rack.

Nearby, two others took turns pounding at a stuck valve with sledgehammers. The valve rang with each blow.

Something whined by Nowek's ear. His neck tickled. He slapped at it, and his finger came away bloody. Arkady Volsky had asked him to buzz around the investigation, just don't get slapped. He rubbed the blood between his fingers. Here was the fate of all troublemakers who don't move fast enough.

He shoved a chunk of the runway gravel into his pocket.

At the operations shack, the man in the hard hat motioned for the other two to remain, then stepped off the deck and made straight for Nowek. He walked from the hips with the rolling gait of a captain on his bridge. His face was deeply lined. A fringe of close-cropped gray hair appeared under the silver hard hat. About fifty, Nowek guessed, though Americans, like Chinese, didn't age like Russians. He wore pointy-toed cowboy boots, not work shoes. Command presence. An aura of authority. Who could he be but the *nachelnik,* the boss?

"Just what in hell is going on here?" He stopped and looked down at Nowek. A picture ID dangled from his breast pocket. The tall Cowboy God of Industry confronting a human imperfection. "This is a restricted access area. AMR ops only. You understand English? You know the word *private property?*"

"It's two words, isn't it?" He put the box under one arm and extended his hand. "I'm Gregori Nowek. Mayor of Markovo."

The American ignored his hand. "DeKalb. AMR tool pusher. Mayor, you say? Of where?"

"Markovo." Tool pusher was an oil patch term that meant the boss of the site. They even used the title in the Russian oil industry, though shortened to a more economical *Tulpusch.* In any tongue, he was the man who made things happen.

"Nowek." DeKalb slitted his already deeply recessed eyes. "You weren't supposed to show until tomorrow."

"My flight was early." He kicked his boot through the gravel. It sounded like a wave breaking over stones, almost musical; a *divertimento* scored for Nepa granite, for explosive glass and blood.

"You're not early. You're out of line." DeKalb's eyes hooded, and not because of the bright sun. "Our memorandum of understanding with Irkutsk gives us power to hold any and all trespassers. That's what you look like to me."

"I'm sure it does," Nowek agreed. "But if you'd permit me to offer some advice, it wouldn't be wise to enforce this rule. You know how complicated things can get in Russia."

"You don't look like a complication."

"Looks can be deceptive." Nowek turned. "For example, I'd heard that AmerRus was doing everything to bring Tunguska back as an oil field. Work-over rigs. Enhanced oil recovery gear. Not to mention the new pipeline. But . . ."

"But what? Pipe's in place."

"I saw it. But what's inside? To look around you'd think AMR had just arrived. You see what I mean about appearances?"

The lines around DeKalb's mouth tightened. "You have some identification?"

"Absolutely." Nowek pulled out his municipal ID and handed it over. While DeKalb scanned it, he examined the American's picture ID pinned to his breast.

The photo captured him in his hard hat, as though it were part of his skull and not something to wear. He had a sour expression that matched what Nowek saw with his eyes. And at the bottom it was signed in a tight, coiled script. A fuse sparking to dynamite.

DeKalb looked up. "Nowek sounds like a Polish name."

"You find all kinds of names in Siberia. Polish, German, Ukrainian. Even Russian."

DeKalb seemed unsure whether he was being needled. Being unsure seemed to bother him more. He looked at the photo, then at Nowek. "All right. What do you want? I'm a busy man."

In Nowek's long exposure to powerful bureaucracies, he found nothing so unexpected, so disarming, as simple truth. "I'm pursuing a criminal investigation."

It worked. The tall American flinched. One mark for messy human imperfections; one down for the Cowboy Gods.

"Sounds like a job for your police."

"You'd be surprised how many people say that."

"What kind of crime are we talking about?"

It worked once. Why not twice? "Murder."

This time, there was no reaction. Dead flat. DeKalb's face might have been carved from marble. "Far as I know, none of my boys have been killed."

"Two of my men were. It happened in Markovo the night before last. Two officers of the town militia and a man who worked for AmerRus. His name was A. V. Ryzkhov."

The American had very blue eyes. They seemed to turn a silver pale as he looked beyond Nowek to the horizon. "I know all the men on my crews, Russian and American. Even some of the Buryats. We treat everybody the same. Work a day and earn a dollar. Ryzkhov isn't a name I know. I'm sorry you came all the way for nothing."

Nowek didn't think DeKalb looked too sorry. "Ryzkhov wasn't on your crews. He was a leasing agent."

"That explains it. Leasing is politics. I don't get involved in politics."

"That's wise. Still, you never met him? He was a prominent businessman in my town. Markovo is small and it would . . ."

"I said I didn't know him." DeKalb was looking genuinely annoyed now. "And if this murder happened in Mar-kovo . . ."

"Murders."

"Then you're a long way from the scene of the crime." He looked at the box Nowek carried. "What's that?"

"Evidence." He held up the box with its bone. "It needs professional identification. You have a specialist here who might be able to help us. Am I using the right word? You understand *expert*?"

DeKalb visibly gelled. In different light, you might see frost streaming from him. "You listen. My company negotiated a set of rules with you people. The Oil and Gas Ministry. Lukoil. The Rossneft pipeline pirates. Those rules say you don't have a lick of authority here. Zero. They say Tunguska is an AmerRus operation as long as the lease lasts . . ."

"How long is that?"

DeKalb ignored the question. "And when it says AmerRus, it might as well say me. Am I communicating?"

"You are. We're not." Nowek turned and looked at the array of silent rigs again. "You lease Tunguska to produce oil. I don't see much activity."

"Crude is cheap. Russian laws are impossible. We're biding our time until they settle out."

"That could take a while."

"Damned right. And because of that our cost structure here is through the roof. We can't rely on local products. Steel, cement, drill mud. Zip. They won't meet spec. Anything we need to bring in from the world costs triple. And it's a moving target. I gave up trying to predict port taxes, value-added taxes, import fees, custom duties, and outright bribes. We have to make our own power here. You see all these crank balance wellhead pumps?"

"I see them." The motionless dipping birds. Black as ravens.

"Every last one was made in Baku. Ninety-nine percent of them never saw a grease gun in their whole damned lives, so guess what? We got a field full of frozen bearings. None of the electric motors are weathertight. They're junk, too. All of it's junk, and there's no prayer of getting parts out of the factory. Seems like those boys are pissed off at Russians."

Baku was Azerbaijan, and DeKalb was right. They were. "What about new pumps? From America? You could run them off wet gas from the wells and forget the electricity."

A new look came on DeKalb's face. "You been around the oil patch?"

"At Samotlor."

"God. Talk about a fuckup. Listen. I'll level with you. We're just gonna sit on these wells until you folks come to your senses."

"That also might take a while."

"In the meantime, the only way to get something in is to bring it here ourselves."

"Isn't that smuggling?"

"You can call it what you want to. See, we're not here to lift oil, Mayor."

"No?"

"AMR's here to make money. When that's possible, we'll work this field. Until then, we won't. Simple as that."

"Does the governor of Irkutsk know this?"

"I imagine so. See, my word is law up here. Your governor would back me up one hundred percent on that."

"At least."

"And so would a man named Gromov. You know him?"

"We've met."

"You'll meet him again if I think you're up here to interfere with AMR operations. Especially over some kind of criminal business that has nothing to do with us. You want to put the squeeze on us? Go right ahead. You'll have to take a number and stand in line."

"We're used to that in Russia. But I didn't come to interfere. The truth is, I came to help."

"Now how is that?"

"In America it must be different, but for us the murder of a rich businessman with deep connections is relatively exciting. Ryzkhov had the kind of name that makes people notice."

"So what if he did?"

"When a crime involving such a man takes place, people look closely. Even more when word gets around that he earned his dollars from foreigners. When it comes to foreigners, I don't need to tell you that Russians are a suspicious people. You know what's being said?"

"I don't . . ."

"That joint ventures are hyenas feeding off the body of Mother Russia. AmerRus is a joint venture, isn't it?"

"Hyenas feed off dead things, Nowek."

"Excuse me. Tunguska is not dead. One look at all the flare gas you're burning off tells me that."

"Does it? You're a real expert, are you?"

"In some things. How things work in Russia is one of them. You see, a murder investigation is under way. Progress reports are demanded." That was a lie, but DeKalb didn't have to know it. "First deputy prosecutors are working late into the night. Someone must feed them with information."

"Bureaucrats."

"Exactly. We're like beetles. Once we arrive, you never get rid of us. On the other hand, after I consult with one of your people here at Tunguska, I can be gone in an hour. A paper is filled in. No more beetles. No more interference. That's how I can help you." Nowek smiled, he hoped, genuinely enough to pass inspection.

"Anything else?"

"Actually, yes. I'd like to finish my work and go home. My daughter ran away a few days ago. I'd like to find her before she gets into any trouble."

DeKalb looked stung. "Ran off? Where to?"

"It's difficult to describe," said Nowek. "But then, sixteen is a difficult age."

Was Nowek deliberately trying to provoke him, or had he just stumbled on the rawest wound by pure, evil chance? "I had a daughter," he said at last. "She would be sixteen this year."

"Then you know what I mean." But then Nowek thought, what did he mean, would be? Had he heard correctly?

DeKalb reached into his side pocket, pulled out a slim wallet, and opened it.

Nowek looked. A family portrait not unlike one he had at home. A dour DeKalb, a woman whose beauty had worn thin, bleached out under harsh light, and a sparkling daughter with huge, innocent eyes. In Russian, "doe's eyes." Not unlike Galena. "Very nice," he said, not knowing what DeKalb had in mind. "You must be proud of her."

"I was." The wallet disappeared. "She was taken from us."

When DeKalb looked up it was with a completely different expression. Pain.

"Taken?"

The two men kept beating their sledgehammers against the frozen valve. A dull bell tolling for the dead.

"It was a break-in," DeKalb continued. "He came looking for something to steal. Police record this long. They couldn't keep him locked up because the courts said the jails were over-crowded. Had to have room for the real bad guys. Thing was, he was a real bad guy. You follow me?"

"I think so." No Russian was accused of a crime unless it was generally established that he was guilty. A defense attorney's job was to inject mitigating factors to make the inevitable judgment less harsh. Nowek knew the American system of treating criminals was more lenient, and not entirely superior. "He was caught?"

But DeKalb didn't seem to hear him. "We figured she heard him tearing the downstairs apart. She was just back from swimming at the pool. Still in her bathing suit. She hid under the bed. Course, that's where a burglar will look."

Nowek didn't answer. He didn't breathe.

"He found her." DeKalb's face seemed to move in, then out of focus. "He did some bad things before she died, Mayor." He took a deep breath, let it out. "I hope you find your daughter before anything like that happens. I really do."

"I'm sorry."

In focus. "Won't help her now. That's my job. So who's this expert you need to see?"

His job? "The tiger researcher," he said, "Dr. Vereskaya."

"Her?" DeKalb cocked his hard hat. "What's her connection with Andrei?"

Andrei. He hadn't used his first name yet. Just the initials. Nowek just held up the box. "I need her to identify evidence of a technical nature."

"I see." DeKalb glanced at his watch. It was an elaborate diver's model, the kind no Russian would ever let near a drop of water. His forearm was tanned the color of old oak. "Tell you what. It'll take thirty minutes to get my chopper fueled and ready. When it is, you're gonna ride it back to Markovo."

"Thank you, but there's no need. I have transport."

"You only *think* you do. Your friend had no authorization to land here. If he tries it again, we'll impound him." He looked up, his pale blue eyes boring into Nowek. "Three zero minutes. That's how long you have with the tiger gal. But remember: if you're up here to start some trouble, or squeeze us, I'll make a call to Gromov and I shit you not, he'll hand you your head. Am I making myself clear?"

"Very." It would almost be worth waiting to see the American's face when he tried to impound Yuri's plane and found himself staring into the muzzles of those Skorpions.

DeKalb began striding back toward the operations building.

Nowek took two steps for every one of the tool pusher's. DeKalb's legs seemed to be built for a different scale of world. How trapped he must feel on this island of gravel floating on top of the eternal frost. Winter was one thing. But with the topmost layer melted, one step off the gravel pads and you sink to your thighs in wet snow and muck. Of course, if something happened to Galena, something like the crime DeKalb had hinted at, he would seek out the farthest place in the world he could name. And then start walking to a place without a name at all.

A place, thought Nowek, a lot like this one.

Andrei. Yes. DeKalb knew him all right. He'd lied. Why?

As they drew closer to the operations building, Nowek saw that the big helicopter he'd spotted from the air was actually a burned-out hulk; a big, fire-blackened machine sitting dejectedly on two pairs of double landing wheels. Five portholes punctured the cabin, all of them plated over with soot-streaked steel. The canopy was yellowed the way old plastic gets when you leave it out under the sun for a decade. Twin rotors sprouted from opposite ends of a long, charred body. Some of the blades were missing.

"Decker!" DeKalb called out. One of the two men standing by the operations shack looked up. He had a small bandage applied to one cheek. "I want you to take the mayor to see the tiger woman. Take you a buggy and be quick. Joffrey?"

"Yeah," said the other.

"You're gonna RTB to Markovo in three zero minutes. Get my chopper ready," he said, pointing to a small, speedy-looking Bell parked at a safe distance from the burned hulk. "The mayor of Markovo needs a ride. We don't want to delay him."

"Yessir."

Decker. The name the dispatcher down in Markovo mentioned. Nowek wondered whether they were the "cowboys" Yuri had rescued Galena from. They were both wiry and dark. One of them chewed a piece of wood and smirked. Possibly. Yes.

DeKalb turned back to Nowek. "Sure was nice to meet you, Mayor. But I don't think we'll have a chance to do it again any time soon." He waved Nowek's ID. "You won't mind if I hang on to this while you're with us?"

"Of course not." Nowek reached over and unclipped DeKalb's ID from his breast pocket. He smiled and put it into his jacket while the American stood there too shocked to speak. The other two watched DeKalb as if he were a gasoline bottle with a flaming rag in its neck. "My memory is terrible. This will remind me to ask for it back."

DeKalb growled something, turned, and went inside. One of the pilots followed while the other walked toward the helicopter.

Nowek waited, ignored. The door opened and out came Decker, a red hard hat in his hands. He still had a white toothpick in his teeth. He handed the helmet to Nowek. A wave of powerful cologne washed off his bare arm. "Company rules. Visitors have to wear them."

"Safety first." Nowek put it on, adjusting the plastic band until it fit snugly. The American's head was bare. He had thick black hair and dark, soulful eyes. Just the kind of American Russian women would swoon over. The dollars in his pocket wouldn't hurt his chances either.

"You say you're the mayor?"

"Of Markovo."

"That was a ballsy move you made on Mr. DeKalb. His ID, I mean. Looks like you're a real tiger all right."

Tiger? Nowek followed him around to the back of the operations building. "What happened to that one?" He pointed at the wrecked helicopter.

"Some locals tried to refuel it without grounding the tanks. Fools put a metal nozzle against a metal skin and a big ol' spark went out and she blew. Mother's too damned big to haul out and fix. Me, I'd guess she'll stay right where she sits."

"Was anyone hurt?"

"Nah," said Decker. "They were killed. Let's get a move on, tiger. I got affairs to finish up."

Nowek followed him behind the operations building to a row of skeletal little vehicles. They had four seats bolted onto a tubular chassis and huge soft tractor tires fat as round pillows, but with a screwlike pattern of spines embossed on the tread. A cylindrical pressure tank was mounted at the back, along with a flat cargo deck. Decker hopped into the driver's seat. With the push of a button, the engine surged to life. He impatiently motioned for Nowek to join him.

Nowek eased in next to him. "What kind of car is this?"

"It's an HMV. High Mobility Vehicle. We call them moon buggies," said the American. His accent was laced with something odd, like a spice in bitter black coffee. "We had them made special for us. Burns gas hydrate."

"You bring it up from the well bore?"

Decker gave Nowek a new look. "Mr. DeKalb said you'd been up at Samotlor."

"Yes. We had hydrate of methane there, but we didn't use it for anything. It was just a nuisance."

Gas hydrate was "ice that burned"; an exotic form of water and methane, fused together by the extreme pressures found at the bottom of a drill hole. Sometimes you struck a thick lens of it and for days tons of hissing ice would erupt from the well casing. The Buryat crews would snap their cigarette lighters and throw flaming ice balls at one another for fun.

"Ain't a nuisance here. Put it in a pressure tank and it'll drive a buggy 'cross just about anything. Ice, snow, open water, even. All weather, any time of the year. But you got to keep moving pretty fast on water. Stop, you like to sink."

He felt the same way about this investigation. Stop and you might sink. "Very resourceful. Are you American? I'm no expert, but your accent sounds different." He found himself staring at Decker's boots. What would the soles look like?

"I'm one hundred percent coonass from Vermillion Parish. That's Louisiana. Except for those Yankees north of I-10, we all sound like this. You know what a coonass is?"

Nowek looked up. "A kind of animal?"

"A real bad kind of animal." He backed out, clutched, and shifted into first. Kicking up gravel and mud from all four wheels, the moon buggy rolled down an embankment, off the roadway, and streaked cross-country over melted ground so churned up not a scrap of green moss remained.

It was a brown soup of mud and dirty ice, though unlike a Soviet oil field, there were no lakes of spilled crude. There were old production wells all around. Nowek could tell by the valving. All shut down, the pumps rusted in place.

Nowek saw the new gas pipes that connected the old wells to a central manifold. Wet gas from the annular casing. Hydrocarbons were flowing. There was pressure. Just look at that flare! Surely AMR could make money with all the Siberian light underfoot. He traced the manifold to one of the big gas storage tanks in the distance.

"It looks like you're repressurizing the wells with gas?"

Decker didn't even turn. "Have to ask Mr. DeKalb."

Nowek eyed the tall stacks tipped in yellow fire. "He said AmerRus is waiting for crude prices to rise before stepping up production."

"That sounds right."

"But the wells don't look like they've been touched in a

while." They passed valve strings rusted to sculpture. "A very long time."

But Decker said once more, "Have to ask Mr. DeKalb."

They passed a big electric pump, its motor the size of an oil barrel. A fat rubber umbilicus connected it to a wellhead, but the pump was silent. The rubber cracked.

"Fracture hydraulics?" asked Nowek. But then, before Decker could answer, he said, "I know. Ask DeKalb."

Nowek held on to the roll cage as they skimmed across the mud at high speed. The engine driving this moon buggy was remarkably quiet for all its power. "I heard I just missed you yesterday."

Now his narrow face turned. "Who said?"

"The dispatcher down in Markovo. His name is—"

"Higgins don't know his ass from a dry hole and you can tell him I said so."

The moon buggy picked up speed. It splashed across a small pond, sending sheets of muddy ice water up from its wheels. They kept right on moving, though a bit slower. Good as the American's promise, it didn't sink.

"How do you like Siberia?"

"Sportsman's paradise," said Decker with a laugh. "Got nothin' but room and no laws sayin' how you're supposed to live. Laws about ruined things where I come from. Can't spit without filing an environmental impact statement. A man can breathe free up here. Just you and God." Decker laughed. "I forgot. You all don't believe in God."

"He's making a comeback. And there are laws, too."

"Not here." But then Decker said, "Other than Mr. DeKalb, that is."

Everything ended with that name! Nowek changed his line of approach. "I understand there are tigers at Tunguska."

Decker grinned. "You know, when tigers fuck the female *screams*. Yoweeee! You know why that is, Mayor?"

"Not really."

"Male's dick's got a bone in it this long." He held his fingers far apart. "And the outside's all covered with spines that go one way. You know what I'm sayin'? Like a porcupine. He can slip it to her nice and quiet, but he sure can't leave without her knowin' it." When he smiled his teeth were very white.

"I can imagine." Nowek cleared his throat. "American tourists may soon come to Markovo. Please, do you like our Hotel Siber? How could it be improved?"

"It could be back in Abbeville." He shrugged. "The hotel's kinda dull. I hang at the Alamo."

The cafe run by the Armenian *mafiya*. Now, there, thought Nowek, was another redundancy.

"They got this little gal who picks up dollars," Decker said with a snicker. "You know what I mean? No hands. You all lay 'em down, she sucks 'em right up. That honey gives old Mr. Washington the thrill of his life. Maybe the clap, too."

This is the way the empire ends, thought Nowek. Not with a thermonuclear bang, not with a gust of freedom sweeping out the cobwebs of seventy years. But with a stripper crouched over dollars, swallowing them, no hands. He thought of Galena's beautiful face, her long, graceful legs.

The buggy chewed up a gravel bank, spun in the mud, and turned up a long raised gravel causeway that ended in a huddle of low metal structures with blue steel roofs.

Nowek eyed the rocks going by. Magnetite and tourmaline gravels. From a different outcrop, a different source. Not Nepa.

They were well beyond the American circle at Tunguska. Well beyond the sheds and storage buildings. Beyond even Dogpatch. The tall stacks stood at a distance; the gas storage tanks lowered to mounds on the horizon. Out here the rigs were all around them, most of them abandoned, a few were new. The old electric rigs were rusted over to a fine brown patina.

Siberia is made on a different scale than the rest of the world. Distances are deceiving. The causeway over the marsh was longer than it seemed. The little blue roofs grew larger slowly, though the moon buggy's speed had not diminished. As they drew closer, Nowek saw that the low buildings stood on pilings, their roofs steeply pitched to shed snow. A satellite telephone dish was bolted to the peak. A sign was mounted above the doorway: TUNGUSKA BIOSPHERE PRESERVE FIELD STATION.

Decker drove up to the building and stopped. Another moon buggy sat parked in front of the main building. He turned to Nowek. "It looks like the tiger lady's in all right."

"Yes." The photo of Nina on his kitchen wall. The photo on Ryzkhov's. The one in the tiger brochure. Melting, overlapping. Three years and he still sometimes heard her voice when it was only the radio; still thought he saw her bringing in laundry hung out to dry when it was just the wind snapping one of Galena's skirts. The sound of her slippers as sleet spattered the windows.

Nowek started to get out, but a loop of thread hanging from his jacket snagged on a sharp weldment of the moon buggy's frame. He moved and the snag only got worse.

"Hang on." Decker slapped at his knee and a slender blade materialized. Made for throwing. Finely balanced, no handle. With a deft snick, he cut the piece of thread caught on the steel tubing. The blade went back wherever it came from so fast Nowek wasn't sure he hadn't imagined it.

"You'll come back for me?"

"Don't worry, tiger," said Decker with a wide, feral grin. "I'll be thinking about you the whole time." The moon buggy reversed, all four wheels canted in a tight turn, and with a hum rather than a roar, drove off down the long, slender causeway, flying like a tiny troika over a snowy field.

CHAPTER
11

THE BULLETS, the orange cloth, a piece of gravel that was common as dirt and terribly specific. And DeKalb's lie about not knowing Ryzkhov. To be Russian is to be suspicious of foreigners. To be Siberian was to be suspicious of *everyone*. It was another ambiguous rule, both bad and good.

Nowek walked to the wooden stairs, thinking of Ryzkhov in his bed, the picture on his wall: a beautiful young woman. Not Ryzkhov's wife, but Anna Vereskaya. And AmerRus, the single largest supplier of dollars to the Markovo economy. Sex, money, and politics. When it came to motives, he had to agree with Kaznin: she combined them all.

Large metal crates were stacked next to the front door, their ends held shut by heavy springs: tiger traps, and big ones. They were longer than Decker's moon buggy.

Her front door had a wooden handle worn to a satin finish. There were no metal doorknobs in Siberia; one careless touch in winter with a bare hand left a glove of skin behind.

The air-lock entry was lit by a cold-blue fluorescent ring. Inside was a second door with a notice to press a buzzer and wait. He was about to do that when he stopped to notice the floor.

Boot prints marked it, executed in dirty limestone dust; the windblown legacy of decades of spilled casing mud. It was gray and extremely fine. It showed the distinctive, heraldic fleur-de-lis pattern he'd seen at Ryzkhov's flat.

A pair of muddy boots stood along the wall. They were small, but heavily built. Like earthmoving equipment. The toes were scuffed to raw suede. The ankles were worn to a glossy smoothness. He picked one up and turned it over. The lugged sole was caked with mud and pieces of gravel. He pried loose enough to see what he'd expected, plus a name. VIBRAM. He put the boot back where he found it, and pressed the buzzer.

The building was well insulated. Ceiling, walls, and most especially the floor. The snows might collapse it. The winds might rip it apart, but the building wouldn't sink into a melted morass of permafrost. He pressed the buzzer again. Still no response. He pushed in.

A calico cat stared back at him from its perch on a desk, alert, calm, in command. It looked up with a disdainful expression that reminded him of DeKalb. The cat raised a paw and began licking, coolly keeping Nowek in sight.

On a bookshelf set against a wall, a sunflower grew up toward a yellow grow lamp. It had a tiny green head already showing a fringe of yellow. A small miracle opening the door to a larger one.

She sat with her back to him, staring at a blank television screen, wearing headphones. A small tape recorder was on the desk beside her and a fancy little laptop computer whirred on the desk. Cables snaked this way and that, connecting the components together.

She hadn't heard Nowek enter. But even with her back turned, Nowek knew her. His hands knew her and it was all he could do to keep from reaching out and touching her, which even he knew would not be wise.

Anna Vereskaya's hair was black and glossy, pulled back behind her ears, draping her shoulders. She wore faded denims with a simple black turtleneck. The sleeves were both rolled up. She wore a watch, a big black affair studded with buttons. On her feet were quilted, insulated booties.

The screen flickered to life in a pattern of white vertical

lines. A still photo? No, because even as Nowek watched, it shifted, jerkily, crudely, to another image almost the same, but not quite.

She picked up the black microphone connected to the recorder and spoke. "Site Fourteen," she said in plain, American English. "First aural trigger at twenty-two ten."

It surprised him. Most Russians who spoke English here used BBC standard. A violinist plays an instrument without frets, without imposed boundaries. Nowek had a very sensitive ear to tone, to nuance. It was how you avoided mistakes. He kept listening.

"Time's twenty-two twelve local. Peter, this is the data file I spoke to you about when you were here. It's the one we're going to nail them with. The bad news is Moscow was no help." She hit a button and the laptop computer whirred. The image on the screen went into rapid sequence, showing the same view of vertical lines against a black backdrop.

Moscow was no help to a lot of people these days, but what did she mean by it? Nowek was about to clear his throat, to announce his presence, but the illusion, the mirage was so delicious he didn't. He couldn't. A man lives in a desert for three years, who could blame him for closing his eyes and savoring the smell of rain?

She spoke again.

"Twenty-three hundred. Just a few minutes now. Keep watching. This has never been recorded."

He turned. The office was decorated with Buryat artifacts, posters, and maps. A reindeer-skin drum, a native knife, its handle aged the color of cream. The posters advertised powders, potions, wines, and balms, all made with essence of tiger. A large map with pushpins showed the vast Tunguska Biosphere Preserve. Bookshelves, the flower and its grow lamp, a desk with a large black rubber biological sample envelope and a glass of red berry juice half full. A portable satellite phone sat in a charging saddle.

And a rifle.

The weapon mounted a large scope on its spine. Except that

you didn't wander off into the taiga without one, Nowek knew
next to nothing about guns. But he could see that this one, all
blued steel, gleaming wood, and polished optics, was lovingly
cared for by someone. A girl, a knife, a rifle.

A trick question: which item didn't fit?

A trick answer: maybe they all belonged.

"Okay?" Anna Vereskaya said. "There's the first second aural
trigger at twenty-three fourteen. It's a helicopter. I ought to
know. I hear them enough." The television screen blinked off,
then back on.

Nowek quietly walked to where the knife hung and took it
off its peg, thinking of Grossman's admiration for the "surgeon" who had operated on Andrei Ryzkhov. The calico
tracked him.

A reindeer-skin thong was woven through the sheath in a
clever fashion. It served both as a way to hang it from your
neck and, with a quick push on a ring of bone, to close it
securely.

The handle was creamy yellow mammoth ivory, so-called
"Siberian Gold." Along with sable furs, the czars had used it to
keep their treasuries filled. Whether the commodity was gold,
sable, oil, or just open, endless space, Siberia had always been a
barge, a freighter, moored to the dock of Russia. Moscow took
what it wanted and then, before the crew was the wiser, pushed
the barge out to sea. He pulled out the bright blade.

It was highly polished; there wasn't so much as a stain on it.
He ran a thumb along the knife's cutting edge. It had the
magical ability to cut without so much as a tug, a sensation on
his skin. It immediately drew a thread of blood. What had Dr.
Grossman said? A knife, exceedingly sharp? He thought of the
Alsatian he'd seen with its neck open to the spine, and quickly
slipped it back into the hide cover. Nowek glanced up. The cat
knew he was here. When would Vereskaya?

"Okay? Watch." The laptop hummed in fast forward, then
stopped. Anna said, "Twenty-three fifty. The infrared trigger
just went off so the camera is shooting double rate and the

sound pickup is continuous. It's almost like video." She paused, then said, "There he is."

He? The screen showed the same scene of white vertical lines, but this time they were joined by an indistinct blob, also white. The screen jerked quickly now, like an old silent movie, but as it changed frames the blob came through the lines like a patch of fog through trees, then froze. Trees? Were the white verticals trees?

The shape began to move again.

"Did you hear him?" she said. "That was his voice. It's definitely American English."

She pointed the remote and clicked. The computer blinked, then hummed. The indistinct shape swiftly grew into the slightly greenish, phosphorescent figure of a man with a ghostly white face. The face turned in the direction of the trees, mouth open in a silent shout.

"Midnight. Keep in mind we're seeing him in IR, okay? Heat shows up white. His skin is actually black. We're looking at a black man in the woods. Note his clothes. He's wearing pants, canvas shoes, and a shirt with some kind of lettering. The white spots under his arms show that he's really sweating. Peter, the temperature that night went down to minus twenty-two. He's not far from shelter. He couldn't be. My guess is he was off that helicopter we heard."

Nowek had the impression she was building a case brick by brick. Of what? And against whom? And what was an American doing out on a bitter night dressed like a tourist visiting the Hermitage? A *black* American, at that.

The man stared at the treeline. You could sense the expectancy in his posture. There was something printed across his chest. The infrared picture made it hard to read. It was mixed in with glowing hot spots that radiated from under his armpits.

She froze the scene.

"There. *CDC Pelican*," she said. "There's more lettering but we can't see it clearly enough to read. Is it a ship's name? A place? I don't know. Does it make any sense to you? See what you can find out. Maybe we can back his name out of maritime records. You know? Ship registry or union stuff."

Nowek peered. Yes. *CDC Pelican*. In English, not Cyrillic. Pelicans were a kind of bird. But CDC? He could read it through the glowing nebulae of heat and sweat that plastered the man's shirt to his torso. Sweatshirts with American names, universities, companies, products, were common enough in Russia. But not at minus twenty.

Siberian rules are absolute: there were no appeals, no special dispensations. Whoever this black American was, he was in real trouble.

"One past midnight. First vocalization," she said.

A new object materialized from the trees; a low, linear shape. Its movements were fluid along the ground. It picked up speed.

Not an object, not a man.

A tiger.

Anna froze the scene and spoke. "Individual is Lena. She's seven years old. Last year she weighed one hundred thirty-four kilos but she's a lot thinner now. See the patches of thin fur? They show up as white, where the skin heat gets through. Lena's denning with four cubs half a kilometer from Site Fourteen. She's hungry and she's used to finding food here. She's not bluffing. She's not even stalking."

Nowek leaned over to watch.

"Plus eighteen seconds."

The tiger accelerated in the rapid-fire blink of the strange camera, covering the last few meters of ground in an eyeblink, impossibly fast. She sailed through the air like a missile, reaching out, the subliminal flicker of long sharp claws, each pad larger than the man's head.

Nowek's mouth opened as the man became a pinwheel of arms and then disappeared below the view of the lens. A ramrod straight tail flicked once across the screen, then vanished.

"That's everything. Lena cached the body. The scavengers cleaned up the rest. We need his name, Peter. If we can get it, they're dead." The screen went dark.

"Excuse me," said Nowek. He took one step toward her, the

sheathed blade still in his hand. The orange calico had been content to watch him. But now it leaped to its feet, back arched, teeth bared in a hissing snarl.

Anna spun, pulling the earphone cord out of the jack. Her eyes went from Nowek to the knife, then back. She stood.

Nina. The hairs on his arms stood out straight. Nina.

It was just like an infrared lamp switched on high. He felt illuminated with invisible heat. The face on Ryzkhov's wall, the woman in the Tiger Trust brochure. The image of Nina that day in the sunflowers. Alive. Eyes the color of green olivine. A triangular face, a broad forehead, a narrow chin. The same lock of unruly hair across one eye. Small gold hoops in her ears. The dark turtleneck was thin, almost painted on. Nowek could see the creamy glow of skin through its weave. She was more beautiful than her pictures, and a lot tougher too. She looked about twenty-five.

"That's a shaman's blade. Give it to me," she commanded him in very rude, uncultured Russian. Nina would never speak that way, not even to a dog. She snapped her finger and pointed.

The mirage popped like a soap bubble.

Anna was rooted to the floor in front of that screen, blocking it. He walked up and handed her the blade. For an instant they both held opposite ends and the cat hissed and snarled; an electrical circuit completed.

"George!" She swatted the calico off the desk. It disappeared underneath and gave a low, feral growl. "Well?" She still spoke in Russian. "How long have you been sneaking around? Are you lost? What do you want here?"

"Forgive me. I used the doorbell, but nobody answered," said Nowek. He couldn't force his eyes away. For Nina, fury and passion had been mysteriously linked. Her face would flush, the red would flow down her neck, her nipples would harden to raspberries.

She crossed her arms across her chest.

He looked away. "I'm Gregori Nowek. The mayor of

Markovo. I was supposed to meet Dr. Gabriel yesterday at my office, but we missed each other."

"Peter is back in Vladivostok." She switched the computer off and popped out a tiny tape cartridge. She pocketed it, but she left the shaman's blade within quick reach.

"I know. The truth is, I came to speak with you." He stopped and saw movement at his feet. The cat was stalking him. It froze, one paw raised, tail straight back. So were the ears. The parallel with the scene on the tape was enough to raise the hair on Nowek's arm again. "Your cat thinks he's a tiger."

Anna stamped and the calico streaked off. "Tigers are the biggest cats. Cats are the smallest tigers. What do you want to speak with me about?"

Her blue jeans fit like they were made only for her. Her black turtleneck was made of silk. Good for warmth, light to wear, it clung to her shape. She was a composite made from opposites, toughness and silk, one woman, another.

"Well?"

"I'm trying to place your accent." Her speech wasn't the contemptuous slur of Moscow, not the husky, rounded syllables of Siberia, but closer to them. Not rounded. Call them octagonal. Nowek waited for her to fill in the rest. Don't explain. Don't apologize. Let the other person fill in the blanks. He'd found it to be an excellent strategy for getting people to talk. "It's almost familiar. Are you from Irkutsk?"

"My parents lived in Irkutsk."

"I went to school there. When did—"

"Is this a social visit? If so, I'm sorry, but I'm very busy. You'll have to come back another time." She looked at the box in Nowek's hands.

So much for strategy. Of course, everyone knew that Russians never won wars through strategy. They won wars by throwing themselves under enemy tanks. "You're right," he said. "I've avoided something because it's unpleasant. I'm sorry, but I've come with very bad news." His eyes kept drifting back to her, staying too long. It unnerved him. What could she be thinking?

"What?" She studied Nowek's face. "A ranger? Did they shoot another one of my rangers?"

"It's Andrei Ryzkhov. I think that you knew him."

"I know him." Face perfectly calm. There was the look of a decision being made in her eyes. "Why?"

"He was murdered the night before last."

Her arms dropped. She looked at Nowek as though he were far away and needed magnification, focus. "I don't believe you." She brushed the lock of hair off her face. It immediately fell back. "We aren't talking about the same man."

"We are. Son of Stalin's interpreter, a brother in the Foreign Ministry. He lived at Rossinka, Number Eight. Perhaps you didn't know it, but he had a wife named Vika." He paused, testing her calm waters. Not a ripple. "Two members of the town militia were also killed. It happened early. About four in the morning. The killers used a knife as sharp as that shaman's blade. Is it Buryat? The workmanship is impressive."

Her eyes didn't flick to the blade. "I can call Andrei and prove you're lying."

"If you can call him, Dr. Vereskaya, then you're wasting your time counting tigers. But don't take my word for it." Nowek nodded at the satellite phone. "Dial the Polyclinic in Markovo. Ask for Dr. Grossman. He did the autopsy. Do you want the number? It's two twenty forty-six. I've called it so often lately I know it by heart."

Her hand rested on the phone, then moved away. There was just the hint of a tremor in it, just as there was a hint of grief in her expression, her stance. "Why would the mayor of Markovo come all the way here to tell me Andrei was dead?"

"For two reasons. You knew Ryzkhov. Perhaps you also knew his friends. Who liked him, even who hated him. Friends sometimes know these things about one another."

"You could have called. Tunguska's a long way from town." But then she said, "Why not ask his wife? Her name's Vika, remember?"

At last, jealousy. Or was it? "She lives in California. It's possible that he didn't share every detail of his life with her."

"All she wanted to share was his money."

And what were you after? Nowek wondered. "A wife so far away lives more independently. So does a husband. But that's no secret to you." He regretted saying it even as the words left his lips.

"What do you want?" She'd gone utterly blank. It was what Galena did when she was lying.

"Your help. When was the last time you saw Andrei?"

She spoke from behind a mask and said, "I don't see why it's any of your business."

"You aren't alone." He took a deep breath. He wasn't good at interrogation. "I understand you often paid him visits. Usually in the evening. You were seen coming and going from his flat at Rossinka at odd hours."

"And I thought the KGB was history."

"The KGB is nothing compared to a curious neighbor."

Anna had the look of a person walking through a minefield. Concentrated. "My trips into Markovo are arranged around the AmerRus flight schedule," she said, measuring each word like medicine, like gold. "AMR flies early in the morning and late in the afternoon. So do I."

"You saw Andrei often?"

"I don't get into Markovo often. My work is here."

"Where the tigers live. The tape I saw when I walked in, what was on it?"

"You watched it behind my back. Answer your own question."

"It looked like a tiger attacking a man."

She crossed her arms over her chest again.

Nowek forced his eyes away from her. "Who was he? Where did it happen?"

"Either you already know and there's no point in telling you, or you don't know and there's no way you can help. You see, there's no reason for this conversation."

"I think there is." He deliberately calmed himself. She was

trying to provoke him. She was succeeding. "It may surprise you, but I want to find the ones who murdered your friend and my two officers."

"Good luck."

"You don't think I have much of a chance?"

"I think Andrei was successful." She turned away and walked behind the desk. She gazed down, her shoulders rising and falling slowly. When she looked back up, her face was hard, not softened by tears. "Russians hate success. They'd rather everyone be miserable than one person live happily. It could be anyone."

Russians? Nowek wondered. What she said was true, but who did Anna Vereskaya think *she* was? "You didn't hate him."

"Andrei was very helpful."

"In what way?"

"The way one friend helps another. End of discussion."

"Excuse me, but not quite." Nowek stepped nearer. "If I learned that a friend had been murdered, I think I would show at least surprise. I can tell you I was no friend of his but it affected me more than it seems to affect you. Of course, I saw him with his neck sliced open. Did I mention that he was tortured? You remember the nice thick carpet in the bedroom? Of course you would. Well, when I arrived it was soaked with blood." He watched her, then said, "They wanted something from him. His safe was empty. Can you imagine what it might be? Was it money? Or something else?"

She looked ready to leap, to bite.

"It's possible you and Andrei weren't such good friends. I could be wrong. Please inform me if this is the case."

Whatever control she had used to veil her feelings before fell away. If her eyes had been X rays, Nowek would have died of radiation overdose. "Who are you to ask? Isn't it enough that you sneak around looking over my shoulder? He was trying to do something good and that's more than any Russian politician I've ever met. Or heard of." Her Russian came at him like machine-gun rounds. Fast and brutal. "I came up here to get away from people like you. Obviously I didn't go far enough. If Andrei is dead, it's because of people like you."

"You suspect me?"

"Spend enough time around Russians, you suspect everyone."

Russians again. Would Galena talk like this someday? "How much time does that take, Dr. Vereskaya?"

"I came to my conclusions early." She glanced over the surface of her desk as though she were looking for a cigarette to light. She pushed a piece of paper aside. "You know, today is the first day I knew Markovo even had a mayor. I thought it was just a place where AMR hired prostitutes."

It made him think of Galena once again. "Was the man on that tape a part of the tiger census operation?"

"Don't be ridiculous."

"Then who was he?"

She took a deep breath, but just as Nowek thought she would say nothing more, Anna said, "He was a poacher."

Poacher? An American man killing tigers dressed in a sweatshirt with twenty degrees of frost? "How did you catch it on film?"

"Not film. On a data cartridge. It's digitized. Tunguska is wired for radiotelemetry, Mayor. At the feeding sites we can actually see them on WebCams. See and hear them."

Web whats? "You keep track of everything from here?"

"No. The raw data gets archived for analysis back at the Institute. It's too bad we don't put it out because it would make good advertising."

"Advertising?"

"The world should know that poaching tigers can be dangerous."

"So you think a poacher deserves to die."

"Absolutely." She nodded at the wall map. "When I'm not collecting tapes, darting animals, and putting radio collars on their necks, I help track poachers for the Biosphere rangers. We've caught a few. Not many. They bait traps with fresh meat and shoot from ambush with high-powered rifles firing exploding rounds. They're made specially to inflict a maximum wound. Ever touch a tiger, Mayor? Her sides feel like steel plate. It takes a lot to stop a two-hundred-kilo Amur."

A special, exploding bullet. He recalled the lump of misshapen lead that Kaznin had shown him at Rossinka.

"What if Andrei was involved with poaching?"

She peered at him, curious. "He wasn't."

"You sound very sure."

"I am. You said you came for two reasons. So far I've heard only one and to be honest, it's not very good."

He put the box down on the desk. "If it's not too much of an imposition, I'd like you to look at something. To identify it if you can. I could take it to Irkutsk, but there's no budget for analysis. I found it at Andrei's apartment."

For the first time she looked uncertain, even fearful. What was it? A hand? A head?

He nodded at the box. "Please."

Anna hesitated, but then she opened the wings of the little box and peered inside. Her hands dove down and pulled out the knob of heavy yellow bone. She had long, slender fingers like his daughter. There were no rings.

When she looked up at Nowek, her eyes were cold as the green ice at the bottom of a glacier. "Where did you get this?"

"I found it under Ryzhov's dresser."

"Bull*shit*," she spat in English. "He wouldn't have this in a million years."

Where did she learn her American English? It was really very convincing. Unsettlingly convincing. "Then it's tiger?" Nowek asked.

She tossed the bone at Nowek. "Upper carpal fragment," she said. "From an older male. Probably six, seven years old."

He held the knot of yellow bone. "All of that from one bone? I was told it would take extensive testing."

"I've seen a lot of bones."

"How can you be so sure?"

She stood and walked to the back door.

"Wait!" Nowek thought she was going to walk out. But the

door led to another room. He could see cardboard boxes stacked inside, some bulging with paper files, others closed.

When she came back, she had a box. It seemed heavy. When she dropped it onto the desk it made an odd, percussive sound. It didn't quite thud, it didn't quite ring. Something in between. "Look for yourself," she said as she opened it for Nowek.

Inside were dozens of heavy, yellow bones. A rank odor rose, much like the one he'd smelled from the piece from under Ryzkhov's dresser, only more, only worse. He picked one out and held it next to the sample he'd brought from Markovo.

Not identical, but close. It had a marking on it, a number code, and a name. *Galia-2*. He looked at the box of bones. If his one fragment could bring thousands on the Asian medicinals market, what was a *box* worth? And the room beyond?

"Any more questions?"

He put it down. "What are you doing with so many bones?"

"Someday I'll call a news conference and burn them."

Burn them? This one box would pay the salary of every militiaman in Markovo for a year, in dollars, and she'd burn them? Nowek wondered what he would do. It wasn't immediately obvious. "There's a lot of money to be made in illegal wildlife. I understand it's many billions each year."

"That's just the CITES estimate."

"Citeeze?"

"The Convention on International Trade in Endangered Species. It's a convention all right," she said acidly. "A trade convention. You have the supplier nations making deals with the consumer countries. Making excuses, too. Like, 'rhino horn harvest is part of the national economic plan.' Or 'the walrus trade is a native tradition we can't interfere with.' They congratulate each other on how green they are, then slice up the global pie in endangered species. Your piece, my piece. It's all politics and money. And the worst thing is, compared to everyone else they *are* the good guys."

"How can you be so sure Ryzkhov wasn't involved with smuggling tiger bones?"

"I trust him. We have an arrangement."

She still spoke of Ryzkhov as though he were still alive. An arrangement. "Who supports your project?"

"The Taiga Wildlife Institute."

"I'm not familiar with it. Is it at the university?"

"Yes. The University of Idaho."

"Idaho?"

"America. We also get grant money and some support from AMR for services in kind. Transport. Electricity. A moon buggy all my own. Why?"

Idaho. Was this where she had learned her American accent? "Ryzkhov also worked for AmerRus. Did you know that, too?"

"Yes."

"But he did other things. Maybe you both talked about it." She didn't answer.

"Well, even close friends don't tell each other everything. Can you possibly remember the last time you spoke with Ryzkhov?"

Another blank look. "I told you. I've been in the field."

But the AMR dispatcher said she'd flown down to Markovo the evening of Ryzkhov's death, and ridden a VIP flight back the next day. "You know," he said, "your picture is on his wall. You, Andrei, and another man. Standing in front of Rossinka."

"His brother was visiting from Moscow. Andrei wanted to show me off."

Finally, something to believe. "I can imagine."

"Andrei liked to show off things even when he didn't own them. A lot of men do that. You probably do the same with your wife."

"My wife?" His words barely came out of his throat.

"Your ring finger," she said. "You can tell there was a ring on it until recently. It leaves a mark, Mayor. A lot of men seem to think it doesn't."

Nowek put his hand in his pocket. "What was the nature of your arrangement with Ryzkhov?"

"Business."

"What kind of business?"

"Mine."

"Maybe you could be more specific."

She could see that he wasn't going to leave without something in return. "You want specifics? Fine. The Tunguska Preserve covers almost twenty thousand square kilometers. We had five rangers to patrol it until the grant money ran out. Now we have two volunteers. They're up against poachers with heavy weapons, fuel, four-wheel-drive vehicles, and helicopters. They buy everything they need, including local officials like you. So if someone like Andrei offers to help, I'm not going to turn him down. I won't allow another Primorsky to happen, and if it means cooperating with men like Andrei, then so be it."

Men like Andrei. Anna didn't sound much like a grieving girlfriend. Still, if poachers saw Ryzkhov as a threat, they'd stop him any way they could. And who was better with a knife than a man used to skinning tigers? A possible fit. Smaller matters than if he'd gotten on the wrong side of Prosecutor Gromov, but fatal enough. He asked, "What happened down at the Primorsky Tiger Preserve?"

"It was way too close to Vladivostok. Access was impossible to control. The Preserve lasted exactly as long as it took the governor to lease it out for timbering."

"The Koreans."

She looked at him and nodded. "The governor said, don't worry, they're cutting trees, not tigers. But if you take the trees, you kill the tigers. That's the first rule of ecology: everything is connected to everything. The second rule is, never trust a Russian politician."

Another good rule. "So the Koreans showed up with saws. Then what happened?"

"First they cut logging roads. That drove off the red deer. Then they cleared the brush. That destroyed the boar habitat. No boar, no deer, no tiger. It's that simple. Tigers were starving. It was a scramble to get the animals up here before the poachers and the loggers finished them off. There's plenty of prey up here for them, the timber density is too low to justify logging. Not too far north the trees run out entirely. Best of all, you can't get here so easily."

Unless you were AmerRus. "How was Ryzkhov going to help?"

She faced Nowek. "You know how things work. If you don't have *blat,* you might as well go home. Andrei knew what was going on around Tunguska. He could make things available to us. Information. People. Whatever. He was very useful. Anything he couldn't manage, his brother could. His father still has connections and he doesn't even live in Russia."

Blat was pull, and without *blat* or money you could forget getting anything done. "Maybe someone knew of Ryzkhov's arrangement with you. Is that possible?"

"You tell me."

"I think that it's very possible. Perhaps they thought they could work through him to make you stop, or your rangers." He thought again of the treasure trove in the other room. A feast of bones. Worth killing for? A twenty-dollar bill was worth killing for. "Perhaps they killed him when they learned he was helping you."

Her lips compressed. But there was no disguising the impact of his words. She thought the same, though she seemed unwilling to say so. "And maybe they sent you to find out whether they have anything more to worry about."

"They're not worrying, Dr. Vereskaya." He thought of Kaznin, of Prosecutor Gromov. That wasn't entirely true. "Could Ryzkhov have been making deals behind your back with poachers? Businessmen make arrangements with many people."

"No." But she didn't look so sure now. She stood. "Excuse me, but I have work to do." She moved out from behind her desk but Nowek stepped in her path.

"Excuse me," he said, "but so do I."

He was close enough to smell the warmth rising from her hair. It was intoxicating. It made him furious.

"Maybe you didn't know, but it's not only tigers who are

being killed. Two of my men were murdered along with your close friend. They had families. Children and wives. In fact, I could make a good case that the Markovo militia should be on the endangered list. If I applied for a grant, if I begged, do you think we could get talented individuals like you to help fly them someplace safe? Where could they go, Dr. Vereskaya? Irkutsk? Idaho? Someone like you would have a suggestion."

"Get out of here."

"I will. But first I think you might be confused about something. You see, I think you were in Markovo two nights ago. If it turns out that you were and you deny it, then a reasonable person might think you were trying to hide something. Do you see the problem?"

"I see you."

"On the other hand, you can help with the investigation into your friend's murder. Especially if you saw him that night. And if you *did* see him, perhaps you might know why I found a tiger bone under his dresser."

"Maybe you put it there."

"Me? I can't even pay my own militia. You think I'd throw something worth so much under a piece of furniture?"

"I think that it's time you left."

"Your friend was murdered and you don't seem to care. Even though he was helping you, you act as though you barely knew him. You pretend you weren't in Markovo, yet someone saw you arrive at the airport. Before the sun sets this afternoon someone will be found who saw you in town. By tonight they'll have you in his flat. Then what will you do?"

The lock of hair fell across her eye. She flipped it away. "You want to know who killed Andrei? Go ask AMR."

"I'm asking you."

"Then you've come a long way for nothing." She walked back behind her desk.

"Dr. Vereskaya, I also have reasons to think someone from AmerRus is involved."

"You bet your ass," she said. "We're missing twenty-eight tigers and it's barely spring. That's ten percent of all wild Siberian tigers left *anywhere*. We're remote. That's what Tunguska had going for it. The poachers couldn't just drive in and set traps like they did down south. It takes organization, money. It takes a punched ticket with the local politicians. Does that sound familiar?"

It did. "Why would AmerRus be interested in bones?"

"They aren't making much money from oil."

That also seemed true. "There's no way they can make enough if they skinned every tiger in Russia," he said. "And a man dressed in a sweatshirt at twenty below isn't poaching. He's committing suicide. I heard you question it yourself."

"Then maybe it isn't the whole company. Maybe it's someone going freelance. They have plenty of time on their hands up here. And they own Tunguska. Who else could he be but AMR?"

Good question. "You said that AMR supports your project."

"I don't mind using bad money to do good work."

"You use them. They use you. You both used Andrei and his brother for *blat*. It sounds like parasites feeding from one another."

"A mayor should be an expert when it comes to parasites."

Nowek wasn't in the mood for irony. He said, "What finally happened down near Vladivostok? With the tigers?"

"What difference does it make?"

"It seems to make a big difference to you."

She stared at him. He blinked and took on the look of something rooted. Something that was going to stay put until he heard what he wanted to hear.

She looked away first. "All right. I told you about the loggers. That's why we were transporting animals up here. We were working around the clock. Tracking, darting, transporting. Then we found Olga."

"Olga?"

"An eight-year-old female. The radio showed she was staying in a very small area about to be logged over. I tracked her and saw why. She had three cubs, all female. That's why she was staying so close to home. After that, we couldn't move her. Not until the cubs were old enough. They'd die."

Nowek thought, look at her. She's talking about a family. It could be her own. They weren't just tigers.

"One day her radio collar stopped moving. Dead stop. I tracked it to a snowbank. I dug down and there was the collar. Cut cleanly. The poachers cut it off her neck so we couldn't follow them."

"What about the cubs?"

"They were too small to survive on their own. We took them back to town and kept them warm and fed. They were about ten kilos. Big enough so that when they clawed it hurt but small enough so that when you tickled their bellies they purred. It was a mistake, but we named them. Vera, Lyuba, and Nadezhda."

Vera, Lyuba, and Nadezhda. Faith, Love, and Hope.

"I tried to line up a zoo that would take them but the damned paperwork . . . I had to inform the Ministry for the Protection of the Environment. I had to get an export license from the local administration. It was taking forever." She stopped, then went on. "I was asked to stop by the mayor's office one morning. He was going to expedite the licensing. I figured he would offer me a quid pro quo."

"What kind?"

"Sleep with him and he'd give me his signature." She shook her head. "But when I got there, he wasn't in. I had a bad feeling about it. I'd been set up."

He watched as her shoulders rose and fell. He wanted to reach out, to comfort her. It was a kind of intoxication, a rhapsody of the deeps, the deeps of time, of memory.

"I drove straight back to the office." She stopped, swallowed. "I . . . I opened the door. There was blood. It was . . . it was all over."

Like Ryzkhov's flat.

"They broke in and slaughtered two of them. I found Nadezhda. She'd run and wedged herself behind some heavy file cabinets. Those bastards probably looked in and saw those claws and teeth and figured two out of three was enough. But she was hurt. Badly."

He could see the way the story affected her. It shadowed her face the way a mother speaks of the death of a child. "Did she survive?"

When Anna looked up her eyes glistened. "The export license came the next day. Hope was the last to die. Isn't that an old Russian saying?"

"Yes." But Nowek thought, they were just tigers. "What would you do to stop it from happening again?"

She understood his thrust and parried it. "Andrei was not smuggling bone."

"But you think someone from AMR is."

"How many black Americans are there running around Siberia? Have you ever seen one?"

"But the man's face was white."

"The camera sees in infrared. Everyone's face is white, unless you're not giving off heat. Then you'd be dead."

He'd forgotten. A *black* American dying under the teeth of a great tiger. Proof, or so she thought, of AMR's involvement in poaching. No. It couldn't be as simple, as strange, as that. "Who else has seen that tape?"

"So," she said. "I wondered when you'd ask. You know, I did my post-doc work in Indonesia. They have fifteen species of snakes, and twelve of them are poisonous. You reach the conclusion pretty fast that if you see a snake, chances are it's not a nice one. Russia's that way. The mayor down in Primorsky? He was the same. You're the same."

"It's possible that you and I are on the same side."

"We couldn't be more different," she said. "One look at you and I see someone available to the highest bidder. You've given up. I haven't. That's all the difference in the world."

It left him without words. Almost without breath. The sound of a motor revving came from outside. Decker in the moon buggy returning.

The clump of boots from the vestibule. A loud buzz. The door opened. Decker seemed different. His face was sweaty and his dark hair plastered to his brow. He looked at Nowek, then at Vereskaya. "You all ready to roll?"

"Yes," Anna answered for him. "He's ready."

Nowek looked at her, his eyes so unwilling to give up even an illusion. She wasn't Nina, that was certain. But hadn't she herself said it?

Hope was the last to die.

12

THE MOON BUGGY glided up to the helicopter and stopped.

"It's been real nice," said Decker. "Come back up and see us anytime." He was smiling. Like most Americans, he did a lot of that. Like most Russians, Nowek didn't think it looked so authentic. What was there to be so happy about?

A bulge in Decker's breast pocket moved like a rippling chest muscle. The word muscle derives from *mus*, Latin for mouse. As though to illustrate the connection, a narrow little face appeared from Decker's pocket. A rodent's face, but no mouse.

Decker grinned and scooped the animal out, holding it under the chest for Nowek to see. "My bro' Harley," he said to Nowek, then to the ferret, "Thank the mayor for everything he's done for us."

"I've done nothing."

"That's what *he* thinks." Decker grinned. "Say bye-bye." He squeezed the ferret's chest. The animal squeaked and tried to bite Decker's thumb.

Nowek got out and the *lunashkhod,* the moon buggy, drove off.

The starter began to whine even before Nowek opened the door. The rotor blades slashed the cool air lazily. There was no sign of DeKalb. Nowek found his municipal ID was on the passenger's seat. He gave DeKalb's name tag to the pilot.

The pilot—was it Joffrey?—reached across and locked the left-hand door. He wore a green headset that was plugged into the bottom of the instrument panel. Nowek looked around for another; the only other pair rested on a hook at the far aft wall of the cabin, out of reach. At least there was a safety belt, and he fastened it tight.

The fire caught hold in the guts of the turbine. The starter's whine became lost in the roar of burning jet fuel. The world began to shake as the rotor blades spooled up to an invisible disk overhead.

A black American wandering around the taiga dressed for the tropics. Sweating at twenty degrees of frost. Running for his life, and finding instead a feeding station meant for tigers. A piece of gravel awash in blood, spattered with glass. And Anna Vereskaya, a woman who lied, who spoke uncomfortable truths. Who vibrated inside him like a sympathetic chord; draw the bow over one note and another one unexpectedly, unasked, softly answers. Not the same note, but related by the unbreakable laws of mathematics, the regulations of hope.

Joffrey fiddled with the radio, switching frequencies and speaking into his boom microphone. He tapped the radio hard, switched channels, then tried again. He smacked the glare shield in frustration.

"Problems?" Nowek had to shout over the roar.

Joffrey looked at him as though he were a mess someone had left on the seat cushion. He snapped the radio off then twisted the throttle on the collective. The engine howled. The machine grew light on its skids.

A fast pounding came from the rear passenger door. Even Joffrey could hear it. He pulled off the power, flattened the pitch, and locked the collective down. Then he turned.

It was Anna Vereskaya. She wore a short denim jacket that left the bottom of her cardigan sweater exposed. She carried a large frameless rucksack. It was mottled in splotches of green and white. Winter camouflage for the taiga. She opened the rear door and threw in her bag, then climbed in after it. She didn't seem surprised to see Nowek. More confirmed in something.

"What's goin' on?" the pilot yelled back.

She ignored Nowek and said, "I'm hitching a ride into town."

He eyed the big rucksack. "DeKalb say okay?"

"It's okay." She pulled the door shut.

With a final glance at the inoperative radio, Joffrey ran the rotor blades back up to speed, pulled in the collective. The Bell swiftly rose into the air and turned south.

"I thought you said you were busy today," said Nowek. He had to turn and lean back. The din of the engine covered their talk. "You're coming into town on business?"

She said something, but Nowek couldn't quite hear.

"What?" He leaned back more.

When she leaned forward, the Buryat blade swung from the leather thong around her neck. "I said, I knew you were working for AmerRus but I didn't realize how much of a VIP you were."

"I'm not."

"This is DeKalb's personal helicopter. He doesn't give people rides for free. What did you have to do, Mayor?" She slipped the sheath under her denim jacket. The ivory handle was still visible.

Nowek looked at the knife, then up at her face. "You've ridden it yourself. What have you done for him?"

She registered the hit, but she didn't respond.

"You said you're from Irkutsk," Nowek persisted. "Is that where you're going?"

"I said my parents were from Irkutsk."

She seemed to be drawing a distinction. "I don't understand. You're not?"

"No."

In geology, a discontinuity is a break in the ordered layering of strata; a place where tectonic forces bend the rock until it can bend no more. A small one is an interesting footnote to the geological record; a big one is an earthquake. Nowek could sense just such a discontinuity, a rush of forces, the plastic deformation of an ordered life nearing the point at which the crystals shatter, the rock breaks, and a rift opens at your feet, in your heart.

"Where are you from, if not Irkutsk?"

Her eyes were cool, the green in them shaded by the blue taiga light. Judging, amused. Willing to play this obvious game a little while longer. "California. La Jolla to be exact. You've heard of it? Palm trees. Beaches. You've watched *Santa Barbara*. It's like that, only more so."

La Jolla? She was taunting him. Provoking again. California? She could have said she was from Jupiter and it would have been just as believable. Was it another lie? Some coded expression that meant something other than what it seemed? All he could say was, "You're an *American*?"

"I said I grew up in California."

"I had no . . . I mean, your Russian is perfect. Stop playing games. You're from Irkutsk. I can hear it."

At this she smiled. "My mother would be happy to know that. She told me I would grow up illiterate because I couldn't memorize Pushkin."

"Pushkin?" Her American English. The things she had said on the tape. It explained everything except that it was also impossible for him to accept. "You're not American. You can't be."

"Whatever."

His head was really spinning. Everything sure, everything reasonable, was thrown into the air, whirling like the rotor blades overhead. "If you are American, why didn't you tell me before?"

"You said you were an expert when it came to accents. I assumed you'd be able to tell. Maybe you aren't as much of an expert as you think."

An underground rumble. Is the rupturing fault here, or is it there? He decided to find out once and for all. "You still think I'm with AmerRus? You still think I'm your enemy?"

"Andrei is dead?"

"You know he is."

"Then what I think about you doesn't matter."

Nowek had taken too big a bite. He'd half-swallowed, half-chewed. He was choking on impossibilities. On competing truths. "The mayor down in Primorsky. The one you thought was offering the quid pro quo?"

"What about him?"

"Would you have accepted?"

She thought about it for perhaps a second, maybe two, then said, "For the lives of three Siberian tiger cubs? Maybe. Maybe yes. But that doesn't matter now either." She reached back and took a heavy green headset from its hook and put it over her ears. She turned her back to him and watched the marshes go by below.

It doesn't matter. An American girl speaking Siberian Russian. A Siberian girl speaking American English. Dream, substance, neither, both, the whole kaleidoscope Nowek had so carefully assembled piece by piece swirled. Nina, Anna, mistress, murderer. Sunflower, knife, and rifle. Who the devil was she really?

The sympathetic note went dead. He felt the burn of shame at being so wrong, so stupid, especially with an American.

Russians were venal, stupid, inferior. They were snakes. She'd said as much herself. It was safer to assume they all bite. That they all were poisonous. Not that she was wrong. No. Being right only made it worse.

Marsh became lake, lake became stands of stunted trees and trees gathered into scrub forest. The silver pipeline, empty, threaded through white snow and green muck straight for Markovo.

She'd also been right when she said that he'd given up, though it amazed him that it was visible, like some birthmark, some brand on his forehead. It was so obvious that even an American could see it. Although not just an American. An

American with Siberian blood. No wonder she saw through him. He thought of his campaign poster.

Be Honest: Could I Do Any Worse?

Well, be honest. He had done worse. Who wouldn't give up? Who wouldn't wish for a return to the days when they pretended to pay you, and you pretended to work? Who wouldn't say, who needs the future? I won't even live in it. Three things were important to a Siberian: first bread, then vodka, and third? Bread again.

He stole a glance at her. Parents from Irkutsk. Had they somehow managed to emigrate? How? Nobody got out of Siberia. Siberia was where they sent you. Siberia was a prison without walls. It was where you could be safely forgotten. A place where even God could hide his mistakes.

She'd said that she would never let another Primorsky happen at Tunguska. Ryzkhov was going to help. Someone stopped him. Then there was the tape. A poacher? Why on earth would a Russian-American joint venture bother with bones? He couldn't accept that. He wished she would answer just one of his questions.

She turned and faced him full, her eyes wide, deep. She didn't look away.

"I can help you," he said in Russian. "But you have to let me."

"As if," she said in English.

"I don't know what your arrangements were with Ryzkhov. But I know AmerRus is involved somehow in this. I need you to—"

"Go away," she said, and then turned her face back to the window.

The scrub forest thickened to a solid green blanket undulating up and down over low, glaciated hills. The Lena appeared, and the pilot banked the swift helicopter to follow the river south. Joffrey stayed mute, insulated by the silence of his earphones.

The flight back was faster than the bumpy, uncertain ride he'd had in *Little Annie,* and that was just as well. It was late, and the sun was already down behind the treeline. The trunks sent long black shadows across snowy, shaded ground.

He saw the column of smoke from twenty kilometers out.

Nowek pointed it out. Joffrey behaved as though black smoke rising from the Markovo airport was the commonest of sights. He didn't say a word. It rose straight up, then leaned over to the south, pushed flat by the wind. Markovo's flirtation with spring was temporarily suspended. A north wind was blowing. It meant weather on the way.

"I can give you a ride into Markovo."

"I don't think that would be wise for either one of us," she said. "Even if you're telling the truth about Andrei." She stopped, thought, then said, "Especially if you're telling the truth."

Even now she doubted him? He looked away. Let her find out her own way. Let her see what's left of her arrangement with Ryzkhov. Let her smell it and then call him a liar.

Closer now. Down, in a long clattering glide. Down below the trees, down to near the surface of the runway. The fire wasn't coming from the AmerRus helipad, though it drifted over it. First one skid, then the other bumped down.

The smoke came from the place where Yuri's hangar once stood. Flashes of bright flame rose within the smoke, then guttered out. The log walls were gone, submerged in gray ash. The metal roof had collapsed. The rotor pitch flattened, the engine throttled back. Joffrey reached across and cracked the door. The rotor blast caught it and sent it slamming open.

She was out, her head down low, heading away from the helipad. The camouflaged rucksack made her hard to see against the dark trees and white patches of snow. She stopped and looked back at him for just a moment, then walked quickly into the growing shadows.

Nowek grabbed the box with its bone and stepped out to the mud of the Markovo airfield, the stink of melted plastics stabbing his nostrils with each breath. Before he could close the door, it was pulled shut from within. The engine rose to a shriek, the rotors sent a hurricane of wind cascading down, blowing away the smoke. Without waiting for Nowek to clear the area, the Bell rose, dipped its nose, and beat north.

The thud of its rotor blades was swallowed by a sky cut from sheets of luminous pearl. Nowek could hear the crackle and sigh of a dying fire. There were no more flames, only sooty gray smoke, dejected and spent, the edges tinged white.

The white Land Cruiser pulled up.

It was Chuchin, and not Chuchin. His face was puffy and scabbed with dried blood, his left eye nearly closed and a huge purple bruise flowering across a cheek. One of Yuri's Marlboros dangled from his mouth. His sunglasses were twisted into a pretzel. They stuck out from the breast pocket of his padded jacket. He was forced to squint. "Well, you missed the show." He tried to smile but it clearly hurt. He watched Anna as she walked down the road leading away from the airport. "I'm impressed. You got her."

"Chuchin!" Nowek jumped into the car. "What happened?"

"This?" He gingerly touched his swollen cheek. "This was just a misunderstanding. They thought a rifle stock was harder than my head." You had to know Chuchin to tell, but another tooth was missing. "Fortunately, it happened *after* I went to town. I saw Nikki Malyshev. I'm happy to report your father will have his birthday dinner." He jabbed a leathery thumb at some tins of food in the back. "I bought some things from him and then I came back here. I should have had a cigarette instead. Five minutes more and I'd have missed those bastards."

"Who did it?" He was furious. "Did Yuri's gang—"

"They tried to stop them. At least *he* did," he said with a quick nod at the wrecked hangar. Plet had appeared out of the smoke. "He drilled one of those bastards into the ground with a wrench. They just stood and watched at first. Even *I* didn't believe it. Then the shooting started."

"Shooting?"

"Plet kept pounding that little OSNAZ shit into the mud. If

they hadn't fired a rocket he'd have sprouted roots and leaves."
OSNAZ was the *Osobogo Naznachenya,* the old KGB's "Special
Forces," the "Black Berets"; unaccountable even to their own
unaccountable masters. They were also officially disbanded.

"There is no OSNAZ, Chuchin."

"You tell them the next time. Or Kaznin. He was in
charge."

"*Kaznin* was here? What for?"

Chuchin gave him a long, sideways look that said, enough
kidding. This is serious. He took a long puff, then slowly spit it
out. "He wanted to know where you were. I said, what am I,
an Intourist agent? That's when things got rough."

Nowek's fists clenched. "I'll kill him."

"You? Listen, just because you're growing a beard doesn't
make you a gangster, okay? So calm down. What could they
do? Make me ugly?"

"What was Kaznin here for?"

"He was headed for Tunguska, the same as you. He said that
he knew who killed Ryzkhov and the militiamen. He was
going to arrest her."

"*Her?*"

He pointed the smoking stub at Anna Vereskaya. She was
walking next to the trees. "But you got her first. That little fat
prick will pop like a tick when he finds out you outsmarted
him. But shouldn't she be under guard?"

Nowek sat back in the seat. AmerRus was involved. But *her?*
She'd been in town that night and lied about it. She said that
she would do anything to protect her precious tigers. Her quid
pro quo. But did it make sense? He shook his head.

"What's wrong?" said Chuchin.

A rumble fell from the sunset sky. Something loose on the
Land Cruiser's dash buzzed.

"Kaznin," said Chuchin. "We should go, Mayor. Now.
Trust me."

"No. There's a complication."

"My head feels complicated enough." He looked at Nowek.

"It's Vereskaya. She says she's American."

Chuchin mouthed the word silently. "You believe her?"

Nowek paused. "It's possible. Yes."

"It's possible that if I had Kaznin after me I would say my name was Eisenhower. Either way you'll have to give her over to him. Either way it's finished."

"No."

"No? You can't . . ." Chuchin grabbed his arm and pointed. Anna was running now. She'd heard the engine.

Nowek opened the window and shouted, "Hey!"

She didn't even turn her head. At his shout she darted into the taiga. In a moment, like a reverse of the tape with its tiger, she was lost in the mottled shadows. Dark green and pale white merged.

"Find her," he said to Chuchin as he got out. "But be careful. She's got a knife."

"And you still think she's innocent?"

"I didn't say that. I just don't think she killed Ryzkhov."

CHAPTER
13

GALENA SHIVERED under the rough blankets, even with the edge pulled all the way up to her chin. Not that she was cold. That would have been easier. It was stuffy and overheated inside the cabin, the air a nasty mix of spilled bourbon, after-shave, sweat, cigarette smoke, and her own fear.

Decker left her numb with the desire to disappear, to evaporate, to die. But then numbness became anger, and his neat little cabin its natural target. Now the place was a ruin of overturned furniture, pulled-open drawers, spilled clothing, and broken glass.

It wasn't enough for what he'd done. Not nearly enough.

The rape was a quick, cold stabbing. That wasn't what frightened her. She'd had boyfriends like that, drunk boyfriends especially, and that described most of them.

It was the way Decker looked when he held that knife, eyes glazed. It gave him more pleasure to scare her, to hurt her. Sex had nothing to do with it. She touched the scab of dried blood on her forehead. What kind of a man was he?

The kind who would place the point of a knife against her head. The kind who would slowly, incrementally, push until she broke, until she fell flat to the mattress, her eyes wide and white, certain of death. Paralyzed with it. That was what he liked best.

I'll put it right through your pretty little head.

And Galena believed him.

She'd tried to stay still as he pulled her torn clothes away and threw them to the floor. She let her mind drift away as he levered her legs apart. She was someplace else when he slapped her. She ignored him, hoped that he would be quick. She shut her eyes.

But Paul Decker didn't like her silent. He didn't want her so easy and accommodating.

The press of his body on her vanished. It was replaced by a sharp, hot tingling. A thin scratch across her ribs that blossomed into pain. Her eyes shot back open. She tried to squirm away, but the more she moved the more the knife cut.

I'm the man, he'd said as the point of his knife scribed a line from beneath her bare breast upward, toward the sensitive center. *Go on and say it. I'm the man.*

She stayed frozen. Steel nicked a nipple stiff with fright. A trickle of blood rolled down her side. She shut her eyes again, imagining a beach somewhere. A beach with a palm tree, though she herself had never actually seen one. She began to climb it as pain flooded below her, rising.

Say it or cut that little titty off and give it to Harley.

The knife bit deeper, rimming the pale pink areola in bright crimson. The trickle gushed hot. She clamped her teeth shut. She wouldn't give this to him. Never. She wouldn't. Let him do whatever he . . .

The blade dug, then twisted. A nerve screamed an electric scream and, despite everything, so did Galena.

"Say it!"

And so she did. Again and again. Begged him with his own words.

Only then did Decker smile, throw both her knees apart, and force his way into her body. He was already inside her mind. He pumped at her as methodically, as boringly, as a machine, no longer caring that her eyes were shut, that she was cold as marble, that her blood was all over the bed, the front of his coveralls. He didn't even look at her.

When he was done he balled his orange coveralls into a heap, tossed them into a corner, and warned her not to move so much as a finger. He whistled as he took a shower.

The water stopped. His cologne flowed out through the open door like a sweet, sick fog as she sobbed too softly for Decker to hear.

Now when she looked at herself in the shattered mirror there was no pose, no smoldering. All of that had been cut away, leaving behind the stain of hate. And hate had driven her to rise from the bed when he left, to rise and rip the cabin apart. If that little rat had been here, she would have torn it to pieces, too. But then the fear came back.

What would he do when he got back and saw what she'd done?

Galena kicked through the shards of glass. They were all too small. She went to the closet and found a pair of Decker's tooled leather boots. He had such small feet. Delicate, even. She took one and smashed a hard heel into the fractured mirror.

Another blow and a long, jagged icicle fell free. She picked it up and looked at the locked door, then went back to the bed and pulled the covers up again. The glass spike warmed to her skin as she held it out of sight.

For the first time in a day, Galena smiled.

Decker would return. She would cut his balls off and hand them to him with a sweet smile. *Oh yes,* she would say, *you were the man. But tell me, what are you now?*

DeKalb's silver hard hat was off. He leaned back in his swivel chair and put his boots up on the desk. The office was impressively bare. Windowless walls covered with imitation wood paneling. A file cabinet. No pictures. No coffee mugs. Not even a calendar. An illustration in an office supply catalog had more signs of human habitation.

There were two wall clocks. He watched the one on the right, the one set not to local time, but to California time.

Home office time. Its hands were straight up. In twenty-two seconds it would be midnight of the day before.

Here was a question: if he never went back east, if he never crossed the dateline, if he never went home again, would his life be one day shorter? Could he choose which day to throw into the sea out by the dateline? He had one in mind.

When the second hand joined both minute and hour, the telephone on his desk rang. Right on time. He picked it up.

"DeKalb." His eyes went up. "Fine on this end." A pause. "I understand." Another pause. "I did. Nowek. Mayor. Yes. From Markovo."

The voice on the other end grew excited.

"I disagree. I know these people. They'll make noise and then back right off as soon as they see where the money's comin' from. That's your end of the stick. Keep it comin' and we won't have any problems."

The line crackled.

"He won't once they have a little chat with him. They'll set it straight. Anyway, I'm here to do a job. Let me take care of the details."

Hell, thought DeKalb, this boy needs some perspective. After all, the man worked for the Company. He ought to know by now that DeKalb was a man he could trust. DeKalb was on the inside. He was a gatekeeper, charged with keeping the rest of the damned world where it belonged: out.

"Eighteen. I copy that."

DeKalb once believed right and wrong were poles apart. Now he knew they overlapped. The borders got fuzzy as the sky before a thunderstorm. Sometimes what *looked* wrong turned out right in the end. And sometimes your whole life got switched upside down and inside out by one day. You had to go on instinct for what was the greater truth. The greater good.

"Watertight," said DeKalb. "You have my word on it. See, the beauty of it is, the locals can't afford to take risks on this any more than we can. We're dancing with the bastards real close. What's your ETA tonight?"

As the voice in his ear read him arrival times and codes, as he jotted them down for later, DeKalb was remembering a girl, fourteen years old, and how he'd found her that day. She no longer looked like his daughter. She no longer even looked human. She looked like a broken doll.

"I understand."

But he didn't. What kind of a man, an animal, would do that to an innocent girl? With the house alarm screaming its fool head off, the cops, the sirens closing in? What kind of a man?

"We'll be waitin' on them."

Like a broken doll.

He made a promise to her and he was here to see it through. Politics be damned. He wasn't here for glory. Not for money, not for oil though it was all around.

He was here for justice.

"All right then." He pushed the notepad away. "By the way, I'm rotating some personnel early. Decker. We'll need to bump up his replacement one week." DeKalb nodded. "Good. We'll expect him. Take my word on the other matter. It's a done deal."

He hung up, then opened the top drawer of his desk. He pulled out a small framed photograph. He passed his rough hands back over the bristles of his close-cropped hair, staring at it. At her. He set it onto the bare desk and imagined her sitting there with him. Having a conversation, the kind of talk no father ever really has with a teenage daughter, but it was nice to think about, wasn't it?

The telephone rang again. He looked at it. They'd never called twice. Even scrambled, it was too risky. Especially now. When it continued, he relented and picked it up.

"DeKalb." His eyes immediately sharpened. It wasn't the home office. It was that dopehead he kept caged down at the Markovo airport. Higgins. "No. Just the mayor. You're sure?" He listened to the reply, the line of his jaw tightening. "Tell Mr. Joffrey I'm anxious to speak with him the instant he gets back." He slammed the receiver down so hard the framed photo of his daughter tipped over and fell onto its face. He gingerly picked it up.

"Well shit."

The cover had a tiny hairline fracture across it. A stress riser, some hidden flaw in the crystal structure.

Like the cover glass on his daughter's portrait, Anna Vereskaya was a stress riser looking to become a break. He knew how to deal with stress risers. With propagating cracks. He carefully put the photo away, then shut the drawer.

The way to cure a stress riser was to stop-drill it. You end the propagating crack in a clean, surgical hole. You removed unnecessary material. It took a good, steady hand, but that was why they offered him the tool pusher's job here at Tunguska. He'd accepted it for reasons of his own. Or more precisely, for a reason of his own.

Like a broken doll.

Justice. Here at Tunguska he was its final arbiter. Its judge, its jury, its trustee and warden. If necessary, he could be its executioner too.

Five in the afternoon. At sixty degrees north latitude, the April sun was already caught in the branches of the trees, sinking fast. Nowek listened to the approaching aircraft. Kaznin. He'd make him pay for every bruise on Chuchin's face.

The north wind had strengthened, and in the shadows the soft snow was reglazed with ice. Nowek found the walking difficult. A solid-seeming surface, he would step through sheets of isinglass only to fall into dense, wet snow up to his knees.

Like Ryzkhov's death. Like Anna herself. Solid, sure, obvious. A *mafiya* murder, a falling-out of thieves, a Russian woman counting tigers. And then what? You step through and nothing is the way you thought it was.

Soaked through, Nowek shivered as he made his way to Plet and the smoldering hangar. The sky filled with a red glow. The roar of the engine changed in pitch.

Nowek looked but Kaznin was too low to see. OSNAZ troopers who didn't exist and a woman Kaznin said was a killer. An American woman. An American woman who had the nerve to look at him and speak the truth: that he had lost and given up. Even now he could hear her saying it.

The smoke rising from the hangar was just a thin streak against the white sky. Embers glowed from shadow. Wooden supports eaten by fire settled with the crackle of gunfire. Plet stood by, his face upturned, the wrench he usually carried now gone and an assault rifle in its place; a parachutist's model with a folding tubular stock.

Before Nowek could ask what had happened, the sound of flying engines fell away and a dark shape whistled out of the sky, touching down on the far end of the runway with a clatter of pots and pans and loose metal sheets.

For once Chuchin had been mistaken. It wasn't Kaznin. *Little Annie* had come home.

The Antonov showed no lights as it rolled up to the ruins of its hangar, air brakes hissing as it slowed to a fast walk. With a final blast of compressed air, a last burst of power that sent a tongue of blue fire from its exhaust, the engine clanked to a stop. Nowek followed it.

The cargo door swung open. Two guards sniffed the smoke like wary wolves before they jumped down. Then Yuri appeared. He stared at the burned hangar a long while before he noticed Nowek. Plet shoved a crate under the hatch and Yuri stepped down. "Who was it?"

Plet said, "Troops."

Yuri scanned the treeline as though expecting a skirmish line to reappear. "What are you saying? The Chinese invaded? What troops?"

"A *Ministertsvo* helicopter," answered Plet. "You know?"

"*Yob tvoyu mat!*" Yuri cursed. He certainly seemed to know who Plet was talking about. He stared at Nowek. "I should have known to stay clear of your kind of trouble. You used me, Mayor. You got a free ride and your friends left me to pay the bill."

A Ministry helicopter. Where did Kaznin come up with one? And which ministry? "They're no friends of mine. What did he mean, a Ministry helicopter?"

"Forget it. I've been an idiot. I even tried to pick you up at Tunguska. Right *then* I should have known. They blocked the runway. Trucks, equipment, a crane. They thought we were partners, Mayor, and look what they did. Now I find you here. Who did you talk into giving you a ride this time?"

"DeKalb insisted I take his helicopter back. He said you had no authority to land at Tunguska. I told him—"

"DeKalb? So now you're such good friends with the Americans they fly you around like you're some golden turd from Moscow? And to me they do this? You know something? It's too bad they didn't kick you out along the way. Too bad *I* didn't. Fuck!" He picked up a half-burned piece of lumber and threw it hard. It tumbled end for end, leaving an undulating trail of smoke. He walked up and jabbed a finger into Nowek's chest. "My only question is, what are you going to do about it?"

"Major Oleg Kaznin was in charge."

"I don't see Kaznin. What I see is you and your Japanese jeep. It's badly worn, but all the same it would make a nice gesture."

"Kaznin is responsible. There are laws about—"

"Stop. They did this to me because of *you*. Pricktwisters burn *my hangar* and you want to talk about laws? That's almost funny." He turned to Plet. "Get the truck. I've heard enough fairy tales."

Plet disappeared. In a moment, from the treeline, a diesel engine turned, turned, then caught in a chuff of smoke. A big Maz military truck nosed from out of a hiding place and stopped next to the AN-2's cargo door. It sat idling in a cloud of blue exhaust. Drab canvas covered its back.

"What are you waiting for?" shouted Yuri. "There are laws about frozen goods! The mayor is here to remind us that fish rot from the head. Let's get this cargo loaded!"

The crew assembled slowly, not sure if there was work worth doing here anymore. Yuri Durashenko was obviously no longer in favor with *someone* with plenty of *blat*. Someone with a helicopter. A Ministry helicopter.

Plet snapped the slide on the assault rifle. It was *blat* made visible, audible, made real.

The loaders went to work.

Nowek said, "This is about Kaznin and his boss, Prosecutor Gromov. We can make them pay, Yuri."

Yuri looked pityingly at Nowek. "Forget I exist. I'll return the favor."

"You didn't help me and they still did this to you," said Nowek. "What about next time? Even if you keep quiet, they can do it again."

"I won't be here next time."

"Where will you go? Kaznin works for Prosecutor Gromov. That takes care of Markovo. Gromov is doing a job for the governor. So much for Irkutsk. The governor works for Amer-Rus, so maybe Siberia isn't far enough. And if Siberia isn't far enough to stay away from this Ministry, tell me, what is?"

"I'll fly *Annushka* to a place those ignorant bitches can't even spell. Who knows? Maybe Alaska." His hands shook as he lit a Marlboro from the embers of his ruined hangar. It was the last in the pack. He crumpled the box and threw it onto the ashes. "We had an arrangement."

"With Gromov?"

"With a client who paid his bills. Unlike you." Boxes began to appear, hand over hand, down the line from *Little Annie*. A pile began to grow beside the truck. The canvas back was pulled aside and the cargo was tossed up and in.

Yuri took a deep pull on the cigarette and let it out slowly. The cloud blew away. "We had a vault full of cash. Rule number one for a new business? Stay liquid." The cigarette faded. He drew it to a bright red ember, then spat out the smoke. "Fifteen, twenty thousand dollars in one-hundred-dollar bills. The new ones. The ones that look fake but aren't. I wonder what they must look like now."

Burned to ash. It reminded him of Anna's treasure room of bone, worth far, far more than Yuri's liquid reserves. And she'd *planned* to burn them.

More boxes appeared. Reindeer antlers. A few glossy black

sable pelts. Then a series of heavy cardboard containers that showed signs of wetness at their corners. One broke open as it was being handed down, and out spilled a meter-long fish frozen into a solid slab. A plank of Siberian white salmon, known as *chir*.

"Watch what you're doing!" As quickly as he angered, his anger cooled. Yuri scooped up the fish. "So why are they after you?"

"They aren't. Kaznin was going to arrest Anna Vereskaya."

Yuri had a pocketknife in his hand. "What for?"

"He says she killed Andrei Ryzkhov and my two men."

"I thought you were doing the investigating."

"Kaznin and I are approaching the same matter from different points of view."

He sliced a curl of frozen *chir* and popped it into his mouth. "Did she do it?"

"No." The suddenness of that made Nowek stop. How did he know? How could he feel so sure? "She thinks AmerRus is involved. So do I."

"Then she's really fucked," said Yuri. "And so are you."

Nowek scanned the treeline. There was no sign of Chuchin or Anna. He'd better find her, he thought. It was a long walk into town from here. Though would it seem that way for a woman used to darting five-meter tigers in the wilds of Tunguska?

"You can't play games with AmerRus. They're wired into everything," said Yuri. "The Americans are like the *mafiya*, except they're better organized."

"Vereskaya told me she was American."

Yuri looked to see if Nowek was being serious.

"I know," Nowek said. "That's what I thought."

Yuri shook his head. "She's no American. She's one of those *Zov Taigi* types who would rather see you pop than take a piss in Lake Baikal." *Zov Taigi* was a Siberian ecology movement, underfunded, without influence, armed only with hope.

"Ready," said Plet. The truck was loaded. The canvas flap at the tail was cinched tight with rope. He was in the driver's seat.

The passenger's door was battered. There were holes that looked suspiciously like they'd been made by bullets. The windshield was made from a spiderweb of cracks.

"Yuri, the troops who did this, my driver said they looked like OSNAZ. Where are they based?"

"I already gave you my best advice. Now let me offer you my last advice," said Yuri. "Don't go looking. You might find them." He climbed up onto the running board. The heavy door squealed open. He swung himself up and into the Maz. He flicked away the stub. "And, Mayor, if she really is American? Don't worry about her. She's got her own way out. It might be wise to think about yourself."

The diesel revved and the clutch screeched into low. The Maz belched sooty smoke and began to roll, leaving Nowek standing in its greasy fumes.

The Land Cruiser chuffed white steam as it rolled up.

Chuchin shook his head. "I followed her tracks to the river and they stopped. The ice is patchy and too thin even for a wolf to walk on. I had the strangest feeling she was there, watching me. I just couldn't see her."

"It's in her blood, Chuchin."

"What is?"

"The taiga."

"You said she's American."

"That too."

Chuchin looked out into the trees. "I asked Nikki Malyshev about those rations."

"What?" Nowek turned.

"Old army rations. You wanted me to ask about them when I bought your father's caviar."

"What did he say?"

"That I'd come to the right place. That he could supply us with all we needed, very cheap, but we should be careful."

"I'm not interested." But then Nowek turned. "Careful?"

"He said there's a lot of competition for them."

A lot of competition? "Who?"

"Semyon Yufa."

Yufa. What on earth would he do with inedible rations? Nowek looked into dark green shadows of the taiga. A place where Anna was very much at home. The shadows verged to black. "She's out there someplace."

"Someplace." Chuchin said it with a perfect appreciation for the true size of a Siberian someplace.

"We have to find her before Kaznin."

"Forgive me, Mayor, but you're sounding desperate."

The day was fading fast.

Nowek nodded. "You don't miss a thing."

CHAPTER 14

FROM THE AIR, the complex looked like a concrete starfish tossed up onto the flats of the Sacramento River delta to dry under the intense California sun. Its radial arms extended from a circular core, reaching out to tall fences topped with coils of razor wire. Gun towers rose from the tip of each arm, but they were unmanned. When asked why, the director replied that he preferred to put his faith in Pacific Gas and Electric. His faith was not misplaced.

The "Death Fence" sizzled with five thousand volts at five hundred amps. Charred birds littered the ground like clinker coal. The bones of unlucky jackrabbits were fused to it, along with the leathery wings of scavengers lured down to feed.

The facility occupied a far corner of an old air force base. Beyond its perimeter the landscape was a drab vista of treeless hills, shimmering flats, and miles of cracked runways. There was no motion except for the lazy circling of birds and the steady stream of traffic on the nearby freeway. San Francisco was forty miles west; from inside the Death Fence, it might as well have been a thousand.

The complex went by a number of names, some gray, some more colorful. To the local mayor it represented taxes and jobs. To state corrections officials trying to keep the lid on bursting lockups, it was an inexpensive safety valve. To prison rights activists it was a cruel and unusual horror.

But to the public speeding along I-80, it was just a small green sign that read TRAVIS ADMINISTRATIVE MAXIMUM FACILITY; a blur that quickly vanished in the rearview mirror.

If its name betrayed little, its mission was more easily defined: Travis Maxi was a privately owned and operated prison designed to isolate four hundred of the most dangerous, predatory felons; a state-of-the-art, sixty-million-dollar holding tank designed specifically for monsters.

Inside the Death Fence, the steel doors and the hermetic cells, four hundred men were warehoused in hard-edged solitude. The windowless cells contained only a single armored skylight well out of reach. Mirrors were made of polished steel deeply riveted into concrete. The zigzagging hallways eliminated all communication, even eyesight, between inmates. Once the doors shut, there was nothing to see and no one to talk to. Solitude was absolute. A Travis inmate could well believe himself the last man, and Travis the last place, on earth.

It was a place where rehabilitation was sacrificed to the rigors of a super-controlled environment, where four hundred dangerous men could be safely walled up and forgotten. The government provided the land, the burgeoning state penal system the inmates. Private industry supplied the rest.

Containment. Isolation. Profit. Cruel and unusual? Perhaps it seemed that way from the outside.

But inside the Death Fence, a Travis inmate quickly learned that no matter how harsh, no matter how inhuman it seemed here, there were other places more cruel, and far more unusual.

The director switched on the tape recorder. "State your name."

His name? Not TMA-103. His name! That more than anything put LeRoy on guard. Despite everything, despite the fact that it was fucking *understood* they were pulling some kind of shit, he answered the director's question. "LeRoy Rogers," he said. "My daddy named me after the Singing Cowboy." A truncheon prodded him hard between the shoulder blades. His leg irons clanked as he fought to stay upright. His wrists were cuffed together to a waist ring. He flexed his arm so the guard could see it. The SS-style lightning bolts tattooed on his prison-pale skin seemed to reach out for something to strike. His sharp-pointed goatee made him look like a minor devil.

"Inmate Rogers, you have been sent to this facility upon a third conviction of murder." The director gazed up over his glasses. "Is that correct?"

"I din't kill no one." Well, that wasn't *exactly* the truth. White nigger, trailer trash they called him. LeRoy was one of the new breed: a superpredator who didn't fear arrest, the pains of imprisonment, or the pangs of conscience. He was born a loaded gun and the world had pulled his trigger many times. But he didn't kill the one they *said* he did. "I'm innocent."

"Hardly. You attempted escape at Pelican Bay. You were found with contraband in your cell here at Travis."

What the fuck? Contraband? Just some metal wire he pulled out the mattress. Dumbass fucks. Who left it there?

"I think you intended to use it as a weapon. I think you were planning to escape, LeRoy. Isn't that so?"

"Wasn't no weapon." That was true. But the escape part, well now. Toss the wire on that fucking hot fence, short out the mother, and go. "It ain't right. I got my rights."

"Not anymore. You committed one murder as a juvenile. A second as an adult. Now a third. You were given a chance. But you didn't take it. What rights do you think you deserve?"

"I din't kill nobody."

"I think that if you had the opportunity, you'd take that wire and stab a guard the instant his back was turned."

LeRoy had to smile. Stick you too, motherfuck.

"You've been a great expense to a lot of people. Extra guards. Extra security. We feel there's a better way to handle your case. But it's your last shot. Your final chance. It's up to you whether you take it."

Rogers looked at the director suspiciously.

"I've explained the experimental program. I warn you: the

camp is no vacation. If you agree to the conditions," a smile appeared, then evaporated, "I'd like you to sign the consent form." He slid a pen across the table. "An X will do."

LeRoy mentally disassembled it. Hard plastic, good for a blade. Grind the tip to a needle, makes a nice tattoo. Spring to jab an eye with. Drink the ink, get sick, go to the infirmary where they kept the sharp things. He turned.

Two guards and at a distance an orderly with some kind of bag. Wonder what was in it. He went back to the form, but his eyes kept rising to that window. Barred, it was still the first clear glass they'd let him see. Fuck, Travis was the fucking hole of all holes. Did he want out of it? Camp. That sounded good. Trees. Cows. Open country and dumbass cracker guards. He was *innocent*.

"Well?"

Outside he could see rolling hills, a buzzard circling. Cars on a busy road, all heading someplace better than here. It looked good, but LeRoy had his pride. The director wasn't going to get shit off him for nothing. "What if I don't?"

"You'll serve the remainder of your sentence at Travis." The director consulted his file, then looked up. "Another forty years. No parole board will touch your case. You'll be sixty-one when you come up for review, LeRoy."

"Uh-huh." No fucking *way*. He wasn't going to spend forty years listening to his heartbeat, only to walk when he had three marbles left inside his old bald head. Using both hands he snatched the pen. It felt real good. The guard stiffened.

He looked at the director and thought of the white coat, the pale skin. Fuck. He knew more anatomy than a doctor. He knew where the ribs were. He knew how to use a sharpened wire to hit a lung from under the arm where they wouldn't be looking for a hole. He knew how. He was the master of disaster, and if this little white rabbit was offering him a ticket out to some camp, well now. Wasn't that something? He'd hit that fucker and be *gone* in a week. One week.

The director watched. "Have you decided, Inmate Rogers?"

"Yeah. I decided my mind." LeRoy clumsily held the pen in

his fist and scrawled his name slow as a first-grader. The words on the page were small as bugs crawling over honey and just as meaningful. Dumb LeRoy, couldn't read, couldn't write. He knew his body parts. Knew his way into them, too.

He finished, then sat back. He kicked a leg and made the chain snap loud in the quiet room. Clang! Loud as a bell. Run for the races. "When do I get out?"

Another jab from the nightstick.

"Sir." Fuck you, James. Gonna stick it up your ass.

"First you need a tetanus booster." The director nodded at the orderly who quietly approached with a hypodermic.

"Uh-huh."

"You'll be headed for the camp before the day is out."

His eyes widened. "Today?"

"Today. Then, if you respond to therapy, and I am sure you will, you'll be home free before you know it. What do you say, LeRoy? Do we have a deal?"

LeRoy smiled as the orderly raised the denim sleeve of his shirt and felt for a vein. "Home free," he said as he felt the tiny prick of steel against the hard, toned muscle of his upper arm. A month at Travis couldn't take away what two hours of weights every day at Pelican Bay had given him. He could snap that fucking needle with a flex. They thought they put a mon-ster man *in*? Camp. He'd be motherfucking *gone* before they called roll. "Home free. I sure like the way . . ." He stopped, puzzled.

"Is everything all right, Inmate Rogers?"

"Yeah. Everything. Free . . ." The window. Shimmering flats. Hills. Cars. Rising black birds, spiraling, spiraling up in the heat, round and round. "Free . . . ?"

The orderly caught him as he fell.

The old DC-8 looked weary after thirty years of hard labor, and with good reason. The four-engine jet still worked for a living at an age when her sister ships had all retired to the scrap yard.

Once she wore the proud livery of a major airline. Now her

interior was stripped to bare metal. Her engines were noisy and illegal to replace. Her spare parts all came from salvage yards. She was crewed by men who were too old or with too many black marks on their records to fly for a better employer.

Yet in spite of all her many obvious faults, she did have two admirable qualities: she'd been dirt cheap to buy and her fuel tanks were oversized, giving her true intercontinental range. From San Francisco she could make Tokyo or Brisbane non-stop. On a good day with light loads and favorable winds she could go farther still.

A day like this one.

The Douglas scribed four trails of sooty exhaust as she made landfall over Half Moon Bay. The evening fogbank was advancing on San Francisco Bay like a slow-motion tidal wave breaking over the coastal mountains. She began her descent. Ten thousand feet above Alcatraz Island. Five thousand over the fleet of surplus warships rusting in Suisun Bay. Ahead were the two parallel runways of what had once been Travis Air Force Base. One was still kept operational.

She touched down in a scream of vaporized rubber. She headed for a cavernous hangar at the far perimeter. There she stopped at last, her engines dying to the loose metallic rattle of worn fan blades spinning in the dry wind.

A big airline catering truck rolled to a stop. The windowless rear raised itself on spindly jacks until it was level with her already-open cargo hatch. First out was a guard with a riot gun. Next came a wheelchair pushed by a white-clad attendant. And then another. More. Eighteen of them rolled across the ramp before the jet's cargo door slammed shut.

A fuel hose was plugged into a wing. The freighter drank deeply. There would be no stopping on her long flight up the northwest coast, far out to sea, paralleling the arc of the Aleutians, making landfall over an alien peninsula named Kamchatka. Finally all tanks brimmed full.

Thirty minutes later the DC-8 departed into the low sun, heading north by northwest, climbing over the bay, the fog. She was light on cargo, but heavy with fuel. The land fell behind as she climbed out over the Pacific; first a city, then a coast, next the bird-limed rocks of the Farallon Islands. North America receded to a line on the horizon.

Finally home was just a distant smudge. And then, as the cold, whitecapped sea spread beneath her wings from horizon to horizon, even that was gone.

Decker found Joffrey in the hallway outside DeKalb's office.

"What's the worry, 'bro?" he asked. "You been eatin' shit or talkin' it?"

"DeKalb wants to see you."

"He does? What about?"

"Stuff."

"What kind of stuff, Mr. Joffrey?"

"You think he'd tell me, Paul?" He tried to laugh and get by Decker but he found himself against the corridor wall. Decker was smiling as he pinned him there with an outstretched arm.

"I asked a question. Be nice to hear an answer if you got one." He pressed Joffrey harder. "What stuff?"

"You said she was a pro."

"Who?"

"The girl. But I saw her. She's just a kid. A little girl."

"You tell the boss? That what you did, Joff? Don't tell me you're that stupid."

Joffrey pushed Decker's arm away and kept walking.

"Shit." He watched him leave. Joffrey was not on the bus, thought Decker. Too busy thinking, and thinking led to worrying, worrying to doing dumb shit. No, Joffrey was not what you'd call an ideal employee. He was the kind who just naturally weeded themselves out. The kind who'd spot an oil slick in the big old Gulf and actually radio the EPA, the Friends of the Fish, the Seagull Association. Dumb shit. A troublemaker. Where the fuck did DeKalb get off hiring him on anyway? Well, no matter. Decker could take care of things. Tunguska was a long way away from anywhere. Most anything could happen.

Decker squared his shoulders, knocked twice on DeKalb's walnut-grain door, and entered.

"Sit down," said DeKalb. "I hear we have a problem with unauthorized personnel on the site again, Mr. Decker."

Decker pulled out a chair. The legs screeched, echoing against the bare walls. "Hell. You got rid of that snoop so fast his eyeballs spun."

"Not the mayor." Hooded eyes. Shooter's eyes. "I mean the girl."

"Girl?" Decker's face went blank.

"Get rid of her. I told you before. We aren't running a whorehouse up here. You remember what I said the last time?"

Decker colored.

"I won't have it, Mr. Decker. Not here and definitely not now. So unless you tell me you can't comply with a direct order, I expect her out of here ASAP. Am I communicating?"

Decker scowled. Joffrey. Sonofa*bitch*. Decker balled up inside hard as rock, cold as ice. She was just getting interesting. Another couple of days wouldn't hurt. The way to a girl's heart was through her rib cage, and that took time. "It's just a little fun. No harm done, Mr. DeKalb. She's a pro."

"This isn't a discussion. Just take her back and make sure she's as dumb as you found her. Now, what about the tiger gal?"

"Last I saw she was with the mayor."

"Then let me fill you in. She rode the bird back to town with Joffrey. You don't know anything about that?"

"The hell you say." Decker looked thoughtful, then shook his head. Two could play the backstabbing game. "Old Joff didn't get the okay to transport her?"

"There was a problem with his radio."

"Worked just fine yesterday."

"Someone snapped the antenna off today. You wouldn't know anything about that either, I suppose."

"Snapped the antenna? Damn. Who did it? You don't think Joff would? Not him, no. Must have been the mayor. Or maybe the tiger gal, yeah. I bet you that's it. Still, I can't believe he didn't put down and ask you. You don't think they planned it out together, do you?"

"I don't know what to think. Not yet. I will."

"I guess anything's possible. Not good coming after every-thing in town, though. Not good at all."

DeKalb sat back. He thought of the cracked cover glass on his daughter's photo. "We should have never let her onsite. That's my fault. I accept it."

Comes to girls, you're too damned soft for your own good. "Can fix it still. Be simple, an accident. Anyone could see it happen-ing. Off in the woods, tigers, poachers, and all. Nobody would wonder. Not a single solitary person. Be a tragedy. Make those eco-assholes think twice about messin' around up here again. Let those fucks stay home and make trouble is what I say. You want me to?"

"No. For now I'm only interested in keeping things smooth. We have another shipment due in tonight. I expect we'll be moving into full-scale operations soon. I don't want any prob-lems left hanging. Not her, not your little whore, not even you, Mr. Decker."

"Me?"

"When are you due to rotate?"

"Next month. R and R to Houston and then I'm gonna glide down the coulee to Abbeville. Why?"

"I'm amending things. You'll ride the next jet out for the beach. I desire your ass off this site. I don't like unannounced visitors asking questions. I don't care for employees who dis-obey my orders, either."

"But—"

"I want you off this site by the end of the week. Now I can think of two possibilities. Riding a jet to the beach is one. You wouldn't much like the other, I expect."

Decker blinked. "Nossir."

"Now we're communicating. In the meantime, I want you to go through the tiger gal's cabin. See if she left any of those goddamned tapes or disks or whatever you call them. Break the place apart if you have to. There's no point in being subtle about it. Not now. I doubt we'll see her again."

"She probably has 'em on her."

"I'm aware of that."

"I could go find her for you. Take care of things."

"No. I'm going to let the locals handle it. They can take the consequences. Until I get things settled down, I want you to stay out of Markovo. Period."

"Yessir." But then Decker clouded. "The hooker's from town. How do I drop her back and stay out at the same time?"

"I don't need the details. Just get it done."

"Yessir." Decker had a strange expression. Not worry. Anticipation. "I have to say, I'm real surprised about Joff. You want me to talk to him, too?"

"Not yet." DeKalb looked at him closely. "I need you both tonight. Just remember, it's going to be like always. You pick up your load and fly it on up. But you best be careful. The Shithook ready?"

"Joffrey's on it. I'll make sure nothin' breaks again. Be real certain about that."

"Well then."

Paul Decker got up, anxious to leave. He was lucky he hadn't mentioned who he had in his cabin. She wasn't some whore, no. He was fucking the mayor's daughter. The snoop's own little girl. DeKalb would go apeshit ballistic. Keep that little bit to himself. Hell, keep it *for* himself, too.

DeKalb seemed to home in on Decker's thinking like a smart bomb. "Mr. Decker," he said. "I want to emphasize that if your taste in whores causes me one iota of grief, I will not be happy. I'm already not happy about too many things. I don't think you want to add to my list. You and Mr. Joffrey both should keep that in mind."

"Can understand that perfectly."

"Just remember I can bury that coonass of yours so deep nobody will find it a month from doomsday. Can and will. Am I being clear?"

"As a big brass bell." Decker nodded. *Goddamned* lucky.

When he got back from the run tonight, her ass would be his, and then her ass would be *gone*.

"Then get you gone."

The first stars popped out of a milky white veil overhead. The western horizon was burnt orange, the east a velvet-purple black. A cold wind blew from the north, driving the leftover warmth of the day before it.

Joffrey twisted a big valve. The pipe clanked once, again, and then the high-pressure hose in his hand stiffened. He let a stream of water as thick as his wrist blast across the fuselage of the Chinook helicopter.

The transformation was both dramatic and rapid.

The opaque canopy turned clear. The black streaks of soot, the char, the bubbled paint, all washed away. He dragged the heavy hose, working his way completely around the nose until the canopy fairly glowed in the last light of sunset.

Decker ambled up, his boots crunching gravel, two pairs of night vision goggles in one hand and a white flight helmet in the other. One hand was bleeding from a deep cut, but he was whistling. "Thanks, 'bro. You got me in some kind of deep shit with the tool pusher. Any special reason for toastin' my ass or was it just something you thought up?"

"She's just a kid. He asked me to keep an eye out."

"Who?"

"DeKalb. Besides, there's laws about shit like that."

"Not up here, bubba. Up here I'm the man."

Joffrey saw the blood. "What happened? That little weasel finally bite you?"

Decker squeezed his breast pocket. The animal popped out, all trembling whiskers and suspicious, sniffing nose.

"You hear what Joff called you?" he said to it. "A weasel. I always thought a weasel was a critter who talked behind your back and bit your ass when you weren't looking."

"Come off it."

"Man talks out of turn, he can dig himself pretty deep. Harley here never did that to me, Joff. I expect that makes him a cut above a weasel. Maybe a whole bunch of cuts." He smiled, then looked at his pet. "How'd you like a little bit of steak Joffrey tonight? Man, you could eat good for a year off his fat butt. Yum yum. What you say?"

The ferret looked at Joffrey with intelligent, interested eyes. He seemed to find the idea worth considering.

"So how'd you get the scratches?"

Decker held up his hand. "I got this at the tiger lady's cabin. I went through her place real good. Had to fight off her god-damned cat. It about chewed me up before I ran it off. But it was worth it. Real worth it."

"You were in her cabin? Man, she'll skin you alive."

"She ain't around to find out. You sure did fuck up in that respect. Might have to *deal* with it, you understand what I'm saying?" Decker stood there with the calm, affectless poise of a snake eyeing a bird.

Joffrey's skin prickled. "What did DeKalb say about the girl?"

Decker handed Joffrey the night vision device. "Kind of a shame, but the boss says to get rid of her."

"To Markovo?"

"Tell you the truth, he wasn't specific." Decker grinned his *I know something and you don't* grin.

"What?"

"Nothin' except I'm gonna retire a real happy man. DeKalb is whistlin' up a bird for me and I'm hittin' the beach. Hit the beach, hit the bitches." Decker shoved a hand into another pocket.

Joffrey tensed.

But it wasn't a knife he brought into the sunset light. Decker flipped the piece of bone like it was a half-dollar. "There's more of it. Plenty more. I got *boxes* of it. Buy me my own helo back home. Hell, maybe buy *two*." He put it away. "We ready to lift? The virgin surgeon's got an appointment tonight." His white teeth glowed in the dusk. "Me, I can't wait to operate."

★ ★ ★

Rotor blades unfolded. Instrument lights glowed bright. The whine of a starter, the hiss of a turbine's fire, the steady beat of steel blades swallowed by the inverted bowl of stars. Joffrey sat in the copilot's seat and looked out the windshield as the engines idled. Decker strapped in on the right side and grabbed the controls. He tested each of the ship's systems, then rolled on throttle and pulled collective.

The Chinook took to the indigo sky like a phoenix. They spoke over the ship's intercom. They showed no running lights, they transmitted no signals. They didn't need them.

High overhead, a constellation of Global Positioning System (GPS) satellites sent ultraaccurate signals beaming down to the Chinook's receivers. The computers triangulated position, azimuth, and altitude to three-meter accuracy.

Low level, Decker turned them south and took up a flight path that could only be described as perverse.

Siberia is wilderness; perhaps the biggest wilderness left on the planet. And wilderness flying is like crossing a wide, wild stream by hopping from rock to rock. The rocks were little islands of civilization. A logging camp, a village. A pumping station. A wide gravel bar in the river where fishermen might be found. Someplace where they could land and not be swallowed up. Even Siberia with its endless taiga, its marshes and muskeg, could be crossed safely given a little planning.

The course they took was the exact opposite.

It ignored rivers, gave settlements a wide berth, and minimized exposure to the intermittent radars that occasionally still came on down in Irkutsk. One misstep, a moment's inattention, a mechanical failure, and the Chinook and its pilots could well be lost forever. A smear of ruin and flame that would heal long before anyone could find them. Neither pilot expected a search and rescue mission. The Russians couldn't mount one; DeKalb wouldn't.

At the terminus of their zigzag course was the Belaya Airfield, an ex-military strip along the Angara River, some twenty kilometers northwest of Irkutsk. The abandoned facility was surrounded by agricultural cooperative land and boasted a runway long enough to handle jets. There was no tower and no services. The ice and snow were kept clear at the whim of the lone guard who lived in the old gatehouse. By midsummer, sunflowers grew chin-high from breaks in the concrete.

The last light faded from the sky, and first Decker, then Joffrey put on night vision equipment. With a click, their world went from dusky purple to brilliant green.

"Seeing good?"

"Okay," Joffrey agreed, though the goggles afforded no peripheral view. It was a bit like peering at the world through two soda straws.

"I been thinking. I ought to throw your sorry ass out the hatch." Decker turned down the lights in the Chinook's cockpit until he could just read the instruments. Only the steady clicking down of miles on the GPS displays showed their progress over the taiga.

"What's one girl? There's plenty more."

"Plenty more copilots, too." Decker jabbed at Joffrey's stomach and the five-point safety harness sprang free. He suddenly banked hard over and Joffrey fell against the side hatch. He reached across and touched the door release. One push and Joffrey would free fall.

Joffrey scrabbled away from it and grabbed on to his seat.

Decker chuckled. "Might need one before the night's done, too. Haven't made up my mind. Ol' Harley seemed to like the looks of your sorry ass. Might get his chance. Yessir. He just might. Yum."

Rank on rank of image-intensified trees swept below as they bounced from one nameless waypoint to another. Decker had his right hand tight on the cyclic stick, the left down on the collective and its throttles.

Their southerly course roughly paralleled the Lena River, but far enough to the west to avoid the scattered Buryat villages along its banks. The taiga sped below them, near enough for the rotor's downwash to whip the tops of the pines. They jogged south, then east, then south again, climbing to cross the thousand-foot hills that formed the Lena's source. The high rim that held back Lake Baikal was just off their left side, a black tidal wave of rock frozen in midfall. Decker pushed over, descending once more, this time heading due east.

A glow appeared ahead and to the right. Irkutsk. Five minutes later, a dark lane strewn with bright green polygons appeared ahead. The lane was the Angara River, Baikal's only outlet. The polygons were floating ice.

"I got the light," said Joffrey. "Listen. I'm sorry about DeKalb."

"You're sorry, all right. Right?" He squeezed his pocket and a little furry head popped up. "Right. Give 'em the signal, Joff. Make yourself useful while you can."

Joffrey switched on the powerful searchlight under the cockpit's chin. He swept it to face the far riverbank, then flicked it off, on, and off again. It illuminated the tail of a parked jet. A big one, four engines, but no windows. A freighter.

"Now that was truly well done." Decker pushed over and dropped to twenty feet, fifteen. Ten. They swept so low over the river that spray beaded the canopy.

As they thundered over the riverbank, Decker twisted off power and yanked the machine into a steep flare, killing their forward speed. An instant later, the rear wheels bounced down, followed by the front pair. He pulled the back power and set the rotor blades to flat pitch as he slowly taxied the Chinook toward the ghostly jet freighter parked out in the open field.

"Fresh fish waitin' on the haul," said Decker. "Tell you what. They's gonna be gris-gris gumbo ya ya tonight."

Two lines of bundled objects sat on the concrete. A guard was positioned at the end of each line. A fifth guard watched from the top of the doorway of the unlit Boeing. Joffrey counted eighteen bundles.

Decker said, "Go on back. I'll drop the ramp."

The copilot left the cockpit for the cargo area.

Decker flipped the plastic guard off the ramp controller and pressed the button. The loading ramp light went from LOCKED to OPEN.

The rotors swished the cold night air lazily. There was a

narrow window of time, even here in Russia where nothing seemed to really matter. It would be a fast turnaround, and there would be no reason, or time, to shut down his engines.

The ramp struck the cold concrete with a distant thump.

Decker switched the searchlight on, then off. Even before the glow faded, men waiting under the cargo jet's wing began to scurry like mice, each one wheeling one of the dark bundles toward the waiting helicopter.

As the first one hurried by the cockpit, the bundle assumed the shape of a wheelchair, and strapped into it was a man, head lolling loosely to one side. It was the only part of him not securely fastened to the frame. Thick leather bands crisscrossed the arms, the legs, the chest.

Decker watched. It was the eyes, the eyes that always got to him. They were open, just like a dead man's. Wide fucking open. Seeing, taking everything in as far as he knew, even if they were supposed to be paralyzed with dope. He sure did have nightmares about those eyes. Those men coming for him, finding him, getting back for what he did to them. Who wouldn't wake up screaming after you looked into those damned, doomed eyes?

Eighteen wheelchairs were rolled into the back of the helicopter. The guards retreated to the waiting jet. Decker raised the ramp. LOCKED. He began his preflight check of the controls and instruments by feel when Joffrey returned. "Got anybody good?"

Joffrey checked the manifest. "Nobody you've heard of."

"They all under?"

"Totally."

"You sure now? Don't want no one to get up and snap off one of my antennas or nothing."

Joffrey held up a straight pin. "I checked 'em out."

"Ol' needle dick, that's what we'll call you. Give them all a stick, did you?"

"Yes."

"Course, you checked the last time." He put his helmet on. Decker remembered the runner. They were nearly to the camp when he heard him screaming in the back and it was lucky he did. A bad injection, some freak resistance to ibogaine hypochlorite, who knew what had allowed that man to snap his leather restraints and rage through the cabin like a damned demon. What choice did they have but to put the chopper down and let the bastard run for it? They were lucky he didn't come forward to the cockpit and kill them both.

"I tell you what. That boy was one surprised coconut," Decker said with a chuckle. "Thought he was heading back to mama. Big fucking surprise how cold it got."

"He wasn't headed for mama. The sheet said he liked boys."

"Boys?"

"Liked 'em so well he ate 'em."

Decker found such dedication truly impressive. "For real?"

"Really real. Twelve they could ID. Found the bones buried under the house."

Decker processed that. "Whooee! I guess that old boy's gonna have to go on a diet."

Joffrey laughed. Maybe it was going to be okay with Decker.

Decker reached for the microphone. "Good evening, ladies and gentlemen. Let me change that to just gentlemen. This is your captain, Barry Friendly, speaking. I'd like to welcome you aboard the continuation of AMR Air's one-stop service to hell. And don't worry about your luggage, folks. You already got everything you need."

"Come off it, Paul. They can't hear you," said Joffrey.

"Now how would you know that?" Decker pressed the mike button again. "Our flight time will be short, so we ask you all to remain seated and, ah, you might as well keep those seat belts fastened low and tight." He pressed the mike to his lips. "On behalf of all your crew," Decker said, "I want to thank you for choosing to fly with AMR tonight. We sure hope we can be of service to you again on your next little trip." He hung up the microphone.

"You're warped. Truly."

"I'm so warped I got this idea." He leaned close, whispering. "You stuck them, maybe they'd like to give you a little poke back. Think so?"

"Let's lift. We got people to move."

"What do you suppose all those boys would do if they found you dropped down like a Christmas package? Bunch of boy-eaters and girl-rapers and scum like that?"

Like you, thought Joffrey.

"Me, I believe it'd be a feeding frenzy. Yeah. Be like chummin' the Gulf. Man, the sharks would be all over you like stink. What do you think about that, Mr. Joffrey? You have an opinion on the matter? DeKalb said I could do it if I thought you were turnin' into a problem."

Joffrey stayed silent. His flight bag contained a pistol. He reached back behind his seat.

Decker hadn't even moved, but suddenly there was a shaft of warm steel pressed against Joffrey's hand. The flat, not the edge. "Hey 'bro, relax. You know I'm the man, right?"

Joffrey wasn't sure what he knew.

"You can say it. Be wise, to, actually."

"Sure, Paul," he said. "You're the man."

"What I like to hear." Decker laughed, a little wildly, then put the blade away and flicked on his own goggles. The world snapped into bright green focus. He twisted on power. The blades spun up overhead, clawing at the cold air. The big machine rose into a hover, turned, and pointed its nose back into the darkness.

CHAPTER
15

DUSK ACCELERATED into evening. Under the trees, full dark came even faster. Flowing water was everywhere, trapped beneath a skin of refrozen ice. Where tributaries emptied out onto the Lena, alluvial fans of white crust spread, building layer on layer. But underneath, hidden, the water was moving, seeking a weak spot, a place to break through, to be free.

When Chuchin switched on the headlights, only one worked.

"Weather's coming," said Chuchin. "I can smell it."

"Your nose is swollen shut. You can't smell anything."

"I spent twenty years in the fucking camps, Mayor," he said indignantly. "I don't need a nose to smell. I don't need eyes to see. And as for my hearing, when someone tells me to keep away from trouble I listen. Of course," he said, "not everyone had the benefit of such a good education."

Nowek looked at him. "You're feeling especially subtle tonight."

"Pah." Chuchin lit a cigarette using both hands. The steering wheel was all but unnecessary, he hardly touched it for long stretches. There was no danger. The road was deserted, the ruts deep enough to trap the car's wheels.

Deserted was also how they found Nowek's father's flat. Deserted, but far from empty.

Standing inside his doorway, Chuchin said, "Where is he?"

When Nowek moved him up from Academic's Village in Irkutsk, his father had filled two heavy trucks with the accumulated belongings of a lifetime. Akademgorodok was no longer a leafy city of professors; it was a dangerous neighborhood where gangs of drunk, unemployed boys ruled the plazas, the unlit corridors, where the few remaining academics cowered behind steel doors. There was no question of leaving him there.

Nowek brought his father to Markovo in the depth of winter, the only time when the frozen river made driving between the two towns possible. Even then there was much that had to be left, to be divided up. First among his fellow musicians, next a few friends on the faculty, and finally by a flock of neighbors who descended like crows onto a newly threshed field.

His father adjusted quickly to Markovo. After a week, Nowek couldn't tell the difference between the old place and the new. The space, the walls, the windows were not the same as the apartment he'd grown up in. But Nowek still found the familiar odor of dust and moldy leather-bound books, the furiously notated sheet music sitting atop the parlor grand, untouched since Tadeus had gone functionally blind.

Nowek remembered when the piano had seemed huge; a monster to be approached with caution in daylight and not at all after dark. It was so small now. He used to play beneath it as his father's chords thundered overhead like fleets of bombers. And from the wall, the same lineup of famous musicians gazed down, their faces, their triumphs, their bright, liquid eyes and clever fingers half a century dead.

Call his father's place haunted.

"Could he have found his own way to your house?"

"He's blind." Nowek felt something cold congeal in him. "Let's go find him."

They drove onto a street that paralleled the river levees. The Lena was grumbling, ice against ice, winter against spring, in conflict, at war. The flow was stronger here and so the ice was weaker. Plates of it rolled over, submerged, only to rise like resurrected continents.

"Maybe he walked," said Chuchin.

"Walking is against my father's principles." But it reminded Nowek of Anna. Where had she disappeared to? Where could an American woman wanted for murder go on foot? "Plet said that the troopers who burned the hangar were from some ministry. It couldn't be Interior. Arkady Volsky would have known about it. He would tell me."

Chuchin touched his tender cheek. "This is no illusion. What about your father's *bufetchitsa*? Maybe she drove him to your place."

"She's his nurse, not his *bufetchitsa,*" said Nowek. "He tells me she won't work nights."

Despite his swollen face, his loose teeth, Chuchin found this funny.

Bufetchitsa meant the woman in charge of the kitchen, though with distinct sexual undertones. Serving wench approximated. Not that Nowek would put it past his father to make use of her in that way. His mother walked out when she discovered Tadeus with an aspiring opera singer, one of her own students, and this had happened just ten years ago when he was sixty-five.

She'd found them out on the couch, intermingled and superimposed, and decided, at my age, who needs this? She decamped to teach voice in St. Petersburg. Tadeus had a veneer of culture. Even blind he could spin magic from the strings of a violin. But he had always been, would always be, a goat.

They drove by the silver oil rig monument. The snow around its base was littered with bottles, and bright fragments of broken glass, glittering like emeralds.

Chuchin turned. "About Vereskaya. You could be wrong about her. Kaznin might be right. Innocent people don't run, Mayor."

"That's where you're wrong," said Nowek as he leaned his forehead against the cold glass. "In Russia it's the innocent ones who have to run the fastest."

★   ★   ★

They were driving through the very oldest part of town, the original river settlement. Here the buildings were all made from wood, the carvings above the windows intact and painted the customary blue, and the streetlights long forgotten. You could see the stars from a neighborhood like this. They didn't twinkle so much as burn.

Astronomy, he thought as he spotted the Great Square of Pegasus. The constellations of spring were testing the waters of the black sky. The stars of winter were low, exhausted in the west. He breathed on the glass, a new nebula exploded. He'd always been interested in astronomy. Even his father thought it was a better choice than geology.

Face facts: his father was the very worst kind of snob. For Tadeus, if you couldn't be a soloist, there was always a chair in a symphony; if not a symphony, then a chamber group might do. Shy of that, an academic's life that left time for cultural pursuits and, naturally, female students. The more useless the discipline the better.

Tadeus had never settled himself into being Siberian. Not really. He lived like exiled royalty. But Nowek grew up with the heroic idea of the "Land East of the Sun" printed on him the way a gosling might spot a tractor and follow it, thinking it's his mother.

Strange as it sounded, Siberia was once a romantic place, a natural place, a place for dreams. A place where an individual could make a difference in a gray, collective society. A place where nature conspired in every way imaginable to thwart the plans of mere men. It was a challenge that sparked a fire in Nowek.

The future lay beneath their feet in the coal, the oil, the diamonds and gold. It rose above them in the taiga forest timber. It roared north in the currents of powerful rivers.

Once, long ago, he'd wanted to be part of that future, that romance. Those dreams. Now they lay shattered like the vodka bottles around the base of the oil rig monument. Glittering and dangerous. To the world, trash; but a weapon in the right hands.

Stars were safer. There were advantages to an astronomer's life. You worked in lofty, isolated domes too far from comforts for Party hacks to visit. You inhabited a world of classical heroes and monsters. Was it Cygnus the Swan, or Aquila the Eagle? A red giant or a brown dwarf? A universe of endless expansion and renewal or one of cyclic cataclysm? These matters were complex enough to keep academics employed with endless debate and theory, and, best of all, they were impossible to resolve. It was better than a pension.

An astronomer wasn't required to know whether bread was better than the rule of law, whether a flood of AmerRus dollars was more important than justice, whether a box of bones was worth a fantastic fortune, or whether a rich man with his throat opened and his knees blown apart was worth anything at all.

The Land Cruiser turned onto a street that led to the Lena. A few weak bulbs hung from overhead wires. Over the bridge, across the river, the newer part of town glowed like those rare mushrooms that give off the strange blue light of decay. A toadstool's garden.

They turned onto a street just shy of the bridge, following the river south. Into the Black Lung.

"Something's wrong," said Chuchin as they neared Nowek's house.

"My daughter wants to be a Hong Kong whore, my father's disappeared, and Kaznin beats you up. You let the only suspect in the Ryzkhov murders walk away while my back is turned, and you're just coming to this conclusion?"

"You didn't even know she was a suspect until I said so." But then he scanned the empty streets. "Where is everybody? Even Nikki Malyshev isn't open and he's *always* open."

The levee rose high off to their left like a dam, blocking the view to the richer side of town. The streets were empty. The alleys deserted. The two-story communal flats wore pinched winter faces, their eyes tightly closed.

"They're afraid," said Chuchin.

"What are they afraid of?"

"You're too young, Mr. Mayor. You don't remember what it

was like when the word went out that the Black Mariahs were rolling." The infamous prison vans run by the MVD, the masters of the gulag, were often painted as meat delivery wagons. It showed a kind of brutal wit. "Believe me, it looked just like this. Nobody knew but everyone knew. It was in the air like a stink. You buried your head and held your breath and hoped you could hold it long enough."

How long can you hold your breath under water? That's how long Ryzkhov lived.

"We're safe from the Black Mariahs, Chuchin. Where would they find fuel?"

Chuchin eyed the needle on the Land Cruiser's gauge. It was firmly asleep against the EMPTY peg. "Good point."

They turned the corner into a small, dead-end street that left the river and the levee behind. Once more all the houses were closed up like barnacles at low tide.

All except his own.

The upstairs lights had been switched on, curtains pulled wide. The ground-level windows were dark.

"I don't know how, but he's here," said Nowek. His stomach tightened in anticipation. "You know what he'll say? He'll say it was a good thing I put away the violin for rocks. He'll say that rocks are patient. Music waits for—"

"The lights are on and he's blind. Maybe it isn't your father. Maybe it's Galena."

Then Nowek saw the lights very differently. "Chuchin—"

"I know, I know. Drive." He stomped down hard on the accelerator and the Land Cruiser lunged ahead.

They pulled up in front of Nowek's house. A curl of white smoke plumed from the chimney.

Nowek opened the door and started to get out.

"Wait." Chuchin grabbed his shoulder.

Then Nowek saw how the upstairs curtains shifted in and out of eyeless frames. Flakes of broken glass were all over the snow. There were tire tracks, boot marks. His front door had splintered wood by the hinges.

As the curtains breathed in and out, the sound of a violin came through the open windows.

It was Kreisler's *Liebeslied*.

Nowek was out and running before Chuchin could stop him. He burst through his front door. His shoes crunched bits of soft wood, scattered metal gears, snapped springs, glass. It was cold inside. Cold as a dacha shut for the winter. He found the light switch. A single bulb illuminated a front hall that was superficially familiar and unimaginably different.

"Galinka!"

The display case was overturned. Chert mingled with fossils, fossils with amphibole. His father's clock lay smashed. The mirror was webbed with cracks. Nothing was left untouched. It wasn't so much thorough as vindictive.

The sound of a violin weaved through the air like a cat walking through rain puddles. It came from the kitchen.

The *Liebeslied* was climbing the final scale to its end. He could smell the raw tang of vinegar in the air.

He rushed back to the kitchen in time to see Tadeus draw the last, aching note from the piece. The silence that followed it was heavy, almost scored, the time ticking away to the click of hot iron from the kitchen stove. It was almost warm in this one room, the stove beating back the perimeter of cold.

Tadeus was sitting at the bare table, the violin tucked under his neatly shaven chin. A bottle of Baikalskaya vodka stood on the table next to him, and there was an empty glass beside it. He was not alone.

Nowek formed the word, but it took a moment to speak it. *"You!"*

Anna Vereskaya put one finger to her lips, then she began to clap. "That was very beautiful," she said.

"It was nice, wasn't it?" Tadeus pointed the bow at Nowek to be still. His father had a brilliant shock of white hair that made his pink face seem even pinker. He basked in Anna's clapping, his nearly sightless eyes magnified enormously behind heavy, useless lenses. His face was illuminated, filled with visions of standing ovations, waves of adulation crashing like storm surf, of concert halls hot with the body heat of a standing-room–only crowd dressed in winter coats and hats.

Anna still had on the short denim jacket over her turtleneck, plus a down vest. It was just about right for the temperature inside Nowek's house.

She stopped clapping. The violin came down.

"How did you get here?" he demanded.

"I called a taxi," said Tadeus. "And told them my son the mayor would pay. You think I'd walk? And don't speak to me that way, Gregori. It's one thing to be *nekulturny*. But it's worse to sound *nekulturny*."

"Not you! Her!"

"I rode the truck in from the airport," she said.

"What truck? Yuri's?"

"I didn't ask who it belonged to."

Clothes had been dragged down the stairs leading up to the bedrooms. Dishes lay in drifts. His records were smashed and the big phonograph toppled. Glass jars of preserved vegetables were swept into a pile in the corner. His violin case was open. The telephone was still on the wall, looking in its rightness terribly wrong. The woodstove radiated heat in shimmery waves. A broom leaned against a wall, standing guard over a pile of swept debris.

"I came and heard her cleaning up," said his father. "There was a fire. I assumed she was your maid working late. Or a new woman in your life. Frankly, it gave me hope," Tadeus said. "Is she pretty, Gregori? Like the last one?"

He glared at her. "So what are you doing here, Dr. Vereskaya?"

"Doctor? Are you a real doctor, or another of these technicians?"

"Father, be quiet. I'm speaking to her."

"Not very nicely but then tone was never your strong suit, was it? You know, Kreisler tried to palm the *Liebeslied* off as an authentic eighteenth-century piece. He got caught, but then, history is inexorable. All frauds are eventually uncovered. Isn't that right, Gregori?''

Chuchin was beside him now, the Nagant pistol in his hand. He looked at Anna. "How the devil did *she* get here?" He raised it to point at her.

Nowek pushed it away.

Tadeus cradled Nowek's violin on his lap. He reached over and found the glass, putting a finger down inside it to test the level, then poured it full again. "Your young lady friend has been very charming to keep me company. Have a drink, son. It makes all of this far more endurable. *Boudem zdrovy!*" He held up the glass in Nowek's direction, then emptied it with a quick jerk back of his head. He turned to her. "I hope you're not some sort of expert?"

"She's a murder suspect, Father."

"Murder?" Tadeus laughed. Even at his age he could sound urbane. "Well, that's no surprise. What intelligent woman hasn't thought of it at one time or another?"

Nowek said to Chuchin, "There's a thermostat by the front door. Switch it on full." To Anna he said, "Well? How did you know where I lived?"

"Markovo is a small place. You're the mayor."

"Who tore my house apart?"

"It was this way when I got here."

"Quite a mess." Tadeus poked a toe at the swept-up pile of glass. "During the war when there was nothing, we never let ourselves live like animals. There was no food, no wood for a fire, nothing but art and you know, it was enough. I remember when Stalin came to review the troops of the Far East Command. Who did he have play?"

"You, Father." He kept his eyes on Anna as though she might evaporate to mist. The heating panel on the ceiling began to crackle. Nowek looked up, hoping it wouldn't black out his neighborhood again.

"Of course Stalin was just a Georgian bank robber. He might as well have been a . . . ." He stopped, reaching for some word just beyond recall. "What is it?"

The heating panel sounded like ice breaking. "Geologist."

"Thank you. What could I play that could be appreciated by a monster like that? Mozart? Bach? No, none of the immortals. I had to find something he might actually recognize. Can you guess what it was?"

Nowek knew, of course. He also knew that Tadeus was playing to his audience, and from the look on Anna's face, it was working. "The *Internationale*."

"Played largo. Very slowly. A funereal rendition, you might say. It would have been satire anywhere else. If he'd half a brain he would have ordered me shot. But with Stalin, you see, I was safe. Do you know, son, he cried as I played up there alone, standing on the turret of a tank. And when his toadies saw his tears, well, what could they do but cry right along with him? Anyone caught with a dry eye would have been arrested. Grown men weeping at the sound of my instrument. Taking garbage, swill, actually, and raising it until it illuminates a heart as black as his. But then, that's art."

"No, Father. That's politics."

Tadeus huffed. "Where's my granddaughter? Have you sent her out to harvest wheat or dig coal?"

Chuchin was back. Nowek said, "Go check the bedrooms."

Chuchin bounded up the stairs, the pistol leading the way.

Nowek turned to Anna. "And you? Did you make another quid pro quo with Yuri?"

"I don't know Yuri," she said. Her taiga-mottled rucksack was on the floor. On top of it was a framed photograph; a family portrait of Nowek, Nina, and a pouty-looking Galena. Three and a half years ago.

"She's young, too," Tadeus said with an appreciative murmur. "I can hear it in her voice. A neck like a swan, legs like two white birches, slim as ballerinas bending over to—"

"Stop flirting with her, Father. Who ripped my house apart? Was Galena here? Did you see her?"

"They were leaving when I walked down your street," she said. "They were in a van. It was too dark to see their—"

"What about my daughter?"

She held the picture up. "This is Galena?"

Nowek pulled her to her feet. The chair tipped backward and fell. The photograph fell to the floor. There was no glass left in it to break.

"Gregori!" Tadeus rapped the bow on the edge of the table. "You will treat the young lady with respect!"

"I'll treat her to a cell unless she can convince me she doesn't deserve one." Nowek snatched the picture from the floor. "I'm finished with evasions. Where is my daughter? Was she here? Did Kaznin take her?"

Anna's face hardened. "Your daughter wasn't here. But I did see her."

He took her by the shoulder and shook her, hard. "Where did you see Galena? I want the truth."

She swiveled her shoulders out of Nowek's grip with an easy sinuous motion. One instant he had her, the next she was standing half a meter away. "I saw your daughter on a flight to Tunguska. Yesterday morning. That's the truth."

"They kidnapped her?"

"No. She went on her own. She flew there yesterday on the AMR helicopter. She seemed too young, I mean, I thought she was just another . . ." Anna looked away.

"Another what?"

Chuchin came back downstairs. "It's like this everywhere. They were looking for something."

Nowek stared at Anna. "Another what?"

"I'm sorry. I didn't know who she was. I would have told you. But she went to Tunguska with a man. An AMR pilot. They knew each other. He's done this before with girls from town."

"He?"

"His name is Decker," she said. "Paul Decker."

CHAPTER
16

DECKER! He'd seen him, driven with him in that strange little vehicle, the *lunashkod*. A strange man, a strange accent, a strange animal in his breast pocket. Was he Galena's friend? Don't be stupid. A man like that didn't have sixteen-year-old girls, pretty ones, for friends.

Chuchin said, "So what are you doing here, then? Who tore the mayor's house apart?"

"She was sweeping up a mess and keeping a lonely old man company," said Nowek's father. "More than my own son."

"They were in a van. A big one. I couldn't see their faces," she said. "When they left I walked in and saw everything. The windows were all broken and it was cold. I started a fire and tried to clean up. When I heard your father drive up I thought they were coming back." She reached out and touched Nowek's arm. "I didn't know who she was. I didn't know. Really. I'm sorry. I would have told you."

Nowek finally spoke. "You're certain? It was Galena you saw on the helicopter?"

"I said—"

"You saw her on the flight from Markovo." Nowek's forehead flushed bright red. "Yesterday?"

"Yes."

The flush descended, coloring his cheeks, his neck. "When I

asked you in your office, you told me you were in the field with your tigers, that you hadn't visited Ryzkhov recently."

She bit her lower lip.

"She's just confused, Gregori," said his father. "Leave the poor girl alone or she'll have nothing to do with you."

"There's no confusion, Father." Nowek's fury was turning icy and if anything, more dangerous. "Why did you come here? Did you plan this with Yuri?"

"I said I don't know Yuri. I saw the hangar burned, then I heard the airplane coming. . . . After what they did to Andrei I knew they were looking for me and for . . ."

"So you ran."

"I ran. Then I doubled back to the road from the river and waited. I didn't know what I was going to do. I had to leave Tunguska."

"Markovo's so safe? Look what happened to Ryzkhov. How did you get Yuri to drive you into town?"

"His truck went by slow enough for me to jump on the back. I rode it all the way into . . . *stop looking at me that way! I had nothing to do with what happened to Andrei!*"

"Nothing? I don't believe that covers the facts. But then we've already established that you're a liar," said Nowek. His tone was so forceful even his father looked. "You refused to help me when I asked for it. You ran away at the airport when you thought you would be caught. Now you're here, my daughter is up there, and you're going to answer me truthfully. If you don't, I'll hand you over to Kaznin. You know who he is?"

"I know you wouldn't do it."

He walked to the telephone, lifted the receiver, and listened. A dial tone. "We have two opposing theories. A scientist must be willing to test any reasonable hypothesis." He began to dial. One number. The next. Rotary dials. If he'd had a modern phone he'd have already been talking to Kaznin. The third. "The scientific method. We progress when—"

"Don't!"

"—the better theory wins." He slapped the cradle down, but

he kept the phone in his grip. "You were in Markovo the night Andrei was killed."

"You already know."

"You were in Ryzkhov's apartment?"

A nod.

He hung the phone up. "You had a fight with Ryzkhov when you found out he was dealing in tiger bone. That your good friend was in fact a seller of bones. Or worse, a buyer."

"No. That isn't—"

"You demanded he turn over his supply. Perhaps he kept bone in his safe?"

"No. Never. Not in any of them—"

"But he refused. You had a fight. That knife around your neck? You took it out—"

"No!"

"You killed him, then when my militia showed up, you killed them, too. But what about the bullets? Who was your friend with a gun? Another person dedicated to saving the Siberian tiger by any means necessary? Another little arrangement you made with—"

"*No!*"

"I'll be honest. I've never been good at interrogations, but I know someone who is. Maybe I can make a trade. You for Galena. What do you think?"

"Gregori!" His father's voice held a shadow of its old command. "You listen to me, you *nekulturny* rock-breaker. I don't know what potato grubber your mother let into her pants while I was on tour, but I will *not* allow you to behave like some ignorant savage to a guest in my presence. *Is that understood?*"

"She's no guest," Nowek shot back. "No one invited her."

"Then you're not only uncultured," said his father, "but you're also a fool."

"I'm telling you the truth," she said softly.

"You said you don't care when a poacher is killed. That poachers should know that killing tigers can be dangerous. Knifing a man who thinks you are his friend must be easier than darting a tiger. He deserves it. And a dealer in tiger bone? What would you do to such a man?"

A tear welled up in Anna's eye. "It wasn't that."

"Then what? Was it a romantic evening that went wrong? Did Andrei decide he couldn't afford you any longer?"

"Don't be an idiot," she said. "I told you Andrei was trying to help. It was the tapes."

The tapes. The black man materializing from the nighttime taiga, shouting in English. The look of surprise, horror, the flash of claws. "What was Andrei going to do with them?"

"He sent a copy to his brother in Moscow. To identify the man. The black man. From visa records."

The brother in the Foreign Ministry. The visa desk. *Moscow was no help . . .*

"And?"

She looked up. Her eyes were full, pleading, but also illuminated, lit with determination. "The man you saw on the tiger tape? As far as the visa office in Moscow knows, he doesn't exist. No record."

"He wasn't AMR?"

"He wasn't *anyone*."

Nowek thought about that face on the tape. The pinwheel of limbs as the tiger charged. *CDC Pelican,* the lettering on a shirt ridiculously ill suited to the cold that night. No visa record. An American who didn't exist. It wasn't so hard to imagine. What had DeKalb said? The only sure way to get things into Russia was to smuggle them? "What then?"

"The rest doesn't involve you." She looked up at him. "Please."

"It's late for asking favors. You can either tell me everything or you can speak with Kaznin."

Anna looked at Nowek. She shook her head hard. "You don't know. You have him. You can look at your father's face and say that's where I come from."

"Don't be so sure, dear," said Tadeus.

Was she playing for time? For his father's affections? "You come from America. Unless that was also a lie."

"*Amerikanka?*" said Nowek's father. "No."

"It's true. My parents were Russian. They were from Irkutsk, just as I said. They lived there in the seventies. But *I* grew up in America."

"But you speak so wonderfully," Tadeus said. "So sweetly. I could swear that I've heard you sing once . . ."

"That's enough, Father." He turned to her. "How did you wind up in America? Nobody left Irkutsk in those days."

"My parents applied for exit visas but only my mother's came through. She left when she was pregnant with me. I don't think anyone else knew. I'm not even sure that *she* knew. Back then they didn't allow whole families to leave."

Nowek tried to gauge her expression. If she'd been Nina, he would believe her. But she wasn't. "Why did they want to go?"

"Who wouldn't?" remarked Chuchin.

"Quiet!" The lights flickered. "Chuchin, go turn the heat down before the fuses blow."

"Up, down," he said as he left for the front hall. "Next time I'll apply for a job driving elevators."

Nowek said to her, "I asked a question."

"Their life was burning down. They had to jump or die. My father was in trouble."

"What did he do?" asked Nowek.

"What does it matter!"

"Assume that it does."

She glared. "You offered to help me."

"And you refused my offer. What about your father?"

She took a deep breath. It was the same thing she'd done before telling him the story of the tiger cubs down by Vladivostok.

"Fidel Castro came to Irkutsk. He wanted to go out on the lake to fish. The Marine Sciences Committee nominated my father to lead the trip. He refused. My father said Baikal was a shrine, not a fish tank for foreigners. He circulated a petition. He even took it to the fishermen. *They* refused to cooperate. There was talk of a blockade of fishing boats. It was an embarrassment to the Party. It was one reason they came back and put that damned cellulose plant on the south shore. To show who was boss."

Nowek thought back. He recalled something, some flap of the sort when he was young. Castro had gone away disgruntled and the cellulose plant to this day spewed poison. Lake Baikal always had a mystical hold on the Russian soul. It was the "Sacred Sea." This small revolt had been the first spark in a movement that made the lake the centerpiece for the Siberian environmental movement.

"They stripped them both of their teaching posts," Anna continued. "They couldn't make a living, not even as janitors. There was an exchange program with an American oceanographic institute in San Diego. Scripps. I can see you don't know the name, but believe me, it was a big step up for them. A one-year appointment. They applied and they both were accepted. It was a political thing for the Americans. They sent out blanket invitations to people they knew would never be allowed to come to embarrass the Russian—"

"Soviet."

"Soviet government. My mother got permission. My father didn't. It was spite. You know how things were. They made the decision that she would go alone. I was born over there. I was their hidden hope. She called me their stowaway to the future."

Nowek recalled a painting, was it a Klimt? A beautiful red-haired woman, nude, very pregnant, a dreamy look on her face. It was titled, *Hope*. "You never knew your father?"

"Only through pictures. Pictures and letters. After a few years, the letters stopped. My mother went to the embassy. They denied that Professor Vereskov existed. Not one man in all the Soviet Union had that name. Not one man."

Chuchin was back, leaning close, listening.

"When the walls finally fell I came back to Irkutsk to find him. The first thing I did was to go to the university. They had no records. He was a lecturer on freshwater ecosystems, a specialist in Baikal endemic species, and *there wasn't one piece of paper that proved he ever had been there.* I went to his old address.

There was another family living there. He was gone. Disappeared."

"That happened a lot back then," said Chuchin.

"I'd given up," she said. There was a small hitch in her voice. An incipient break. "Then I visited the old Lystvyanka aquarium. You know it?"

Nowek knew it all right. In the summer, with a picnic lunch packed, he and Nina had visited its cool green confines many times, letting the filtered light of the great tanks cast an intimate spell across them, shutting out the world as they walked together on the bottom of the sea.

"There was an exhibit of *omul,* you know, the Baikal fish? It had an old plaque so corroded you couldn't make out anything. I don't know why I started rubbing at it. I knew it was his specialty, his area of expertise. I just wanted to touch something, some piece of him. That's when I saw it. *S.A. Vereskov.* That's when I knew that he was real."

Nowek had seen it. He'd touched the glass with his own fingers. Touched her father's work. "You doubted it?"

She looked bitter. "He was just a face on a photograph until I saw that name. Then I wanted the rest." She unzipped the down vest. With the woodstove and the electric panels it was almost warm in the kitchen. "I couldn't know his beginning, his life. But I wanted to see his grave."

"How was Ryzkhov going to help you find a grave?"

"There are records in Moscow for everything. Andrei's brother found him listed as a volunteer laborer. I knew that was a lie. A man who spent his life studying Lake Baikal? They sentenced him to die cutting trees."

"They did a lot of that, too," muttered Chuchin.

Yet another Russian irony, thought Nowek. A police state dedicated to the elimination of law, of rights, spent an astonishing amount of effort keeping meticulous records. Give me anarchy any day of the week, he thought. But records? They were frightening. "Did you find out where they sent him?"

She nodded. "It was a Forestry Administration camp," said Anna, known to the world by its acronym: GULAG. "It was

called Elgen 9. He died there. The records said it was smallpox."

"What was the name?" It was Chuchin. His leathery face
suddenly seemed to take on a new color, the creases deepened.

"Elgen 9."

"Elgen?" said Chuchin. "You're certain?"

"What is it, Chuchin?" asked Nowek.

"I was *na narakh* at Elgen," he said. Behind the wire. There
was something odd in Chuchin's expression. Something in-
completely masked. It showed through his old wrinkles, his
new bruises. "I lived there two winters. If it had been three I
wouldn't be alive. I was lucky. I was good with a saw. They
transferred me. The camp shut down after I left."

"The Main Administration closed it?" asked Nowek.

"Like she said. Smallpox closed it. Everyone was wiped out.
Inmates. Guards. Everyone. Maybe even the ghosts." Chuchin
breathed in, out, his face too blank. He looked at Anna.

The iron stove clicked. The wood settled with a sigh.

"You might have known him," said Anna. "You could have
been his friend."

"You don't make friends inside the wire. Not with politicals.
You know what Elgen means? It's not even Russian. It's a
Buryat word. *Place of Death*. It was a good name."

"Buryat?" she said. "It's in Buryatia? That's near the Biosphere Preserve."

"It's not near anything. Elgen is up north where the trees
stop and the ice begins. But if you're looking for a grave, forget
it. The river goes by the camp. We used to stack bodies in
winter. When the ice broke, we'd shove them in." He looked
at her. "There was no wood to waste on markers and no way to
dig through frozen ground. The river was your father's grave."

"What river?"

"The Nizhnaya Tunguska."

She cocked her head. "But it flows . . . I mean, I know
that river. I've walked in it."

"That river's a thousand kilometers long," said Nowek. "It
empties into the Yenisey. The camp could be anywhere and it's

probably gone." Though as he said it he thought back to the one he'd flown over this morning. The white depressions, the fallen posts, the stripped cable and barbed wire. The snowy field.

"No, Mr. Mayor," said Chuchin. "She's right. It's up there above the oil fields. Twenty, maybe thirty kilometers north. Why do you think I wouldn't fly there with you?"

"I thought you hated airplanes."

"That's the other reason."

"All these months," she said. "I could have seen it. Driven a buggy there and . . ." She looked up. "I still . . ."

"Not anymore." He could see what was in her mind. Tunguska. The gravity, the black hole exerting its pull. "You said that Ryzkhov had more than one safe."

Her eyes saw a silver river, rounded pebbles, stacked bodies. "What do you mean?"

"When I asked whether he kept bone in a safe you said that he didn't. Not in *any of them*. How many are there?"

"Andrei had to be cautious. He kept maps of properties AmerRus was interested in leasing. You have to keep these things very quiet."

"Properties for oil exploration?"

"That's what he did for them."

But why hunt for new oil when you were already sitting atop an elephant field? "Where are these maps?"

"Nobody else knew, but he told me. Andrei could be very clever."

"You know about the wall safe? The one I found open?"

Anna nodded. "He called it his giveaway. Anyone who broke in would find it and not tear the rest of the house apart."

Maps stashed in secret places. Would the police know about them? Would the neighbors? What about his murderers? "At Andrei's flat. What happened after he told you about your father?"

Her look of determination receded, but not much. She'd made up her mind. "He said the American, the black man on the tape, must not be in the country legally. That it was odd because the Americans liked to do things legally. It surprised him."

"Why did you want this American's name so badly?"

When she looked at Nowek her eyes burned. "If we could establish that he worked for AMR, I could nail them."

"For poaching tigers?"

"There's an international conference coming up on endangered species. We were going to hold a news conference and blow AMR's poaching operation right out of the water."

"They'd laugh."

"They wouldn't. All the dollars AmerRus invested in Tunguska are underwritten by the United States Commerce Department. Proving that they're using taxpayer funds to poach endangered species would kill AMR's Tunguska project."

And Markovo, too, he thought. "What time was this?"

"Ten. Maybe a quarter past. Andrei said that I should stay there, that it was too dangerous to leave. He offered me a drink. We talked. He wanted me to stay with him."

"I can see why," said Tadeus.

"You're blind."

"Not to everything."

Anna said, "I told him if I could handle a two-hundred-kilo tiger, I could handle Markovo and, besides, we weren't involved that way anymore. At least I wasn't."

Anymore. But once? "You had your knife."

She touched the leather sheath hanging from her neck. "I always carry it. We had a drink and I left. I walked back to the hotel afterward. The project keeps a room there for visiting investigators. I used it."

"You were seen going in?"

"There was a guard at the door. But the front desk was empty. The *dezhurnaya* upstairs was asleep."

"And of course you were alone."

"Alone." Her eyes finally overflowed, and a tear trickled down a cheek. "I thought, after you told me what happened, if I had stayed with Andrei it might not have happened. I could have stopped it. I might have been able to . . ."

"I don't think so." Nowek thought back to the scene at
Ryzkhov's flat. The bullets, the dog, the blood, the dirty glass
syringe sliding into dead flesh.

"Now look what you've done," said Tadeus with a click of
his tongue. "You've made her cry."

"Do you believe me?" She looked up at him and the powerful sense of contact, of past and present overlapping, melting,
was enough to make Nowek draw in his breath.

"Why didn't you tell me this when I asked?"

"I didn't know which side you were on."

Nowek wondered which side he was on, too. It wasn't a
coin, one face, another. It was more like those non-Euclidean
geometries that mathematicians play with; a universe of sixteen
dimensions and spheres of sides. "And now?"

"You knew AmerRus was involved with Andrei's murder. I
could see it in your face. It's why I came here."

Flattering, but hardly true. Where else would she go to find
a new *kryusha,* a new roof? If she only new how badly his was
leaking. "Who else has copies of the tape?"

She nodded at her rucksack.

"All of them?"

Another nod.

Nowek saw his own kitchen with new eyes. This wasn't just
vandalism. It wasn't a warning to stay out of the case. They
were looking for something. Nowek had visited her. They
thought he'd taken a copy of that tape away with him.

What did that make it? Proof of AMR's poaching Siberian
tigers? Kill and sell every tiger in Tunguska and you wouldn't
pay for a month of drilling operations. No. Something, some
factor of ten, was missing.

"Will you help me now?" she asked.

He turned to her. "You say that you and Andrei were just
friends now. But I have a neighbor who saw you visiting with
him often, and at strange hours."

"Before. But not since his wife—"

"I also saw your picture hanging on his wall. His arm was
around you. I wonder. Did his wife ever see that picture?"

"She refused to leave California. She only wanted a check each month. She didn't care if he ever visited her."

"What was the bone doing in his flat? If Andrei wasn't involved with poaching, if he was helping you save tigers, who put it there?"

"It was AMR. They wanted to make it look like—"

"You killed him?"

"I didn't!"

"You asked me to believe you," said Nowek. "I'll tell you. I believe you were there with a knife. Ryzkhov was killed with a knife. You have a fortune in tiger bone up at Tunguska. I found a tiger bone under his furniture. I picked up a piece of granite gravel from his carpet. I found identical examples of it at Tunguska."

"It's not—"

"Now I'm no prosecutor, but even I could send you to prison with all of that. And I have to tell you, being American won't help. Kaznin will take you to Gromov, and frankly, Gromov can do what he likes. So what do I believe? I believe that either there's an elaborate conspiracy to make you appear guilty of the Ryzkhov murders, or else you *are* guilty. With the name of an accomplice, the one who used his gun, we'd have this all wrapped up in a ribbon."

"I came here because I thought I could trust you."

"Or fool me. Why not? I'm just the mayor of a little town filled with ignorant savages. You're an American used to getting everything your way. Maybe you killed him. Maybe you didn't," said Nowek. "I don't know the answer yet. But I'm not letting you out of my sight until I do." He held out his hand. "Give it to me."

"The tapes?"

"The knife. I've seen the work it leaves behind."

She looked at him a long time before she blinked. She reached down, pulled the thong over her head, and held it out to him.

"What about Kaznin?" asked Chuchin.

Nowek took the knife, then tossed it to Chuchin. "There

aren't many places to hide in Markovo. He'll find her eventually. We need to know a few more things before we let him."

"I'll keep my eye on her," said Tadeus.

"Which one, Father? I'm sorry about your birthday. I'm afraid we'll have to postpone the celebration. You should be safe here for the moment." He nodded to Chuchin. "Go bring his caviar."

"Sturgeon?"

"What else would it be? We'll leave the heat on so you won't freeze."

"That's very accommodating."

"You're welcome. Someone tore my house apart and I'm going to find out who they are. I think when I do, I'll be closer to getting Galena back." Chuchin came back with four blue tins of caviar. "We're all going for a little drive."

"How little?" said Chuchin, mindful of the nearly empty fuel tank. He dumped the tins onto the table and peeled open a lid with a tiny key. Inside were fat black marbles, first-class Caspian caviar, rich and greasy.

"Rossinka," said Nowek. "Number Eight. Dr. Vereskaya is going to show me just how clever Andrei Ryzkhov was."

CHAPTER
17

THE LAND CRUISER LURCHED as it drew a bubble of air through the fuel lines. They bumped across the stone bridge spanning the Lena. Snow had melted from the daytime sun and the flow of the river was getting stronger. It accelerated as it was channeled through the concrete embankments, rushing like a chute. Plates of ice swept by, spinning, splintering into chunks, into fragments, and finally a greasy skim of crystals. Black eddies swirled around the footings.

They left the old part of town behind and headed for the brightly lit center, the Hotel Siber, the old KGB building and Rossinka.

Nowek looked up into the sky. No more stars. Clouds were scudding in from the northeast. That meant low pressure to the south over Lake Baikal. It would pick up moisture there and swirl it up here as rain. And if it rained, the river would flood.

"There's probably nothing left," said Chuchin. "What the militia missed the neighbors wouldn't."

"Probably," said Nowek. The green lights washing up from the dashboard cooled Nowek's blood. He had to think. His brain felt like the near-empty tank. Sucking air. Running out of time. Anna sat in the deeper darkness in the backseat, her rucksack pushed down beside her boots.

"I could describe him for you," she said to Chuchin. "From photos."

"Him?"

"My father. You might have seen him at Elgen."

"Tell me that he looked cold and unhappy," said Chuchin, "and I'll say that I saw him every day I was there." He looked at Nowek. "What do you think you'll find, Mr. Mayor? You saw how many militia were there. It was like a bazaar. And don't forget who was bossing them. He would know what to look for if there was something we shouldn't see."

"They don't all work for Kaznin."

"True," Chuchin agreed. "Just the ones who are still alive."

The guard booth at the Rossinka gate was steamy, a blue, flickering light illuminating a man seated at a tiny desk. A small Japanese television was playing a tape as the Land Cruiser rolled to a stop. The window slid open.

"What?" the annoyed guard said. Behind him on the desk a tiny color screen showed a sailboat on an azure sea, and on its forward deck a man and woman entangled and coiled, knotted as the ropes beneath them. Limbs rising, opening to a score of insistent moans, astonished little seagull cries.

Nowek wondered, who's steering the boat?

"Who are you here to see?"

"Who are you to ask?" replied Chuchin.

He trained a flashlight first at Chuchin, then Nowek, finally at Anna. It lingered there a while before swinging back to the front. Behind him the lovemaking was building to a wild crescendo. "You can't come in here without an invitation."

"Go back to your film. You're missing the best part." Chuchin rolled up the window and before the guard could say anything more, drove off.

Number Eight Rossinka was dark. The elaborate arched window over the door had actually been removed and replaced with planks of wood. The front door was locked.

"He'll call someone," said Chuchin.

"I know. We'll have to be quick." Nowek looked at Anna. "So?"

"Go around the back," she said. "To the garage."

"The car's long gone," said Nowek.

"We're not looking for his car."

The driveway was embraced by curving town house walls.

"Citizen Geraskina is awake," said Nowek as they went by Number Ten. A car was parked in front. "She's the one who called the militia about Ryzkhov's dog."

"Czar," said Anna. Her voice was hushed. As though the town house walls were tombstones standing shoulder to shoulder, as though the heaps of ice and snow they rode over were graves. "He was a good dog. He even got along with George."

"Who?"

"My cat. The calico."

At the back, they came to Ryzkhov's garage door. Anna got out. Nowek tried the rolling door. It was steel made to look like wood with embossed graining. Solid enough to thunk when rapped, it was firmly locked from within.

"What are you doing?" he asked her.

She was running a finger along the underside of a metal clapboard. She stopped and pried up the bottom lip of the sheathing. A small key dropped out into her other palm. "For emergencies."

"What kind?"

"In case I came by when he wasn't in."

"You did that often?"

"Sometimes." But she had already put it into the circular opening beside the door and twisted it. She put her shoulder to the heavy door. It began to rise with the squeal of unlubricated wheels. She stopped and left it partly open, then ducked under and inside.

Chuchin had the silver Nagant in one hand and a flashlight in the other. He got down on his knees and aimed the light in.

"The light must be burned out," she said. "It used to come on when the door opened."

Chuchin stepped under and swept the beam to the ceiling. "The bulb's not burned out," he said, "it's been *privatized.*"

Nowek joined them inside.

The garage was four bare walls and an equally bare ceiling. Muddy tire tracks and oil drips showed that someone had once kept a car in here. Empty storage racks had been toppled and ragged holes punched in the unpainted Sheetrock. Copper pipes dressed in heavy insulating rubber coats snaked overhead, all neatly labeled GERACHAYA and CHOLODNA. Hot and cold. White chunks of Sheetrock lay crushed on the floor. The steel bar that did all the damage had been left behind.

She stood at the back wall. Here, too, the covering had been punched open with the bar. The studs, raw and oozing with pine pitch, showed like fractured bones. "Shine that light back here."

Chuchin pointed it at the back wall.

In the white focus of Chuchin's light, Anna stood beside a white plastic cap that extended a few inches from the rear wall. It was threaded onto a black iron pipe with the neat label KANALIZATSYA above it.

"That's the shit pipe," said Chuchin. "You don't want what's in there."

"I said Andrei was clever." Anna grabbed the cap and twisted. It wouldn't budge. When she tried again, Nowek saw the roped muscles in her forearms stand out, then recede. She looked at him. "Help me."

Nowek grabbed the steel bar.

Looks were deceiving. The plastic cap was remarkably sturdy. It took three blows to open a crack in the end of it. One more. A miss. The bar struck the iron waste pipe and rang like a dull gong.

Another blow and the white sewer cap split open.

Nowek stepped back, half expecting a gush of filth. There was none. "Give me the light, Chuchin."

He took it and aimed it up the iron pipe. It was filled with something, all right. "I think I see the blockage." He reached in and grabbed something. "Here's your hidden treasure." He pulled out a fistful of windshield wipers bound with string. He let them clatter to the cement floor. Anyone with half a brain kept a supply of wipers safe from marauding fingers, though stashing them up a sewer pipe seemed extreme.

"You'll never make plumber's apprentice," said Chuchin as he quickly snatched them up. "I think these could be made to fit. Keep looking. Maybe he's got a spare battery up there."

"There's more," said Anna. "He told me that's where he kept his secrets. He called them his state secrets."

"His money," said Chuchin.

Nowek stuck his arm far up the pipe. He was up to his shoulder, even a little beyond when he felt it. A string? "There's something inside."

"Money," Chuchin solemnly pronounced again. "How much?"

Nowek eased his arm out of the sewer cleanout. In his hand was a white string. He pulled it clear of the end of the pipe, then drew the length of it out as though he were reeling in a fish. A tight roll of papers emerged, then fell out into the circle of Chuchin's flashlight.

Nowek picked them up. Dense. A small log of papers half a meter long, tied up with heavy cord. He pulled the knot apart. The tightly wadded papers sprang open.

Nowek snatched the flashlight and aimed it down.

Maps?

At first he made the mistake of thinking they were all duplicates. Each one had the same title block printed at the bottom:

PETROCONSULT SA: Foreign Scouting Service PETROLEUM ACTIVITY, EASTERN SIBERIA

On familiar ground at last. Nowek kept looking. Five were of a different scale from the sixth and last map. They were detail views keyed to the broader territory displayed on the final chart.

This one encompassed nearly all of north central Siberia;

from the upper shore of Lake Baikal at the map's bottom to the fanlike delta of the Lena River and the Laptev Sea at the top.

To the unprepared eye it was a curious sort of chart, one that combined surface features, rivers, towns, roads, with underground geology; the Aldan and Tunguska Basins, the Anabar Shield, the Lena Trough. Nowek held the map close.

Spattered across its length and width were exploratory wells, oil, gas, plus the known outlines of producing fields webbed by a skein of pipelines.

Tunguska was a huge, irregular splotch that dominated the entire region. A true black hole. It was connected with Irkutsk by the new pipeline that ran by Markovo. Nowek followed the route with his finger. The map was heavily marked by hand and covered with Ryzkhov's notes. Five squares, each about twenty kilometers on a side, had been drawn in red. They corresponded to the five other detail maps. Clearly these were tracts that Andrei, as a leasing agent for AmerRus, hoped to acquire for his American benefactors. His state secrets.

"So what does it mean?" asked Chuchin.

"It's Ryzkhov's business plan," said Nowek. "These were areas he hoped to sell to AmerRus. Or did sell. I don't know which."

"He didn't own them," said Chuchin. "How could he sell them?"

"It would take a while to explain that, Chuchin."

"Let me see that map," said Anna. She took the flashlight and beamed it on the headwaters of the Nizhnaya Tunguska River, tracing it from its source down by Ust Kut.

The river rose close to the Lena; at one point it was separated by only a low hummock of ground not ten kilometers wide. But from there the destinies of the two great rivers were irretrievably distinct. The Lena surged northeast to the Laptev Sea; the Nizhnaya Tunguska trended northwest to the Yenisey River, which emptied into the Kara Sea.

The flashlight went north, then west. It came to the black splotch of the Tunguska Fields, moved up, then paused.

Nowek said, "Wait." He flipped through the detail charts,

then back to the broad map. Stare at nothing long enough, it becomes something. Notes on a page, black marks hung from the barbed wire of a staff, the wiggles of an electric well log.

"You see something, Mr. Mayor?"

"Andrei Ryzkhov might have been a great businessman, but he wasn't much of a geologist. These black shapes? They look like lakes and in a way they are, only underground," he said. "Someone has drilled there and found oil." He moved to a nearby zone. "These dotted lines show geologic traps where oil might be hiding. The structural geology is favorable. This is where AMR would want to sink a well. Not that anything is guaranteed. Even in a place that looks good, it's more likely to come up dry than not."

"So what?" asked Chuchin.

"So these properties Ryzkhov marked off? None of them are in places where you'd expect to find oil. There are no geologic traps. No hint of any oil-bearing structures present."

"But Andrei said that AmerRus would pay him for—" Anna began, but Chuchin cut her off.

"Wait. You see that one?" He was pointing to a red square directly north of the Tunguska oil fields. "You see the way the river curves? That's the Nizhnaya Tunguska." He jabbed a finger to the damp paper. "These hills? That's where Elgen used to be."

"My father's camp?" said Anna.

"More than him."

A shout came from outside. "Who's in there?"

Anna snapped the flashlight off. The map glowed subliminally, then faded.

"I'm going to call the militia now!"

"It's the guard from the gate," said Chuchin. "He has his pants back on."

"Let's go," said Nowek.

"What about upstairs?" Chuchin asked.

"Forget it." Nowek rolled the maps tight again. "I think we may have what we came for."

★   ★   ★

The guard was gone when they shut the garage door and got into the Land Cruiser. The sky was heavy, crowded with sowbellied clouds that picked up the lights of town. Anna sat in the back.

The engine turned, turned, and finally caught.

"We don't have much more gas for little trips," said Chuchin. "Where to now?"

"Home. It was a mistake to leave my father. Kaznin could return."

"You have a strange look on your face, Mr. Mayor."

Nowek said, "Chuchin, I'm thinking a very strange thought."

They drove back over the bridge and into the Black Lung district. Snow was piled high alongside the buildings where it had been plowed off the road.

"Why did Andrei arrange to lease an old camp to Amer-Rus?' asked Anna. "What could be left of it after all these years? Why would AMR pay for someplace where there's no oil?"

He turned around to face her.

She looked at him long. Her eyes reflected the dashboard lights. Rippling, a stone breaking through black, moonlit water. "You believe me about AMR now?"

"Believing is easy," said Nowek. "Trust is harder."

Chuchin peered ahead. A lone streetlight burned halfway down the block. He slowed. "Mayor." He switched off the Land Cruiser's lights and coasted to the curb. The wheels splashed icewater up in a filthy spray.

"Are we out of gas?"

"No," he said. "Up ahead. Nikki's back in business."

A van was parked like a black raft in the pool of yellow light cast by a single hanging bulb. It was parked in a pool of melted ice that nearly covered the wheel hubs. It blocked the mouth of Nikki Malyshev's alley.

As he looked, two men got down from the cab of the van and splashed around its front. They climbed up the snow mound. They paused, leaned together, their black shadows merging.

They suddenly parted and began moving in the direction of the alley. Black shadow, black figure, moving fast against a backdrop of mottled snow and silver water.

Anna leaned over the back of the front seat. "That's the van I saw at your house."

One van might look like another in a poorly lit street. But even at this distance, Nowek could see that each of the men carried a length of pipe.

CHAPTER
18

A SHOUTED QUESTION, an answer in breaking glass that ended in a heavy thud. It echoed from brick walls slick with melted ice. A scream of outrage, then one pitched higher and more desperate; a man pleading for something he knew he would not get.

Nowek threw open his door.

Chuchin was already out, the silver Nagant pistol in his hand. He stepped carefully, moving from firm place to firm place, without looking down. His "feet knew ice," as the saying went. His breath flagged white in the cold, damp air.

"I'll be the hammer and drive them out. You be the anvil and stop them." Chuchin cocked the pistol.

"Just the two of you?" said Anna.

"Stay here. Don't move," said Nowek. But belief wasn't the same as trust. He grabbed the keys from the ignition, slammed the door shut, and began to run, slipping, cracking through the ice, heading for the van.

There were no more screams. The sounds of a terrible beating filled the alley. The two *byki* were working hard. Nowek heard it in their breathing. Like city-bred men confronting a country labor, anxious to not seem soft, to see it through to its end. Splitting wood. Gutting a carcass. The blows were low, steady thuds like the beating of a giant heart, the steamship thump of a rock crusher.

Nowek went to the driver's side of the van. Unmarked and empty. He peered into the cab. There were no keys in the ignition. He started to move around the front.

Ice cracked with each step. Beneath it lay cold black water. A plow had cleared the street of the heaviest snow by pushing it into a bank along the side. There it hardened to granite. It would hang around until July. It made an excellent dam. Another step, another crack. The breaks webbed out and then both feet went through. The water was knee deep. His feet fell into a fossil rut. Here the water was deeper. Nowek stepped up, then broke through again. He didn't need boots; he needed a boat.

He heard another shout from the alley. Chuchin, this time, then two loud booms; an unmistakable punctuation that brought all sounds to a halt. A third shot brought the neighborhood dogs to life. The hammer had dropped. Now for the anvil.

The snow mound blocked his view into the alley. But Nowek could hear the muffled crunch of running boots. He was around the front of the van when a figure came sailing over the snow.

The pit bull threw up his arms as he collided with Nowek, dropping an iron pipe. They both fell, tangled, breaking through into the water. Jagged chunks of ice slashed at Nowek's cheek as they rolled, parted. The man staggered to his feet. He had the pipe back in his hands. His fur hat was gone, revealing a sharp, V-shaped hairline and a red face. "Vanya!" he shouted, and then faced Nowek. "Get out of here."

"No."

As the second pit bull came over the snow mound, he swung.

Nowek turned into the blow. It hit his shoulder rather than his head. His arm went instantly numb. He rolled away, flattening himself to the front of the van. The pipe slashed down again. Nowek spun and grabbed at it, pulling the pit bull in to him.

Headlights came on. The van's horn blared.

Nowek was blinded, sight and sound. He held on to that pipe as though at its end was everything, all the answers. The red squares on Ryzkhov's map, the piece of gravel dusted with comet glass. Everything. The pit bull pulled suddenly and very hard. Nowek lost his balance and fell.

He wasn't struggling so much as swimming on his back, his head the prow of an inefficient icebreaker. Something eclipsed the headlight. He sensed the kick coming, too late. It caught him on his side, nearly lifting him out of the water. It drove his breath out, an explosion of white bubbles.

The boot came at him again, though not a kick. It pressed down on his chest, hard and heavy. Neck, cheeks, then nose submerged. Nowek's hair floated up like seaweed. Broken panes of ice covered his face. He tried to reach around behind to find the bottom, to push his way up and out. Just darkness. He clutched at the boot on his chest. It was made from stone. A piling jackhammering him down, down. His lungs burned. They screamed. He realized he should have taken a deep breath. Tingling. Swirling black dots like bats against the head-lights above.

How long can you hold your breath?

And then some traitorous signal, some idiot impulse, forced his mouth open.

He gasped for air and filthy black liquid poured in. He was directly in front of the wheels. The pressure on his chest re-mained. He gagged again, completely out of control, and felt the cold radiate through his chest like pooled mercury. Over-head the sky was eclipsed by the wedge of a black hull.

It was her wool skater's cap that he most remembered. Camel-colored and very fine, it looked beautiful with her bril-liant red scarf, her cold-scalded cheeks. The cap had strands that caught the snow. Near her skin they melted to diamonds that flashed fire in the sun. Her face was surrounded with an aura, a halo. But at night the lights of the rink made a galaxy of them. She would draw him close for a kiss, that half-melted look on her face, and Nowek would pass through a field of stars.

"Come on!" she called back over her shoulder. She was waving at him to follow. But it was spring, the ice windowpane thin. It stood up to her weight, but Nowek would . . .

"Come on!"

On faith, he took one step and heard the ice begin to give. He stopped and looked down, then up again. Nina was gone.

"Come on!"

Cold. Someone was shaking him. He opened his eyes. Nina. Nowek closed his eyes, then opened them again.

Her hair straggled down her cheek. Drops fell from her clothes. The down vest she wore over her denim jacket looked deflated. The denim was black with water. She wiped her face.

"Jesus. Come on. Breathe!"

He tried to say her name but something was in the way. A cold weight. A heaviness. He tried and a gout of water came up his throat for his trouble. He coughed it out.

"Breathe, dammit!"

He gagged, gasped. She wasn't touching him. He was shaking. He was very wet. And cold from the inside out.

Her face came close, her fingers pulled his lips apart. Her lips, warm. A kiss. Finally.

Nowek's chest inflated against something alien. He gasped another gusher half from his mouth, half from his nose. The air burned as it went down. Burned as it came out. Another. He heaved, choked, spat.

"Come on! Again!"

Nowek felt water lapping at the back of his neck. He forced his mouth open, sucked down another mouthful of air.

"Help me!" She took him by the shoulders and pulled him toward the snowbank.

He slid up its side like a penguin on a floe. Nowek reached up and gripped her arms, or at least he tried to. His hands wouldn't close. He couldn't make them.

"Mayor!" Chuchin came running from the alley. "Mayor!" He pushed Anna aside and lifted Nowek up. He put him down on dry snow and rolled him in it. It drew the water away from

Nowek's body, it fell off him like dead skin. It was not enough. "Go get the car!"

"*U menya nyet!*"

"Where are they?"

"He took them!"

Chuchin cursed as he rubbed Nowek's cheeks hard. The ice cuts began to bleed, not much. There was no feeling in them, like rubbing wood.

Nowek's skin was very cold. He rolled both eyes in the same direction. "Chuchin."

"You're alive? That's a start," he said. He reached into Nowek's jacket and found the Land Cruiser's keys. He tossed them to Anna. "I thought you rolled under a wheel to keep them from getting away. It would be just like you to use your head as a wheel block. Come on. Sit. You aren't as dead as I thought."

The shaking was all over him. Inside him. "How . . . long?"

"How long what?"

The stars were back. His brain, too. Nowek looked down into the dark alley. Dogs were howling. They sounded remarkably like a wolf pack closing in. He thought of Kaznin. "How long was I . . . under the water?"

"What am I, a clock? You were supposed to stop them, Mayor. Remember?"

"Malyshev . . ."

"Forget Malyshev."

His brain was barely firing. He looked up. "Help me."

Chuchin dragged him to a sitting position.

Where his legs were under snow they felt strangely warm. That he could feel them at all seemed a tremendous accomplishment. "I . . . I want to . . . to see."

Chuchin scowled. "If Nikki's head was as hard as yours he'd still be alive."

"Chuchin . . ."

"All right. Here." He hauled him to his feet, then let Nowek lean on him, step by step, into the alley.

The brick walls seemed to curve in overhead, leaving just a thin strip of night sky. Nowek belched and a sour trickle came up. His clothes were plastered to him, cemented. He was shaking, and that was a good sign. But he wasn't feeling the cold, and he knew that was not good.

Lose five degrees of core temperature and you begin to shake. Lose ten and the shaking stops, but so does thinking. Lose fifteen and everything goes. Where did that put him?

The snow was deep. It still had the granular feel of winter in it. A long extension cord slithered up and away to some invisible plug. An overturned electric heater sizzled as snow touched red coils. Nowek looked around.

Made from old wooden crates, the kiosk had been splintered, the glass windows smashed. On the pockmarked snow were cigarettes, airline bottles of liquor, Snickers bars, and a scattering of small dark boxes that Nowek mistook for rats except that they didn't move.

Neither did Nikki Malyshev. He lay at the center of it all, arms out, swimming across the snow, legs apart in a kick stroke. Head to one side, ready to suck in air. Nikki's head looked melted, almost flat. His lip was drawn up in a sneer. A broken white tooth showed. His wares floated around him; the chaotic, bubbling dreams of wealth and enterprise, caught streaming from his head, blood and brain condensed by the cold night air to merchandise.

Nowek leaned over. If Chuchin hadn't grabbed him, he would have pitched face first into the snow. He picked up one of the dark boxes and held it. His hands seemed cased in heavy gloves. There was no feeling. Claws good only for crushing. He managed to bring the metal tin up to his face. Too dark.

An engine started out on the street. The Land Cruiser nosed its way over the snow, its sole headlight illuminating the alley.

Nowek read the markings in the light.

DON'T EAT AFTER 1991

And on the other side a label. Prune and cottage cheese. He looked at all the others scattered across the snow.

"Bespredl," snarled Chuchin. Anarchy. "It's not even safe for thieves. Look at this. It's . . ."

"Chuchin."

"What?"

He held up the tin.

"You're hungry? Forget it. One of those boys was Yufa's son. He ran when I fired. Typical thieves. Inside their leather jackets they're all just boys." Chuchin seemed insulted. "You were supposed to stop them."

Yufa. Kaznin. Nikki, and Yufa again. A tin of obsolete army rations. Red squares outlining nothing but space. He shook as he gripped the tin. "I . . . I stopped one of them."

"Briefly."

"Yufa," he said again. Nowek trembled as the cold reached through him. Hypothermia killed more people in spring than in winter. In spring they were trying to forget the cold, to prove that it was gone forever. They froze to death by the score. In winter they didn't have the luxury of pretending.

The Land Cruiser stopped.

He thought of the stove back at his house. If it had been a real stove, a Russian fireplace, he could have crawled onto it and slept like a muffin, slowly baking. "What about Nikki?"

"If you stay out much longer, Mr. Mayor," said Chuchin, "you can ask him personally." He shoved him toward the car.

Anna was in the driver's seat. The dome light came on as Chuchin pushed Nowek in. She was as soaked, but she seemed not to care, nor notice.

"You need to get dry," she said. "You drowned. Do you know that? You were almost gone. You've got to get out of those wet clothes."

She was right, but he wasn't paying attention. Ryzkhov drowning in blood. Kaznin. Yufa. The Ministry. Prosecutor Gromov. Squares on a map. Elgen. The names kept spinning in

Nowek's mind. The American caught on videotape stumbling through the snows. Army rations. Yufa.

Chuchin opened the driver's side and motioned for Anna to get out. She slid across, closer to Nowek instead. "Is there a blanket in the car? We're going to lose him if we—"

"Take my jacket." Chuchin stripped it off and tossed it to her. She peeled her soaked down vest off, then unsnapped the denim jacket. Worse than useless when they were wet. Her turtleneck was silk, terribly thin but it trapped body heat better. She wrapped Chuchin's padded coat around both their shoulders. She rubbed his hands, his wrists. He tried to say something. His lips wouldn't obey.

"What is it?" she asked. Her breath was warm.

"Dream. Just . . . just a . . . dream." He could feel the boot on his chest as he spoke, pressing down hard. But he could see Nina's face.

The cold was in him now and it made him giddy. She pressed against him. He could feel her muscles, their hardness, and when she turned slightly, the softness of her breasts through her turtleneck. Hard, soft, cold, and warm. He felt her radiate. He forced his lips to stop chattering. It worked for a few seconds.

"You're lucky the water was cold," she said.

"Cold water is . . . easy to find. Warm . . . would be lucky."

"You were almost dead. Is that so funny? You're here making bad jokes because of the mammalian diving response." She pressed against him. "The systems shut down. Respiration, heart, everything. The brain can keep going for a long time when it's cold. It's how whales can stay underwater for hours. It's why you aren't dead."

"Hours? That's nothing," said Chuchin as he backed out of the alley. "The mayor's been holding his breath for three years."

CHAPTER
19

"YUFA'S BOYS MUST have seen me at Nikki's this afternoon," said Chuchin. "I was buying *ikra* for your father's dinner, but maybe they didn't know. Maybe they didn't give Nikki a chance to say I was buying caviar, not something else."

Something else? thought Nowek. DON'T EAT AFTER 1991. Why would Semyon Yufa care about old army rations?

"You called me a name," she said as they drove out of the Black Lung, heading back for Nowek's house. "When you were on the street. You called me Nina."

Chuchin looked at him, then away. The heater was dialed up full. The warm air blast barely penetrated Nowek's skin. But her name, that made it.

"There's not much fuel left, Mr. Mayor." Chuchin tapped the fuel needle which stubbornly refused to budge. He shrugged and lit a Yava instead.

"Nina's your wife?"

"She was." To say more was somehow wrong, a betrayal.

She looked at Nowek and saw something there that told her not to ask anymore. She shivered, then said to Chuchin, "Do you have another one of those things?"

Nowek put his hands in front of the heater grille. His fingers tapped the plastic uncontrollably. Rising core temperature. It was heat, but not like having Anna pressed near him. "I thought . . . Americans didn't like to smoke."

Chuchin handed her one lit from his own.

"I thought all Russian politicians were corrupt."

"You're . . . almost right."

"Both of us."

The red eye of her Yava glowed hot in the darkness. She seemed to burn in reflected self-righteousness. "What do you think Kaznin will do?"

Nowek said, "He knows you're here. Markovo is small."

"What if he finds us?"

Us. It was an interesting expression. And, he thought, probably accurate. Us. The word spun through him like a flywheel unbolted from its mount. The duly elected mayor of Markovo, running from a former KGB major, now a private security consultant who worked for the governor of Irkutsk and his right-hand man, Prosecutor Gromov. Markovo was no longer safe. And if Irkutsk, if Siberia, wasn't far enough away to be safe, then what was?

And Galena. They almost certainly had her. They'd know it was their best chance to control him. Worst of all, they were right. He'd hand them this woman, this woman who had just saved his life. Whatever he owed her, he owed Galena more. For a moment, his shaking stopped. He said to Anna, "At best you would be deported."

"My project . . ."

"The tigers can take care of themselves."

She let her eyes linger on him, gazing through wisps of smoke. "At worst?"

"Gromov holds a trial. You're convicted."

"Of killing Andrei?"

He nodded. "And . . . my two men. It's economical. There's no reason to let an opportunity go to waste."

"Maybe I need to hire a lawyer."

"Don't waste your money."

"You're honest, anyway."

He thought of his campaign poster. "Honesty has always been one of my main flaws."

The Land Cruiser was hot enough inside to grow bananas. Steamy. And it still was barely enough. The shaking was almost gone. His brain was moving and his lips, his teeth, were not. An improvement.

Another bright ember, a wash of smoke. "Why was Andrei arranging those properties for AmerRus?" she said. "Are you sure there was no oil potential?"

"Yes."

"Who owns them?"

"Who controls them is what counts."

"Gromov," said Chuchin. It sounded like a growl.

"But what for? What would AMR want with them?"

Nowek gritted his teeth together hard to keep them from chattering.

"Your father told me you became mayor because you're drawn to the impossible."

"He may be right," he told her. "At Samotlor I saw men work at temperatures that turn steel brittle as glass. But the crews were tougher. I saw men do the impossible every day for a dream that not one of them believed in."

"Because of corruption," she said.

"Because of stupidity."

The red eye glowed. "You complained?"

"I noticed."

"Keep talking. We're almost there."

Did she think he would pass out now? He'd been resurrected. Brought up from the blackness, swimming toward the light the television psychics jabbered about. He was not about to fall back in. "I tried to get the Oil and Gas Ministry interested in making changes at Samotlor. They told me to do my job. I said I was. They disagreed."

"You were fired?"

"I was encouraged to discover new opportunities."

"So you ran for mayor?"

"The main party of reform was looking for someone. Arkady Volsky was in charge. He's still the presidential representative for Irkutsk. Don't ask me how he does it."

"He's a friend?"

Nowek nodded. "He used to be a leader in the coal miner's union."

"That only means he used to be honest," Chuchin noted.

"He asked me to run. I agreed. I thought maybe here in Markovo, in this one small place I could make . . ." His hands trembled. She took them and held them together. "I thought I might make a difference. I would keep . . . another Samotlor from happening."

"In other words," Chuchin piped in, "when it came to the impossible, his father was absolutely right."

How were her hands so warm? They felt hot. "Tons, tons, and more tons. That's all that counted. How many tons of oil you pumped. You know, up there they break off chunks of frozen oil to burn in the winter. There are lakes of spilled crude. Deep enough to float a ship. Nobody cared. I . . . I refused to let it happen here."

"That sounds familiar."

He remembered what she had said about the tiger preserve down near Vladivostok; how she would never let them get away with doing here at Tunguska what they had done to her tigers down there. "I agreed to stand for election. I won. Not that it's meant so much."

She let her grip on his hands loosen. "How did she die?"

"She?" But his eyes betrayed him.

"Nina. Your wife."

Nowek's legs trembled. So did his voice. There were limits. "It's all in the past. That American. The black man. You know he wasn't poaching. It can't be that."

"Then what was he doing? Why would he be there?"

"I don't know yet," said Nowek. "But AmerRus does. Gromov does. And so does Major Kaznin."

"They won't talk," said Chuchin.

"There's someone else who might." He said to Chuchin, "You have another Yava?"

"You? I thought you said smoking was slow suicide."

He was on a keen edge, an after thrill from near death. And from her sitting so close to him. Which was more powerful? Chuchin handed him one, got it lit. The foul smoke was familiar, reassuring. Only a live man can kill himself.

"I'm getting used to the idea."

The stove had burned its load of birch to ash. With the electric panels turned down, the house had taken on the chill of the wet, cold night. It was spring, but it was still Siberia. With the windows broken, no stove could compete with the cold. You could see your breath.

Chuchin spun the thermostat up full when they walked in. The ceiling panels crackled with energy.

Nowek's father was huddled in a chair right next to the iron stove, his heavy overcoat draped around his shoulders, asleep. The violin was by one of his feet, the empty bottle by the other, all four tins of sturgeon roe opened, emptied.

Nowek opened the flue, then pried up the steel lid. He tossed in the cigarette and dropped a log of paper birch onto the last coals. The wood smoked, crackled, and popped, then began to burn in earnest. He put the lid back in place. Overhead, the electric panel radiated softly.

Tadeus shifted in his chair.

"I'll get it going," said Chuchin. "You should change."

Anna watched from the doorway to the kitchen. She had the rucksack with her. She carried her soaked vest and jacket.

"You brought dry clothes?"

"There wasn't time."

"Come on," he said to her as he walked to the stairs at the back of the room. An icy flow of air cascaded down the steps.

Clothes had been pulled out of the upstairs rooms and dragged down the stairs. One of Galena's T-shirts lay with a muddy boot print on it; a shimmery dress crumpled like tissue paper into a ball. A single high heel shoe broken flat. Nowek picked them up as he went.

There was one nightlight at the far end of the hallway. The door to Galena's room was open. A cold draft billowed out. He tossed her things in and shut the door.

At the end of the hall was his own bedroom.

"I'm sorry they did this," said Anna. "You're right. I should try to get out of the country. I don't know how but staying here isn't fair to you."

"You saved my life. The least I can do is offer you dry clothes."

"I don't mean that. You don't have to stay involved."

He thought of Ryzkhov, his two men. The way everything else, everything outside seemed to be falling apart. "Too late." He stopped at his own door and turned. The nightlight was behind him, darkening the hallway. A brighter light came up the stairs from the kitchen. She was a silhouette, and she was no longer Dr. Anna Vereskaya, saver of tiger cubs, instigator of murders. She was the face in its halo of diamonds, warm lips, a kiss of life itself. "Anyway, my father was right," he said to her. "I'm drawn to the impossible."

"I like him."

"Wait. You'll change your mind."

The bedroom was pulled apart and its window broken. A dank breeze filled the heavy drapes and shifted them uneasily. The overhead heating panel was like a third person in the room. An invisible source of warmth. Nowek could feel it as he walked in to draw the drapes closed.

Clothes, books, shoes, everything orderly in Nowek's life was strewn across the floor, across the bed, the chair. Even the pillows had been razored. They spilled foam entrails across the rumpled sheets. The dresser was toppled, the drawers pulled out and overturned.

He picked up a pair of heavy felt pants, a shirt, a wool sweater as he walked to the far closet. He was shivering again, but not from the cold.

"It's like Varykino in here."

He looked back at her as she stood in the door. "Where?"

"Varykino. The house where Zhivago went with Lara? It was cold like this when they went there to hide. Cold and filled with ice and snow. It was the scene I most remember. The icicles hanging from the chandelier. You remember?"

"Sadly, my chandeliers are all out for repair." He looked up at the heater. "And there aren't any icicles. Not yet."

"My mother wanted me to memorize Pasternak's poetry, but I couldn't keep it all in my head. He was her hero."

"His poems were better than his books."

"Do you remember the scene in that house?"

He did. And more. He closed his eyes.

"It snowed and snowed, the whole world over, snow swept the world from end to end. A candle burned upon a table, upon a table, one candle burned."

"What was that from?"

"*Zhivago*. He's sitting at his old writing table. It was one of the poems he wrote at Varykino while the wolves howled at the moon. You don't recognize it?"

"It wasn't in the movie," she said uncertainly.

"You never read the book?"

She shook her head.

"Now I believe you really are American." He shoved away a pile of clothes and found a wooden locker at the back of the closet. Amazingly it had been overlooked by Yufa's men. When he opened it, the sweet smell of verbena, of camphor, came out. He lifted one of Nina's sweaters out of the darkness, into the light. "I think this will fit." He knew it would. He hunted for a pair of Nina's pants.

"Three years." She very carefully put the rucksack down. A small puddle of water had collected between her feet, falling from her soaked jeans. "Why did you keep her things?"

He stopped and stared down into the closet. "It was a plane crash. There was no body. Nothing." He looked back at Anna. "For the first year I could imagine her showing up, imagine that it was all a mistake. She'd taken a different flight, she was alive, back home. She'd need her clothes. The second year I stopped imagining. Now I keep her things because it's all I have to keep. Except for Galena."

Anna stood with her arms at her sides. "I'm sorry I didn't tell you about her up at Tunguska. I would have. Really. I'm sorry."

"You know, my father says the violin is the most expressive instrument. The one nearest the human voice when it comes to emotion. Only an operatic soprano surpasses it."

"I'd like to hear you play sometime."

"Here. This should do." The thick cardigan sweater had once been a deep red but had aged and faded now to an eggplant purple. He found some of Nina's pants, the wool steeped in the invisible liquor of memory. A belt with its crease where Nina had always fastened it. Then, at the bottom, the camel-wool skater's cap.

He held them tight, fingering the wool, the felt. A sacrifice to memory. To life. He tried to feel the woman in the fabric, but it was empty as a discarded shell. A deep breath. "You should dress warmly tonight. The air smells like snow," he said. "It could be rain. This time of year it's hard to predict."

She stood directly under the radiating panel.

"Do you remember the rest of it?"

The walls seemed suddenly closer. The ceiling lower. There was a pressure in the air, in his ears. "The rest?"

"The poem."

He looked away, then back. There was a flash, like sunlight caught inside ice, when her gaze crossed his. "We *had* to memorize it. Pasternak was an approved poet by then, an example. A hero with a Nobel Prize hanging from his neck, though they wouldn't let him go and accept it. They . . ."

"I don't care about that. How does it go?"

"How old are you?"

"I'll be twenty-eight next month. Why?"

"I wanted to know." He paused, remembering how he would say the words of *Winter Night* to Nina as a kind of a lullabye, their bodies close, sharing heat, the blankets drawn to their necks, as a storm shut down everything in the world. How the horizons themselves would gather close around them, until beyond the room, beyond the feel, the sight, the sense of each other, the world simply ceased. Don't call it a poem. Call it an incantation. An invocation. A spell.

The heater clicked again. The lights dimmed.

"Distorted shadows on the lighted ceiling, shadows of crossed arms, crossed legs, crossed destinies. A candle shed wax tears upon a dress. All things vanished outside in snow while a candle burned upon the table; upon the table a candle burned."

He looked at her. "I don't remember the rest."
"That's a lie."
What else could she tell?

"The snow will bury roads, will cover roofs deeply. If I step out to stretch my legs, I will see you from the door. Snow melts from your lashes. Sadness is in your eyes. It's as if your image were being etched forever with a strong acid onto my heart.

A corner draft fluttered the flame and the white fever of temptation upswept its angel wings to cast a cruciform shadow. It snowed throughout the month of February while a candle burned upon the table; upon the table, a candle burned."

Water was all around her boots. "You're as wet as I am but you don't seem to notice," he said. "It's the Siberian in you. You'd better change into these." He held out Nina's clothes.

She pulled the wet turtleneck over her head and stood there beneath the heater panel. Her hands went out to him.

Her bra was a delicate tracery of fabric, the sort of finery that Nina would have traveled in to Irkutsk, waited in line for a day to have the chance to own. Anna's breasts were higher than Nina's, higher and heavier. The cold had hardened her nipples. Like a violin, her waist was narrow, her hips gently flared. A red flush extended down her neck. A spell. An incantation. An invitation. No.

Yes.

Two steps. One. Nowek pulled her tight to his chest, Nina's clothes trapped between them. Her arms were cold. His head was hot with memory. She turned her face up to him. "I never actually saved a person before."

"Just tigers?"

"I didn't know if it would work. I didn't really know what I was doing."

"Maybe I wasn't so dead."

"You don't know how you looked."

He said, "There was a dream I had. In the water. Back on the street. We were skating."

"Where?"

"A lake. The ice was dangerous. Too thin. But if she could do it, I could follow."

"It wasn't me with you."

"I know."

"Did you follow her?"

"But I came back." Here was Chandrasekhar's Limit; the ghostly shell surrounding a black hole. Come too close, fall through and nothing, no force in the universe, can pull you back. Not Tunguska. Here. This woman. Now. He bent down and kissed her.

There was a moment of resistance. Like stepping through a thin skin of ice to deep waters. Warm lips, warmer tongue. Sight and scent, the words of the poem circling, spinning through him like snowflakes flying outside a frosted window.

And then, a breath. Tiny, just the hint of air moving from her mouth to his, then more. He pulled back. "What . . ."

"Sssh."

He reached for her waist. Her jeans were icy wet. They kissed again, longer, deeper than the first. She breathed in through her nose, then slowly exhaled through Nowek's lungs. A delicious, warm flow from deep inside her. It made him dizzy with implication. He drew a breath and sent it back.

Was anything more intimate? Air from deep inside her, deep inside him. A bubble trapped between them like Nina's clothes. He was losing himself, the blood thundered in his temples. How easy it would be. So very easy to let the world spin off, to forget Ryzkhov, to let the faces of his two militia blur. And Galena. Everything. It would be so easy. So impossible. He pulled away.

"What is it?" she asked, frightened.

"I'd better wait for you downstairs."

There was a puddle of water on the floor at their feet, as though they had both half melted. She picked up Nina's clothes.

He held his breath as he walked by her, then gently shut the door.

Chuchin waited downstairs while Tadeus quietly snored. The stove crackled and shimmered with heat. He looked beyond Nowek. "Where is she?"

"Changing."

"Into who?"

"Funny." Nowek stripped off his sodden jacket, the shirt that stuck to his skin, the dripping pants. A black bruise had already blossomed on his side, just below the ribs. He stood close to the stove, letting his naked skin soak up the waves of heat that spilled from its iron sides.

The hairs on his legs crinkled as they dried. He held his palms over the stove and rubbed. He was feeling almost human. And almost too much.

Nowek pulled on the dry pants. "We'll have to find fuel someplace," he said. The last shake subsided as he buttoned the wool shirt. With the sweater on and standing so close to the stove, he actually felt warm again. Alive. But not so alive as he'd been upstairs. Well, his father had said it: he was drawn to the impossible.

"Where are we going? Who will you get to talk now?"

"In Siberia there are few roads," said Nowek. "Only directions." He reached down and put the violin back in its case.

"Which direction are we going now, Mr. Mayor?"

His head snapped up. "Forward."

He walked to the telephone and picked up the receiver. He dialed Arkady Volsky's home number down in Irkutsk. It clicked.

A rough, gravelly voice came on. The presidential representative said, *"Ya sluchayu."* I'm listening.

"It's Nowek."

"Grisha! I've been trying to find you all night. Your phone is out of order. Did you know?"

"It's working now. Listen. You were looking for a real scandal up at Tunguska? I may have something."

"I have something for you, too."

Nowek wasn't listening. "The Americans came to produce oil. There's one problem. They aren't producing much and they aren't looking for it either."

"How do you know?"

"I went to Tunguska this morning. Everything is shut down up there. There's plenty of wet gas flowing, but they're using it to power their equipment and burning off the rest. As for oil, it's just a trickle. But there's more. I have a map of their leases. Ryzkhov was their *makler*." An arranger. "I think it got him killed."

"Why?"

"The properties he arranged to lease have nothing to do with oil. One of them is an old camp, Arkasha. There are four others. All in places that couldn't possibly have oil. The geology is exactly wrong."

There was a silence, then, "Why would AmerRus do that?"

"I don't know yet. They're making money from it, though. And so is the state. That I *do* know."

"The state is Gromov. What could that bastard be up to?"

"You tell me. I'm no investigator. I just know how to make trouble, remember?"

He could hear Volsky's breath begin to accelerate. "If Gromov is doing something extralegal up there then maybe we can slam the door on his prick. Gromov. The governor. Throw them out of office once and for all. Moscow would back us one hundred percent."

"Name one thing in Russia that's *not* extralegal. Anyway, politics are your concern. I have a simpler worry. My daughter's at Tunguska."

"Galena? Now? What is she doing there?"

"I need your clout on this, Arkasha. Not to mention your helicopter. I want you to order a raid. Even if I'm wrong about AMR, there's still a law against kidnapping children in this country. I want—"

"Stop. I know you have a personal stake in this but we need to take small steps before we run. I need to think. What the devil would AMR want up there besides oil? There's nothing there worth stealing."

"Except space. Maybe Gromov needs a place to hide inconvenient people and AmerRus lets him."

"If that were true you'd be the first to go and I would be the the second."

Volsky was right, of course. "All I know is Galena's in danger. I'll go bring her back myself if I have to."

"From Tunguska? I wouldn't. Not in your state of mind. Listen. I looked into your friend Kaznin. Did you know he was involved in some nasty business with covering up mass graves a few years back?"

"He didn't cover them. He netted bodies from the river. That's why they call him the Fisherman. I mean it, Arkasha. I'll bring her home myself. Will you help me or not?"

"The best help I can give you is to remain calm and let me speak. Kaznin's file has his medical records . . ."

"Believe me, he's healthy. Kaznin flew up to Tunguska to make an arrest on the Ryzkhov murders."

"Who is it?"

"Dr. Anna Vereskaya. She's an academic involved with counting tigers at Tunguska. She knew Ryzkhov," he said. "She was with him in his flat the night he was killed, too. But there's a wrinkle. A big one. She's American."

There was a pause. "You say her name is Vereskaya?"

"Her parents were Russian. Ryzkhov was helping her get to the bottom of something that involves AmerRus. She thinks they're poaching tigers but they aren't. Or at least, it's not just that."

"Where is she now?"

"Here."

Volsky whistled. "What if they're right about her?"

"Then I have the suspect in custody. But they're not right. She didn't kill Ryzkhov. I think AMR did."

"Naturally you can prove it."

"Not yet, but I will. There are Americans running around up north without proper documents. Vereskaya had a kind of videotape that showed one of them. He was . . . he was lost in the taiga. She took the tape to Ryzkhov hoping he could help identify him. Then he's murdered. There's a connection."

"All right. This is progress. This illegal American, you've spoken to him?"

"He's dead."

"Dead?"

"He was killed by a tiger."

Another pause. "Grisha, have you been drinking?"

"Not nearly enough." He told Volsky about the chunk of Nepa gravel, the tin of rations, Nikki Malyshev, the ransacking of his own place, the destruction of Yuri's hangar. "Kaznin had a squad of troops with him. My driver said they looked like OSNAZ."

"There is no OSNAZ anymore."

"That's what I said. Have *you* ever heard of the Ministry? Is it some kind of private army the governor's established?"

A long silence roared out of the phone like the tallest wave of a set. It curled, fringed in white foam, toppled.

Finally, Volsky said, "Grigori Tadeovich, I know a lot of things. I know that your friend Kaznin has dirty hands." There was the rustle of papers. "I know when he was born, when he entered service. Even the kind of blood he has, which if you'd keep quiet for only a moment I'd tell you . . ."

"You're changing the subject. I want to know about this

Ministry. You know them. I can hear it in your voice. Who are they? Is it Prosecutor Gromov's private army?"

"Sometimes being stubborn helps. But not all the time."

"You asked me to make trouble. Who are they?"

Volsky sighed. "This business with your daughter has upset you."

"She's sixteen. What do you think?"

"I think you're too emotional," said Volsky. "Too close. Back away for a moment. Calm down and in the morning we can discuss it again. I'll look into the matter of these questionable leases. I'll speak with someone tonight. Keep the woman in custody. Whatever you do, stay clear of Tunguska."

"Arkasha, what is the Ministry doing up there? They're working with the Americans. What is it? Some sort of secret mining project? Is there uranium up there? Diamonds? Gold nuggets big as potatoes? What could be so valuable?"

"How long have we been friends?"

"Since the election. Before."

"You trust me?"

"Sure, but . . ."

"Then trust me now. Don't go up there like a hero to rescue anybody. Trust an old friend to tell you the truth."

"An old friend? I would have said good friend. Why won't you answer me directly about the Ministry?"

There was no pause. *"Tibye ni nuzhna znat,"* he said. "It's not necessary for you to know. Not yet."

In a great earthquake, the most profound distress comes from seeing everything reliable, everything known, suddenly thrown into doubt. A street, a building, a roof, a friend.

"Grisha? Where are you?"

"I'm going to get her back."

"Don't. Stay put. I'll send someone. I'll *come myself* if I have to, but . . ."

"You'll go to all that trouble to stop me, but you won't do anything to help? No thank you."

"Where will you be in an hour?"

The answer was obvious.

"Tibye ni nuzhna znat." Nowek put the phone back on the hook. Volsky. His old friend. He sensed her on the stairs. Sensed her. He could still feel her breath swirling in him. He picked up the phone again and dialed.

"Who are you calling now?" asked Chuchin. He looked worried.

"Someone I still can understand."

Chuchin looked at Anna and his mouth opened.

There was nothing so provocative in the way Anna Vereskaya presented herself. A drab, almost colorless pair of wool pants drawn tight with a cheap belt. A dark sweater buttoned up the front. It wasn't that.

It was as if he were looking at her for the very first time. Seeing her standing at the foot of the stairs, Nowek felt himself divide, and divide again like a microscopic view of a multiplying organism. Standing there dressed in Nina's clothes, Nina was gone. She was not coming back in a fantasy, in a hope. The mammalian diving response. It could work only so long before you had to surface for air.

The phone at Mercury Condom was answered quickly. Nowek forced his eyes away from her. "Put Semyon Yufa on."

"Who is this?"

"Tell him it's the mayor. He offered me a tour of Mercury Condom if I was interested."

"So what if he did?"

He looked up at Anna as he spoke. "Tell him I'm interested."

CHAPTER
20

"HE KNEW," said Nowek. "I could hear it in his voice. Damn him, but he knows about the Ministry." He gripped the rolled-up maps, Ryzkhov's "state secrets," and said, "When I told him about the maps, about AMR and illegal Americans running around, all he could think about was using it as a club to hit Gromov over the head with. He wouldn't do a thing to help me get Galena."

"How do you think he's still such a big shot?' said Chuchin. "He knows who he can piss on and who can piss on him. It's valuable information, Mr. Mayor. And anyway, you have no idea what AmerRus is doing."

"What I don't have is proof." Nowek rubbed the unshaved stubble on his cheek. "Volsky knows about it already. My friend. Can you believe it?"

"Easily," said Chuchin. "Where I went to school the first lesson is this: first the grub, then the morals."

He could feel her eyes, two warm circles on the back of his neck. Anna was talking to his father, too softly for him to hear. There was a momentary pause, he turned, and found her looking at him. His father was smiling indulgently.

Tadeus had his hand on her knee. She shook her head

slightly, signaling Nowek that she knew what the old goat was up to, that she could take care of herself.

Nowek thought of that moment back in his room with her in his arms. Galena gone. Two of his men murdered. Nikki Malyshev clubbed to death and his oldest political ally Arkady Volsky holding back on him. All of this and what does he think of? What does he feel, what does he most remember?

The smell of her hair. Like bread baking on a winter day. The way her breath filled him. Summoned him, made him alive again. Marx said religion was the opiate of the people, but religion was nothing next to Anna.

A low moon lit the eastern horizon; a flattened red crescent that broke away from the earth, floating up to poke a horn into a bank of scudding low clouds.

They took Tadeus back home and made sure he was safe before driving off. The town was silent under a lowering sky.

Nowek watched rows of darkened houses go by as they drove in the direction of the old Mercury Condom factory.

"What makes you think Yufa will say anything?" said Chuchin.

"It's like a good oil prospect," said Nowek. "You look at the underlying structure, you examine the records, you pile evidence on evidence, and then you make a wild guess. Anyway, you said it yourself. We live in *Vorovskoi Mir*."

"Thieves World?" said Anna.

"Absolutely. If you need to find something out in such a place, you don't ask the mayor. Forget the government. You ask a thief. In there," he said to Chuchin.

Chuchin backed them into a narrow alley, barely wide enough for the Land Cruiser to fit. The brick walls to either side were high enough to keep the snow on the ground from melting, and the car slipped and skidded. Across the street was the main gate of the Mercury Condom factory.

Mercury Condom was at the eastern edge of Markovo's bleak industrial district. Gray drifts of asbestos fibers blew over from the waste heaps of the nearby metallurgical mill. The factory itself was a small complex of low buildings and chemical storage tanks enclosed by a perimeter wall.

Yufa had taken over the three-story main administration building at the center for the same reason generals prefer hills. A small thicket of radio antennas sprouted from its roof, illuminated by the bright red MERCURY CONDOM sign.

By day, the plant could be mistaken for a medieval village, the administration building the local church, the sacred center of gravity. By night, with the red sign shedding a bloody light over everything, Mercury Condom resembled an abandoned slaughterhouse, minus the charm.

Nowek looked across the narrow street. The factory gate was open, with frozen-over tire tracks converging, threading the needle's eye beside the empty guard kiosk. The booth was empty, the glass opaque with dirt. The Land Cruiser's engine sucked another bubble of air and stumbled.

Chuchin killed the motor. There was no telling how much fuel was left, but there was surely none to waste. The silver Nagant revolver was on his lap.

There were no working streetlights, but the red moon illuminated the factory's perimeter wall. There was a big billboard on the wall, kept in perfect shape. On it a loving couple, hand in hand, marched across a field of flowers to a bright and confident future. MERCURY CONDOMS it said, then below, THE BEST PROTECTION AGAINST INFLATION!

Anna said, "You aren't going in there by yourself."

"Actually, I am." He faced her and felt the jump, the pull once again. An elixir. An invitation. Yes? No. "Chuchin will keep an eye on you."

"Mayor," said Chuchin. He'd offered the Nagant.

"Yufa has more. Besides, what do I know about guns?" Nowek swung out of the Land Cruiser and quietly closed the door.

Nowek felt revived in his dry, scratchy wools. Invigorated. Not only by being alive, though there were distinct advantages to that. No. By something more. Something new.

He took a deep breath. Years after the factory closed and Semyon Yufa took over, Nowek could still smell latex rubber.

Nowek made his way inside the walled compound. Beyond the gate was an open courtyard, and in the middle of the space was a broad square of snow delineated by four red cones.

Cars were parked in front of the main building. A dark BMW, Yufa's. Several smaller Japanese sedans and, at the end, Kaznin's trim white Volvo.

Two larger vehicles were backed against a loading dock; a large cargo truck and beside it, the van. Both were familiar. One he knew from Malyshev's alley; the other belonged to Yuri.

The bright red MERCURY CONDOM sign atop the administration building sizzled, blotting out all but the brightest stars. The sky was heavy with vapor. He tasted the air. Snow. Definitely snow. Soon.

Lights were on in the main building. Nowek could see shadows moving behind the curtains.

The condom production sheds surrounded the courtyard on three sides. They were low and crude as chicken coops. He was halfway across the open yard, near one of the red cones, when he felt the first vibrations tickle his ear. A seismic trembling in the atmosphere. Nowek stopped, hunting for the source.

A contrabass note from heaven. A celestial string vibrating slow and deep. It became stronger, more resonant. From beneath it grew a screaming undertone.

A helicopter.

A brilliant finger of pure white light stabbed down. It lit the entire courtyard. It threw his black shadow onto the snow. He held up a hand. The hot light poured through his fingers like boiled milk.

Nowek started to run, slipped, fell, got up, and ran again for the loading dock. He made it as the first wind struck. He squeezed between the van and the truck. The beat of the rotors and the screech of jet engines built to a crescendo loud enough to vibrate inside his chest.

The bleaching light turned the snow violet. The helicopter

came to a hover. Trash scurried. The machine began to descend. A wheel. Another wheel. A fat belly, a cabin hung beneath steel blades with portholes glowing like the yellow eyes of a sea monster hauled up from the abyss.

It was a Mil-8, a troop-carrier built to haul thirty soldiers, painted the customary mustard brown. It took on a tinge of red from the MERCURY CONDOM sign. Nowek stayed in the shadows and watched.

The helicopter's wheels touched down and sank into soft snow. The rotor blades kept spinning. The jet engines screamed. The olive drab canvas covering the rear of the truck snapped in a wild drumbeat of wind. The hairs on Nowek's arms stood at attention when he saw the insignia painted on the machine's tail.

The Mil had once belonged to the Interior Ministry. Somewhere along the line it had been requisitioned by another agency; one that had taken the expedient of daubing out the word INTERIOR with brown paint, leaving MINISTRY behind.

A private army. The Ministry. Kaznin, his boss Prosecutor Gromov. And Semyon Yufa. An alliance that combined the very worst of Russia's mistakes: the secret police, its corrupt *vlasti,* its thieves. Not that they were so very different.

The engine sound changed, the rotors went flat. The helicopter blocked his view of the building and its hatch was on the side away from where Nowek stood.

He saw movement in the lit portholes. A moment later the rotors spooled up, coning as they lifted the Mil into the air. The helicopter climbed, then the nose dipped. The landing light snapped off and the machine thundered north. In a few moments, it was just a lingering tremble.

Nowek eased himself up onto the truck's running board. The courtyard was deserted. The helicopter could have all been a dream except for the ruts pressed into the snow, the cones knocked flat.

Nowek didn't bother with the van. He'd last seen Yuri driving toward town out at the airport, the back stuffed with frozen slabs of *chir* salmon and boxes of reindeer antlers. The one with the big wrench and the half-shaved head, Plet, had been at the wheel. What were they doing here? Conducting business with Yufa. Who else was there in Markovo to do business with?

He dropped off the running board and walked back to the loading dock. Old tires cushioned the rear where it snugged up to the wall. His shoulder protested when he pulled himself up.

There were three bays, with three steel curtain doors leading into the delivery shed. They were pulled down tight to the deck and secured with locks. Two were rusted solid. They might have been that way for years. Surely there'd been no legitimate deliveries or arrivals since the plant shut down. But there were footprints in the snow and even more interesting, dark wet splotches on the concrete. They led to the third rolling door, and this one Nowek found unlocked.

It rose with an alarming rattle. He stopped. A strip of yellow light spilled out across his feet. And with it came a peculiar sound.

How different the world seems to a dog, all smells and invisible trails. An owl can distinguish the slightest movement on the dark ground from a hundred meters up. Even a shark, not the smartest animal, can isolate a single drop of blood from a cubic kilometer of ocean.

It was the same for a musician: the world possessed sounds that ordinary people didn't hear.

This was a noise like the chuffing of a poorly tuned engine running loaded, uphill. Slower than a diesel. An ancient steam locomotive pulling out of a station.

Whuh! Whuh! Whuh!

The puffing grew louder and faster, and ended in a grunt. Nowek slipped under the door. As he rolled inside, the grunt became a scream.

"Where are they?" A new voice shouted from another room. New, but also familiar. "I asked a question, *suk*. You know."

Suk? It was slang for traitor. Literally, "bitch." Nowek let his eyes adjust to the room.

The loading shed was unheated and filled with crates, cartons, and along one wall a stack of aluminum beer kegs. The cartons wore a large red star and the name of a processing plant west of the Urals. They were familiar. He'd seen one recently, and he remembered where: in the back of Yuri's airplane. He went to them and pulled up the flap.

It opened easily. The cardboard was half rotted with age and dampness. It came apart in his fingers. Inside, stacked like rows of soldiers ready for inspection, were hundreds of tins of army rations. Some were rusted at the edges. A few had leaked some undefinable liquid onto the others, and that liquid had hardened to a gray crust. Many looked almost normal, if decades-old cottage cheese and prunes could be considered normal.

DON'T EAT AFTER 1991. Thousands of tins. Who were they for?

He let the wet cardboard flap fall closed.

Nowek heard a faint hiss like a leaking balloon. He sniffed. A musician knew his sounds; an oil geologist knew his gasses. Propane? No. Sweeter than that. Acetylene.

"You cold? Wait. I'll turn up the heat."

The hiss grew louder. Another bellow.

He moved toward the door to the next room. It was ajar.

The rhythmic panting began again. He'd heard that sort of sound before from weight lifters preparing for a press. Nowek's hand found an iron hook on a dusty workbench; the sort workmen used to grapple wooden crates. It had a leather wrist strap, a heavy iron handle that sprouted a shaft and a wicked curved point, sharp and bright. Like the weapon they'd used on poor Trotsky. Its weight was comforting. He came to the door, leaned close, and peered through it.

Three more aluminum kegs were stacked one atop the other on the near wall. Beer was a valuable commodity; like tiger bone, like empty space far from anyone's attention, the harder it was to find, the more it was worth.

But on the other side of the room was a man. Two men. One dressed in a dark jacket with his back to Nowek, the other with his arms over his head, belted together.

He was naked to the waist, arms fastened together high enough to keep him barely on his toes like some ballet grotesque. Half his skull was bald, the other half dense with black hair.

It was Plet.

The one with the dark jacket had a lit welding torch in his hands. The brilliant blue fire sent his own distorted shadow flickering across the walls, across the kegs, the ceiling, his dancing image an animated cave painting.

The burner was fed from a big tank on wheels. There was propane enough to last a week. Plet's outsized pipe wrench stood in the corner. Even from here Nowek could see the charred skin. The shadows shifted, elongated as the burner head moved in. The hiss of the gas resolved into a wet sizzle, a puff of smoke. Plet erupted into another wild shout.

When he looked up, he caught sight of Nowek. His eyes opened wide like a shipwrecked man sighting land. It was salvation, if only you could make yourself believe.

The pit bull with the torch sensed him. "Vanya?" He started to turn.

The sharp V of his hairline. Razored. Nowek knew him all right. They'd met just outside Nikki Malyshev's alley this very evening. The one who'd pushed him down into those icy waters.

Nowek rammed the door open. It hit the kegs with a full, low thud. The pit bull turned the blue jet at Nowek. His mouth opened. Nowek swung the hook by the leather wrist strap. It caught the black hose and yanked it free. The burner hissed to the concrete and writhed like a cut snake. Nowek swung again.

The pit bull ducked back, crouched low, then rose, reaching into his jacket. The small pistol was compact and angular. It reflected no light. It was aimed at Nowek's face.

Nowek raised the hook.

The man stepped back to fire. As his finger curled around the trigger, Plet lifted his body off the floor, using the arm restraints for leverage, and pulled the guard back and into a leg lock. He leaned forward and clamped his teeth around the pit bull's ear, then yanked back.

A brilliant white flash, a sharp crack, a scream, and a metal clang; a jet of cool liquid flowing out under pressure from the middle keg.

Smell it. Not beer at all. But kerosene.

The guard bellowed as blood gushed from his torn ear. He twisted, trying to escape. Plet pulled him back again and slammed him into the wall. He hiked his legs up, waist to neck, and swung him again into the cement. The gun dropped into an oily puddle. Again. There was the wet thud of bone striking cement. He sagged, leaving a red trail.

The air reeked with raw fuel.

The propane jet hissed. The air was a noxious blend of gunsmoke, burned hair, charred skin, and petrochemicals.

Nowek dove for the valve on the tank and twisted. The hiss subsided, then went out with a soft pop.

A blue ring of fire still glowed around the head of the extinguished torch, fed on kerosene vapors. As more fuel splashed onto the floor from the leaking keg, there was more vapor. The ring expanded. The puddle grew wider, the blue ring brighter. It glowed softly, without malice, without fury. Patient in the knowledge of what would come. Nowek tried to stomp it out.

His shoe caught fire.

Plet pulled against the ropes that held him and said, "Get his knife! *Bistra!*"

Nowek beat out the fire on his shoes.

"Get his knife!"

Nowek reached and went through the fallen guard's jacket. Holster. Wallet. Keys.

"Hurry!"

The man's clothes were sopping with fuel. Nowek's hand closed around an oily shank.

Nowek slashed at the rope suspending Plet's body. Up close he could see that the marks on Plet were not all from the torch. His chest was a composition of tattoos; a Virgin Mary cradling a baby rose up the center, angels at each side knelt in profile, their huge eyes made from Plet's nipples. Down his forearms to

his fingers were daggers, teardrops, and cryptic letters and numbers.

The gas torch had burned away the Virgin's face and one
angel's eye.

The last strand snapped and Plet collapsed against Nowek.

The blue ring of fire was fringed with orange. Growing.
Little gusts of sonic air rose and curled around them, half oily
vapor, half smoke. Nowek could feel the heat.

He put Plet's arm over his shoulder and led him into the
adjacent storeroom. He parked him against a table. "Why were
they doing it?"

"You. They wanted you."

Nowek went back in for the guard.

"Where are you going?"

Nowek stood in the doorway. The blue ring and the black,
oily puddle seemed to crawl to one another, amoebalike.

They merged.

There was a puff, a flash of yellow, and a boiling cloud of live
fire that drove Nowek back. The flames parted and he saw the
inert body of the guard, then it too was veiled in a curtain of
heat that suddenly grew, driving Nowek farther out the door.

"Leave him!"

Nowek went back in.

The fire had a voice. A hungry, bawling roar of youth, of
vigor. A heat detector triggered a spray of water from the ceiling. At first it was a trickle. It grew. First one spray head, then
another, then a row.

Nowek waited until the flames shifted to one side and dove
through.

He was surrounded by light. There was no air. His skin
prickled.

The guard was moving now, half sitting, trying to stand,
falling. His skin rippled like the surface of the sea in waves,
rising, falling, dissolving into a suit of pure light. Nowek yelled,
but his voice was drowned beneath the hiss and crackle. The
guard held up one arm. Fire dripped from it in hard white
marbles. Nowek moved toward him.

There was a chuff. A flash. Nowek was lifted off the ground and shot backward, slammed against the door, spinning and sprawling. He rolled against a wooden worktable as a ball of greasy smoke boiled out of the open mouth of the furnace and spread along the ceiling.

He got up, swaying in the heat. He looked around the storeroom.

Plet was gone.

Another gust of heat knocked him back. He retreated toward the loading dock doors. There was a shout. A voice from somewhere nearby. An answer. The sprinklers rose to a steady hiss. Nowek backed up against the loading dock door. Outside the night was cool and the air clean as new glass.

Inside was hell.

More sprinklers joined in the battle. A second row. A third.

Nowek eased under the metal door. He could feel the cool night on his skin. A hand, an arm. His own body. He stood up.

"Borya?"

Two men in dark leather looked up from the driveway below. They looked at one another, then back at Nowek.

"Who the fuck are you?"

One he recognized from the day at Kaznin's office. They were more of Yufa's *byki,* and before Nowek could answer, they both pulled out guns from beneath their jackets and pointed them at his eyes.

CHAPTER
21

LeRoy Rogers was drifting, except that his arms and legs were chained. Weightless above some kind of dirt floor, a single white bulb burning overhead. Chained, except he couldn't feel any shackles. Like a spirit, like he was dead. He couldn't move, couldn't even roll his eyes. They were dry as dirt, like they'd been left open for days.

A voice. He tried to turn his head. No way. He tried to listen. Nothing made sense. Nothing at all. His body ached like he'd been beaten. Must have hit him on the head. Shit, he didn't say nothing bad. One minute he was signing up for that program, the camp. Where the fuck was he? Why'd they up and hit him for? A man, even an inmate of Travis Maximum Facility, had a right to know.

The voice again, and then a face. It blotted out the bulb. Slit eyes, leathery skin. A hat made of greasy fur with a star. Who was he supposed to be? Some kinda guard.

The face disappeared and a metal tube took its place. A tube with a forked end, and a wire. And light, blue, dazzling, dancing light at its tip. Hot light. The guard shoved the wires up next to his cold pale skin.

A snap. An electric waterfall big as a building, an elevator running him up so high, so fast, then throwing him into space. LeRoy's body went into convulsions that left him shuddering uncontrollably. Blue skin flushed pink. One leg was bent underneath his body. He could barely feel it.

LeRoy remembered a dusty church, a shouting preacher. Swaying women overdressed for the heat, swooning in it. He'd been a child then, a frightened little kid. Then the words came back. Jesus, oh, sweet Jesus, forgive me for I have sinned!

The shaking worked its way down his body, his thighs, his legs, his feet. He rolled his eye down.

He was naked as a baby. Not even his shoes.

"You get up!" The same voice as before.

The tube was back, dazzling, snapping blue fire.

"You get up!"

He tried to. Honest to Jesus, he tried to. Almost did, too. Got a leg out from under, an arm in motion. But not fast enough.

Screeeeeeesnap!! Overload. This time LeRoy *was* flying. He landed against something soft. He shuddered as he stared up at the naked lightbulb. He felt the cold for the first time. He collapsed against the softness. A pillow. Get some rest. Just give me a—

"You get up! Get dressed! Up!"

LeRoy managed to prop himself on an elbow and turn his head to face the slit-eyed fuck with the bang stick. He was thirsty. His eye kept wandering around the room.

The softness, his pillow, was a man. No. Not one man. There was a *pile* of people slumped on the floor, dead asleep, or maybe just dead. Blacks mostly, though that wasn't a surprise. LeRoy had spent so much time inside he was surprised when he saw his own white skin in the showers.

And the others. Three men with rifles plus the one with the bang stick. There was a pile of dirty brown clothes by their feet. Bang Stick was moving. He was coming for him again.

"No. Don't. I can't . . ." LeRoy's eyes pleaded even as he knew he wasn't speaking loud enough.

The cattle prod smoked as the charge sent him flying, jerking, coughing for breath. He urinated.

The ones with the rifles laughed.

"You get dressed! Now!"

LeRoy crawled at the pile of clothes. He could smell them before he could touch them. He grabbed the cloth and a crust of caked dirt cracked off. And bugs. Movin' around like watchin' the exercise yard from up high.

He draped the rough, stinking shirt over his shoulders like he was dressing somebody else, somebody dead. What if all the rest, those men on the floor, what if they were dead? What if this was hell? The pants were beyond trying. He couldn't make his legs move that good. He saw a pair of some kind of boots. They were stiff felt, not leather, and they smelled even worse than the shirt.

"Up! Get up!"

He got to his knees in time for one of the other guards to swing the butt of his rifle against his chest.

He toppled back like a suit of empty clothes. He hit the dirt hard.

He felt someone run some cloth up over one foot, then the other.

They worked the pants up over his penis. There was some quiet conversation among them, then a command. Silence.

"You get up now!"

He staggered upright, then stood, weak as a colt, swaying side to side. They had the pants on him. Bang Stick pointed at the boots.

"Valenki!"

Was it something he was supposed to do? To know? His name?

"Valenki! Valenki!" Bang Stick was screaming his slit-eyed head off and LeRoy knew that was not a good sign.

LeRoy put on the boots. They were rotted out from sweat. But they fit, sort of. They wouldn't be no good for running. Where the fuck were his shoes? He had them on a minute ago in the director's . . . then he saw them.

They were on Bang Stick's feet.

"You come! Come!"

The three guards made an opening. Bang Stick moved in but

LeRoy had the drill now. He moved. One leg after another, stiffly, headed for the opening, the door. No cuffs on him anywhere. Open air, cold, coming through. He walked outside and faced a field of brilliant, floodlit white. He stepped out into it.

Sand? Was this the fucking desert? He looked down. His boots. His whatchamacallit. Valenki? They were already soaked through. It was nighttime. He took a breath and smelled cold, smelled trees. Smelled men, too. Not sand.

Jesus. Not sand. Not dirt.

It was snow.

Nowek's green shirt was measled with burn marks and holes. His face was smudged, his bare skin slick with raw kerosene.

"Keep going," said the guard behind him.

"Where?"

"Don't worry. You'll see."

The lobby ended in a stairway, the stairway led up to a long corridor. It was softly lit. There was a beautiful oriental runner stretching its length. The doors were wood, carefully polished and unmarked. The fire extinguishers were missing from their nooks, the glass doors left open by Yufa's men. The smoke had risen, collecting up here on the third floor. Each breath sliced your throat, like swallowing fish bones. Nowek tried short breaths. Smaller bones.

"In there. He's waiting." One of Yufa's *byki* poked him with the barrel of his gun. The second guard reached ahead of Nowek and opened the final door at the end of the corridor. A flow of air was sucked into Semyon Yufa's office. Nowek followed it.

Inside Yuri Durashenko sat on a small, three-legged stool. A guard stood behind him with a machine pistol.

"So, Mayor," said Yufa. "I've been wasting time with your friend here trying to find you and your girlfriend. Then who shows up? You. Life is funny sometimes, don't you think?"

"No, but comedy is a personal thing."

Despite everything, Yuri laughed.

Yufa glanced at the guard standing behind Yuri. The guard swung the machine pistol like a club. Yuri went sprawling.

Yufa said, "If he sneezes, shoot him." Then, to Nowek, "You see what comes from having no respect? Sit down."

A steel poke and Nowek found a stool next to Yuri.

Yufa looked every bit the *vor,* the *mafiya* lord, here in his office. He sat behind an empty desk padded in green baize. A samovar steamed behind him, sending wisps of vapor into the air. The smoke from the fire was thinner in here, sucked out through the open window. The curtains filled and bellied out; Mercury Condom setting out on a voyage under full sail. He had a decorative letter opener on his desk; a sword embedded in a fist-sized chunk of rose quartz, a miniature Excalibur. At the very center of the room, set apart like a sacred object, there was Yufa's famous roulette wheel, a massive marble disk balanced on a carved pedestal.

"Where's Borya?" asked Yufa.

One beat, two. A look exchanged, but no answer.

"What, nobody saw him?"

"He was supposed to be in the shed."

"I didn't ask where he was supposed to be." Yufa swore, picked up a handheld radio, and spoke into it. He slammed the radio back onto the desk. "You," he said, motioning for one of the guards. "Go help the others. That little bastard better be somewhere."

He was, thought Nowek. Borya. Boris, more formally. The one with the sharp, shaved hairline. The one who'd beaten Nikki Malyshev to death with a pipe. The one who had taken his own house apart. The one who had stepped on his chest and pressed Nowek down into the dark, cold water, pressed him nearly into another world.

Yufa's anthracite eyes glittered. "So tell me. What are you doing walking in here and starting fires?"

"I didn't. One of your boys was playing with a welding torch in a room full of fuel oil. He should have been more careful. Accidents happen."

Yufa's eyes went dead. He stared at Nowek unblinkingly,

lizardlike, his olive skin flushed even darker. "Kaznin said you were a suicide. I think he could be right."

"I'm not an expert in psychology."

"You're an expert in making trouble. There's too much of that already. It's time to stop it."

"You and the Ministry? I thought thieves were above cooperating with men like Kaznin and Gromov."

"*They* cooperate with *me*."

"I always suspected you and the Party had a lot in common."

Yufa jabbed a thick thumb down to the desktop. "The Party looks out for the Party," said Yufa. "They used to be big shots. Now they're just another gang. *We're* the ones who keep the country alive. It's a heavy burden in troubled times."

Troubled times. An *apparatchik* explaining why he'd missed his quota could hardly have said it better. "So now thieves are in the public service sector?"

"We always were. Look around. You let everything fall to pieces. Even the Chinese live better than we do. So who makes sure there's gasoline to buy? A little warm water to drink? Medicines? You? *No*. Us. Business is business. That's how Russia works." He sat back in his chair. "That's how it's always worked. You understand what I'm saying?"

"I understand why Gromov needs you. Why do you need him?"

"A little looseness is good. Too much is bad. A prosecutor can puts limits on things."

"Like unauthorized theft?"

"Exactly." Yufa nodded at the open window. "Out there there's no order. But in here we're like a family. One finger looks after the next. We're a *bratsky krug*." A circle of brothers. His wide face seemed to bud from his shoulders without need for a neck. His black hair gleamed. "Borya's missing."

"You said so."

"Borya's my son."

Nowek felt the impact of Yufa's words. He could see the pain on Yufa's face. His son. His future. Wrapped in fire. Burned to grease and bone. That was going to complicate things. Nowek knew that once they found Borya there would be no room for negotiations. There would be no room for anything. "I have a daughter," he said. "She's also missing."

"Why tell me?"

"I came to offer you a deal."

"Don't—" Yuri began, but the young pilot was cuffed into silence.

"One more word, that's it," said Yufa. "So? Talk."

"Your boys paid Nikki Malyshev a visit tonight."

"Little Nikki's a *fartsovchik*," said Yufa. A street vendor beneath the contempt of a *vor* like Yufa. "What business is it of yours anyway?"

"It's your business I'm curious about. You bought things from him. Things nobody else would buy. Food nobody in their right mind would touch much less eat."

Yufa gave him a measured look and then said, "Why should I buy anything from a piece of garbage like Nikki?"

"Because you're the only buyer in Markovo for old army rations."

Yufa smiled, then snorted. "Listen. Nikki was a poodle who thought he was a wolf." The smile vanished. "He tried to sell things that weren't his. They were mine. That's against the law. *My* law."

"So you had him killed."

"When someone steps on your prick you do something. You can't let it go by. Not in my world."

"Your boys also visited my house."

Yufa's eyes showed nothing. No emotion. No recognition. Dead flat.

"They also broke into Andrei Ryzkhov's place. You wanted something. It wasn't there because I have it. I'm prepared to make you a deal. You can have the tapes. You know the ones? Of course you do. But I want my daughter back. Tonight."

"Deals." Yufa snorted. "Ryzkhov wanted to deal but he wasn't such a good businessman. He didn't understand that when there's just one person in the market, the buyer sets the price, not the seller."

"Ryzkhov tried to sell the tapes to you?"

"Don't ask me why he thought they were so valuable. I tried to help. I mean, as a favor. But in the end, we were unable to reach an acceptable agreement. I put him in touch with others. Negotiations broke down. Think about it."

Nowek was thinking about it. Would Ryzkhov try to cut a side deal with Yufa for Anna's tapes? It wasn't even a question. Who did he put him in touch with? AMR? "Forgive me, Semyon," he said, "but you're wrong about there being only one buyer. I think there's a whole world of buyers interested in a man who doesn't exist."

Yufa stuck a thumb down onto the green desk again. "This is the world, Mayor. I run it. Talking about other worlds, it's like a color neither one of us will ever see. Especially you. Especially now. I don't know anything about your daughter except that she's going to be sad tomorrow if you don't give me what I want tonight. I want the American. Right here. That's it. I'm doing you a favor to even talk. So. Is this acceptable?"

"Not if it's the same deal you offered Ryzkhov."

Yufa leaned forward. "We didn't touch him. On my word, we didn't touch him. You could say that he killed himself over those tapes. What about you?"

The tapes. The American wandering the nighttime taiga. The old army rations. Anna. Nowek could feel the night sharpen to a point, a narrow, slender needle of time, terribly brittle, ready to break like an icicle rotted by the sun. "Maybe they're worth more than you think."

"No."

"Maybe they're worth a great deal to AmerRus. Or is it Prosecutor Gromov? You're his business partner. You probably know how much he gets paid to let undocumented Americans into Siberia."

"Go ask him. He's been asking for you all day."

"I'm asking you. Who are they, Semyon?" asked Nowek. He leaned forward. The guard stiffened. "What are they doing up at Elgen? Who are they throwing behind the wire? Not thieves, surely. You look out for one another too well. You're a circle of brothers. Who is it this time?"

"I don't know what you mean."

"Please. A man like yourself has no reason to lie about this. This is your world, remember? You know about Elgen. It's an old camp. We never throw anything away in Russia. We never know when it could be needed again. And Siberia has always been a tough place to leave. Think. The last Japanese prisoners from the great war? They left Siberia in 1992."

"So what?"

"The Koreans run camps down south today. We still had *Americans* from the Korean War sitting in prison in the seventies."

"Maybe you should write a history book if you get the chance."

"Who are they putting behind the wire now?"

Yufa shrugged. "It's amazing to me, Mayor," he said. "You have the Americans biting their own tails, a smart boy like Ryzkhov dead, a couple of militia. The prosecutor general himself wants your head on his wall. Somehow here you are alive and you *still* don't know anything."

"I know they're using Elgen for something. The Americans are involved. A place like that is only good for one thing. It used to be a gulag. I think it still is."

"Go ahead and shout. Nobody would believe it. A tape. Ryzkhov, some old rations. Malyshev. Nobody would put those things together and come up with a gulag. Nobody."

"You're wrong," said Nowek. "I did."

"That's a problem, but it's your problem. Not mine."

"Who are they throwing inside?" Nowek demanded again. "Is it Baptist missionaries? Korean lumberjacks? Mormons? Chechen rebels? It's someone. I don't have to put it together. I can smell it. Who is it this time?"

The radio chirped. Yufa picked it up. He listened, his eyes shifted to Nowek, then he slowly put it down. His face might as well have been chiseled from basalt. To one of the guards he said, "Go bring the van."

"Semyon—"

"No," said Yufa. He swallowed, his face no longer blank. He seemed on the verge of tears. "My son. My . . ." He stopped and shook his head. "There's no deal."

A metallic crash came from outside the building. Everyone stared at the drapes for a stunned moment.

"Go," said Yufa.

Nowek's guard went to the window and shoved the curtains aside as another *crump!* ended in the sound of shattering glass. Another smash, then a crunch, this time punctuated with the frightened honk of a car's theft alarm.

Yufa got to his feet so fast his chair tipped over backward.

Yuri's eyes darted. The letter opener on Yufa's desk. Yuri had been watching it, waiting. He'd nearly acted too soon when the fire alarm had gone off. Now one guard was looking out the window. The other stood behind him with the autopistol. An HK SP89. A valuable piece of plumbing. Worth three thousand dollars on the market. But just now it was worth a lot more. Wait and be killed. Act now and it was only maybe.

Forget the odds. Maybe was good enough.

He jumped and swung an elbow into the guard's gut. It was like punching brick. The HK didn't even waver as it turned in Yuri's direction.

Yuri leaped at Yufa. He snatched the letter opener from its crystal sheath as he vaulted over the desk. The Ukrainian boss stood against the wall, arms spread out. He was in the direct line of his own guard's fire. "No!" he screamed as a burst of 9mm rounds tore through the wall above his head. Plaster dust showered down, mingling with yellow gunsmoke.

The guard at the window was turning, his hand beneath his jacket.

Yuri grabbed Yufa and stuck the point of the letter opener in his neckless neck. Yufa was as soft as the guard was hard. A trickle of blood leaked over his tight collar. "Tell them to drop the guns."

The pit bull by the window had his pistol out.

"Tell them or I'll roll your head down the stairs!" Yuri sheltered behind Yufa's bulk. He jabbed the letter opener deeper. Yufa's eyes glistened white.

He couldn't speak. He tried. He blinked.

The young pilot jabbed the little sword deeper. "On the floor! Tell them!"

Yufa nodded fast.

Both weapons went down. Nowek was nearest to the HK. He picked the ugly thing up like a snake that might or might not be dead. It was heavy, easily three kilos, and greasy in his kerosene-slick hands. The barrel was warm. The curving magazine showed plenty of brass.

The guard at the window was balanced on the balls of his feet. Ready, almost trembling. If he moved, Nowek would have to shoot. He looked at the guard, pleading with every psychic ray he could muster. Don't. Don't move. Just stay.

He moved.

Yuri threw Yufa at him. Pit bull and boss fell against the window frame. "Shoot!" he yelled at Nowek as they disentangled.

Nowek turned the weapon on them.

"Shoot them!"

Another metallic smash echoed up from outside. The car alarm shrieked.

"Stand still," Nowek told Yufa and his guard.

"You can't do it," said Yufa. "I can smell it on you."

An owl, an eagle, a shark. A musician. Yufa was right. Nowek said to Yuri, "Run."

The pilot sprinted for the door.

Yufa had moved to the edge of his desk. "There's no place for you now. Not here. Not Irkutsk. Not anywhere. And your daughter? I know a place where they'll eat her alive. Even then it will be better than my Borya had."

"Don't move."

Yufa laughed as he dabbed at his neck. "Your friend was right. You should have pulled the trigger."

"Stop."

"You aren't a leader. You're no father. You aren't even a man."

Maybe his finger moved. Maybe the trigger slipped. He couldn't have pulled it. But the weapon exploded in his hand, bucking and hosing a spray of bullets across the room. When the hammer finally fell on an empty chamber, Yufa and the guard were on the floor. The smoke was thick. When it cleared Nowek saw that his crime had been just attempted murder. They were both alive, stunned.

He pulled the wooden door closed and ran after Yuri.

Down the stairs, out the lobby. He saw Yuri go out the front door, then heard a sharp, short whistle.

"Plet!"

Nowek joined Yuri outside. He threw the empty autopistol into the snow and watched Plet smash Yufa's BMW with the pipe wrench.

Still naked to the waist, the big man worked diligently with his favorite tool. He was all iron arms and sweaty brow, using his big wrench to smash the evils of capitalism personified. The rear window crumpled. The alarm shrieked. Plet reared back and took out the taillights. The angels tattooed on his chest were no longer worshipful. They were avenging.

Nowek looked up and saw shadows moving by the curtains again. A muzzle poked them aside.

"Plet!"

A brilliant gout of yellow flame belched through Yufa's window. A metal hailstorm riddled good German steel.

The roar of an engine.

A white Land Cruiser with Chuchin at the wheel skidded to a stop. Anna threw open the door as another burst from upstairs raked the courtyard.

Chuchin leaned out, pointed the pistol, and three white flashes lit the courtyard followed by heavy, echoing booms. The window went dark.

Nowek dived in as Chuchin floored it. Plet leaped onto the rear bumper and grabbed the roof rack. He pulled himself up and held on.

A whine of slipping tires, a sudden lurch as they bit, and they took off. Yuri ran after them. Plet held out his wrench, one arm wrapped around the roof rack. Yuri got a grip and Plet hauled him up beside him.

They rocketed by the gate and out into the night.

Chuchin swerved around a corner. The low moon careened from one window to the next, then behind a wall. When it emerged, it was just a glow lost in cloud.

"You're getting a raise," said Nowek when his breath began to calm. "Where did you find fuel?"

Chuchin reached down and held up a long rubber hose. "From each according to his ability, to each according to his need. Kaznin's Volvo was full. I figured he wouldn't need it. Did you see him?"

"No."

"That helicopter, it was the same one. It was from—"

"I know." He turned. Yuri and Plet were still hanging on. He looked at Anna, then turned to Chuchin. "Pull over. Find someplace dark."

Chuchin steered them off the road and into an empty, snow-covered lot. Frost-crumbled brick walls sheltered them on three sides. The snow cover was still deep, almost up to the Land Cruiser's floorboards. The car skimmed across the crusted snow like a sled. They stopped. The lights went out.

Yuri and Plet staggered in next to Anna. Plet still gripped the wrench. It seemed part of his arm. A lobster's hard, crushing claw.

"Mayor, I owe you," said Yuri, out of breath. "But you should have shot him and done everybody a favor. He'll come after you now. He talks like a human being, but he's a monster."

"So was his son."

Plet grunted.

"Why did you tell him a story about your daughter?" Yuri asked. "He wouldn't care."

"It wasn't a story."

Yuri's eyebrows raised in unison. "They have her?"

"She's at Tunguska," said Anna.

Yuri seemed to notice Anna for the first time. "She was right here all the time. I thought you were bluffing. You really could have made a trade with that bastard. Why didn't you?"

"Trade?" she said.

Nowek faced Anna. "Your friend Andrei. You gave him a copy of that tape. He was supposed to send it to his brother to find out who the man was. A name. Yes?"

"You know all of that."

"I also know that he was trying to sell it back to Yufa."

"He wouldn't—"

"He did. Yufa put him in touch with AmerRus and you know what happened next. Yufa said he didn't kill him and you know, I believe him. A thief has his honor, after all. Unlike Kaznin. Unlike Gromov."

"Andrei wouldn't lie to me."

"After all this you still would trust him? Why? Because you used to be lovers? It's not enough of a reason. His wife could say the same thing."

Her mouth tightened.

Nowek wasn't finished. "Ryzkhov knew that Yufa would understand what was on that tape, and why no one could ever be permitted to see it. The problem was, he thought he was important. Too important. Ryzkhov had a nice, thick roof over his head. His 'state secrets' would protect him. Only a paper roof wasn't good enough."

A militia jeep turned the corner, its blue strobe flashing. It sped by in the direction of Mercury Condom.

"I keep asking myself," said Nowek, "how does AmerRus make money without finding oil? How does Yufa make money selling old rations? Why would Andrei Ryzkhov arrange for the lease of an old camp? Three mysteries, plainly. But with one answer. It's a puzzle." Turning to Yuri, he said, "Perhaps you can help me solve it, Yuri."

"Me?"

"You," Nowek replied. "You're part of this little arrangement. You did business with Yufa. You flew those rations north. You and Yufa, you're partners. I don't have him to ask. But I have you."

"Partner? What are you talking about? Didn't you see me in his office? Did I look like a guest?"

"I saw you," said Nowek. "I also remember seeing a crate of army rations in the back of your airplane."

"Listen. All of that was in the past," said Yuri. "We don't work for Yufa anymore. What is this anyway, an interrogation? Who got us out of there?"

"You know about AmerRus. You know what they're doing."

"All I know is you'd be dead if I hadn't grabbed that Ukrainian bastard. Now you're acting like *I'm* the criminal?"

"I think you are. There are laws against participating in corrupt enterprises. Maybe I can get a judge to enforce them in your case. If not, then I'm certain you could be held long enough for Yufa to find you. Or Gromov. It could become difficult. I'm sure you understand."

"Better than you. Face facts. *They're* the judges. *They're* the laws. *You're* the outsider. Those pricktwisters in Irkutsk have their fingers in everything. Wait and they'll have their fingers in you. Which is why I don't advise waiting." He looked around nervously. "Listen. When AMR first showed up we flew for them every day. Geophysical surveyors. Supplies. Some hunting trips for investors from America. Things were really moving. There was a lot of activity. They acted interested in finding oil."

"What kind of hunting?" Anna asked.

"What do you think? You stocked their hunting preserve for them. Then all of a sudden, everything stopped dead. No consultants. No surveyors. Not even any hunters. As far as they were concerned, we no longer existed. We couldn't even get in the front gate. We couldn't haul shit from a latrine if we paid them. So it was do business with Yufa or starve."

"What kind of business?"

Yuri shook his head. He reached for the door but Plet was faster. The big red wrench came down like a gate.

"Tell him."

"Tell him what?" He tried to pull the door handle, but the iron wrench pressed down harder. "We're getting out of here."

"No." Plet didn't move. Yuri couldn't.

Yuri appealed to reason. "You want to share his cell? He'll be dead tomorrow. Why should I?"

"Because if he's dead tomorrow," said Plet, "he'll outlive you by a night."

"What is this, an attack of morals?"

"I have reasons."

"I'd like to hear just one."

Plet shoved the heavy wrench across Yuri's chest.

Yuri stopped struggling. "This is mutiny."

"Well?" said Nowek.

Yuri glanced at Plet, then back. "Three times. Okay? Three times. They had us fly down to the BAM," he said, meaning the Baikal–Amur Mainline. "We landed next to a railroad spur and waited. A train came by. It never even stopped. It didn't have to. You know how slow they have to go. They kicked boxes into the snow and kept on rolling. We loaded them and flew."

"Where?"

"Where do you think? Tunguska. Whatever AmerRus did with these boxes, they never told me. My part was finished."

"So you admit to being a part of Yufa's organization."

"Do you eat? Do you breathe? *Everyone* in Markovo is part of his organization. Everyone except you and that idiot Malyshev. If he'd been more careful he'd still be alive. One day they'll say the same about you."

"I can wait. You sold some of those rations to Nikki?"

Yuri looked at Plet again. "Okay. I'll be frank. We kept a few crates for ourselves. I figured, there must be more to this than meets the eye. Who would want to eat them? Nobody. They were bad when they were new. DON'T EAT AFTER 1991. Think what they must be like now."

"I saw."

"So did I. There was no one at Tunguska who would touch

it. The Russian crews eat better than people in Markovo, and the Americans? Please. I mean, they have steaks. They have lobsters. They shit Dove Bars still in the wrappers. I figured it had to be something bigger."

"Smuggling," said Nowek.

"Obviously. But I opened a dozen and there were no diamonds in those tins, Mayor. No drugs. Nothing but what the labels said. Junk. So I sold the rest to Nikki. What he did with them was his business. And what you do from here on is yours."

What had Yufa said? That Nikki was trying to sell something that didn't belong to him?

Yuri mistook Nowek's expression for disbelief. "It's true. What could I do? There was no choice. A businessman must go where there's business."

"I have good news for you. If you're looking for work, you're in the right place," said Nowek.

"What work?"

"I have some business for White Bird Aviation. You're going to fly tonight," said Nowek. "You're going to take me to Tunguska."

"Fine. Only why not go to Paris first? The weather's nicer."

"It's no joke, Yuri. My daughter is up there and you're the only pilot with an airplane I know."

"Don't beg him! Commandeer the aircraft!" said Chuchin.

Nowek shook his head. "I need a pilot, too."

"It's a good idea," agreed Yuri. "A plane, a pilot. And if you had ham you could make an omelet. If you had an egg. See you around, Mayor." He reached for the door. "Let's go."

"Wait!"

They all looked. It was Anna.

"How much would it take to get you to fly there?"

"It's ridiculous to even talk about it," said Yuri.

"Tiger bone sells for five hundred dollars per gram. That's not ridiculous."

"Anna!" said Nowek, but she hushed him.

"Retail," Yuri broke in. "It's more like three thousand dollars a kilo here. Why do you mention it?"

Nowek glanced at Anna again. "What are you saying?"

"He wants to be paid." She barely whispered through her tightly drawn lips. To Yuri she said, "So a hundred kilos would bring three hundred thousand dollars?"

"More or less. Where's this hundred-kilo tiger?"

"In a box. In several boxes. They're waiting for you. At Tunguska. But you have to take us there to get it. You have to take us there tonight."

Us, thought Nowek. Why was that word so small, so large?

Yuri looked at them. He wasn't inclined to believe Nowek. But Anna Vereskaya was another story. She was the tiger woman. A hundred kilos of bone? Enough to buy some new airplanes. To start all over someplace else, someplace where they never heard of the Ministry. Never heard of Prosecutor Gromov. A place where lobsters spent their summers, not their winters.

Nowek said to Anna, "You can't give him those bones."

"I'm not giving him anything. I'm selling them."

"How do I know these bones even exist?" asked Yuri.

"You don't," said Anna. "All you know is the offer's good now. In the morning, after Kaznin finds us you won't have a cent. You'll have nothing but a lot of angry people wondering where you are and how you helped us. On the other hand, you take a risk, you reap a reward. Take it or leave it. Do we have a deal or not?"

Yuri slowly smiled as he pulled the door shut. "You know something, Mayor? I was wrong. She *is* an American."

Nowek looked at Chuchin. "Drive," he said.

As the car moved off, a spatter of wet snow fell from a small cloud, showering the windshield, the world, with melting stars.

22

WET PINE BARK glittered in the single headlight's beam.

Nowek unrolled the oil exploration map they'd found in Ryzkhov's basement. He handed it to Yuri.

"I don't need maps." Yuri gave it back. "I said before that I can find Tunguska with my nose. But one pass is all you get. That's it," he said. "If we can land, we pick up your daughter, my bone, and we run. If we can't, if they still have the runway blocked, then . . ." He shrugged.

"We'll land." Nowek wasn't going to Tunguska just to leave Galena behind.

"Now you're a pilot, too?" said Chuchin.

"I'm thinking in new ways, Chuchin." Nowek could see the tension in his driver's face. "I may even start driving myself around. Who knows?"

"Pah."

"What is AmerRus doing with a place like Elgen?" said Anna.

Ideas were cheap. Proof was hard. Nowek could afford to spend a little common currency. "They're using it. Or allowing others to use it."

"For what?"

Who would be willing to eat obsolete swill? Who *else*? he

thought. "Prisoners. I've thought about it. It's the only thing that makes any sense. It has to be prisoners."

The word swirled like a gas, like smoke, dispersing into silence. Finally, Anna said, "Then that American on the tiger tape could be . . ."

"A guard. Someone brought in. Some kind of a consultant," said Nowek. "There are a lot of American consultants in Russia these days. Though to be honest, when it comes to gulags we don't need them."

"Absolutely," said Chuchin. "When it comes to jails and jailers, Siberia already leads the world. We could send consultants to *them*."

He was right, of course. Centuries of experience. Endless space. Cheap, available labor. Who needs consultants? wondered Nowek. Then who was that dead American?

"Well, whatever they're doing," said Yuri, "we'll have to be very fast. Remember, AMR runs Tunguska like their own country. But if there's as much tiger bone as you say . . ."

"I've been collecting it now for almost two years."

They all looked at her.

"Bones from forty-three animals. There's more than two hundred kilos."

"Two . . . hundred? Do you have any idea what that would bring on the market?"

"Yes."

"Get it to Vladivostok and it's worth more than half a million dollars." Yuri's voiced was hushed in awe. "And you were going to just *burn* it?"

"You're forgetting one thing, Mr. Businessman," said Chuchin. "The same thing Ryzkhov forgot."

"What's that, grandfather?"

"You have to live to sell it."

Chuchin took a drag of a cigarette Yuri had given him. The Marlboro smelled better than his customary Yava. "Elgen. It's been a memory for so long. Sometimes even I wondered how it could have happened. Or whether it even did." Chuchin paused. Thinking of the lights, the barracks, the towers, was not so easy. He'd spent twenty years as a citizen of the invisible empire.

"Tell us what you remember," said Anna, and everyone in the car, even Plet who had his own stories to tell, leaned close to hear better.

"I won't tell you why I was there. Who knew? I wasn't a thief, that much I'll say. If I had been, I would have had a better time of it. Thieves were king inside the wire."

"Now they just supply it with food," said Nowek.

"They put us on big river barges at Norilsk and sent us south on the Yenisey. Upstream. You see, I was getting a promotion. The Norilsk mines were the worst place they could send you."

"Except Kolyma," said Plet.

Chuchin nodded. "He's right. DALSTROI was hell," he said. It was the acronym for Far Northern Construction Trust. "Norilsk was just purgatory. Anyway, the lumber camps were a step up from either one. The work is outside, there's room to breathe. I'd been inside already nearly ten years, so in a way I had seniority."

"They sent you to cut trees?" said Yuri.

"They sent me to disappear. What we did when we got there was not their concern." Chuchin shrugged. "The barges were nothing but steel boxes with a diesel engine. They threw us into the hold and locked it. It was dark. It was filled with men. Who knew how many? You could hear only breathing and moans. It was . . ." he paused, "it was something you could not begin to imagine."

The car swerved as the tires ran in the hard, frozen ruts in the River Road.

"There was no food. No sleeping planks, no water, no insulation. We drank what condensed on the iron hull." He stopped, then spoke. "Some academic prick told us we were drinking our own water back, that it came from our breath, so we were all doomed to die of thirst."

"What happened?"

"We made sure he was the first to go. Anyway, he was half

right. We piled the dead ones against the steel and used them as beds. When the barge stopped at the Nizhnaya Tunguska, they opened the hatch. In the light . . . well, it was beyond what the eye can see. You stop seeing. That's all I can say."

"They marched you over the taiga to Elgen?" asked Anna.

"No. They transferred us to open boats and chained us together. Anyone who tried to jump had to drag twenty others with him. It was tempting."

"To escape?" asked Anna.

"To die. But we wouldn't give in to those bastards. We wouldn't let them win. Taking the next breath was a kind of victory. So we kept breathing. We went two days like that. No food, although we could scoop river water when the guards weren't looking. The river was getting too shallow. We kept grounding on rock. Finally, we went around some strange hills. Right in the middle of nowhere. They're covered with . . ." He made a fist and shook his head. "I don't know what they're called. Rocks, but with animals inside."

"Fossils?" said Nowek.

"Why ask me? You're the expert. The camp was built at the base of those hills. It was an old one. Stone barracks two stories tall. A shed for cattle. The czars may have opened Elgen, but the fucking communists, they kept it going."

Another cloud of smoke, a jet, a ring.

"I remember the first thing I saw when we arrived. You spoke of laws? We had laws. They posted them at the gate. Everything was simpler then. There were only five:

1: NEVER EXPECT BREAD AND SOUP TOGETHER.
2: WHAT'S GONE FROM YOUR HAND IS LOST FOREVER.
3: YOU WILL REPAY WITH SWEAT YOUR CRIMES AGAINST THE PEOPLE.
4: THOSE WHO DO NOT FULFILL THE PLAN ARE SABO-TEURS."

When he stopped, Anna said, "You said there were five."

"So I did." Chuchin barely nodded. "The fifth is the one that made sense of all the others."

"What is it, Chuchin?" asked Nowek.

"5: SABOTEURS WILL BE SHOT."

★   ★   ★

The guards herded LeRoy by a large billboard covered in red letters. He looked, but they made no less sense in Russian than they would have in English. They came to a large hut made from hewn logs. Smoke curled from the chimney. Some men were in there, and even if he hadn't seen the smoke, he could smell them; a smell beyond rancid. A lot of dirty, sweating men. Who were they going to have him bunk with? He felt weak from the shot. Weak like a strong wind might bend him double.

"In!" Bang Stick shouted.

Took my shoes, motherfuck. You're gonna regret that.

Inside the low wooden shack the odor doubled, then doubled again. Every corner he looked into, every shadow, contained a man dressed in dirty rags. Ten clustered against a wall. And in the middle, near the hot iron stove, stood four more. Brothers. Black as eggplant.

"You a fast boy, catcher," said one of them. "You the first awake."

He wasn't no catcher. It was slang for an inmate who became the sex slave of a man who would protect him, the "pitcher." But he would have to prove it to these men, that was also for sure. "Whassup?"

No one answered. They stared silently at the iron stove in the middle of the room, keeping careful distance from it as though it would burn them. They all wore the curious felt boots that LeRoy now had on his feet. Their eyes caught the light of the single bulb overhead, glittering in resignation, with fury, with cunning. Most were black, some were Latino. But here and there were a few truly petrified whites. The four in the center dominated the space without trying.

"Hey," LeRoy said to them. "I asked a question."

They stared back as though he were a dog that talked.

"What the fuck is this place anyway?"

Someone sniffed. "Fresh fish don't smell."

"Not yet," said someone else.

Laughter like racking coughs filled the tiny, fetid room.

"You in the deepest kinda shit is where you at," said one of the men in the center. His ebony skin was clean. He looked almost normal, dressed as he was in a uniform not unlike the one the guards wore, fur hat and leather boots. But no weapon. The man. The boss. Guaranteed.

"I been there." LeRoy knew he needed to impress them with his cool. With his *fuck with me at your own risk* attitude. He knew the rules. Old hands, new hands, and the way to survive. His eyes, his ears, his fists. He knew the penalties, too. A knife in the back. A wire around the throat. Or hide out as some jock's catcher. No way. He'd never let anyone get that close and live. His breath was coming faster. "I spent my time at Pelican Bay."

"Oh, my. Some kinda *bad* dude we got," one of the men in the center echoed. The lieutenant. More coughing. Or was it laughing? "What you got on your arm? Look like Aryan Brotherhood shit to me. You a long way from your friends."

He looked at the twin lightning bolts of his tattoo, then back up. "They ain't none of your concern." The hot stove felt good. There were open tins of food piled nearby. He was hungry. LeRoy stepped into the center.

One of the lieutenants shoved him back.

The room went dead quiet.

"You want to try me?" LeRoy felt the monster in him struggle to rise. Fucking medicine. It flickered, unsteady as a candle in the wind. "I ain't afraid of you," he said.

"Time you learn," the one in the uniform said. "Take him."

The walls erupted in a seething mass of rags and filth.

LeRoy stood there, stunned for the instant it took for the

men to swarm him. He swung and broke the jaw of the first. He smashed the nose of the next one flat to his face. He got his fingers into an eye and jabbed deep, then pulled. There was a bellow, but they were many, and LeRoy, even with his monster, was few.

His legs were kicked aside. He was down, struggling, his head bashed by feet, by fists. He fought back, then his face was pressed to the dirt as they held him down. His mouth was filled with grit. They held LeRoy Rogers all the way down and did over and over what he'd never let anyone do to him before and live.

He cried for his monster to come back, to fill his arms, his legs. He cried for God. His voice was smothered by wheezes, by rooting grunts and sudden groans. Catcher. Punk. Goat. They used him over and over until he was soaked in his own blood.

He even prayed, and when it went unanswered, LeRoy cried out for his mother.

The lights of the airport showed up ahead as they left the dense stands of Siberian larch and Korean pines behind.

The low clouds had solidified into an overcast by the time they pulled up to Yuri's ruined hangar. Plet fueled *Little Annie* from a score of heavy drums he rolled out of the shadows. White Bird Aviation had lost nearly everything when the hangar burned; these came from a cache kept in a shed behind the ruins.

"We'll overfly Tunguska, check the runway, and land. You can get your daughter," said Yuri. "I'll go collect my bones. I only hope they cleared that runway. I'm not sure there's another place that's long and smooth enough to land. Though for two hundred kilos of tiger bone, I'd swim there with *Annushka* on my back."

"There's a place."

Once more, they all looked at Anna.

"The gravel causeway that goes to my building. It's almost

six hundred meters long. Dead straight. Land there and you're that much closer to the bones."

"I like it," said Yuri.

One by one Plet rolled the steel drums to the Antonov, set them upright, pried open the bung, and rammed the hand pump down into the hole. He worked like a machine, steadily, never stopping, never resting, and without a word spoken.

"There's another little problem," said Chuchin. He pointed at the AmerRus building.

Behind its security fence, there were lights on. As they all looked, the front door was just now closing.

"Tell me, Chuchin," said Nowek. "Should we go kill them?"

"Only if we're smart."

"How much?" asked Yuri as the last liters gushed into the Antonov's tanks.

"Five and a half." He spoke in hundreds of liters; *Little Annie* burned almost four hundred liters of high-octane fuel each hour.

Yuri did the calculation. "It's almost enough."

Plet stepped back as they gathered at the Antonov's door. He had one of the Czech Skorpion machine pistols in one hand. His wrench in the other.

"You're not coming?" asked Nowek.

Plet handed Yuri the weapon. "Don't worry," Yuri said quickly. "Plet's always been afraid to fly. It's his policy never to be higher than he likes to fall."

Plet tapped his forehead in a kind of salute. Then stepped back into the shadows.

"So?" said Yuri. "Let's go. By this time tomorrow, with two hundred kilos of bone, we'll all be rich."

DeKalb slammed his telephone down. Higgins, his dispatcher down at the Markovo airfield, was a squirrel. But he was a squirrel with enough sense to keep one eye propped open. He stood up and grabbed his hard hat, then made his way to a locked cabinet at the back of his personal quarters.

He cursed as he spun the combination. He liked things smooth, and this was threatening to get all wrinkled up in a furball. The lock sprang free. He yanked the metal door open. This was not supposed to be his responsibility. It was hard enough explaining how an old oil man could sit on wells and not get his fingers so much as greasy. He knew it had to be done. He knew why he was doing it. The locals were supposed to keep his ass intact. And now look where *that* had gone.

Inside the locker was a collection of serious weaponry; sporting rifles, handguns, plus a few more exotic pieces of hardware. He thought of them as tools, each one made to do a certain job and do it well. He thought of himself that way, too. Especially after the break-in back in Houston. Take away a man's future and what was left? Hard metal, a keen edge. In other words, a tool. DeKalb examined each of the guns with that clear, simple idea firmly in mind. It was better to keep things clear. It was better to keep things simple.

The Ruger with its big scope was made for the long shot. Perfect for tigers, where you didn't really want to get close. His hand traveled across polished walnut and blued steel.

The bolt-action Heym Safari was too light for anything larger than boar. A Weatherby shotgun was ideal for the clouds of eiders that came over each season. Close in, it was the best personal defense device this side of a blunderbuss; nothing made a bigger bang or a bigger hole. His hand kept on moving.

The right tool for the right job. You don't pound nails with a screwdriver. You don't take a hammer to a bolt.

His hand gravitated to the last item on the rack.

If the other guns were specialized tools, the M-209 was something of an adjustable wrench; good for many different applications. Nail, bolt, near and far.

He lifted it from the rack.

It was an over-under weapon; a standard M-16 assault rifle on top mated with a stubby shotgun barrel below. Only it wasn't a shotgun. The single-shot tube fired a 40mm fragmentation grenade, either in a direct trajectory like a rocket, or lobbed high in a ballistic arc. Anyone inside the lethal radius of the grenade's detonation found himself efficiently aerated by high-speed slivers of good American steel.

He took a canvas sack and carefully fitted twenty grenades inside. Like stubby olive drab sausages. He drew the top closed and slung the hybrid weapon over his shoulder. He shut the locker and spun the lock.

Outside it was snowing softly from a broken deck of clouds. The snow turned to pellets, to wet drops with a hard core. The air was confused, the season was poised on a narrow beam, ready to tumble either way.

He walked to the radio room at the helipad.

The room was hot with the smell of electronics. There was no one on duty there tonight. He leaned the M-209 in the corner and flipped the sophisticated burst transmitter on. De-signed to slice up a transmission into a blizzard of bits, then squeeze them into an impossibly fast spurt of noise, the radio was his guarantee that no matter what he said, no matter who might be listening, nothing would be overheard nor under-stood.

When the red STANDBY light extinguished, he keyed the microphone.

"Rattler, Rattler, where the hell are you?"

Decker started at the sudden transmission. They were almost back to Tunguska after dropping off the evening's cargo.

"He's on the burster," said Joffrey. He switched the audio panel to the number-three position.

"I got ya. Say again your message?"

"What's your ETA back at the pad?"

"We're inbound, fifteen klicks north," he said. "About six minutes."

Decker's voice trembled as though he were speaking through water. DeKalb could hear the slamming thud of the rotors through the loudspeaker.

"I just talked to Markovo. We may have another inbound."

"Shit. Who is it now?"

"I'll explain when you get here," said DeKalb. "Pick me up for a fast turnaround."

"No can do, boss," Decker said. "Been a long night in the air. We don't have the gas." Shit, he thought. He had some work to do with that little honey back in his cabin. If he had to dump her like DeKalb said, he wasn't ready to let her go entirely to waste.

"What about the Bell?" asked DeKalb.

"It's flyable," he said.

"Good," said DeKalb. "Just get here quick and we'll take it. I'll brief you when we're airborne. Out."

"I wonder what it's about?" asked Joffrey.

"Bet you one of those boys woke up early," said Decker as he bent on more speed. "Nobody jump when you stuck 'em with that pin?"

"Not a twitch."

"Don't know why they just don't dump their sorry asses in the ocean and be done with it."

"Easy," said Joffrey. "They'd float."

DeKalb snapped off the transmitter and went back outside. He brought the M-209 and carefully set it where it wouldn't feel a drop of wet snow. The canvas sack he carried himself. The wet flakes fell quickly. Half ice, half water, they didn't drift. The Russians say that snow "walks." This snow was running. Corn snow, they used to call it. You'd get it sometimes back in Houston when a Blue Norther turned bluer than normal. He felt the heavy flakes strike his cheek and run cold down his neck.

Nowek. Again. Why? What on earth could draw him to come up here at night, in this weather? It could blow everything up. Could ruin it and DeKalb was not about to see that happen. Not on his watch. Not for other reasons, too. Nowek was becoming a problem. A problem demanding a solution. And solutions were what AMR paid him for.

★   ★   ★

The lightly loaded Antonov leaped off the Markovo runway. Nowek kept Yuri company in the cockpit while Chuchin sat in back. Anna stood behind the pilot's seats, her head up in the greenhouse bubble overhead, her hand on the back of Nowek's seat. She could look left and see a red navigation light blur as they swept through a snow shower. A faint green glow came from the opposite wing tip.

Below, barely visible, the silver thread of the Tunguska pipeline glowed subliminally against the black taiga. Yuri snapped on *Little Annie*'s landing light to make it stand out more sharply against the blackness.

Yuri scowled as he watched the snow showers ganging up into something bigger, something more definite. Real weather. Well, you didn't get rich by avoiding risk. Risk was part of the deal. Still, he wasn't entirely happy. How far could he fly with a load of bone? Where could he unload it safely? East. It had to be east. All the way to Vladivostok? No. The Armenians would slit his throat. Someplace else.

China? They were even worse than the Armenians. Maybe Irkutsk, Chita, then Khabarovsk. Or north to the Bering and across the divide to Alaska. He could trade bone for fuel at any one of a hundred little airports and still have a fortune left over. But it had to be fast. It had to be before those bastards in Irkutsk could put out a warning to stop him.

"How far?" asked Nowek.

"Mayor, in all the history of Russia, you are the most anxious to arrive at a place like Tunguska. We have a head wind. I'll get you there, don't worry." Yuri's face was lit by the glow from the instrument panel. "What are you going to do while I load the bone?"

"I'm going to find Galena," said Nowek. "I'm bringing her home."

Anna's hand moved from the back of his seat to his shoulder. "I'll show you where Decker's cabin is."

He put his own hand on top of it.

Yuri was about to say something when they bored straight into the black flank of an invisible cloud. The landing light surrounded them with blinding incandescence. He snapped it off and pitched them over violently. The view ahead lightened a bit as they popped out underneath the murk. He turned on the landing light again. The pipeline was slanted at an unfamiliar angle. He banked back to follow it.

The forest below was as black as the clouds above. "Here." Yuri motioned for Nowek to take the wheel. "You're so anxious to get there? You fly."

"I can't fly."

"Sure you can. It's easy. Even a mayor can do it. Just follow the pipe." Yuri reached under his seat and pulled out a small tube and fiddled with it.

Nowek gripped the wheel like he was strangling a snake. It vibrated like something alive! But where were they? The pipeline dangled like a thread hung just beyond the windshield, white against the dark swamps. The plane began to tilt. Were they too far left? Or was it right? Which way was up? Nowek felt something odd in his ear, like an elevator moving just a little too fast. He cranked the wheel over slightly. The feeling got worse. He moved it the other way. Too much!

A distinct shriek of air whistled through holes in the Antonov's skin. The wheel seemed to be fighting him, pushing back against his hand. He shoved it harder, but it was getting more difficult. It was getting away from him. The pipeline was nearly horizontal. Which way was . . .

"I have it." Yuri pulled back on the yoke and leveled the wings. He had the tube up to his eye now. He snapped the light off once more. "I have a suggestion."

Nowek wiped a bead of sweat off his face. "What?"

"Stay with politics."

The windshield went from gray to black. They were under the cloud deck again. Yuri came level at eight hundred meters. He had the tube up to his eye like an old spyglass a sailor might use to see a reef. He took the tube and shook it hard, then looked through it again. A primitive nightscope.

Nowek thought of the invisible landscape going by below.

The trees giving way to marsh, the marsh to tundra, and farther north the tundra ending in pure ice.

Yuri checked his watch against the panel clock, then peered closely at the big compass mounted atop the vibrating glare shield. "Ten minutes more to the turn. It's a good thing they built this pipeline."

"You can see it with that?" asked Nowek.

The blackness outside was absolute.

"Enough."

"Enough for what?" asked Nowek.

"Relax, Mayor." Yuri put the nightscope to his eye and scanned the ground going by. "At White Bird Aviation we make a solemn promise to all our passengers: for every takeoff there will be a landing. It's practically guaranteed."

"Might as well start looking," said Decker as he handed a pair of night vision goggles back to DeKalb.

DeKalb put them on and scanned below. "All I see are green clouds."

"Yep. They're working good all right. Nobody busted them on us, did they Joff?"

Joffrey didn't answer the taunt. He knew DeKalb wasn't happy about letting the tiger woman offsite, and it had been his fault. What would come of it, that was what worried him most. That and Decker. Deeper and deeper. He was in too far hauling DeKalb around so he could plink some poor bastards he didn't care for. Didn't that make him the same as Decker? He stole a look and watched as the pilot fed some tidbit to his pet. Damned rat is what it was. A furry damned rat.

Down below them, the clouds were almost a solid white blanket bathed in white moonlight. The Bell cruised fast and easily above it all. But Joffrey knew they weren't going to accomplish much up here. At some point, they'd have to go rooting around in the muck. Soon.

Joffrey checked the GPS satellite navigation set. It showed strong winds from the northeast. A wet direction. "Winds are from zero four five at fifteen," he said over the intercom.

"What's that mean?" DeKalb asked.

"It means we got a tailwind and they're taking it on the nose," Decker replied. "We're already faster than that old garbage scow, so my guess is, we're gonna see those boys real soon."

"Higgins said they left forty minutes ago."

"Higgins," said Decker with a snort.

"How far are we from base?"

"Thirty-four klicks," Joffrey answered.

"All right." DeKalb gripped the M-209. "You just get me close."

"Yessir. I'll do you just that." He pushed over on the cyclic and the Bell ramped down toward the tops of the clouds. So solid. They looked as unyielding as granite. It was always a shock when they *poofed* into them with nothing more than a slight jar.

"Picking up some ice," said Joffrey. He thought, *Good.*

"We'll break out of the clag here in a minute," said Decker.

They tunneled through the cold guts of the snow cloud.

"Through one thousand feet," said Joffrey. "We might not break out, Decker. Maybe we should RTB and wait for—"

"We'll break out." Decker nudged the stick a little more forward. The altimeter unwound faster. There was no reason to dawdle inside some ice bag of a cloud. "Keep talkin' to me."

"Eight hundred." Joffrey switched on the radar altimeter. "Radar's showin' six forty. Six. Five hundred feet. Paul . . ."

Suddenly, the clouds unwrapped themselves from the Bell's windshield.

"Give us some defrost, 'bro. I can't see."

Hot bleed air from the jet engines rushed across the inside of the glass. The ice was almost melted anyway, the precipitation falling from the clouds more rain than snow. It cleared up quickly. They were underneath, in clear air. Where the Antonov would be.

"Black as a nigger baby's bottom," said Decker.

"You see anything?" DeKalb asked, anxious.

"Not yet." Then Decker got a tickle. "Hang on." He didn't make the mistake of looking straight at it. He used the side of his eyes, the sensitive part, and looked a bit askance at the sky ahead. "Well, how about that?"

DeKalb's pouch of 40mm grenades clattered as he shifted forward in the backseat.

"Twelve o'clock and level," he said to DeKalb. "That fool's running with his lights on. See him out there? Dead on."

DeKalb left the image-intensifying glasses on. A tiny constellation of lights that even as he watched blossomed into a hot white supernova. "Decker!"

"He just switched on his landing lights to see where he is." Decker banked away from the oncoming Antonov. "Hell. I could tell him that. That boy's in a world of hurt."

"Another fifteen minutes and we'll be over Tunguska," said Yuri.

The glow of *Little Annie*'s landing lights faded on Nowek's retina. The world was reduced to that silver thread surrounded by meandering streams, islands of tuft pine, and mounds of ice heaved up into eerie prisms. "You're sure we're on course?"

"Would you prefer to navigate?"

"What about our lights?" asked Anna. She was still standing behind them with her head against the cabin glass.

Yuri reached down and switched them off.

"I lost him," said Joffrey. "He's gone."

"I got his exhaust. Hang on to your shorts there, Joff. I'm the man. Remember?"

"I remember."

"Hell. Those boys are makin' it easy." They didn't need radar; they didn't need a beacon. A blue-white flicker strobed the night ahead of them as the Antonov's radial spit fire into the wet sky.

"We're getting close to base, gentlemen," said DeKalb. A

red glow pulsed through the low clouds from the burning flare gas.

"Go ahead and run your hatch back. Be ready, Mr. DeKalb. We're a lot faster than they are. Be about twenty seconds and you all can shake hands."

With the side hatch open, the wind rampaged through the Bell's small cabin. "Keep it coming," said DeKalb. He was getting soaked, not that he felt it. He was hot, set on fire with something burning from the inside out. "Keep it coming. I see 'em."

They lofted above the Antonov's altitude. Decker left the power where it was. The turbines screamed as they burned in from behind.

Decker turned his head. His neck glistened with sweat. "Okay, boss. Lock and load."

DeKalb broke open the grenade launcher and dropped a 40mm cannister into the breach. It snapped together with a *clack*. He had to be careful. The wind could rip the thing out of his grip. He wrapped the sling around his forearm.

Decker rolled on full throttle and the Bell surged forward.

"Easy, easy," he said as the big biplane became a black, three-dimensional form against the tundra below, a party-favor sparkler burning where the big radial engine blew fire from its exhaust. "I'm gonna cut the engine when we get close and coast on up to them. Just drift on up like a big ol' gator snappin' up a goose for breakfast. They won't hear nothing before you thump 'em. You ready?"

"Ready." DeKalb pushed the muzzle of the M-209 into the gale. He could see details on the plane now. The tail, the braces that kept the antique from shivering apart. Even the splotchy paint job. Despite all the whispers to the contrary, hunting men was not in the same league as killing a tiger. A tiger was a force of nature. One you had to respect or pay the consequences. Compared to that, this was dead easy.

Yuri put his hand on the glareshield, then moved it to the window beside him.

"What's wrong?" asked Nowek.

"Something's vibrating."

"Everything's vibrating."

Yuri put a finger to each of the instrument dials.

Anna bent down. "Is everything all right?"

Yuri checked the engine instruments. The one-thousand-horsepower radial was a brute, but it was a dependable brute. Still, out here small vibrations were not things to ignore. He shrugged his shoulders. "I guess so. I thought . . ." He stopped. "Hear that?"

It was a low thud. Was it a cylinder coming detached? A rod ready to explode out through the crankcase? Despite the rumble, all the dials were normal. He put an ear to the window glass. The new sound became even stronger.

"Here she comes," said Decker. "I'm gonna pull up next to it then yank and bank. You'll have a clear shot straight down, Mr. DeKalb, but you'd best be strapped in if you don't want to go out the door yourself."

"We're too close!" said Joffrey. His hands were itching to grab the stick. "Decker, you're way too—"

The Antonov rushed backward at them.

"Get ready. Get ready." Decker twisted off the throttle. Their speed was still so much greater that even now, engines silent, the Antonov seemed stopped in midair. "Go for the cockpit. Get 'em where they live, boss."

DeKalb had his finger around the trigger. The safety was off. The fat little sausage in the bottom barrel ready to fire. Fragmentation round, 40mm. Lethal radius twenty feet. He could toss a rock and hit the damned thing with better than twenty-foot accuracy.

They passed *Little Annie*'s tail. The wings. The cockpit. Decker looked across and could see the glow of instrument lights. "Here we go!" He twisted on full throttle and pulled them up and over.

The Bell leaped and banked over onto its side. DeKalb's

hatch faced straight down to the black earth. But in between was the Antonov. "Now! Shoot!"

DeKalb hung from his seat belt, struggling to center the cockpit in the top sights. He braced his boots, steadied his arm against the one-hundred-knot wind, and pulled the trigger.

There was a disappointingly small burp. A flash. The pop of a champagne cork.

Decker pulled the collective and cyclic. It mashed them down hard in their seats as the Bell soared up and away from the impending disaster.

CHAPTER
23

THE HELICOPTER'S JET ENGINES screamed back to life so close and so loud it seemed to come from inside the Antonov, from within Yuri's own skull. "It's going to blow!"

Yuri meant *Annushka*'s engine, but even as he yelled he knew the sound was all wrong. There was no way to mistake the shriek of a turbine for a radial's rumble. He looked up and saw something so strange, so unexpected, that he blinked, half expecting it to disappear.

A flash, and then a soft, leaden *thump* from out on the right wing.

A helicopter?

"What was—" Anna began.

"Get down!" Yuri threw an arm against Anna and she fell back. He slammed the wheel far over. The heavy biplane began to roll. At once the control wheel began to shake, to vibrate.

"What was that?" asked Nowek, but Yuri wasn't answering.

He rammed the big black throttle lever forward and hauled back on the shaking yoke and stood *Annushka* on its wing, curling around in an impossibly tight spiral. The big radial engine spat blue flames and stumbled, then surged.

A brilliant flash erupted down on the ground below and behind; it illuminated the silver pipeline, then surrounded it in

a white spherical shock wave. At its heart was a red tongue of
fire that faded as the grenade's blast dissipated.

"Hold on!" He pulled back and pointed the nose of the
biplane toward the belly of the clouds. They were close to
them, because even before he could explain what he was doing,
before he could say that someone was out there, someone who
meant them harm, they were enveloped in cold, clammy gray.

A loud drumming filled the cockpit. It wasn't rain beating
against the windshield. It was coming from the upper wing, out
on the right side. The yoke trembled. The engine needles
might be healthy, but something was coming apart. They could
stay inside the cloud for as long as they had fuel. Or until
something out on the damaged wing broke in earnest. Or until
whoever had fired at them would go away. It was all a question
of which would happen first.

"Did you get him? Did you hit him?" Decker held the Bell
in a hover as the biplane vanished behind a curtain of snow and
rain.

The lights of Tunguska were a red glow defining the northern horizon. When the clouds opened, the flickering candles of
the three tall flare stacks appeared, then, ghostly, vanished.

"I don't know." DeKalb put the night vision goggles away.
"He started moving. I think I got a piece of him."

Joffrey let out a long breath. Good, he thought. Next week
when the Air Alaska charter showed, he would be on it. He
was out of this zoo. He'd had enough of the damned project,
sneaking around. Get free, take a shower, and wash off the dirt.
Wouldn't that be something? They could keep the money.

"A piece?" Decker hunted for the missing plane. "Hell. He
was close enough to chuck rocks at, boss. I mean, I put you
right in there. Could of spit in his ear."

The slipstream fed a torrent of icy wet air into the helicopter.
DeKalb felt the M-209 begin to slip. The wind was snatching
at it. He pulled it closer to his chest. The wind! He'd forgotten
the wind! The target had only looked motionless. Between the
M-209's muzzle and the Antonov a river of one-hundred-knot

wind was flowing. A hurricane and then some. He hadn't accounted for it, and it made his grenade curve away from the cockpit. His fault. "Turn us around. Let's make sure of him."

"No can do. He just up and flew into a cloud." Harley tried to escape from Decker's breast pocket. The pilot slapped the ferret hard. With a squeak, the animal dived back down.

"There's no radar? Nothing we can use to spot them?"

"Nossir. What you see is what we got. If that old boy's any good on instruments we'll never know where he is till he decides to come on out."

"He can't stay inside that cloud forever."

"Paul." Joffrey tapped the fuel counter.

"I see it," said Decker. "You have an idea?"

Ideas? He wished he'd kept that woman the hell off his site. He wished he'd told the home office that public relations was their problem, that Tunguska, and Elgen, were his. But it was too late for that now. Too late for ideas. "Okay." DeKalb nodded. "He was headed for Tunguska. We'll do the same."

When LeRoy came to, the room was empty again. He might have imagined everything, the fight, the stink, the press of bodies, the rapes, except for the fact that he burned inside like they'd poured acid into him. They'd made him their catcher, their punk. They'd hurt him badly. He rolled over.

The medicine, he thought. It had to be that shit they'd given him back at Travis. Took away his mind, his powers.

He pushed himself up. The rags they'd torn off him were in a heap. The stove was still warm. There were tin cans underneath it, some sealed, some peeled open. He reached out and snatched an empty one.

It was dark brown, covered in some kind of weird writing. But all writing was foreign to him, so it didn't matter. There was a metal key still attached and this got his eyes into focus. This drew his professional interest.

He eased his pants back on. They busted him up bad. He could feel the steady trickle of blood down the inside of his legs. *Fresh fish* . . . He licked his lips. His throat was dust.

There was a bucket filled with filthy snow melt. He cupped a hand into it and brought it to his lips. He drank it down, feeling his strength return. Metal. He grabbed the tin. The edges were good and sharp. He unrolled the key from the pried-up lid, carefully flattening the metal, folding it quickly into an elongated triangle.

The piece gradually assumed a more lethal shape. *Catcher . . . punk.* When he was done he examined his work.

It was narrow and long, the edges sharp where he wanted them, rolled blunt where he could grip it. It was light. No good for shoving through ribs. It might bend in half. But the edges would cut.

A noise.

He smothered the shiv beneath him and squatted as a man came in. A guard. He saw his own tennis shoes on his feet. Fuck. Bang Stick, only this time, he didn't have the cattle prod.

He felt the buzz, a tingle that started down low in his belly, reaching up, filling him. His monster.

LeRoy sized him up in an eye blink. Rifle. Pistol. His own shoes, shoes that LeRoy could *fly* in if he got the chance. Took the chance. Payback time, motherfucker. Guess who's gonna cash your check? His buzz was *ringing*.

"Up! You get up now!"

LeRoy groaned. He didn't move.

The rifle came up. "You get up now!" The guard swung the wooden stock. He was aiming to smash LeRoy's teeth out. Instead, LeRoy grabbed it. The lightning bolts on his forearm bulged as LeRoy yanked him off his feet. The tin flashed in the dim light: silver, silver, pink, red.

He let the guard down and took his own shoes back.

The rifle was empty. The pistol was not. The shoes felt real good on his feet. So did the uniform, the sheepskin coat, the fur hat, the heavy felt pants.

LeRoy wrapped him in his own bloody pants and pushed the body into a corner. The gun in his pocket, he walked right out the door and into the snow.

Perimeter lights. Chain-link fence. Beyond it nothing but

black forest, ghost silver trees catching reflected light. No sound but the crunch of his feet on dirty ice. Where was this place? Cold. Mountains. Had to be the motherfucking mountains. He waited, watching, taking in everything. He kept coming back to that fence, and what he saw made him smile.

He'd seen better security fences in reform school. It was a double course of chain link separated by a moat filled with a tangle of razor wire about five feet wide. At the top of each fence a single naked strand of copper conductor was strung, isolated from the posts by ceramic knobs. Juiced. Cheap motherfuckers, he thought. You made that fucking moat too narrow. He took another deep breath of clean air.

Mountains. The Sierra Nevada. He'd seen them as a kid growing up in the blue-collar oil towns of central California. White snow shimmering above the valley dust, the valley heat, floating like some kind of dream. Like Shangri-la. Always said he'd go up to where it was clean and cool, but this wasn't what he had in mind. His breath flagged white.

"Where the fuck you goin' now?"

LeRoy spun. It was the big black. The boss. He was standing in the shadows, leaning on the wooden siding of the hut. Alone.

"Ain't no place to run. Don't even think about it."

"I ain't thinkin'," said LeRoy, snarling it. He smiled as he gripped the pistol in his pocket. "I'm *doin'*." He could feel the tingle again, louder, clearer than before. A big tuning fork buzzing in his crotch.

The boss laughed. "You don't know a damned thing, do you?"

"I know you're all by yourself." He took a step. "I know you're gonna help me outta here."

"The fuck I am." The boss emerged from the shadows. "You in kindergarten. Time you graduated." He reached into his pocket.

LeRoy tensed.

A bright reflection. Not a shiv. Not a gun. A whistle.

The black started to put it to his lips.

LeRoy felt the buzz go right up his spine, right into his brain, then echo down his limbs. Lightning bolts like the ones on his arm, only for real. An electric jolt that sent him flying through the air straight at that taunting voice. The guard's pistol came out. Finger through the trigger guard, thumb off the safety. Got to get closer. No noise.

LeRoy rammed him back into the shadows, flat against the rough wood planks. The whistle fell to the snow. The black man's arms went up and gripped LeRoy's shoulders, trying to fend him off. He was remarkably thin, strangely weak. Elgen had drained him. LeRoy was fresh from CDC Pelican Bay, a prison equipped with a gym, with weight machines, with time to work out and food to make you strong. The difference was telling, and it was immediate.

LeRoy batted away the man's arms and thrust the short-barrel Makarov deep into the folds of his overcoat. Then without the slightest hesitation, he gutshot him.

A muffled pop, a hot white cloud of cordite and the black man flew backward against the wood, his eyes wide, his hands holding his belly, his mouth opening in a scream.

LeRoy moved in again. He smashed the man's head back into the wood, once, again, a third time, once for every groan, for every wheeze, for every time those men had taken him down and put his face into the dirt. For every time they'd made him their catcher, their punk. Blood and spit flecked the dead man's mouth.

His arms were hot, sweat beaded from his face. The buzz was on him good. He lifted the body like it was weightless and took it to the fence. The right distance. The right angle. Like putting a fucking ball over home plate. Measuring with a careful eye, he threw the man up over the top.

The feet snagged on the inner fence with a jolt and snap of blue fire. The body quivered and jigged as it bridged the moat. A bright shower of sparks, a smell of burned meat, and then a big relay clunked and the camp lights flickered. An alarm horn began to hoot.

It was time.

LeRoy stuck a toe into the fence and climbed right straight up, onto the body, clambering over it, over the moat with its razors, and over the bloody head to the outside fence. He vaulted over the final hot wire and landed in snow.

Outside.

Voices. Shouts. LeRoy Rogers scrambled to his feet as first one, then another searchlight blinked on. They swept the fence, stopping at the body. He ran for the darkness, ran for the forest that lapped Elgen like an ocean. Running, running. He'd run all the way down this mountain if he had to. He wasn't home yet. But LeRoy, and his monster, were free.

Yuri lit a cigarette with shaking hands as he flew through the murk. He hated instrument flying. Depending on little needles, gears, wires, and tubes to live. But tonight he was grateful. He considered them deities, good gremlins, living in *Annushka*'s guts. But gremlins that could turn to imps, to devils, at the snap of a spring. He drew half the Marlboro down with a single drag. Only then did he pull the engine back to a more normal setting. Tunguska was near. Off to his left somewhere, and very close.

"What did they shoot at us?" asked Anna.

"A rocket. It hit something." He checked his watch. His hand was trembling. "We're there."

"Tunguska?"

"Right below." He turned until the gyro compass showed the number 335 in the smudged window.

"I think I can see where it hit." Anna had her head up against the overhead window. She could see something out there on the wing. "Something's moving out there. Flapping."

"Wonderful." He looked at Nowek. "Take the wheel. Don't do anything but hold it. See this needle?" He pointed to the gyro. "Keep it on three thirty-five. Okay?"

"I'll try." Nowek took the wheel. Down below, down underneath the clouds, in some American's cabin, was Galena. Could she hear him? Could she sense him? As a child she would cry when the wind began howling, the snow hissing against their house like it had been fired from a sandblaster. He would leave Nina, rise, find a robe, and go comfort her.

Yuri grabbed the primitive nightscope, let go of the wheel, and stood up.

"There's definitely something moving out there." She stood back and let Yuri peer out.

He trained the nightscope on it. The image faded green to black, to dim green. The batteries were dying and he couldn't waste them . . .

"Yuri! I can't fly this thing!"

"Try harder." He flicked off the scope and looked at Anna. "I'm going to turn the lights on, then off. You watch and see what's out there." He dropped back into his seat and took the wheel back. Nowek let go as though the wheel were scalding hot.

Yuri reached down to the navigation light switch, then looked back over his shoulder. "Ready?"

He flicked them on, then off.

In the flash of green light, Anna saw a great black flag of fabric whipping in the wind, streaming back from the upper wing panel. "It's a loose piece of skin. About three meters by two. It's pretty big."

Nowek remembered how the fabric covering had seemed loose to begin with. Like his own green suit. Now it was ripping apart at the seams. "Can we still land at Tunguska?"

"Mayor, landing is the very least of our concerns."

Ice pellets beat against the windows. The Antonov was a biplane. It had four fat wings. But that didn't mean he could afford to lose one of them. He touched the throttle. He was about to nudge it forward.

And then there was no more time to decide. With a rip and a swerve, *Annushka* pivoted hard right. She slewed drunkenly, her rear fishtailing as Yuri fought the skid with full rudder. When he straightened them out, the wheel in his hands was fully deflected to the left and his leg stood out straight, pressing the right rudder pedal to the floorboards. It was not a condition the Antonov was designed for. Even with the engine roaring at full throttle they began to drop. "You remember rule number one?" he shouted at Nowek.

"Never crash?"

"I think we're going to break it."

The Bell darted through the sleet at twice the speed of the Antonov. The lights of Tunguska showed as a furry smudge against the streaked canopy glass. The burning flare gas was clearly visible; three orange cones of fire licking the bellies of the clouds. They were very close.

"Five klicks," said Decker. He turned to DeKalb. "You want me to put down at the pad and wait?"

"They can't just disappear."

"Lot of dark country out here," said Decker. "If they went down, it's gonna be tough to find them. Even in daylight. They find a reasonable spot to land they might walk away."

"That's not going to happen."

"Yessir. I mean no. I hear you." Decker banked away from home and began to hunt the clouds again.

The rain fell off to a spatter as they dropped down into clear air. Yuri was fighting the controls, balancing them like a broomstick on his palm. His right leg shook with the strain, the fatigue. One instant of inattention and they'd fall off on the damaged wing into a spin from which there could be no recovery. He risked a quick peek and saw three flickering candles loom out of the blackness ahead. "Mayor!"

Nowek saw it, too. Flare gas burning. Tunguska.

Yuri wedged the shuddering wheel against his knee, put the nightscope to his eye and flicked it on one final time. The world went from black to gray to green to black. The batteries were dead. He threw it to the floor. "Where is your road?" he yelled at Anna.

They swept over the outermost rig towers, dark and abandoned.

"Northeast! Over there!" She pointed to the right.

Yuri let the damaged wing pull them around to the right. "Okay. I'm going to have to use the lights. You understand?"

He reached for the silver toggle switch. He turned the lights on.

Gravel roads, ponds filled with drilling mud. Outbuildings and pipe racks. Piles of expensive oil recovery gear rusting to sculpture. Then, the long causeway leading to the Tiger Census building appeared at the far range of the light's beam.

They were below the three high stacks.

"Get set," said Yuri as he frantically spun the trim wheel. "This won't be a pretty landing."

Decker spun the nimble Bell in a quick pirouette to face the flash of white light off to their left. "Damn. That boy's landing on the road." He rolled on throttle and dipped the nose. The Bell accelerated.

There was no way to stretch a glide. The gravel roadbed seemed impossibly far. Try to haul the nose up to reach it and all you do is stall into the ground. Or spin. Gliding took speed. He pushed the nose over. Would they make the causeway? It reminded Yuri of the old saying that when forced down at night, you put on your landing lights. If you don't like what you see, you turn them off.

They were losing altitude. "Brace yourselves!"

Anna crouched behind Nowek's seat. She wrapped her arms around his chest, linking her fingers like the buckle of a seat belt.

"We're landing! When we stop, throw open the hatch and run. Everybody run." He looked at Nowek. "You know? Maybe Plet was right about flying."

"You can do it."

"We'll see very soon if you're right."

One hundred meters; then fifty. Thirty meters. Altitude they would never reclaim. Not with *Annushka*'s wing peeled back. How would he fly home? The bones . . .

Fifteen meters.

"Get ready!" he shouted.

Nowek saw no difference in the blackness outside. Only the red glow of the flare stacks seemed to have risen into the sky.

Anna's arms tightened around him. So tight he could hardly breathe.

Yuri could smell the ground; the ice had melted enough to release the gassy stink of the marsh and mud. He pulled back on the yoke and broke their descent into a flatter glide. Fifteen. Ten meters.

"Brace yourself!"

Nowek braced his legs against the instrument panel.

Anna whispered something. He couldn't quite hear it.

Humps of reeds and black marsh braided with water, drifts of snow, all racing by in the glare of the landing beam. The illusion of speed was no illusion. They were fast. Yuri hauled full back on the yoke just as the wheels struck a hummock. Yuri killed the throttle. It popped like gunfire.

The Antonov bounced them up into the air, high, slowing, slowing, then they struck again, this time on the edge of the gravel road. Yuri kicked them into a swerving turn and aligned them down the causeway's length. The lights swept across the Tiger Census building, a photographic flash that burned an image into his retina: the signs, the stacked box traps, and two of those strange little vehicles, the moon buggies. Then darkness.

The wheels struck. They dug into the gravel and held. The tail rose. Yuri pulled back on the yoke but it was no good. The propeller dug in. They began to swerve. The tail went up, up and over, tumbling them in a vicious snap. The lights shattered. The canopy glass burst from its frames, scooping in raw wet mud and the buckshot of granite gravel. They were upside down. A wing crumpled with a rip of wood and fabric.

A final jounce and then silence. Raw fuel was everywhere. It dripped through the upside-down cockpit. Raining petrol.

The linked hand at his chest disengaged finger by finger, and Nowek fell, landing on what had been the cabin roof. Gasoline flowed onto his face, cool, poisonous.

Yuri was already there, bent nearly double. He looked over
at Nowek and said, "I hope those bones are there, Mayor. I
need a new airplane thanks to you and your . . ." He stopped.

"What is it?" asked Nowek.

"Listen."

A low thud. Growing louder.

"Run." Yuri grabbed Nowek's shoulder and spun him out
of the inverted cabin. *"Run!"*

"Chuchin!" Nowek tumbled out of the hatch expecting a
jump down and instead finding the ground. The upended fuselage was level with the gravel, the tail either buried in the muck
or sheared off entirely. The helicopter was no longer a thump.
It was a whine. It was close. The Tiger Census building was too
far. "Chuchin!"

Yuri pushed him off the gravel and into the bogs, then
jumped down beside him. They came up next to Chuchin, but
there was no sign of Anna.

"Where did she go?" Nowek shouted as the Bell swung to
face them, its tail high, the rotor an invisible steel disk.

Chuchin pointed at the buildings.

"They're down on that road, Mr. Decker."

"Looks like they busted up getting stopped. Yeah. Flipped
right on over," said Decker. "They might be alive. Might be
armed and they sure as shit know we're coming. I'm gonna
give you a high pass. I won't hover. You got that, Mr. DeKalb?
You gotta hit 'em on the run and I sure hope you do a little bit
better than last time."

Joffrey sat with his hands still clear of the controls. As though
it absolved him.

"Lock and load."

There was a new 40mm cannister in the breech. DeKalb
snapped it shut, locked it, then wrapped a finger through the
trigger guard. The hatch was open. He was soaked, cold, and
angry. But DeKalb was ready. He ran the illumination on his
night vision goggles up full. The world was brilliant green. The
Antonov sat at an odd angle, flat to the gravel road or half

buried in it, he couldn't tell. Wheels in the air, upside down. They were probably dead already. Or too smashed up to move.

Excellent. All those problems tucked away in one basket. He thrust the muzzle into the slipstream and leaned far out. Hundred knots of wind. Speed. Angle and distance. The human mind was the greatest killing machine the world had ever known.

As the Bell swept overhead he fired. The grenade popped with a bright flash. One second. Two seconds.

There was a small white flicker, followed by a tremendous secondary detonation. As he watched, pieces of the Antonov flew up and tumbled, propelled into the air one last time on a column of greasy, gasoline fire.

"Well," said Decker. "I guess that's about all the damage we can do for one night." He came to a hover as the pieces slowly dropped back to earth.

"Put down by the building," said DeKalb. "I want to see for myself."

The ruddy light of the burning Antonov lit Chuchin's pale face. He aimed the old Nagant at the hovering helicopter. He was about to squeeze off a shot when Yuri shoved the pistol away. "Don't!" He wanted to kill them too, but right now he preferred to live, and living depended on those bastards believing him already dead.

They sheltered in the icy muck off to the side of the road. The wind blew the stink of burning fabric, gasoline, and rubber over them in a pall. The fire was hot on their faces.

"Well, now we're really stranded." Yuri watched silently as his prize possession was reduced to ash. "You know how far it is to walk back to Markovo? It's even farther with a hundred kilos of bone on your back."

The helicopter swept low over the fire, then peeled off in the direction of the Tiger Census Building.

"Fuck," swore Yuri. "They're landing."

The Bell settled, bounced, then dropped again. The side hatch was flung wide. Nowek could make out one figure emerging, then, after a few seconds, another. How many were in there?

The rotors kept spinning, the turbine howled at high idle.

"This time you'll let me shoot," said Chuchin.

Yuri had the little Skorpion out. He raised the machine pistol, sighting over the tiny black pips on its snub barrel.

The two from the helicopter advanced down the gravel toward the burning biplane. They stayed apart, sweeping the area ahead of them with their weapons.

"They don't see her," said Nowek.

"So? They'll see us," whispered Chuchin.

It was pitch black except for the light of the flames. How were they seeing anything? Nightscopes? Something. They came steadily, moving quickly from one side of the road to the other, peering down into the icy muck on either side. Closer. Fifty feet. Thirty.

Any second.

Chuchin raised the Nagant and held it steady. He sucked in a long, deep breath.

Suddenly there was movement by the Tiger Census Building.

The two stopped and turned. One of the moon buggies was rolling toward the helicopter.

One of the figures let loose a burst of automatic fire, raking the little buggy. A jet of escaping gas erupted from its high-pressure fuel tank.

The *lunashkhod* tracked straight and true.

Another burst of fire. The buggy trailed a white cloud of vapor from the leaking fuel.

The two men began trotting back toward the Bell.

Yuri said, "She's going to ram those . . ."

The moon buggy crunched into the tail rotor. Its blades ripped into the already punctured tank of gas hydrate. A white mist enveloped the Bell's tail. It expanded into a foggy sphere; a petrochemical cocoon. It reached the helicopter's turbine exhaust.

"Anna!" Nowek stood up. Chuchin grabbed his knees and

pulled him back down as the Bell erupted into a fireball that expanded forward, reaching the machine's own fuel tanks, breaching them.

A second detonation tore through it. The rotors, suddenly free of the weight of the aircraft, spun up into the sky, higher, higher, like a maple seed rising, like a child's toy. They crumpled and fell against the metal roof of the Tiger Census Building. The rumbling blast ebbed as white heat receded down the spectrum to yellow and purple.

Yuri spotted movement by the building. "Someone's coming!"

Another moon buggy.

It was rushing down the gravel road, straight for them.

Yuri stood up, the Skorpion level braced against his waist.

A flicker, a flash of light. A familiar flag of dark hair streaming back in the wind. Nowek knocked the weapon aside. "No!" he shouted as the *lunashkhod* pulled up.

Anna was at the wheel. In her lap was George, the calico. Tigers were the largest cats. Here was the smallest of tigers.

Nowek jumped into the moon buggy beside her. "How did you do that?"

There was something wild, something unexpectedly feral in her expression. Something furious. "It was easy," she said.

The fire was spreading to the Tiger Census Building. It licked its way up the wooden stairs. It ate through the roof, papers rose on the heat, burning, flying, rimmed in gold.

The rifle Nowek had last seen on her wall lay across the rear cargo deck of the buggy.

Yuri stared at the building. "The bones," he said.

Nowek watched corrugated metal peel back as bright flames flooded up the wooden structure within.

"I'm sorry, Yuri," she said. "You'd better get in."

Yuri did, sniffing the smoke. It smelled like money burning. His future burning. The mouths of so many American presidents screaming for his help, for rescue. White Bird Aviation. His dreams. All of it gone.

Chuchin jumped into the moon buggy.

"Galena," said Nowek. "We have to—"

"Hang on. We're going to get her." With a surge of power, she accelerated away from the Tiger Census Building, dropped off the gravel road, and flew across a pond of standing icewater and mud. There was another flash from far behind, another detonation, but it didn't matter now. They were beyond stopping. The little moon buggy's tires whined and churned up sprays of slush as they flew across the snow, heading for Decker's cabin.

CHAPTER
24

THE GRENADE ARCED high into the night, tipped over, and dropped behind the fleeing buggy. It flashed white, and then a low detonation rumbled across the frozen ground like summer thunder. DeKalb could no longer spot them. They were off the causeway, taking off cross-country. He shouldered the M-209 and stood in the white hot heat of what had once been a two-million-dollar helicopter, and one of his own pilots.

The insulation in the Tiger Census building was burning, letting off a poisonous stink. There was an organic note to it, a strange, cooked flesh sort of smell. Could someone have been in there? Too late to wonder. The wooden pilings the building rested on burned from the top down like candles.

He moved to escape the acrid smoke and found Decker.

"They took them a buggy," said the pilot. Night vision goggles dangled from his neck. His eyes were two white circles surrounded by soot. The little ferret in his pocket was squirming to escape. It put its sharp nose into the air, smelled the fire, and began to claw. Decker slapped it back down. "They rammed the bird and then they up and *ran* off."

"But where to? Why come back up here?" DeKalb looked at Decker. "You talked with him. Any idea why the mayor is buzzing around me like a goddamned bee?"

"Me? Nossir." But that wasn't so. He had a pretty good idea

why Nowek was back, and where he was headed. He also knew what not to say to DeKalb. "Any which way they go we'll get 'em. Even if that buggy's full of gas they can go only forty, fifty kilometers in a straight line. They can't make it back to Markovo."

DeKalb didn't share Decker's optimism. He was drawing a circle on a map in his head. Fifty klicks wouldn't get them back to town, but it could be a problem.

Decker saw the thought behind DeKalb's worried look. "Buggy won't get them up there and back, Mr. DeKalb. No way."

Elgen. It could get them there, thought DeKalb. One way. No return. Who in God's name would head up there *knowing* they'd have to walk out? And where could they walk *to*? Unless they made an arrangement with someone for a pickup. An aircraft? Jesus. It was possible.

DeKalb stared into sweeps of rain, the occasional wet flake mixed in for interest. He turned and peered into the blackened cockpit. Joffrey, not that the charred, misshapen object sitting in the seat could be identified at a glance. He had both fists up and balled as though sparring with the flames. Teeth, wrists, and ankles, white shimmered in reflected firelight where the fire had eaten him all the way down to bone. Kerosene burned hot.

"Dumb fuck. Wouldn't have happened if he'd asked about transporting the tiger gal," Decker said.

DeKalb didn't turn. "It wouldn't have happened if you had done your job, either. I asked for those tapes. Not a goddamned mayor on a goddamned investigation." He turned. "Let's go."

"Go?"

"We're gonna call this one in to the locals."

Galena heard a sound and woke from a fitful sleep. Decker. He was back. She blinked, listening to the whine grow strong, grow near. One of those little cars. She pulled the blanket off. She'd found a pair of his overalls, the orange overalls with the moon and oil-rig insignia of AmerRus on them. An old pair, because they had a long rip in the upper thigh. A hole.

She swung her legs out of bed and with the spike of glass in her hand, she jumped to the door and flipped off the lights. She was sore, her inner thighs bruised. The pain brought her full awake. It brought everything back. The pain brought back the fury.

The whine subsided. She heard a voice. She stepped back so that when the door opened she'd be behind it. The neck, she thought. First the neck, then his balls. She touched the tip of the glass shard and imagined thrusting it right through Decker's heart. Afterward. She'd save that for last.

The doorknob turned. She tensed on her feet, waiting in the darkness. The outside bolt slid free with a *clack*. The door cracked open. Cold spilled in around her naked feet.

The door swung wide suddenly and violently. It struck her bare toes and she yelled.

"Galena?"

She threw the door back off her and heard it strike something solid. She raised the chunk of glass and charged around. A shadowy figure inside the door. She screamed and slashed at it before her brain could register that the voice calling her name was not Decker, it didn't even belong to a man, or that the other voice belonged to her own father.

"Galena!"

She twisted the shard. The glass snagged, then snapped against something soft, something yielding. She raised it again to strike. It didn't matter who . . .

But now a hand gripped her arm and held it.

"Galena! Stop it!" shouted Nowek. "Stop it!"

Galena was trembling with rage, powerful with hate. She was possessed by the adrenal demons that permit men to lift cars. To raise impossible boulders. She tried to break free but her hand was getting squeezed hard. Very hard. Painfully hard.

A hand struck the light switch. The fluorescents buzzed on.

Nowek had an iron grip on both her arms. She dropped the glass and balled her hands to her mouth when she saw a woman dressed in her own mother's clothes. She fell back against the wall.

Anna's sleeve was sliced open. A piece of glass was caught in the fabric of Nina's heavy sweater.

Galena's eyes filled. She was going crazy. She was already dead. How else could this happen? Her father, her mother three years in the ground . . .

"Galinka." Nowek's face seemed to melt. He held her tight, so tight it was hard for her to breathe except in short gasps.

"I've come for you."

"We should go," said Anna. "Right now."

Nowek didn't hear. Galena looked over Nowek's shoulder as he swung her side to side. Her eyes tracked Anna silently. He wanted to say, no. It isn't what you think. But he wasn't so sure anymore. Not so sure at all. There was something hard, a lump, pressed between them. He put her back down onto her feet. He saw a bulge in one of the zippered pockets at her breast and thought of Decker's animal, his rat.

He saw the tear in the orange fabric, too. The rip. The hole that suggested a missing piece of fabric that he knew perfectly well. "Where did you get this?" he asked her.

"It's Decker's. I got it here."

Decker. Nowek remembered the way he'd made that silver knife appear when he'd snagged his coat on the moon buggy's frame. It had just materialized, cut the looping thread, and vanished. Why had he not noticed that? Why hadn't he seen?

"What's wrong, Father?"

That was all for later. "Where are your boots?" he said. "Get them on."

Galena couldn't look down. Couldn't look away. What if she did and this woman who looked so much . . . what if she vanished? "Who are you? Why are you wearing my mother's clothes?"

"I'll explain everything later," said Nowek. "We're going home." How? He didn't have to say it. It was on his face like shame.

But Galena stood rooted. Miracles were rare. Everyone said

so, though Galena had never lived one to know. She wasn't letting go of this one so soon. She ran to Anna, burying her face into the sweater with its smell of camphor, of wool, of home. She began to sob, not in the throat, but from deeper inside. "Who . . . who are you?"

"Come with me. Inside." Anna guided her back into the cabin.

Galena wouldn't let go. She took her to the bed, but Galena suddenly stiffened. There was no way she would sit on it. She looked up at Anna, her eyes not seeing, her brain remembering.

"You can call me Anna."

"Anna? But . . ."

"Sssh." She found Galena's boots in the ruin and wreckage. A pair of mismatched socks, both Decker's. She made Galena put them on, all the while nervously looking back at the door. She picked the sliver of glass from her sleeve. It had sliced the wool, but not her arm.

"Where . . . where are we going?"

Anna saw the hard yearning in Galena's face. She wished she could come back for her the way Galena wanted. Needed.

"You heard your father. You're going home." She looked up at Nowek. Somehow.

Nowek saw something poke from Galena's overalls. The hard lump he'd felt when he'd hugged her. "What's that?"

She pulled out the ornate cigarette lighter she'd taken from Decker's drawer.

"Where did you get that?"

"Here. Right here." She pressed the tiny metal stud and the clever door flipped open. "Who is she, Father? Why does she look like Mother? Why does she have on her clothes? How . . ."

"I'll tell the story, but it's not yet over." Nowek saw a photograph inside the secret compartment. He took the lighter and peered in.

Stalin laughing with his mouth wide open, his "iron teeth" on display. Two generals at his feet, stolid, unsmiling, worried.

Who wouldn't be? And next to him a young man with wheat-blond hair and a look of nervous exhaustion.

The man with the nervous look? Andrei Ryzkhov's father.

He snapped it shut, feeling the sudden acceleration of a river finding the weak place in a concrete wall, discovering its own true course, rushing with the energy that comes from truth. A tape. A negotiation. A knife. Now this. Decker.

"Mayor!"

It was Chuchin.

Nowek stuffed the antique lighter into a pocket and took Galena's hand. He held it as though he were welded to her. Even outside in the moon buggy he refused to let go. Yuri and Chuchin were in the back. The rifle with its big scope lay across their knees. The cat sat in the driver's seat, of course.

They clambered onto the overloaded vehicle. It sagged on its balloon wheels. The rain hardened, congealing.

Anna pushed the calico aside. It took a swipe at her hand, but she didn't notice. Nowek and Galena shared the seat next to her.

Nowek showed the lighter to Chuchin.

"No thanks. I'm giving up habits that are bad for health."

"It's Ryzkhov's. It came from in there." He nodded at the cabin. "You know what I'm saying? The American had it. Decker. And look." He pulled Galena's overalls away from her slender body to show him the rip, the hole.

"So." Chuchin snorted. "Being right is nice. Being alive is even nicer. What do we do now?"

"How far will this machine go?" Nowek asked Anna.

"We don't have a full tank. Thirty kilometers at most."

Thirty. It wouldn't take them even halfway home. He reached down into his padded jacket and pulled out the knife Anna had given him. The shaman blade. The ivory handle glowed like the moon through a cloud. The cold steel blade, wickedly sharp, glinted. Sharp enough to cut without feeling, a mysterious miracle of some native Buryat armorer. He held it out.

"You're sure you want to give me that?"

"You could say that events have overtaken my suspicions."

"Excuse me," said Yuri, "but it's no suspicion that we're five against all of AmerRus. We're alone in the middle of Tunguska and this little car may be remarkable, but it won't fly. Forget tiger bones. I'm starting to worry about mine."

"We could steal a helicopter," Chuchin suggested.

"Better steal a helicopter pilot while you're at it," Yuri replied. "I can't fly one."

"I have a better idea." Anna opened her rucksack. She pulled out a small box and placed it onto the moon buggy's dash. She pressed a button and a small LCD display lit up in soft, golden light.

"What's that?" said Chuchin.

Yuri answered before Anna. "GPS," he said. "Satellite navigation. You know how much those things cost? I could sell them all day for five, six thousand. Why didn't you show it to me before when we were flying? I could have used it."

"I got it from my office. With the rifle. We can still use it to make a straight line course. That will maximize the buggy's range."

"It won't maximize it all the way to Markovo," said Nowek.

"No." Anna looked at Nowek. "But it may take us far enough. It may take us all the way out of Siberia."

"What's that mean?"

"It can take us to the world."

The world? What was she talking about? Yufa had said it: this was the world. His world. He and men like him controlled it. Nowek was the trespasser. "This is no time for riddles."

"I know. Will you trust me?" she said.

He held Galena tight. For himself, sure. For Chuchin, for Yuri. They could decide for themselves. But for his daughter? Did he trust this woman with his daughter's life? His own stowaway to the future? He remembered Anna in his arms, her smell, her feel, her breath bringing him back from the thin ice, the blackness. To life. Nowek looked at her. The space between them shimmered, melted again, though he didn't so much as move, didn't so much as breathe. "I trust you. But you'd better be right."

She nodded. "Okay." Anna punched in a quick set of coordinates, then pressed the DIRECT-TO button on the GPS unit. "We can use the river for a road. The buggy will make better time on a solid surface. We might squeeze a little more range from it that way."

An arrow appeared in the display, along with a direction, a distance, and a time en route. She swung the steering wheel to match the arrow and pressed the accelerator.

"I don't like this, Mr. Mayor," said Chuchin as he held on.

Sluggish under the heavy load, the moon buggy set out over the dark, frozen marshes. A quarter kilometer elapsed on the tiny display, then a half. At just under two, the path entered a thin forest of stunted pine. Only here did Anna switch on the headlights. The path through the trees was well worn. It emerged at the banks of a river: the Nizhnaya Tunguska.

A thin wet fog had risen in response to the rain; battling elements, spring and winter. The river ice chilled the air to the dew point. Nowek could watch the fog rise, swirl, solidify.

The moon buggy bumped over the rocks along the banks, then tipped down to the wet ice. The low-pressure tires did not sink through. Two bright tunnels of light beamed ahead; a black, empty hole cut through the mist swirled shut behind. Anna switched the headlights off. The flat, open river was easy enough to see, to steer by.

Following the arrow on the little navigator, she turned north.

LeRoy's foot struck a hidden root and he fell face first to the snow. Half an hour of running and his feet were nothing more than stumps. No feeling. Nothing. He willed his foot to pull out from under the root. He started walking again. Fucking snow. Mountains. He'd never look up at them again and make a wish. The beach. That's where he'd live from here on. Palm trees. Bikinis. Fuck. *No* bikinis. One foot. Another.

He found the frozen stream not fifty meters later.

The surface was good and hard. It wasn't too slick from rain. He pressed down and heard a faint crackle. Real good. But which way? Had to be someone he could find. Someone meant food. A warm house. A car that would drive him out of this motherfucking ice and snow. He'd be in the city by daylight, if he could just figure out which way to go.

It was black. Clouds low and heavy. Spitting ice pellets. Low trees clung to the bank of the ravine. A wind shook the branches.

He started walking along the solid ice. In another fifty meters, the stream opened out onto a river. Out in the middle he heard the ripple of moving water over rocks. Along the edge the ice seemed sturdy enough. Clumps of reeds were caught in dead vegetation along its stony bank.

Left or right? Inside prison you ran the exercise yard to the left. Nobody knew why. It was just what everyone did. Counterclockwise. For that reason alone, LeRoy turned right.

LeRoy was correct; right was his lucky direction. North would be a thousand-kilometer walk to the Arctic.

Right would take him to Tunguska.

Decker emerged from the communications shack and immediately saw something he didn't like: across the runway, the door of his own hut was wide open. He carried DeKalb's big Ruger hunting rifle. He put his goggles on, dialed them up and looked into the darkness at his cabin. Nothing. Gone.

"What is it, Mr. Decker?" asked DeKalb. He turned and looked. "Who's over there?"

"Damned if I know." Decker yanked the goggles off.

"Your whore taking a walk?"

"She can't go nowhere."

"That better be true." DeKalb carried a fresh bag of grenades. "Kaznin is on the way."

"Solo?"

"With a squad. Call sign 'Berkut.' I alerted Gromov as well." He looked at Decker. "Let's get the Chinook turned around. We're going hunting."

★   ★   ★

The Ministry helicopter touched down in the courtyard of
Mercury Condom. The rotors kept spinning as two of Yufa's
men approached it, their heads bent low against the fierce, wet
wind. The rain was constant now, not heavy, but persistent.

Each man carried a short-barreled assault rifle. The two *byki*
joined the six white-clad troops under the command of Major
Oleg Kaznin. The new arrivals settled into their canvas sling
seats. They immediately lit cigarettes and chatted excitedly.

The two were dressed for a night of raising hell in town;
leather jackets, simple pants, and thin gloves. Their weapons
made a lot of noise but had no accuracy.

Up forward, just behind the cockpit, Kaznin had the tiny
VIP cabin all to himself. As the Mil-8 lifted off he had the
oddest sensation, the flicker of a shadow across his sureness, his
confidence. It was doubt, and Kaznin wasn't accustomed to it.

The rotors beat a steady thud overhead. Yes, he thought. It
was like blotting up mercury. First a small spill. Ryzkhov. Then
Nowek, the woman, now this. You jam your finger down and
it escapes. Soon you have little silver beads everywhere. And
failure had a price tag that Kaznin appreciated all too well.

The Mil-8 flew north under a thickening roof of clouds.

His roof, he thought. His *kryusha*. His protection. How well
constructed was it really?

As firm as Prosecutor Gromov, he thought, and just as pre-
dictable. Gromov could be trusted to always do what was in his
own best interests. So long as Kaznin's interests were the same,
there was no problem. Was that still true?

The helicopter dropped, bounced, shoved by gusts of wind.

They'd spoken on the telephone this evening, and Gromov
had not been the least bit subtle.

*"Frankly, I don't understand why the mayor has not been dealt
with in a conventional manner before this."*

"Nowek's an unconventional man. I tried to explain things
to him. He refused to understand."

"He's stubborn is all."

"He's Polish. They're more stubborn than smart."

"He's been smarter than you. You had one little salesman to worry about. An entrepreneur. Now look."

"The Ryzkhov issue was addressed."

Then why, Major, are we having this conversation? Either you finish this or I will find someone else who can. Posadit na piku. Panimayich?"

"Ya panimayu."

Nowek, thought Kaznin as the machine thundered north. Gromov had ordered him to bring his head back on a pike. Could he? He realized that a lot hinged on this night. A lot, and maybe everything.

Water sprayed up from the wheels. Rain was carried on a bitter wet wind that drew the mist across the river in sweeping curtains. Galena huddled close to Nowek, curled inside the curve of his body.

Suddenly, without any warning at all, the blue river ice turned white. A tributary fed into the Tunguska, weakening the solid surface, turning it thin and treacherous.

White turned gray. They sped off the ice and splashed down into a black, braided passage of moving water. The *lunashkod* slowed, settling.

"We're sinking!" Chuchin shouted. "We're . . ."

Anna accelerated. "We're not."

"Father!" Galena clutched Nowek as they drove straight across the water, the spines on the wheels churning the icy sludge.

They kept moving. They did not sink. The surface congealed, dark to light, and they bumped back up onto firmer ice once more.

"What powers this thing?" asked Chuchin. His fear was momentarily diverted by professional curiosity.

"Gas hydrate," Nowek answered. "How far have we come?"

Anna glanced at the GPS display. "Eight kilometers more."

"To what?"

But Anna didn't answer.

The *lunashkod* hit forty miles an hour as it whined over the ice. It was firming up as they went north, not because the temperature was colder here, but because the river was growing deeper. The powerful engine whined.

"How is driving into the wilderness leaving Siberia for the world?" he asked her at last. "What did you mean?"

Anna eyed the fuel gauge. It was down to the yellow caution zone. "This is going to be hard for you to believe," she said as she steered away from a hummock of broken ice, then back to the middle of the frozen river. "But getting out to the world? That's going to be the easy part."

"Can we stop?" asked Galena. She was nestled close, tucked into the curve of Nowek's body, the calico cat in her arms.

"Stop? What for?"

"I have to pee."

"You know what a Siberian toilet is, Galena? It's a stick."

"A stick?"

"To beat away the wolves."

"There's no stick."

He put his head over hers and smelled her hair, stroked her wet cheek. "Then let's not stop."

Fourteen kilometers upstream, the GPS indicated a turn to the left. Anna swung the wheel, heading for the bank.

They crawled up and under the cover of the dwarf cedars. Away from the river the character of the taiga was completely different; here it was more obvious that this was a wooded desert, a place where less water fell from the skies than in Arabia, a frozen sponge that trapped enough moisture in permafrost to maintain the illusion of a forest. She turned on the headlights. There was no path to follow.

"We're almost there."

The trees were more closely spaced now, and the little cedars had no light to grow by. Still the GPS arrow pointed confidently ahead. One moment Nowek was looking at the stunted, twisted shapes go by, the next, the satellite navigator was blinking ARRIVAL.

He was about to say something when they broke into a small clearing.

"We're here," said Anna, letting the buggy slow.

"Yes, but where are we?"

"You've seen it before."

"I've never been here." And then Nowek realized she was right; they both were right. He'd never been here. And yet he'd seen it.

They were headed for a large, windowless box that sprouted a pole and an antenna. A camera was mounted on the pole, looking down. There was a padlocked door in the box's side. There was a number painted on it: *14.*

Right here, he thought. It was right here that a black man, that man without a name, had wandered looking for shelter, and had found instead a tiger. He twisted in his seat and scanned the treeline, half expecting to see a low, flowing mist materialize. That's why the forest felt so different.

This was tiger country.

Anna pulled up next to a fallen tree that partially blocked the doorway to the feeding station.

"You've brought us to *this* place?"

"We're about out of fuel," she said. "Where would you have gone?"

Nowek was about to answer when he heard two sounds. The first he knew, but it was the other that made him tremble and hold Galena even tighter.

The first was the low beat of a helicopter. Rising, then fading as the sound fell from the spitting sky.

The second was a sharp, questioning cough from the darkness beyond the treeline.

He looked at Anna. Yes. Tiger country.

The helicopter became louder. "We'd better get inside the shack," she said.

Nowek stared at the treeline. "We can't hide in that box from them."

"No, but maybe we can stop them. Come on." She scooped up the calico, grabbed the rifle, and said to Yuri and Chuchin, "It would be better if you didn't wander too far."

Anna went to the padlocked door.

Nowek was beside her now. Galena shivered. "Was that Lena?" he asked her.

"Yes."

"Who's Lena?" Galena asked.

"Don't worry, Galinka," said Nowek.

The lock was frozen. She put the cat down. The calico stood there lifting one paw after the other, trying to get them out of the wet snow. Finally it gave up and mewed.

Anna took the rifle and gave the lock a smack. The hasp popped open. "There's emergency supplies in here. Food and heat sticks, even clothes. You never know." She ducked down and went through the small door.

He followed her in.

It was cold inside. Cold and dark. Anna's hands knew the place well, though. She found a flashlight stuck to the wall with magnets. She switched it on, then used it to find another one. With both lights burning you could see most of the interior. They were spelunkers, stumbling through a glittering cavern of electronics and ice.

"Welcome to my Varykino," she said with a quick smile.

Icicles streamed down from the low roof. Cables snaked from a massive battery pack out to the camera and to a solid-state recording device. Against a wall was a rucksack like the one Anna had carried, mottled green and white. She opened it and emptied out the contents, hunting for something. She found it. "Here." She held up a cloth-wrapped pad to Galena.

"What?" Her lips were blue.

"Take it." Anna folded the cloth pad in half with a quick snap. She held it out. "Put it in your pocket."

It was already warm when Galena touched it. She smiled.

"What is all this equipment?" asked Nowek.

"Radiotelemetry. The tigers have collars that transmit their location and their heart rate. The whip antenna on the roof picks them up, then rebroadcasts it up to a satellite on a cellular phone link. It gets bounced back down to the Taiga Institute in Idaho."

Idaho? She may as well have said Andromeda.

Anna found a small briefcase. She popped it open. Inside was a small telephone handset studded with buttons. She hefted the unit. It looked very heavy. There was no obvious antenna.

"That's a telephone?"

"It's a NEC M-5000." Anna nodded. "A satellite phone. But the power is marginal and the antenna is very small. We have to point it precisely to find a satellite." She folded the top of the briefcase up and down. "The antenna's built into the case."

Nowek stared. "You can just make a call? Just like that? The satellites will work even out here?"

"Even out here."

Nowek was about to tell Anna to be serious. They were stuck in a place that made Markovo seem like the center of civilization. There was a tiger roaming around in the dark, silently, and a helicopter hunting for them more noisily. He was about to say all these things when he heard the moon buggy's engine start with a swoosh of compressed air and a thrum of power.

Anna stood up. She nearly dropped the phone.

"Mayor!" Yuri yelled. *"Mayor! Stop him!"*

Nowek hit his head on the low roof as he scrambled to get outside.

He made it in time to see the moon buggy fly across the snow, heading for the trees.

"Chuchin!" he shouted. He looked at Yuri. "Chuchin!"

Yuri stood atop the fallen tree trunk. "That old *strafnik*! He left us for the wolves." The sound of the helicopter swelled. "And you accuse me of treachery? Leaving us out here like this? If we make it back, Mayor, I think he should be fired. He called us *suki*." He hopped down.

It meant bastards. "What exactly did he say?"

"Bastards. Can you believe it? He took the Skorpion with him."

"The gun?"

"The *only* gun."

"What happened?" Anna came out. "Where did he go?"

"He left us. Abandoned us," said Yuri. "Can you believe it? Called us all bastards."

"No," said Nowek. "He didn't."

Anna swept the snow with her flashlight. The beam fell on an object half buried in snow. The Skorpion.

"Hey! It must have slipped off." Yuri collected the weapon.

"It didn't slip," said Nowek. "Chuchin did it on purpose."

"Purpose?" said Yuri, indignant. "What purpose?"

As the sound of the helicopter grew close, Nowek said, "He meant to give us something. He meant to give us time." He looked at Anna. "We'd better use it."

She unfolded the briefcase top and tilted it to face the southern sky.

CHAPTER
25

"NOT A DAMNED THING," said DeKalb.

"They're down there someplace." Decker kept the big Chinook above the east bank of the river. The downwash of its twin rotors flattened the treetops. It gave him a clear look along the river's length, and across to the west, into the forest beyond. The rain streamed back along the windshield. The fog filled the riverbed bank to bank like a milky glacier.

"Hell of a night," said Decker. "Rain, sleet, now we got us an ice fog. Weather's gonna make finding them kinda sporty. Who they bringin' up from town?"

"Kaznin and some of his men." DeKalb checked his watch. "Time we gave him a call."

Decker handed back the microphone to DeKalb. "What's a *Berkut* anyway?"

"A big bird." DeKalb pressed the microphone. "Berkut, Berkut, how do you hear Rattler?"

Decker thought, now that's funny. A big bird? The locals were lucky to get anything into the air, as piss poor as their maintenance and oper—what was that? He jerked his head to one side. Motion. Below. On the ice. His goggles didn't have enough resolution to tell just what it was but it was something where there shouldn't be anything.

He reached up and switched on the spotlight. It lanced down and to one side, a white tunnel of light. He locked the collective in place, put his hand on the spotlight controller, and swiveled it. "Hey now. Look at what we got."

DeKalb put the microphone aside. "What's wrong?"

"Down on the river. See over there? Headin' south."

"South?"

"Yessir. They're . . ." The buggy scuttled underneath them. He wheeled the thudding machine around and put the beam back on target. The vehicle began to swerve, trying to escape. He grinned. "You want to take a closer look?"

"I want them stopped." He pressed the transmit bar. "Berkut, Rattler has a buggy headed upstream about fifteen klicks out of Tunguska." Heading south! He paused, listening to the reply. "All right," he said. "We'll rendezvous with you in zero five. We're going in." He nodded at the pilot. "Kaznin's on the way. Let's see if we can't nail them first."

"You got it." Decker rolled on more power to the engines. The Chinook thundered after the moon buggy, nose low to the river, skimming to ragged tops of the fog. "Something funny." Decker was having a hard time keeping the beam on the target and flying the Chinook. The moon buggy's dodging and weaving didn't help. "Damn! Hang on a second. I can't see." He needed a good copilot to fly this beast and keep the buggy in the spotlight. He couldn't do both. He tried leading the moon buggy, anticipating its jinking. "Can't be sure. But I thought I saw just one person down there."

"One?"

Frustrated, he hauled back on the controls and slowed. From a distance it was easier to keep watch on the buggy, but too far to see what he needed to see. "Can't fly and talk and run this damned light all at the same time. Where's our backup? We could use 'em. Box that bugger in and take him down from two sides."

DeKalb thought for a moment and then said, "If you can get me close enough, I'll use these." He tapped the night vision goggles. "Get me close and then kill the light. You fly. I'm gonna clean this mess up myself."

"Sounds like a winner."

Chuchin swung the wheel and the moon buggy slewed away from the hot light. It seemed to know where he was going before he did. The beam was on his back like a bead of sweat. The fat bastard of a helicopter was behind him. Loud, but hanging back. Why? What were they waiting for? Could they tell he was alone? He turned in his seat.

The *lunashkhod's* soft tires struck a rock and absorbed it, but the blow sent the machine sliding toward the trees. Chuchin slammed the wheel over and steered out of the skid. He didn't want to have that damned light on his back. But he didn't want to lose them, either. He bumped back onto the river and slowed until the spotlight caught him again. He pressed the accelerator. With a whine the buggy shot across the fractured ice, the slushy snow. A tributary opened up to the left. Open channels of braided black water flew beneath his churning wheels. The buggy started to slow, to settle.

"Not now, you foreign bastard!" He slammed the top of the dash. The tires caught hold of solid ice again.

Well, maybe it wasn't so bad. If only it had a roof to keep off the damned rain. Of course, if he had a wish, he would press a button and wake up in his bed. He swung the wheel, plunging into darkness. The darkness went white as the beam quickly adjusted. "Come on," he said. "Keep following."

The thud of its rotors grew louder.

Chuchin looked over his shoulder. One hundred meters. About right. The helicopter kept coming. Just as Chuchin was about to swing out of the spotlight and head for the trees, the light blinked off. It startled him.

The buggy hit an invisible rock and staggered, bouncing, landing sideways, sliding to a stop against a larger boulder that rose like a breaching whale, half drowned in ice.

The helicopter was close, invisible against the low, woolly sky. Impossibly loud. Each beat of the rotors sent an individual blast of wind across the ice, drilling a wide hole in the rising fog. They weren't using the light. It thundered overhead. The rotor wind enveloped Chuchin and the buggy like a whiteout blizzard. Chuchin backed away from the rock, the noise of the Chinook drowning everything, even the sound of his own heart. He looked up, straight up, and saw the belly of the hovering machine, light gray on charcoal. It slewed aside, tilted slightly. A hatch opened.

He took out the old Nagant, cocked it, and fired blindly at the sound. The muzzle blast lit the ice. It caught raindrops in midfall, freezing them, releasing them to the dark. The shots themselves could not be heard above the engines.

The helicopter scuttled sideways.

"Hah!" he yelled. He hadn't felt this good in years. Thought he was a toothless old wolf they could hunt down from the air? He hit the accelerator pedal as a white flash erupted above, followed an instant later by an immense *crack!* that seemed to come from deep inside his chest.

Moment becomes moment. Chuchin was trapped inside a blizzard of white-hot metal. An eerily silent snow. His ears felt stuffed with cotton. His head rang like a dull bell. He shook his head and warm liquid leaked down his neck. He thought he'd hit something, been thrown from the driver's seat and tossed to the ice. But he saw that he was sitting where he had been sitting, stopped in the middle of the river, completely in the open, exposed. Acrid smoke hung low to the ice. Rain dripped down and blinded an eye. He swiped it clear. It flooded again. He felt around on the seat and found the reassuring weight of the Nagant.

There was the sharp, rotten smell of gas. Sulphurous. A jet of it spouted from the buggy's punctured pressure tank. Leaks? The right side of the buggy was . . .

A brilliant light snapped on, smothering everything. It came from above. In its blue harshness, Chuchin saw the blood.

He blinked, cleared his eyes, and looked up.

The helicopter. Was he seeing double? The one light was now joined by a second. Why couldn't he hear them? Two machines closing in from opposite directions. He pressed the accelerator. Like a half-crushed insect, the moon buggy began to drag itself slowly over wet ice. It went five meters. Ten. Then came to a stop. He jammed his boot down. Nothing.

Both helicopters danced around him, low, their wind rampaging. It felt cold on his wet cheeks. He leaned over the steering wheel as though ready to take a nap, to rest. He was tired, so very tired. He put his head to the wheel, and then, as one of them landed on the harder ice by the edge of the river, Chuchin closed his eyes.

"Did you hear that?" Yuri whispered.

The muttering of the helicopter, the grenade's blast. Nowek didn't answer. Chuchin. The silence that followed made his ears burn. Chuchin.

"I've got someone!" Anna said as she crouched next to the satellite phone. It clicked in her ear. "Peter! It's Anna!" She paused. "Peter?"

". . . offices of Dr. Peter Gabriel of the World Tiger Trust. Our normal hours of operation are . . ."

She looked up with tears in her eyes. "There has to be someone. You must know someone we can call. Think!"

Think. Someone you can call. This more than anything made Nowek realize how far out on a branch he'd crawled. Who in Markovo would come to his aid? Who in Irkutsk? Who in all of Russia? Everything, his rebelliousness up at Samotlor, his running for mayor, his stubborn pursuit of the truth, his trust in Arkady Volksy, had come down from trunk to branch to limb to twig. Beyond lay nothing. Nothing but a long, final fall. He looked at Galena. She'd been right to want to leave. She'd been right, and he'd let her down because the truth was simple: there was no one to call. There was no one.

The helicopter sound doubled, echoing, louder now.

"Father?" Galena's voice was very small. The sound of rotors and Decker's face went together. "I'm frightened."

"So am I. Go inside the shack."

"What's going to happen?"

"Go inside the shack!"

"Galena," said Anna softly. She had the calico cat in her hand. Its legs draped down. "Will you take care of George? He gets upset by loud noises."

Galena reached out and took the cat.

"Now go inside the shack," said Anna.

Galena bit her lower lip. She looked five years younger than the overconfident young woman standing in high heels outside the Hotel Siber. But she went back inside. Nowek shut the door behind her.

"Amazing. Me she ignores. You she obeys."

"It's not what you say," said Anna. "It's how you ask."

"Mayor?" said Yuri. "We're running out of time for great ideas. I'm sure you must have at least one."

"Actually, I don't." Nowek stood there. He heard a noise in the trees. A cough, fainter than before. "Even your tiger is leaving us."

"She's not leaving. She's denning. She's got four cubs to guard. She won't leave them. She's not giving up." She glanced back at the small shack. "Neither am I." She stood there for a moment as the rain fell. She was looking up at the camera that covered the clearing. The camera that had captured the final moments of a black American man who had no name, who could not exist. It was capturing them now. Her mouth opened, then shut, then she nodded.

"What is it?" Nowek asked.

"I remembered the telephone," she said. "But I forgot the camera." She looked at him, then pressed the button that killed the link to Peter Gabriel's answering machine and began furiously punching in a long string of numbers.

"Who are you calling?" asked Nowek.

She looked at Nowek and said, "Moscow."

"You said it yourself. They're worse than useless."

"Not that Moscow," she replied as the phone clicked, then began to ring.

★   ★   ★

Decker put the Chinook down on the banks of the river, the blades invisible disks that caught the spitting rain and sent it out in a furious spiral. Its spotlight held the motionless moon buggy in its focus.

The Russian machine, call sign "Berkut," landed nearby. It was the same Mil troop carrier bearing the name MINISTRY on its brown tail. Its own light joined the first. The buggy seemed tiny, insignificant, a specimen caught on two pins of converging light, fastened to a fabric of blowing mist.

Kaznin put down his handheld radio and pulled the curtain that walled off the troop compartment from his own. "They have one of them out there in a disabled car. Bring him in if you can."

"Only one?" the squad leader asked.

"If it's the mayor, try not to kill him."

"And if it isn't the mayor?"

"Then bring me an ear." He pulled the curtain closed.

"All right," the troop commander said to Yufa's two men. "There's one man out there so you better be careful and creep up on him." The troops in their white snow camouflage suits snickered. "Watch out. He might twitch and hit you."

Semyon Yufa's two pit bulls jumped down from the Ministry helicopter to a chorus of laughs.

The rain was falling more steadily. It was dispelling the fog, though it made the river-ice slick. The two *byki* split up and approached the brightly lit buggy from opposite sides. They slipped in their city-smooth leather shoes. Soon they were paying more attention to their feet than to the wrecked moon buggy. Why not? They could see from here that slipping on the wet ice was the more obvious danger.

The twin spotlights sent long, double shadows out before them. Both tires on the right were blown flat, the windshield was shattered, and a man was slumped across the wheel. The blood. They didn't speak, and in any event couldn't have been heard over the two idling helicopters. They both carried their little snub-nosed machine pistols, fingers curled on the trigger.

Closer. Their shadows merged with the buggy. The grenade

had peppered one side of it, punching black, irregular holes in the frame. Gas? You could smell it from here. The fuel tank was torn, leaking.

Closer. One stayed back and covered the other. His slow, stealthy walk became a trot. He moved in and shoved the bloody body with the muzzle, hard. No reaction. He reached in and touched Chuchin with his own hands, then shouted, "Dead!"

The other nodded and walked up to the ruined machine. Ten meters. Five. The machine pistol was at his side.

There was a bright flash. The first of Yufa's men seemed to fly straight up, then slowly, slowly, his arms pinwheeling like wings, he fell to the ice.

"What's goin' on?" Decker snapped. "What are those two assholes tryin' to do out there?"

"Was that firing?" asked DeKalb.

"Two rounds. I sure hope they—"

Suddenly the moon buggy erupted in the fast, staccato flash of a machine pistol fired on full automatic.

"Jesus Christ!" DeKalb hollered.

TICK!

A hole magically appeared in the windshield not two feet from Decker's eyes. Another. A third. A hard, aluminum slap, and then the bullets found the spotlight. *TICK! TICK!*

"Goddamn it, he's—"

The lamp blew in a great smoking crash of glass and hot filaments flying.

"Get us out of here!" DeKalb screamed. *"Go! Go! Go!"*

TICK!

Decker twisted the throttles but the engines took time to respond. They slowly surged to takeoff power. The twin rotors had a lot of inertia to overcome. The night was alive with little invisible droplets of death. He wanted to get away from the gun that was taking his machine apart. Now. But it was only after he had yanked on the collective and pulled the Chinook into a dangerous, vertical climb, that he realized the gunman had shifted his target, that he was no longer in the crosshairs.

The spotlight on the second helicopter went dark.

"What in hell is happening down there?" DeKalb demanded as he got his headset back on. It was down around his neck, shoved there by the hard climb. "*Berkut, Berkut!* What's goin' on? Who's shooting?"

Kaznin pressed himself flat to the floor, willing his body into two dimensions. He screamed for the pilot to take off, but there was no answer. He reached for the handheld radio. DeKalb was shouting through it. The troops were yelling in the back.

The VIP cabin had five holes ripped through the curtain that separated them from the cockpit. The Mil's engines were slowly dying. So was its pilot.

Kaznin threw open the torn curtain. He stood there, looking out through the shattered windshield, then slowly pulled it shut. He turned to the back and roared, *"Get him!"*

The squad knew an ambush when they smelled one. They were already on their feet, leaping through the cabin door, landing, spreading out, keeping low to the ice and snow, leapfrogging from ice prism to rock.

Kaznin watched them melt into the dark, fanning out. White on gray, white on gray. One more silver bead of mercury dividing, dividing, dividing.

Bring me his head on a pike.

That's what Gromov had told him. The shadows eating into his confidence were back. They had a name: Nowek, he thought. Nowek.

The squad commander shouted an order, heard a response. The hiss of rain on the river ice smothered their sound.

Then, from the darkness ahead, a single shot. Not even aimed. Probing, testing. Bait? Who had fired? How many of them were there?

The commander listened, straining, trying to make tactical sense of the sounds. He ordered the white-clad trooper to his right forward to find the source of the shot.

Another shot flashed from the fog.

This time he was close enough to see that it came from behind a big bastard of a rock. Rounded, humped, gray fringed with splintered ice. They couldn't shoot through stone. They'd have to surround him. He motioned another trooper forward, this time on the right. A classic pincer. Careful, now. Very careful. A moment of uneasy quiet, of shuffling boots, shifting white shapes and shadows.

The commander clicked his assault rifle on single-fire and took aim on the boulder. He caressed the trigger. The heavy bullet struck and sparked away into the darkness.

There was no answering volley. Had their quarry escaped, or was he just waiting?

Now what? One man with a gun against six was not the walkover it might seem, not in the darkness. There was hardly a more dangerous place for several armed, nervous men to be than chasing after one; it was too easy to be shot by your side in the confusion. But he was a professional, a veteran of Grozny. A survivor, more accurately. Where were the two men he'd sent ahead?

The beat of rain on ice became louder. And then, motion. A thump, a flash from behind the rock, and the rolling thunder of a single shot. A pistol, not the blast of a rifle.

Once more, silence.

He squinted through the rain. What was going on up there? Why did they not have those fancy goggles that could see through the night like the . . .

Suddenly, a dark figure rose from behind the boulder. The commander swung his rifle. A man, a man in a dark jacket. Not snow camouflage. *"Fire!"* he bellowed.

A bedlam of muzzle flashes and exploding cordite. All weapons were trained on the dark figure. It staggered back against the rock under the impacts. Each strike gave the body new life, making it jerk, turn, rise, arms flailing, legs kicking in a futile attempt to escape.

The volume built to crescendo as their target was torn to pieces, butchered crudely, one bullet at a time.

★   ★   ★

Kaznin peered across the rain-swept ice. He couldn't see anything. First one trooper materialized, then another. A third. Their white hoods drawn tight around shocked, surprised faces. At last the commander. Bright red blood splotched his white uniform. He was holding a wounded man by the arm. He eased him down and started dressing the ragged, red tear in his leg.

"Where is he?" asked Kaznin. "Where is the mayor?"

"I don't know."

"You don't know?"

"That devil, he tricked us into killing one of our own men. We never got a look at him—"

"You don't even know who it was?"

"He's wounded. Badly. Here." The commander tossed a blood-soaked identity booklet to Kaznin. "He put his jacket on my man and let us all shoot. This was inside."

Kaznin opened it delicately, allowing blood to drip onto the metal floor. "So," he said after seeing the face of its owner. He dropped it. "You let one old man, a *toothless pensioner* fit only for driving a car, fool you into killing each other? Do you know what Prosecutor Gromov will say when I make my report? I promise you will find out. Where's the body?"

"He's probably already dead. I put a bullet in him myself. Let him drag himself into the woods to die."

"All right," said Kaznin. "We still have the others to find. We'll come back and if he's still alive I will give him his bullet in the customary manner. But if we don't find the others, Commander, I promise you, there will be enough bullets to share." He picked up the handheld radio, pressed the transmit bar, and began to speak.

They were orbiting over a point upstream, safely away from the vicious firefight. A ringside seat. A trap, thought Decker. They must all be down there waiting. Smart. Not that it would do much in the end. Whittle us down, but they can't get away. No how. Where the hell could they go?

The radio crackled. They both listened.

Decker looked at his boss. "What he say?"

"Kaznin wants us to land."

"Land? What for?"

"Their chopper's been damaged."

They orbited once, again, finally Decker said, "I don't know, boss. Must be more of 'em down there than just one. Tear up a chopper and a squad? They about ate us up as well." He stuck a finger in the hole in his windshield. It was leaking cold rain. "Has to be. What do you want to do?"

"If he's right about there being just one of them, the others are still a problem. That's my job on the line. But it seems to me your exposure is a bit larger. It could become a problem, Mr. Decker. What do you think is best?"

His exposure? His ass. Decker slapped the collective down and the big machine began to settle. "I guess we land."

They left the wounded trooper behind in the Russian Mil, sedated with a quick stab from the medical kit, his leg wrapped tight and a hot thermos of tea beside him. The red night lights glowed forlornly from the grounded machine, its rotor blades tilting back and forth, teetering as they caught the dank wind.

The larger American helicopter swallowed the rest whole; the four remaining soldiers plus Kaznin. The troopers were angry at the night, at the shock of seeing their friend wounded, of leaving a dead comrade out on the ice. They were ready to see someone hurt, and hurt badly.

Kaznin went forward to the cockpit.

"Well, hey. Long time no see," said Decker with an appraising look. "Been doin' any fishing?"

Kaznin didn't bother to answer.

Decker rolled in both throttles and the steel blades bit the air. The heavy helicopter rose, pirouetted around, and climbed back to the south.

"What the hell happened?" DeKalb demanded.

"Ambush," said Kaznin. "We lost some men and the pilot."

"You all were supposed to ambush *them*," said DeKalb.

"That ol' buggy left a track," said Decker as he scanned the ice with his night vision goggles. "We can follow it all right. Bound to see where they split up. Gonna be tough to do it without a spotlight, though."

"Then we'll do it the hard way," said DeKalb. He looked at Kaznin. "On the ground."

Kaznin felt that nervous ghost shimmer in his belly again. "We're down to four troops."

"Against the tiger gal, the mayor, and his girl?" said Decker. "I don't see a problem."

DeKalb said, "His girl? What's that mean?"

Decker grinned, a bit too quickly. "Nothin'. Just . . ." he stammered. "Just nothin' at all, Mr. DeKalb."

His girl? DeKalb mused. Hadn't the mayor said his daughter was missing? His sixteen-year-old daughter? *His girl?* Why was the mayor buzzing around him? Why wouldn't he give up, roll over, and play dead like he was supposed to? Decker. You little coonass shit. You and your dick, thought DeKalb. When this is done I'll cut it off and feed it to your weasel. He turned to Kaznin. "I called Gromov. He wasn't happy, but he'll come if we need him."

"That's probably wise," said Kaznin, though he didn't really think so at all. Gromov. Hauled out of his warm bed and brought out here to do what Kaznin had assured him could be handled, and handled quickly. A helicopter damaged, its pilot killed. One wounded and another dead. Yufa's thugs. No, this was not at all good. The flicker, the shadow grew bigger, stronger. It congealed like cold grease in his gut.

Decker was peering down at the river. The moon buggy's tracked swerved to the right and dived into the forest. "Well," he said, bottoming out the collective and settling the machine onto the ice, "this is as far as I go. All out." He killed the engines.

DeKalb waited as the troopers got off, then told Decker, "You're coming, too."

CHAPTER
26

"YES! I CAN. Can you? It's . . ." Anna waited for a burst of static to clear. The signal was weak, the distances immense. "How's this? Can you hear me better?"

Yuri put a hand on Nowek's shoulder. "They're landing. They'll track Chuchin back here. It won't take them forever."

Anna's voice made him turn. Eleven time zones and half the earth distant, a young student researcher at the Taiga Institute in Moscow, Idaho, listened to the weak signal beamed up from the Siberian night.

"Is this some kind of a joke? Is this Linda?"

"No!" Anna shouted. "This is Dr. Vereskaya. Anna Vereskaya. I'm calling from Tunguska, Siberia."

"You know what time it is? You're sure this isn't Linda? Come on. I'm going to hang up in a—"

"Just listen," said Anna. "Don't hang up. Are you familiar with the data acquisition system for the Tunguska project?"

"Sure," the young man replied huffily. "They have me copying it onto backup. That's why I'm working so late—"

"Listen. Don't talk. I want you to go into the system and select the telemetry feed from Feeding Station Fourteen at Tunguska. Drop out all the others and don't let it go back to sequencing. Just Site Fourteen, all right?"

"Why do you—"

"*Don't ask questions!* I want that channel on record. There's going to be a video signal that you have to get onto tape. Can you do that quickly?"

"Sure, but we'll lose everything off the other feeds."

"I know. We'll keep an open line on the telephone in addition to the site mikes. I want everything sent to tape backup. Everything. Can you make it happen?"

"I think I better check this out before I monkey with—"

"Look. If you don't know how to do it, then find someone who does. Now. I don't have time for a conversation."

His technical expertise challenged by some *girl*? "I can do it in my sleep. I can even put it out on the Web if you ask nice. Link it with a hot button and anybody dialing into the Taiga home page can see it too. Live, from Tunguska. You want a *real* audience? Just say the word."

Anna's eyes brightened. "Yes! Please!"

Satellites. Nowek looked up at the gray belly of the clouds. It was a kind of prayer, actually. Sending your words, your hopes, into the sky, hoping that someone, somewhere might listen. She could be speaking with God, thought Nowek. For all it matters here. For all it matters now. Perhaps it would be enough to make a difference to the world. But to him? He turned and looked at the tiny white shack.

What would happen to Galena? They'd find her. What had Yufa said? He knew of a place where they would eat Galena alive. Nowek looked at the line of trees, thinking back to when he'd seen a tiger materialize, accelerate across this very piece of frozen ground, and sail through the air with claws extended.

Voices now, coming through those same trees.

Yuri racked the lever on the Skorpion and trained it out toward the sounds, resting the barrel on the fallen tree trunk.

Anna left the antenna pointing south and pulled out the phone cord, stretching it to the door of the tiny hut. She opened it and waved for Galena to come. The calico was now draped like a fur stole over her shoulders, asleep. To the young student in Idaho she said, "I'm going to leave an open circuit. You're recording?"

The distant voice mentioned the price of a satellite call was three dollars per minute.

"Don't worry," she said. "The bill won't come till next month." She said to Galena, "How'd you like to practice your English?"

"Cool."

"Here." Anna handed the phone to her. "You're talking to America."

"America? What do you mean?"

"Get back inside. On the floor," Anna ordered her. "Now talk!"

Galena shyly took it and said, "Hello?"

Nowek took Anna aside after he shut the door. "I won't let them take her. You understand?"

"I understand." She nodded up at the camera. "It's going out on the Web."

"What web?"

"The Internet. Do you know what that means?"

"Some computer is watching?"

"It means when they come, the *whole world will be watching.*"

The troops followed their commander more cautiously. He'd led them into some kind of a trap once already. They found the buggy track at once and fanned out, heading for the trees that grew beside the iced-over river. And Kaznin's threat carried weight, too, even if they all worked for Gromov, even if they all would share in failure. Some shares would be bigger than others.

Kaznin kept watch on the two Americans behind the skirmish line. DeKalb carried his hybrid weapon with a satchel of extra grenades. Decker was armed with the big Ruger hunting rifle. His night vision goggles dangled from his neck. Kaznin carried his service pistol, a 9mm Makarov.

The troops hit the treeline and stopped. From the man walking point came a whispered, *"This way."*

★　★　★

The taiga was alive with sound. The squad commander listened to the steady drip, the occasional shower of water off a rain-soaked bough. The gurgle of melted snow flowing under the ice. He stayed in the middle of the track left by the buggy. Around each tree was a ring of thin snow, sometimes even bare earth. Drips, splashes. He motioned his men on. The moon buggy had come this way, and somewhere back along its track, they would find the others.

Two men and a girl. If they were smart they would each go a different direction. More likely they would struggle through the snow, leaving a trail a meter wide, until they fell exhausted from their efforts. Then he would find out whether they would rise and fight, or stand and take their bullet. He looked left. The flanker was just entering the treeline. The trooper to his right was already invisible.

The right flanker entered the trees and blended his body against the gnarled trunk of a dwarf cedar. He was looking for tracks, and he quickly found some, then more, though they were strange. Men left a wide swath. These were distinct, shallow. He cautiously followed them to an area of disturbed snow. He snapped on a flashlight.

Mother of God.

He bent down and spread his gloved fingers wide. It covered only half the print. What kind? A bear? No.

And over there, more, though much smaller. He was about to straighten when he heard a sound. He turned his light to it.

Two golden stars burned from beneath a fallen trunk not ten meters away. The snow had been scooped out to make a deep depression. There was a hiss and the two stars blinked and became four, though the new ones were far more widely spaced, and they burned a deeper amber.

A low warning growl made every hair on his body stand straight. It resonated through the forest, through his chest.

The new stars began to move.

He dropped his light and ran.

★   ★   ★

Nowek was listening to his daughter. He was about to quiet her when he heard the tiger's chuffing cough, and then the roar of her charge.

An instant later, a single gunshot. Then a wild, savage snarl that could not mask the terrified screams of a man.

"Lena!" said Anna.

A staccato burst, then another scream. Shouts, excited, frightened voices, and then the yowl of a cub.

"Oh God!" Anna could see with her ears. It was Primorsky. All over again. The slaughter. "No!"

A sustained burst of fire and then silence.

Anna was standing, staring into the trees with her rifle.

"What are you doing?" said Nowek.

"She had four cubs."

"We have more important things to—" But Anna was moving. "Anna!" He grabbed her.

"Let me go!" She wriggled away.

"You can't go out there alone. I won't let you."

"I didn't ask for permission." Anna swung her rucksack off and handed it to Nowek. "Take good care of the tapes. I know you will. Remember. You have to let them get close."

"Close?"

"Right into the camera's field of view. You have to make them say everything. Make them say what they've done. In English if you can. You believe in laws? Well, now the Internet's your courtroom, Gregori. Only you can make them confess in front of the world. You can do it. I know."

"I'm no lawyer. I'm no good at solving mysteries."

"You're wrong." She shouldered the rifle and started to walk down the trail left by the moon buggy. But she stopped and turned, reaching down the front of her jacket.

Nowek ran to her. "Listen to me. For just a second—"

"No. Here." She gave Nowek her shaman's knife again. Once more they both held on to it, and once more it was as though an electrical circuit had been completed. "I'll be the hammer. You be the anvil," she said, repeating Chuchin's words. "Don't forget George. Don't leave him behind."

"Promise me you'll come back."

"I promise you I'll try." Anna let go of her end and hurried down the trail, quickly disappearing into the trees.

He saw her, he saw his dead wife standing at the airport gate, turning, waving, he heard all the things he had never said, never thought to say, echoing in his memory. Now it was happening again. Dressed in Nina's clothes, she was Nina, and not Nina. More, different. But the pain was the same.

"How could you let her go?" asked Yuri.

How could he let her go? He could still feel her in his arms, taste her breath, smell the warmth rising from her hair. She'd fallen into his life, blazing like a meteor. Like a column of fire, soundlessly descending from the east, detonating like a ten-megaton bomb, not over the taiga. Swift, brilliant, sudden, and brief. How could he let her go?

He drew the blade from the sheath. Wickedly sharp. It felt like he'd pulled it straight from his heart.

LeRoy Rogers wasn't walking. He was falling step to step. The river, this motherfucking frozen river, was endless. It went nowhere. He'd heard engines. Trucks on a freeway? Something. It gave him reason, it gave him motion. But just as each bend in the river promised lights, promised warmth, promised a way down off this mountain, each time he expected to see a bridge, a railroad, something, he'd come up empty.

Until now.

He stopped dead in the middle of the ice and stared at the apparition. He blinked and rubbed the cold rain away from his eyes. When the helicopter remained, he slowly, slowly grinned. He was beyond wondering why a flying machine might be parked out in the middle of the ice. Or who might be inside it. There was a red glow from its windows. People. It didn't motherfucking just grow there.

He began to walk again. A whisper of caution told him they might be out hunting him. That they might have missed him back at the camp by now, might have seen that dead body stretched over the wires for what it was: a bridge. But that red light, that man-made object, beckoned him on like smoke from his mama's chimney. Like a smile on a woman's face.

He stopped and listened, watching the grounded Mil for a while. No signs of movement. No signs of life. Had to be somebody. Had to be. People wouldn't just leave a machine out like that. He felt the cold weight of the pistol in his pocket. People he could handle. He'd convince them to fly him away from the mountains. Fly him all the way home.

And food. Be something good to eat in it maybe. And some new clothes, too. Boots. His feet were solid blocks of stone now. No feeling. He didn't know much about cold, not real cold, but he knew he didn't have much walking left in him. He was gonna make it, he would have to make like Superman and fly.

He began to make his way over the fractured ice again, lurching, staggering, one foot after the other. He fell, fell again. The ice cut his cheeks raw. Close now, he drew the pistol. Go in quiet. The red glow was bright to his light-starved eyes. Quiet as a cat. Go in, point the piece at the pilot and tell him there's been a little change, see, and we're gonna go for a ride. Take this boy home, James. Got an appointment with a hot meal.

He tried to put his stone-cold finger through the trigger guard. It was like shoving a block of wood into a hole. Dead. No feeling. He remembered how he'd felt back at the camp when he first woke up. This was the same, only different. He tried to grip the pistol's handle. Could he use it? Could he pull the trigger if he had to? Never had been a problem. Have to rely on what comes natural.

He was next to the machine, so close he could touch it, so close he could hear the sound of rain falling on its metal skin. He listened. Where the fuck were they hiding? He took another step and slipped.

LeRoy fell against the machine with a dull thud, sliding down to the ice. Shit. He scrambled back up. No surprises now. Pistol in hand he staggered back to the hatch. It was partly open.

He slid it back the rest of the way and stood there, swaying, looking into the red light. He was close to the end. His brain was spinning. He didn't have another mile left in him. Not another foot. But he'd put a round through his head before he went back, before he let them do what they did to him again.

He reached up to grab something, to pull himself into the helicopter, when suddenly LeRoy was flying. He landed inside and rolled up against something soft, something alive.

Someone booted him from behind, sending him sprawling against a curving metal wall. Another kick and he was on his back. He still had his gun. He swung his arm and tried to point it at . . .

The gun was gone, clattering to the floor. He looked up into the red and saw a white-clad trooper standing above him, hooded like some kind of Klansman. There was blood all over his jacket. It was flowing from open cuts on the side of his face. A nightmare face.

The man reached down and picked up the pistol, then pushed his hood back away from his face. There was a quizzical look to his narrow, oriental eyes. Finally, he leaned over and stuck the heavy barrel of a gun, a big silver mother, against LeRoy's temple.

"Aht koo da vwi?"

"Go ahead, motherfucker," LeRoy spat back. "Go ahead and pull that motherfucking trigger. I've about had it with all this Chinese chinko jabber. I'm a fucking member of the Aryan race! I don't have to listen to this shit. So go ahead and shoot me, asshole. I ain't goin' nowhere." LeRoy began to shiver with cold.

Suddenly the pistol pointed away. The man in white kept his eyes on LeRoy as he reached back and grabbed a canvas sack that hung from the cabin wall. Inside it was a silver thermos. He took it out and tossed it to LeRoy.

Using both hands, LeRoy managed to get the top of it un-screwed. He wedged it between his wrists and put it to his face.

Steam. Hot, sweet smell of tea. Hot. Hot!

He scalded himself drinking it down. It would have hurt any

other time, but not here, not now, not after all those miles of snow, ice, and rain. He drank the thermos dry, feeling the warmth sit inside him like a stoked furnace. When he was done he let it drop to the floor. It rolled away. He looked up at the white figure, and when he did his eyes, despite himself, despite his monster, despite everything, began to swell with tears. "Ain't nobody ever done that for me . . ."

"Where did you come from?" Chuchin demanded again. He couldn't hear anything this stranger was saying. His ears were plugged up with something, some aftereffect of the explosion. They still streamed blood. But he knew that despite the ragged uniform the half-dead stranger was wearing he was no trooper, no militia. He prodded LeRoy with his boot. "Who the devil *are* you?"

CHAPTER

27

ANNA KEPT TO SOLID GROUND as she paralleled the buggy tracks. She came to a long, wide bog. She could hear the sound of running water under its skin of ice and snow. She tested it with the toe of her boot, the snow visibly deflected as she stepped. Near the edge it would take her weight. In the middle? Not a chance. She untied her boot, then laced it to the barrel of her rifle. Leaning out over the bog as far as she could, she pressed a series of prints into the snow.

She found a fallen log that spanned the bog and crossed to the far side. She moved on hard ground back to where she'd left the first marks, and made a new set to join them. Only then did she jam the wet boot back on. To a casual eye, her track appeared to cross the bog, or at least, she hoped so.

She turned back to Lena's den.

There were flashlights ahead. Then excited, angry voices. She could smell the guns. She knew Lena would never tolerate the presence of men so close to her four cubs. She knew that meant Lena was dead. And without their mother, the young cubs would also die. She thought of Galena.

No longer bothering to mask her tracks, she noiselessly approached the small clearing, tree to tree, the rifle cradled in her arms. It was her claws, her teeth.

Once she'd made a promise down in Primorsky to never let

them massacre cubs again. She'd also told Nowek she would do
her best to come back to him. It was time to keep one promise
in a way that might violate the other.

Decker stood over the lifeless body of the big female. Kaznin
was hanging back, close to a tree as though he might be ready
to scramble up it at the snap of a broken twig. Tigers did that to
the imagination. It wasn't rational. It was something, some reaction buried deep inside the brain, the same little circuit that
made the hair on your arms rise to attention at the sound of a
growl in the night.

"Only *Amba*," said the troop commander. He looked to
Kaznin.

"They're here," he said. "The tracks will take us to them."

Decker prodded the dead tiger. He had a well-calibrated eye:
she weighed about three hundred pounds, more than eight feet
from whisker to rump, and the tail went another three. But she
was torn up bad. Troopers had just blasted away in a panic. Not
at all prime condition. Nobody would buy a pelt like that, not
the Chinese, not even the Arabs. Not all full of holes. But the
bones, they'd be worth something. He reached down with his
knife and snicked the radio collar from her neck. He held it up
to DeKalb.

"Throw that away. Her project is over."

Decker tossed it into the snow.

"That bitch," DeKalb swore. "That goddamned irresponsi-
ble bitch. She led us here. She knew what would happen. She's
trying to whittle us down. Used a tiger to do it."

"Should of let me take care of her," said Decker. "Saved us
all a serious bunch of grief."

"Your whore," said DeKalb. "I should have taken care of
that, too."

Decker shook his head. "What's that mean, boss?"

"The mayor's girl. His daughter. You thought I didn't
know? You're turning into a problem, Mr. Decker. You might
want to think on that."

"I'm turnin' into the only chopper pilot in a thousand square miles, too. Might want to think on that yourself."

DeKalb strangled his reply. Later, he thought.

The cub was still moving, making small mewing sounds as it tried to crawl back to its den. About the size of a cocker spaniel, its flanks bubbled red with each labored breath. Both hind legs had been paralyzed from a spine shot. The snow was spattered red under the sweeping lights of the soldiers; where the rain diluted it, the color bled to pink.

Decker walked over to the cub. It looked up at him with pain-rimmed eyes and snarled. He kicked it until it bared two long triangular fangs and hissed like an angry cobra.

"Stop playing games," said DeKalb. "We have more important matters."

Decker casually pointed the Ruger at its head and pulled the trigger. The *crack!* echoed and it went flat to the snow in a spray of blood.

"Shit." Decker swiped at his face. His breast pocket shifted and out popped the ferret, its whiskers twitching, its tongue tasting the cold air, the blood, the rain, flickering almost too fast to see. Its eyes gleamed with excitement. Decker edged near the den. He tossed in a ball of wet snow.

More hisses, a snarl, and the scrabble of claws.

Decker was at the shallow depression, the trampled snow that marked the entry. "Here, kitty kitty," he said, the rifle at the ready. Head shot. Save the pelts. Buy him a couple of months on the beach. Ten, fifteen thou apiece.

"Step away from that hole," said DeKalb. He had the M-209 broken down. He inserted a grenade into the breech.

Decker stayed put. "You gonna waste 'em?" He meant it literally.

"What are you doing?" asked Kaznin. "We don't have time for this."

"I'm gonna take care of business," said DeKalb. To Decker he said, "Do as I say."

Kaznin stood back.

A low feral growl came from the darkness under the tree.

DeKalb slammed the breech shut and locked it.

"Hang on a sec, boss. You know what one of those little critters will bring? And I'm talkin' dead. Don't—" Decker saw the barrel swing his way. No *way* did DeKalb have the balls to blow the den right out from . . .

A white flash, a loud, single *crack*.

DeKalb dropped the M-209 into the snow, stumbled backward, clawing at something behind him as he fell.

There was no warning. One moment Anna was loading another ketamine dart into the rifle, the next brought a subliminal sense of scuffling boots. She started to turn when a tremendous blow to the back of her head sent her sprawling. The rifle flew from her hands and she dropped face first to the wet snow.

Goddamn. They shot DeKalb. Shot him dead. Decker heard the commotion out beyond the small clearing. Kaznin was hiding *behind* the tree trunk, his little pistol out in the air. The other Russian had run in response to a shout. DeKalb was down, motionless, back shot. He wasn't struggling. He wasn't breathing. A dead man sure as shit. Hell. There's a heaven after all, I guess. He knew about the bitch. He knew about the mayor's little girl.

He collected the M-209 and safed it. The last thing he needed was that damned launcher spitting out a grenade at him. He rolled DeKalb over onto his stomach to check the entry wound.

There wasn't one. Not so much as a spot of blood.

He ran his hand down the parka's slick, wet fabric. Decker's hand stopped when it came upon a distinctly foreign object.

A tiny nylon syringe was embedded into the muscles of his lower back. Decker reached down and yanked it out. The needle dripped liquid as amber as a cottonmouth's venom.

"Well, shit," he said. He looked out into the darkness. She was here and she took out DeKalb. "Well, shit," he said again. He touched DeKalb's neck, and as he felt for a pulse he stared into the tool pusher's pale, waxy face. He had to wait several seconds. Weak, thready, hardly there at all.

DeKalb was alive, but you had to pay attention to know it. The ketamine hydrochloride had been designed for a tiger, a large animal with a different metabolism entirely. Instead of relaxing an Amur to the point of drowsiness, it sent DeKalb straight into the world of the unconscious.

A yell made Decker look up. A woman's voice, followed by a curse. Fuck, he thought. Now we're gonna have some fun. He unhooked the night vision goggles from DeKalb's neck and looped them over his own. With the M-209 in one hand and the big Ruger in the other, he stood over DeKalb and watched as they brought Anna Vereskaya in.

"Vwe govarite pa Russkie," said Kaznin. It wasn't a question, it was a command.

Anna didn't answer.

"Please. Don't pretend you can't understand your native language. I know you. I know all about you and your family," said Kaznin. "You must be exhausted. I know I'm very tired chasing you and your friends. I hope this chase will have a swift conclusion. With your help."

His Russian was polite, and this more than anything, more than the soldier with his gun, more than the blood streaming down from her open scalp, this told Anna that this short, stocky man with the inappropriate smile was going to kill her. Kill her like they killed Lena, like they killed the cub, like they murdered her own father. Murder was their way. She tasted her own blood in her mouth.

"None of this was necessary. It's all been a matter of great exaggeration. The wild fantasies of Mayor Nowek. He's with you? Of course he is. Where?"

Anna's head was throbbing. Open her mouth and something might crack, something might shatter and fall.

"You must understand my position," Kaznin said earnestly. "The prosecutor general has given me complete authority in pursuing Ryzkhov's murderer. He believes that you may have been involved. Frankly, so do I. You were seen at his flat. You were seen leaving it at a late hour, not that this was so unusual." He stopped, gauging the effect of his words. "The next thing we know he's dead, and so are two militia. Do you understand?"

"*Ya panimayu*," she spat back in Russian. Each syllable hurt. She swallowed. More blood.

"Excellent. It would be helpful if you cooperated. Now aside from any damaging evidence, we must also recognize that you're American. Nobody wants to harm relations with the United States. Where would we be then?" He waited for her to agree, but when she didn't, he said, "You could be on a jet heading home by tomorrow night. You'd like that?"

"Don't fuck with her," said Decker. He didn't understand one word of Russian. But he could tell that Kaznin was snowing her, or trying to. He could also tell that it wasn't working. He knew how to find things out. He could do it. He was the man, after all.

Kaznin waved him quiet. "Here is the alternative: you will stand trial for Ryzkhov's death, plus two militia. And that barely begins to cover what's happened tonight. I assure you, Dr. Vereskaya, American or not, you could be found guilty. I can say that an American who murders Russians will not be treated very well in prison. Do you know what I'm saying?"

"I know you've already lost," she said, glaring. "Your little secret? It's no secret anymore. Not to me. Not to Mayor Nowek. Not to the whole world."

"Secret?" Kaznin answered, but inside he was shaken. What did she know exactly? Who else might she have told? Was there time for her to get word out? He looked at her again. No. Unlikely. Not up here. Siberia had many advantages, after all. It was a place where secrets remained frozen and untouchable. A place far from the eyes of the world.

"We know who killed Andrei." She looked at Decker and said in English, "You should have left his father's cigarette lighter where it was. But you were too busy raping children to worry."

"You don't know shit," said Decker, though with a scowl.

That doesn't seem to be the case, thought Kaznin. Not that it would matter. "Now that you say so," he said to her, "some important thing was missing from Andrei Ryzkhov's flat. Videotapes. Whoever has them is tied to a murder, of course, but—"

"It's murders, not murder. Even a *nekulturny* thug like you should understand the difference."

His neck twitched. He ran his hand over the thin hairs plastered to his scalp. "Forgive me for not being so cultured as your friend the mayor. I'm just a common man who serves his country. Now I can tell you that our investigation will reveal the former mayor of Markovo to be mainly responsible. With your help we might find a way to minimize your role. With your help we can wrap this sorry matter in a ribbon."

"He's still mayor," spat Anna.

"Actually, he's not. I have papers, signed by the governor of the state of Irkutsk, removing him from office. Prosecutor General Gromov has vowed that corruption will be weeded out ruthlessly. You had the tapes. You were with the mayor. Let's assume they are both in one place. Where?"

Finally Anna said, "Maybe they evaporated. You're familiar with sublimation? Ice can go from solid to vapor without ever going through a liquid phase. A person can too, but it takes more effort. You of all people should know what I mean."

"I'm not familiar with that principle, Dr. Vereskaya," said Kaznin. "But I know enough about genetics to see the connection between the daughter and her father. The disease that took his life has not been entirely eradicated in Siberia. It's easy to catch but hard to cure."

"His disease was seeing people like you for what you are." Her eyes burned back at Kaznin. Her father had sublimated, gone from life to memory, because of men like him. "And you're right. I've got a real bad case of it."

"Let me explain something to her," said Decker. He stepped up next to Kaznin and gave him the big Ruger. He held up the M-209 for her to see. "You know what this is? It's a grenade launcher. Nice little piece. Makes a big bang. That's why you shot the boss, right? Save those little kitty cats from gettin' scattered."

Anna glowered.

"This tube right here? Just made for takin' out bunkers. Now, where's the bunker? Good question." He pretended to turn, to search. He stopped and smiled when he faced the hidden den. "How about that. We got us a bunker. You must be wondering if it really works the way they say. I know I am." Decker smiled. He broke open the tube and stroked the little green grenade. "Frag round. Makes a lotta metal, Doc." He snapped it back shut, rotated the lock, then flipped the safety off. "How many little pussycats are down that hole? You have an idea? Yeah. I bet you even have names for 'em."

"Don't." She said the word as though it had to be squeezed by her lips.

"Why not?" He shouldered the weapon and pointed it. "Give me a reason, bitch. Just give me a reason."

"Don't!" She twisted in the grip of the two troopers.

"Where are the tapes?" Kaznin demanded, all courtesy gone from his voice. "Where is Nowek?"

"Time to come to Jesus," said Decker. "We gonna have some tiger gumbo here in a second—"

"No!"

Decker pulled the trigger. A single shot cracked from the rifle, not the grenade launcher. It burrowed into the den and immediately set up a cacophony of snarls and hisses.

"Next one's for real," said Decker, seeing that he had already won. "You want to see if I can do it?"

"No!" she said. "All right! Don't kill them. I'll show you the way." Her shoulders slumped. "They're all together. At a feeding station."

"Feeding station?" asked Kaznin.

"For tigers. It's just a kilometer that way." She pointed at the trees.

Decker turned to Kaznin. "See? It's like I always said." He grinned. "Best way to a woman's heart is straight through her rib cage."

28

THEY TOOK COVER behind the fallen tree trunk in front of the shack's open door. The tree had been a young one. Its trunk was terribly slender. Any position more than flat on their stomachs put their heads above it.

Nowek listened to the rain, to the low, conspiratorial sound of Galena speaking with the American boy in Moscow, Idaho; a prayer sent soaring to a distant, rich life that was now more remote than a star. He'd lost Galena that morning in front of the Hotel Siber. Lost her and saved her. Now he stood to lose her again. And Anna? The same.

Violinist, geologist, father, mayor. Nowek's slide had accelerated. He looked up at the camera on its pole. It was a rich enough irony, even for Russia: here, in the wildest, most remote part of a wild, remote land, they were under the stare of the whole world. Nowek thought, I have one last career move ahead of me: to play the role of bait.

From the shack, Galena said, "Eighteen. How many years old are you?"

"She's sixteen," Nowek said to Yuri. It irritated him that she found the truth so hard to tell. "Why does she lie?"

"It's not a lie exactly," said Yuri as he shifted the weight of the Skorpion in his arms. He let the snub-nosed muzzle rest on the fallen tree. "You could say that she's accommodating herself to a larger truth." He checked the magazine. Ten empty holes, twenty filled with bright brass.

Voices from the trees. Closer now.

Larger truths. Ryzkhov murdered. His two officers. Nikki Malyshev, even Semyon Yufa's son Boris. All to hide the fact that camps were open once again in this bitter, dark country. It didn't matter whether they were throwing Baptists or poets inside. Chechens or renegade Chinese. As Chuchin said, the only theory that mattered was *Who beats whom?*

Who beats whom? He could hear Kaznin laughing at him.

Nowek said to Yuri, "You know why I took this on? This investigation? It just came to me."

"It's a little late."

"Deep down I knew that there would be no real reform for Russia. How could there be? The same people who ruined us before are still in charge."

"Everyone knows this."

"I wanted the investigation into the Ryzkhov murders to work according to real law. To be right. I thought it could be my last opportunity before everything is lost to *Vorovskoi Mir.* To chaos."

"It seems like a safe prediction," said Yuri. "But you're wrong about chaos. It's just a phase."

"A long one. In Russia, it's gone on for a thousand years."

"No. Look at the big corporations in the west. They're all fat now, but just a hundred years ago they were wolves tearing each other apart. They did what they had to do to survive. The ones who were quickest, who had the biggest teeth, the best connections, lived. This is our starving wolf phase. Who knows? In five years we could all be pissing cream."

"No."

"Why not? Once a market begins, it develops a life of its own. The free market will always be with us because greed is part of our natures."

"Maybe in other places, but not Russia. You know why?" Nowek leaned close. "Because envy is also a part of our natures."

They stopped and listened to the rain, to Galena's giggle over something a boy thousands of kilometers away had said.

Yuri said, "But this isn't the only reason you've been so stubborn about Ryzkhov."

Anna. Was it so obvious? "That came later. For now all I can think about is this: AmerRus killed Ryzkhov and my two men. They did it to keep evidence of Elgen from reaching the world."

"Why would Americans care about Elgen?"

"You said it yourself. AmerRus controls everything. They run Tunguska like a colony. But they depend on the state, our state, to protect their investments in the oil fields."

"AmerRus doesn't care much about finding oil," said Yuri.

That was true. That was the problem. The one fact that refused to fit the others. Do you crumple the last anomaly into a ball and toss it away, or do you toss away the theory and find a better one? "It's something. I know it is. I'll make them say it." He paused, then said, "Somehow."

"You still have hope, Mayor?" Yuri asked.

Nowek glanced at the camera on its pole. "There's infinite hope." He looked back at the young pilot. "Just not for us."

Decker led the way with the M-209. Anna followed, flanked by the three troopers. Finally, with DeKalb's prized Ruger rifle in his arms, Kaznin.

The commander of the Ministry squad could feel his own heart beating through his white camouflage snowsuit. He could feel the throb in his ears, his neck. He could hear his own labored breathing. He was steaming like a draft animal hauling a cart. The tiger's den was behind them; the taiga forest dark ahead. He risked flashing a light, swept it across the wet ground, then switched it off again.

Anna's trail was impossible to miss. It required no great skill; what did you expect from a woman stumbling through the snow? But the others were around, close, perhaps. He was worried about them. In the trees. Hiding. Running for their lives. Waiting in ambush. Which?

Decker moved confidently, quickly. The forest was dull green in his night vision glasses. The marks in the snow were perfectly visible to him, as was the outcome.

Galena. He remembered how she'd tried to go cold on him, how he lit her up with a little poke. Lit her right up. He thought of Vereskaya. How much could she stand before she broke? Be fun to find out. He could taste it, taste it like biting into a big old peach plucked straight from the tree, still hot from the sun.

The tracks moved straight across an open area. The trees were heavier ahead. A little stream for sure. He could hear it moving under the ice, beneath the snow. The tracks went straight across. The tiger gal was light. Would it take his weight? He stopped.

"*Shto eta?*" asked Kaznin. Then he remembered Decker spoke no Russian. "What is it?"

He cautiously stepped out, keeping to Anna's own prints.

The ice crackled. He took another step.

Kaznin turned to Anna. "Where are they?"

"Just beyond those trees," she said.

"Then we might as well get this show on the road." Decker took another step. Okay. He scanned the far trees. Nothing. Hell. She did it. So could he. He took another step, then another. He moved to one side of Anna's boot marks, keeping fresh ice underfoot. The crackling was muffled by wet snow. But there was a springiness that kind of . . .

The cracks webbed out. An instant later he crashed through, water to his breast pocket, the night vision goggles' battery pack submerged. They winked out as Decker blindly struck the ice, beating a path back to the bank with the stock of his weapon.

Harley, with all the self-serving instincts of a rat facing seawater pouring into a hold, jumped ship. The ferret leaped from Decker's pocket and made for the edge. His weight left nothing behind but tiny pawmarks swept one side, then the other, by his tail. He shot up a tree and sat there, glowering down.

"Shit!" Decker crashed his way back to Kaznin. The night

vision goggles were shorted. He hauled himself out, soaked from the waist down in water that had been ice and snow not half a minute before.

She prayed Nowek had heard and that he'd made the necessary preparations. "You have to watch where you're going," said Anna. "The taiga can be tricky this time of year."

Yuri leaned close to Nowek. "You heard?"

Nowek nodded. A shout, then another. The camera. The all-seeing eye, broadcasting to the world. He would have one chance. One chance only. All his life he'd made his way with his mind, with words, not with violence. Somehow, in some way he'd have to do it again.

Decker tossed the over-under weapon to a trooper and grabbed Anna by her sweater, pulling her to the edge of the frozen bog. She stumbled, she fell. He shoved her face into the broken ice and black water.

"No!" shouted Kaznin.

He held her down as she clawed at him, her boots kicking, her body squirming to be free, to breathe.

"Decker!" Kaznin looked to the three troopers. "Stop him!"

It took all three of them to pull him off. When they did, Anna rolled onto her back, gasping.

"You can have her after. We still need her," Kaznin said under his breath.

"Bet your ass she's mine," said Decker. "You can take that to the bank." He felt a strange emptiness in his breast pocket. He tapped it, then looked up, searching. "Harley!"

"Quiet!" said Kaznin.

"I don't give a good fuck what they hear. I lost my 'bro." He whistled. He looked up into the low branches. Too dark. He whistled again. "Get back here you little sonofabitch!"

"This way. Over here," called the squad commander. He'd found a second set of boot marks leading to a log that spanned the stream.

Kaznin watched Decker look forlornly at his pet ferret. It

seemed a mystery how a man so willing, so anxious to cause pain, to hurt for no reason beyond his own pleasure, could grieve over vermin. It was so childlike. It was how Kaznin thought of most Americans. Smiling at nothing, they were children who were either innocently foolish, like Vereskaya, or innocently dangerous like Decker. Kaznin was capable of worse, but his violence was harnessed to a higher cause. A larger truth. "We'll come back for your pet," he said, handing him the M-209.

Decker glared at Anna. "This time the bitch goes first."

The young research assistant at the Taiga Institute sat with his feet on the desk, his eye on a computer monitor and a telephone pressed to his ear. His screen was blank; the camera looking down on Feeding Site Fourteen was sensitive to heat and there was none to see. He thought, maybe I'll ask her to stand out where I can see her. Check her out thermally. She sure has a nice voice, sort of low, sort of growly.

Galena had Anna's cat in her arms. She stroked its ears and asked the American boy a question.

"My favorite group? Hootie and the Blowfish," he answered. "What about you?"

Blowfish? Galena had never heard of them, but she couldn't admit that. "In Russia technorock rules."

"Technowhat? I never . . . wait a second." He sat up. Something was moving on the screen now. "You have something out by the treeline. Galena? Something's moving. Can you see it?"

He heard voices on the other end of the transglobal call. Then, Nowek came on.

"What is it?"

"Two heat sources . . . wait, three. Four! You got a whole bunch of heat out there all of a . . . there's another! Six in all. You can't see them yet?"

"No." Six. It wasn't as many as he'd imagined. But plenty enough. Anna had been right. The satellite link was working.

What would happen in the next few moments would be sent around the world.

Nowek held the phone close. He pointed at the floor of the little shack. "Down," he whispered to Galena. "Get down flat. All the way."

"Why?" Galena started to peer out the door when Nowek shoved her down and put his boot onto the small of her back.

The calico cat snarled at him. Arching its back, fangs bared. Nowek swatted it and it ran out the door. "Keep telling me what you see," he said to the distant voice. "They're moving."

The trees opened onto a small clearing. The troops stayed low, keeping cover between them and what might be ahead. Decker put the M-209 down and grabbed Anna. A blade touched her neck. "Too bad you didn't get to see your old boyfriend after we were done with him," he whispered. "We fucked him up good. He woulda' sold your sweet little ass for a minute of air. Just one more minute of air, yeah."

She shivered against the steel.

"What about the mayor? His little girl said he was a real tiger. Said he'd kill me if I hurt her. You think so?"

"Yes."

"I'm lookin' forward to seeing him try." The point of the blade pierced her skin, ever so slightly. "What about you? You a fighter or a lover? Me, I'm both."

She struggled to get free of him. She cried out.

"Quiet!" Kaznin scanned the clearing with DeKalb's night vision goggles. A small shack, its door ajar. Movement inside. Yes. Definitely movement. He saw a large figure dive out and come to a stop behind some low obstruction. A fallen tree. The snow around the door was tramped down. The moon buggy's trail arrowed straight for it. He looked at the squad commander and nodded.

Without words, two of the troopers began to spread out, to surround the shack and its occupants, to place them in the focus of their fire.

"How you want to do this?" asked Decker.

"Quickly. Tie her up first."

"Now you're talkin'." Decker pulled Anna's belt off and looped it tight around her wrists. He pulled them down between her ankles, nearly folding her in half. He wove the laces of her boots through, then together. When he was done he kicked her onto her side. "We gonna have some fun, girl. Just the two of us. Don't you worry 'bout it."

She spat out a mouthful of snow. "I thought you only liked children."

"I always say, love the one you're with."

Kaznin eased himself up, still sheltering his body behind a gnarled pine. He cupped his hands to his mouth and shouted, "Citizen Nowek!"

Yuri jumped and pointed the Skorpion. He thumbed off the safety.

"No." Nowek clamped his hand over the barrel. "Not yet."

"Citizen Nowek! You know who this is. I'm here to arrest you by order of the governor of the state of Irkutsk. Come out now and you'll live to stand trial for your crimes."

"Which crimes are you speaking of?" said Nowek. "If you mean the murder of Andrei Ryzkhov and my two officers, then you've come to the wrong place. But you already know that. You know who killed them. You've been protecting him from the beginning. And I'm not *citizen* Nowek. I'm the mayor."

"Not anymore. And what I know is not important. We have Vereskaya," said Kaznin. "There's no reason for her to pay for the mistakes of others."

It took everything inside to keep from rising to his feet, walking over to Kaznin, and strangling him. He reached down deep inside him, searching for coolness, for clarity. He needed something he could poke into Kaznin. Something that smug bastard would feel. "That's the problem with Russia. No one's willing to take responsibility for anything."

Kaznin gritted his teeth. Nowek had no respect. None. Even here, at the end of his life, a joke. "If you had done as you were ordered, none of this would have happened. You insisted on running out of control. Now you are my responsibility and I promise, I will take it."

"I'm not so sure. This is bigger than fishing dead bodies from a river. This isn't about the past, and keeping it buried. It's about the future. You're the criminal. You and your American friends."

"What I know about the future is that if you do not come out, unarmed, yours will be short."

With an eye to the camera, an ear to the microphones, Nowek suddenly switched to English. "You know, it's amazing. The KGB picked its people well. Even here, now, you can't force yourself to speak the truth. You're incapable of it. You know that the American pilot is guilty of killing Andrei Ryzkhov and my two men. His name is Decker. Paul Decker."

The American tensed. "How'd he know?" asked Decker. The barrel of the M-209 was drawn to that taunting voice across the clearing.

"Nowek is still playing games." But Kaznin was troubled. Why did Nowek start speaking in English? To prove he was better educated? More culturally advanced? He was wrong. "Citizen Nowek!" Kaznin called back in English. "I said investigations should be left to a professional. Now you see where your mistakes lead."

"What about your mistakes? Where will they lead?"

Kaznin was losing his patience. "There is no reason to talk. I see many of my friends here, but none of yours. Come out now, *with the tapes,* or we'll shoot."

"Unfortunately, there's a small problem. *Ani ni zdyes,*" Nowek answered.

Kaznin paused. Not here?

"And I think it's safe to conclude that you have no idea where they are, either. Trust me. They're in a place that will do me more good than they will you."

"Let me do this the right way. We got all we need," he said, looking at Anna.

Kaznin nodded. "Nowek! If you come out, if you hand us the tapes, you have my word. Nothing will happen to Vereskaya. She'll go home within the week. You can trust my word."

"I don't think so. You miss the old days, Kaznin. You miss the secrets. The powers. You miss being able to make inconvenient people like Anna Vereskaya disappear. That's why you've allowed Elgen to happen again."

Kaznin felt the word sting. *How much does he know?*

"You've opened the camps again because in your heart they never closed. What's a Fisherman without a net?" Nowek gathered himself, then spoke again. "Tell me that you don't know about Elgen. Tell me that you aren't using Siberia again as a place to make inconvenient people disappear." He raised his voice and faced the invisible men in the trees. "Tell me that you haven't tried to bury that fact to protect AmerRus. Tell me this and then perhaps I might be able to trust you."

Why is he using English? It was unnerving Kaznin, confusing him.

"Grisha! Don't bargain with them!" Anna shouted.

Decker had the knife out. She was on her side, down in the snow. The point of it pricked the skin of Anna's neck. "Scream, bitch," he whispered into her ear as he knelt beside her. "Let your boyfriend hear you scream."

She clamped her mouth shut.

"No?" He reached down and found her breast. "Damn. You cold or is all this too excitin'?" He caught her stiffened nipple between thumb and forefinger and pinched down hard.

A whimper escaped. He was pulling and twisting. She bit down even harder.

"Scream, baby," said Decker. "Be wise to, actually."

She felt faint. The pain radiated up her chest, down her arm, along her side. Another whimper, louder.

Decker knew he was close. He could sense it. "You're too easy," he whispered, then gave a savage yank.

Her scream welled up and exploded into the night.

Nowek was on his feet when Yuri pulled him back down.

"If you hurt her, Kaznin, I swear I'll . . ." Nowek stopped at the new sound.

A muffled throb. The heavy beat of a helicopter.

"You hear that, Mayor?" Kaznin called, comfortably back in Russian. "That's Prosecutor Gromov with more troops. There won't be any time for negotiation."

The sound built, faded, built again, riding the winds.

"Just the opposite, Kaznin. Your time is short, not mine. He'll expect you to hand over Vereskaya, me, and the tapes. What will you have to give him when he arrives? Gromov has sent you to take care of a problem. Not half a problem. Without the tapes you're still in danger. You know I'm right."

Kaznin looked back into the woolly, rain-spitting sky. Damn it! Gromov would be incensed at being summoned to Tunguska. It would already reflect poorly on Kaznin. Gromov would want an end to this, not a standoff. A decision. He wanted more than just bodies. He wanted those tapes.

"Well?" called Nowek. "Did I say something wrong?"

"You've presented complications. It's your specialty." Kaznin listened. The helicopter sound faded, swallowed by the rain, the mist rising from the river ice. "But there's still plenty of time. For me. But sadly not for you."

LeRoy Rogers listened to the sound of the rain on the hard metal skin of the disabled helicopter. The red lights that had drawn him to the Mil from across the ice were noticeably dimmer. The hot tea the bloody-faced man had given him was gone. He was feeling the cold coil through his gut again. He shivered, then looked to his left: Chuchin, asleep—drunk more accurately—still bleeding from his ears and his scalp. To the right was the wounded Ministry trooper, unconscious though now and again he'd moan and try to move. His leg was puffy around the tightly cinched tourniquet and his face was looking gray. LeRoy knew what that meant.

An empty bottle of medicinal vodka lay on the cold metal deck, another fallen soldier. LeRoy kicked it and the clatter was loud inside the silent machine.

But then it wasn't silent anymore. A new sound. One that made him forget all about the cold, about everything.

A helicopter.

Try and run? They'd nail him sure as shit even if he could run, which he couldn't. Stay and let them drag his ass back to that camp? No fucking way.

LeRoy backed himself into one final corner, hemmed in by fear, by shame, by a lifetime of violence. Violence given, violence taken. It always came naturally before. It came naturally again.

The sound deepened into the throbbing beat of another helicopter.

"Shit." LeRoy managed to get to his feet. The dim red lights swirled. He reached up to grab a metal handle to keep himself from falling. Pistol. Got to get my hands on a motherfucking gun.

Chuchin had one tight in his grip. He had the one LeRoy took from the guard hidden someplace.

One was all he would need.

The beat was loud enough to feel inside his chest. The disabled Mil began to shudder and sway in a new wind. A brilliant light flooded the ice outside, it scalded LeRoy's eyes as it poured through the portholes.

Voices joined the turbine's wail.

"Fuck." LeRoy reached down for Chuchin's Nagant. He leaned closer, closer to Chuchin. Sleep, baby. Be just a second now and . . . he touched the oiled metal. It was warm with Chuchin's body heat. Now. He grabbed the barrel and yanked the heavy old pistol away.

Chuchin jerked awake like he'd been stabbed.

The muzzle swung down. LeRoy let him look up into the barrel. Be easy to waste his ass. Easier than not. But he'd given him that hot tea. He'd been a human being to LeRoy, and that was uncommon. Uncommon enough to win his life, unless he decided to act stupid. "Listen, old-timer. I won't shoot you," he said. "Just stay put. I got my own business to take care of."

His gun. He'd never lost it. It was the drink, that was it. The vodka he'd swilled to numb the pain. It was back. It felt like a

spike being driven right into his skull. Chuchin stared up at the
wide black mouth of his pistol. "So? What now?"

LeRoy couldn't understand Chuchin's Russian. He didn't
need to. He could still feel those men on his back, hear their
grunts and wheezes, feel the burning shame of it. No way. Let
them shoot. Be a better way. A better way entirely. A man's
way out. *Home free.* He smiled. "Stay put. Don't move. You'll
be home free."

Chuchin couldn't understand why the man's lips were moving but there was no sound. The world was muffled silent as a
midnight snow, his shattered eardrums useless. But he didn't
need ears. He didn't need eyes. He reached over with his other
hand and touched the cabin wall. Vibrations.

LeRoy turned and made his way back to the hatch. He
reached down and touched the metal handle. There were men
outside on the ice. Close. Surprise their asses. Go out like
Jumping Jack Flash, let 'em see the piece. Would they shoot?
Of course they would. What would it be like? A flash, a quick
blackout like that motherfucking needle back at Travis? Or
would he feel the bullets? Either way. Didn't matter. Not one
bit.

He took a final breath, let it out slow, then looked at
Chuchin. "Thanks for the tea. But I best be goin' now." He
threw the handle and pulled. He slammed the hatch back and
jumped out onto the ice, the pistol in plain sight. He saw a dark
figure ahead and aimed at it, then, for a reason that felt new and
strange, he moved the Nagant away from the man and pulled
the trigger.

The pistol flashed, then boomed, then kicked itself right out
of LeRoy's grip.

He didn't see the man beside him. He didn't sense the swing
of a rifle in his direction, the shout in a language he couldn't
understand. Only an obliterating white flash and a blow that
sent him skidding across the slick ice, and the thought, the final
luminous thought that glowed from within his dying brain like
a firefly in a sealed jar, that maybe he'd done right not shooting
that man. Maybe, after all this time, he'd done right.

★ ★ ★

"Why are you so stubborn, Nowek? Don't you know that AmerRus dollars have fed families in your own town?"

"Have you asked Ryzkhov's father? His wife?" Nowek almost stood again, but thought better of it. "I tried to make Markovo a place where laws mattered. Your American friend Decker broke the biggest law of them all. Murder is the one thing that can never be forgiven, Kaznin. It's not like robbery. We can never hand the money back. We can never apologize."

"Don't lecture me. Ryzkhov was a thief! He was trying to make money selling those tapes back to us! And for a man like *this* you would condemn yourself, and your woman, to die?"

"I'm not dead yet."

"A distinction without a difference." Kaznin pounded a fist into his hand. "What is it you hope to accomplish, Nowek?"

He looked across the darkness to the trees. "I'll tell you something that I've only now learned. Hope is a funny thing," said Nowek. "It's stubborn. Like me."

CHAPTER
29

THE GRADUATE STUDENT at the Taiga Institute watched the screen as the confrontation developed in the distant arctic clearing. Galena wasn't answering him now. What was happening? He clicked his mouse on an icon and sent the entire scene hurtling into the ether, out onto the Worldwide Web.

At first there were few watchers dialed into the Institute's home page. After all, it wasn't as interesting as the MIT student who wore a camera all day in order to broadcast his life to the world, or the elephant in Kenya wired for sight and sound. And many of those who did amble through quickly clicked off the black and white scene in favor of more colorful places.

But some remained, wondering what kind of drama this might be, and why a staid, scientific institution was putting out such strange visuals to the world.

Curiosity was their prime mover, but the whiff of the illicit, the inadvertent, that rose from their monitors was the most powerful lure of all. They were seeing something they weren't supposed to see. More than anything else, that made it irresistible.

It was like nuclear fission. Once begun, it doubled, quadrupled, on a schedule of its own making. The clearing at the northern edge of the Russian taiga was reproduced on two, then five, then eight, then a dozen screens. A hacker in Finland broke into the voice channel and heard Russian spoken. It was like waving a bunch of fragrant flowers in front of a beehive: in a very few minutes, the hive was buzzing.

The helicopter throbbed at the edges of Nowek's hearing, a reminder that Kaznin was right about one thing, that time was not on his side. Nowek raised his voice and said, "Gromov directed you to plant evidence in Ryzkhov's flat to make it appear that Anna Vereskaya was guilty of his murder."

"Nobody had to order me."

"I forgot. You're a good consultant. A good consultant doesn't wait to be asked. He anticipates. The truth is, Anna Vereskaya is innocent."

"Yes! Anna Vereskaya is innocent! Why do you need to hear it?"

"I'm a condemned man. It's a sort of last wish and I don't smoke. The governor knows about the camp at Elgen?"

Kaznin gritted his teeth. "Of course he knows."

"Louder!"

"Yes! He knows! Gromov runs it for him!"

"In other words, the governor and the prosecutor general for the state of Irkutsk conspired with a foreign company, Amer-Rus, to operate a prison camp for—"

"What's illegal? It was completely authorized by the state. *You* are the one who has broken laws."

"Stalin authorized them, too."

"For people like you. He was ahead of his time, or perhaps you are only late."

The helicopter sound was almost inaudible now. Had they gone away? "You sent Decker to Ryzkhov's apartment to keep that tape from ever . . ." He stopped.

This clearing. The tape in Anna's office. The tape that Ryzkhov had tried to sell, the tape that had killed him. What was on it? An American. An illegal American. A man without a name and a company willing to kill to make sure he never got one.

He looked across the clearing to the trees. It was like a mirror held up to his own thoughts, bouncing, reflecting back and forth, gathering clarity with each echo. A laser cavity.

"What's wrong?" Yuri whispered. "Don't stop. You're doing a good job of pissing him off."

Finally, the light broke free. "My God," he whispered.

"What?" Yuri thought that Nowek had seen something, and in a way he had.

"That tape. An American was on it. Why would AmerRus care whether an American showed his face to the world? My God," he said again. "It's not Russians. Not Russians at all . . ."

"Of course they're Russians. Kaznin is—"

"*Not Kaznin*. The camp. *Elgen*. It's not being filled with *Russians*. My God," he said. "They're putting *Americans* up there." The anomaly. The balled-up fact that did not fit. Straightened, pressed flat. It slid into place now with a chilling ease, the glide of a needle into cold flesh.

Americans. In a Siberian camp. Run with the connivance of the state, which meant they were being paid off. Like the North Koreans down south. Illegal, yet they'd never been shut down. Why? They were too lucrative for the local politicians. But Koreans thrown behind the wire was one thing . . .

"You've reached the end, Nowek," said Kaznin.

"You're right," he said to Kaznin. "Before I could see only the edges. The pieces of your crime. Now I see it for what it is. I even know why you did it."

"Know this!" Kaznin shouted. "I have an executive order removing you from your position as mayor. As far as the law is concerned, you are a criminal, nothing more."

Nowek sat in the cold, the wet. "I've been fired before."

"I want you to come out. If you don't, I'll explain what has to be explained to Gromov without you."

Yuri whispered, "You have something else in mind?"

"Yes." Nowek slowly stood up. He heard the click of weapons in the darkness, from the trees. He didn't want one word lost. He was delivering a lecture to an attentive class of muzzles, of gunsights.

"I admit I've been mistaken," he called out. "I thought everything began and ended with Ryzkhov's murder. But now I see that I'm guilty of thinking too small. What's the murder of one Siberian compared to what you and AmerRus are doing at Elgen? Siberians are born dead as far as the rest of Russia cares. What's one more? What's three? Or three hundred? But Americans. That's certainly a new approach."

"What's that supposed to mean?" said Decker, but Kaznin waved him quiet.

"Tell me, Kaznin, when did AmerRus stop looking for oil and start smuggling in American prisoners?"

"Shit," said Decker. "How the fuck did he—"

"He's guessing." But why? Kaznin wondered, what does he hope to gain? What can he possibly hope to gain?

The silence, the whisper of a wind through the trees, the drips of rain falling from dwarf cedar.

"Does the American government know what AmerRus is doing? I know they're paying. Do they know what a bargain they're getting?"

Finally, Kaznin said, "You're wasting time and you have no more of it to waste. There's no evidence anywhere for anything you've said, Nowek. None. Only in your head and to be very honest, that evidence is not in the safest of places right now. Tomorrow AmerRus will go on the way it has. So will Elgen. So will I. Now tell me where the tapes are or I'll order you shot where you stand." He nodded at a trooper.

Nowek looked up at the camera on its pole. It was a kind of a prayer, a plea to the invisible forces. A mariner whispering to calm the waves, a violinist asking his trembling hands to steady.

"Where are those tapes!"

"Relax," said Nowek. "I have them here. All of them." Nowek looked back at Galena on the floor of the shack.

"No more stalling!" shouted Kaznin. "Throw out your weapons first!"

He looked down and said, "Yuri, give them your rifle."

"They'll kill us."

"True. But maybe not here. It's Galena. I can't give them a reason to shoot her, too."

Yuri sighed. He thumbed the safety back on and tossed it to the snow in front of the log. It sank half out of sight.

"All of them!"

"That's it," said Nowek. "We're unarmed. But there is one other thing. One additional fact you should know. The evidence you mentioned? About Elgen? You're wrong. It exists. It exists in so many places you'll never erase them all. There are too many fish for the Fisherman's net. You can have the tapes. Your secret no longer belongs to you. It no longer belongs to me. It belongs now to the whole world."

Decker had the M-209 to his shoulder. He centered Nowek's chest in the iron sights. "I can do him now. All of them. Can blow that little shack back to Tunguska."

What did Nowek mean, it belonged to the world? Why were they standing so still, looking up? Why was Nowek speaking English? Something was crawling up Kaznin's back, some signal, some omen. Something he did not understand. Something that he feared.

"Take two men and bring them to me." He held the big Ruger up. "I'll watch from here."

"You afraid of the mayor?"

"I'm careful."

On dozens of computer monitors around the world, five ghostly white figures moved toward one another on a dark field of cold, wet snow; Yuri and Nowek from the left, three other forms from the right. The near-simultaneous translation provided by a curious student at a language training school in Monterey, California, stopped: there were no words to translate. The figures closed in on one another at the center, full in the camera's unblinking eye.

"That's close enough," said Decker. He held the M-209 so that its muzzle faced the shack. "Anything makes me twitch, I'll turn your little girl into a crispy critter."

One trooper kept his rifle pointed at Nowek's belly while the other collected Yuri's Skorpion, then Yuri himself.

"Take him back to Kazzy," said Decker. "I can deal with the mayor. Him and me have a lot in common." He grinned at Nowek. "Just so you know, Mayor, Kazzy's watching from cover. He's got a rifle. Drop that sack where I can see it. You say the tapes are inside?"

"It doesn't matter anymore." Nowek held the rucksack in front of his chest. "You killed Ryzkhov. I know it. The world knows it."

"There's no way anybody's ever gonna know squat."

"You're wrong." Nowek slowly turned and nodded at the camera. "You see that pole beside the shack? You see what's on top of it?"

Decker looked warily, as though it were a trick.

"A video camera. Some highly technical piece of equipment I'm sure you'd understand better than I. It's recorded everything that's happened tonight. It's recording everything right now."

"Hell you say."

"Forgive me. I'm mistaken. It's *transmitting*. Right now your face is going up to a satellite, down to a scientific institute, then out onto the worldwide network. You might say that you and Kaznin have testified to your own guilt, and now the entire world knows it. The world knows about you, about AmerRus. Everything. Kaznin once said that modern methods are more effective and you know? In the end, I have to admit he was right."

"You don't know what the fuck you're saying." But Decker eyed that camera. Could it?

"No? I found the cigarette lighter you stole from Ryzkhov. You also left a piece of your uniform in the mouth of his guard dog. Where did I find them? On my daughter. In your cabin. At Tunguska. You had her there."

Decker laughed. The M-209 wavered, but only slightly. "I had her a couple a times." He looked beyond Nowek to the small shack. "Me, I think I'll have her again before too long.

She begged me to take her away. Anyplace was better than Markovo. Fact is, your little girl'd spread her legs for a bus ticket."

Nowek felt his heart trip over itself.

"See, I know where she belongs better than you. Flat on her back with her little feet up ticklin' my ears. Yeah. Can you picture it?"

Nowek felt the hairs on his neck rise. "You're a murderer. You'll go where murderers belong."

"I broke her in good. That's why they call me the virgin surgeon . . ."

Nowek felt the explosion. It was a new feeling. It didn't belong inside a man who played violin. It didn't belong inside a geologist who made his living with his mind, a man who didn't know violence. But it was inside him, here, now.

". . . though just between you and me, she's been under the knife before. Yeah. Little girl on the outside, pure professional on . . ."

The growl that came out wasn't Nowek. It wasn't even human. He threw the rucksack at Decker's chest.

The M-209 flashed. The grenade burst through the rucksack and sailed like a sparkling party favor over the roof of the shack. It bounced off a tree and buried itself in snow, the nose fuse crushed too soon to arm.

Nowek reached into the neck of his jacket and pulled out Anna's Buryat blade.

Decker reacted fast, but the rucksack was tangled with the M-209's barrel. He dropped the weapon but by then, Nowek was on him, pulling him down to the snow.

As he fell Decker slapped his knee and a slender silver blade appeared. The rucksack was trapped between them. The American brought his knife hand up and the sharp steel cut through the nylon, sinking deep into its folds, hunting for Nowek's skin. Tapes spilled out of the gaping cloth. The knife caught on webbing for just an instant, then slit it apart.

They rolled. Nowek landed on top. He felt something slap against his belt as Decker tried to slash him through the rucksack. He brought the Buryat knife up. One of Decker's hands closed around his wrist but Nowek forced it down.

The blade sliced the American's cheek open. Blood gushed into Decker's eye. It seemed not to hurt him so much as surprise him. He grunted, bucked, and shoved his own knife straight up through the rucksack.

Nowek felt the bite, felt it melt through his jacket, prick through his skin and sink deep. It was hot, and cold.

Nowek willed all his strength into his arm and pressed the shaman's knife down against Decker's neck. He was ready to saw off that laughing, obscene head and roll it into the river.

Decker's eyes were white. He stopped thrusting his knife. Instead he pulled it upward, upward toward Nowek's ribs, his heart.

Nowek gasped as he felt a sensation of ice deep inside him. Something gave way, something parted in a gush of heat. Suddenly he couldn't breathe.

Decker threw him off. Blood streamed down his face. He grabbed the Buryat blade from Nowek's hand. He stood back. His eyes glittered. "You don't know shit," he said, panting. "You think it was all me? You think I'm the one who did that boy Ryzkhov all by myself? You ignorant fuck. You cut me." He put a hand to his cheek and pressed down hard. Blood seeped by his fingers. "You cut me."

Nowek pulled at the air. It was like breathing fire. An alien atmosphere. Each breath made him feel more dead, more open to the rain.

"All this time and you still don't know. You might as well, since you're gonna take it into the dirt. You listening? It wasn't even my idea to off Ryzkhov. I helped out is all. He was—"

The flash of the Ruger, its thunder. Decker's scalp seemed to roll up like loose fabric, bottom to top. His glossy black hair was gone, replaced by an uneven, bloody crown. He tottered on his feet, back, forward, then pitched over onto his knees, then down to the snow.

Kaznin emerged from the trees. The sound of the helicopter was back again. Approaching now. Kaznin kicked the M-209 well out of Nowek's reach. He leaned down and saw the tapes. He ground them into the snow with the heel of his boot. "This is the end of it, Nowek," he said. "Maybe you can think of another joke to commemorate the occasion. Looking at your condition, I would say that time is of the essence."

Nowek pushed himself upright. He held his belly together with his hand. His life was leaked out through his fingers. He was breathing around red-rimmed pain in little gasps. It was like breathing through a straw. The rumble of the helicopter grew loud, immediate.

"I knew you would have at least one surprise left for us," said Kaznin as he racked the spent shell and sent another into the breech. "A camera. I must say, even I am impressed. The camera is really transmitting everything? Every word? Or is that just another of your little jokes?"

The helicopter passed over the clearing, then turned, looking for a place to land.

"Why—"

"Decker? A professional avoids taking unnecessary chances. Suppose your story about the camera were true? A lifetime in intelligence breeds caution. Something you never learned."

"Ryzkhov . . ." Nowek stared up as Kaznin stood near. "It was both of you . . ."

"Another black mark on your record." Kaznin smiled. "I told you to leave things to a professional. Though I admit, you did very well finding out about Elgen. I respect your abilities. In another time, another place, we could have been comrades. Now there's very little left for you to worry about. Only one thing. Where will you take your bullet?" He stood over Nowek, triumphant. He put his boot on Nowek's chest and kicked him flat onto his back.

Nowek gasped as he felt his belly fall open. Staring straight up, the helicopter. Its rotors shimmering in reflected light. Its wind rampaging down across the clearing. Its thunder filled his ears. A shocking white light flooded down. A rope uncoiled from its belly and a figure appeared, another, sliding down to the ground.

"Gromov will appreciate a tidy end to things. We're wrapping this matter up in a ribbon, Nowek. Thanks to you." Kaznin let the muzzle drop until it pointed at Nowek's head. "The head, I think. It's the customary place. Unlike you, I'm a man who respects tradition."

Nowek tensed. Tensed as though he could deflect the bullet by the power of his will alone. He drew in a lungful of pain, of air, and into the teeth of the helicopter's spiraling wind, he roared *"Anna!"*

The truth was free, even if he was not. The truth would live, even if he would—

Another flash, another detonation.

The monitor went black. "Galena? Are you still on?" The student at the Taiga Institute tapped a few keys before he remembered he was still linked to Site Fourteen by telephone. "Galena? What's happening? I lost the video."

A thump, a high-pitched voice, then others. Finally, *"Khto guhvareet?"*

"Where's Galena?"

A click, and then a steady disconnect tone.

CHAPTER

30

BY ALL ACCOUNTS, heaven was not supposed to look like this. True, his experience with the subject was purely theoretical. The communists said that both heaven and hell were opiates for the weak, that the only thing that mattered was cold gray fact. Take stock: he was cold, it was gray. Hell was a better fit with the available facts. His ears were assaulted by powerful subterranean rumbles, the high-pitched screams of the damned. The world jostled, shifted. The noise got worse.

Nowek floated, controlled by some inner gyroscope that kept him a few centimeters above his body. If only he could turn and look, he might peer down into his own face, as gray as the walls that arched overhead.

A voice, garbled, like something coming from deep under water.

"How is he?"

Nowek listened for the answer. He couldn't make it out above the thunder. He wanted so much to know the answer to that single, simple question.

Later, pressure on his hand. He blinked. A face swam out of the gray. Dark hair. Her sweater, the woolen skater's cap. Holding his hand. Nina? He blinked again. No.

Anna smiled, though she looked frightened, too. She squeezed his hand again and disappeared.

His heart pumped and his belly turned warm, wet with blood.

Her voice. "Can't you do anything?"

"Not here."

Pressure on him, pressure and pain, but he didn't care. The pain proved he was still alive. He tried to turn to find out where she had gone but he'd been strapped tightly, fastened down like cargo. The straps had kept him from floating away.

"Blood."

"We're losing him."

No, he thought. You aren't.

Later he smelled something foul, sulphurous, something burning.

Something familiar.

And then a new face. Dried blood overwashed with new, fresh red. A face from a horror movie. Then a gap-toothed smile. Chuchin? He had stained bandages around his ears, around his forehead. He wore a white soldier's snow jacket that showed signs of being present at some recent butchery. Chuchin risen from the dead with a cigarette dangling from the corner of his mouth.

Chuchin put the lit Yava to Nowek's lips. For no reason other than to see what might happen, Nowek sucked.

Too much. A sharp electric jolt girdled his midsection. He spat it out.

". . . kill him?"

Chuchin snarled something.

"He can't hear you." A gruff, male voice. Authoritative.

But he was wrong.

Needles, needles and slow, amber floods of opiates. Nowek's heart slowed. Galena was still there, in and out like a figure in a dream, still wearing the horrible orange outfit with Decker's name printed on the breast. His eyes filled. If he was alive then so was she. If he was dead, being dead had its merits.

"Anna."

Her name, though it was more a puff of air than anything. There was a sudden reaction, a bustle.

"Grisha! So you've decided to live?" A booming voice.

An eclipse. Arkady Volsky rocked back and forth, his fist clenched around an overhead strap. The big helicopter was being buffeted as it fought its way through layers of cloud.

"I told you I would come for you. You couldn't wait?"

Volsky had a pure Slav helmet of golden hair. His skin was splotched a florid red as though he'd tried to run too far too fast. Volsky still wore a necktie, though it had been roughly pulled aside and in any event looked at odds with his fur-lined leather jacket.

He looked away. "Is he awake? He really spoke?"

Someone said, "In and out."

Volsky said, "I told them you were too stubborn to die. I knew I could trust you to get to the heart of things. Didn't I say you were better than any investigator?"

No, you said I was a troublemaker. That point had certainly been proven.

"Actually," Volsky continued, "you're too stubborn in general. When you called? I could have saved you a lot of pain if you would have kept quiet for only a minute. But no. You wouldn't listen."

Nowek's lips were dry as bleached wood. He managed to wet them.

Volsky looked up. "Bring him something to drink."

The same, faceless voice demurred.

"Sto gram!"

A flask tipped against his lips. Vodka. It tasted hot. Then cold. Then good.

"Do you know where you are? Do you know what you've done?"

It wasn't modesty that made Nowek shake his head.

"I apologize for arriving a little late. We saw the machine down on the ice, the Ministry helicopter. We thought we'd find you there. Fortunately your driver knew where you were."

Chuchin. It hadn't been a dream, a mirage. He whispered a word that rose up on greasy vodka fumes. "Kaznin."

"He'll wish we'd shot him twice before this is over. Now listen. The Anti-Corruption Task Force has been investigating the governor of Irkutsk for months. Moscow doesn't like the idea of governors setting up their own private armies. They don't like governors setting up their own foreign policies either. That's what they pay me to look out for . . ."

A true politician's first job, thought Nowek, is justifying his own position.

". . . There was just one problem. The governor, Prosecutor Gromov, they have the whole state of Irkutsk in their pockets. They're connected to everyone. Everyone depended on them. Everyone except for me and of course, you."

It didn't sound like an enviable position.

"We knew about the Ministry. But there was no place to drive the wedge. You gave us the place. We'll bury that prick of a prosecutor, Grisha. And the governor, too. You and me."

Private armies and foreign policies. What would Moscow think of a private, foreign prison? Did Volsky know?

Volsky looked aside, as though to see who else might be listening. "We found someone. Frankly speaking, someone very strange. He attacked us with your driver's gun. Do you know who I'm talking about? Was he one of your men?"

Nowek shook his head.

"Too bad. I hoped you could clear that mystery up."

Nowek fought his way up through an opiate haze, through air made thick as glass. "Elgen . . . Americans . . ."

"Don't worry about Americans," Volsky said. "AmerRus will be taken care of in the proper fashion."

"Not . . . AmerRus." He started breathing, his chest heaved.

"Give him something!" Volsky ordered.

Another needle.

A soft curtain was pulled across Nowek's consciousness. Not solid, but sheer. It seemed to sparkle a bit where it caught the light. The world narrowed, faded. He fought it. "Kaznin . . .

he was there . . . Ryzkhov's. He . . . they both . . . murdered my men . . ."

Volsky shook his head. "I was trying to tell you this when you called. You wondered about type AB negative blood? How it was so rare? Well, I looked at Kaznin's service record. Can you guess what I found?"

Nowek stared, fighting to keep the perimeter of light open, his ears above water. He was floating. Floating away.

"Type AB negative. This time it's the Fisherman who won't get away."

Muffled sounds. The light seemed tinged with a new color, some chemical hue. He let go. Adrift, he looked over and saw Anna. "Sorry . . ." he told her. "I . . . lost . . . your tiger."

"Sleep," said Volsky. "Don't worry. We're landing."

The ferret waited for Decker to return. It was growing light. The animal was cold and hungry. Finally, Harley climbed down from a perch in the branches of the dwarf cedar and began to follow his master's scent. Decker's cologne was a bright ribbon to the ferret's sensitive, anxious nose. It grew stronger as he crossed ice, then snow, then to a tree at the edge of a clearing where the snow was trampled. He stood on his hind legs, sniffing.

He leaped in the snow like a dolphin frisking in the sea. The smell was growing, though there was something else, a rich red scent a wild animal would know at once. Ahead was a dark shape, lit by the pearl glow of Siberian morning light. He stopped, stood, and squeaked.

There was no answer from the shape in the snow.

He leaped, leaped again. The blood scent was overpowering so close to the body. The cologne, the blood, the smell of burning, the . . . Harley froze. He twitched his head in the direction of the soft, padded sound and saw a new shape flying through the air. Claws extended, tail ramrod straight, eyes burning golden.

The calico's pounce smashed the ferret against Decker's

body. It struggled once, then as the cat's needle teeth clamped down hard into the back of its neck, it surrendered to the unbreakable demands of natural law.

Dr. Grossman pulled the curtains wide. "Actually, it's refreshing to have a live patient."

Nowek blinked in the sudden brilliant light of a spring morning. One last icicle let diamond drops fall with the sincerity of a metronome. The Markovo clinic. Grossman's white smock was smudged brown, as though he hadn't changed from that morning in Andrei Ryzkhov's apartment. Nowek could see the syringe with its thermometer sliding into his own white flesh, a silent count, and then a quick pull. For establishing the time of death, liver temperature, he remembered, was an infallible indicator.

"How . . . how long?"

"A few days. Nothing to worry about. The only difference is that now your stomach is a little smaller than it used to be. I hope you don't mind."

"I'm not hungry."

Grossman turned, trying to decide whether that was a joke. He checked a drip tube that sent some liquid the color of straw into Nowek's forearm. An ancient black toad of a telephone squatted on the table by his bed. "Your driver was lucky. I picked a piece of metal from his head this big." He held his fingers apart. "It was coiled like a watch spring, stuck into his skull like steel hair."

"He's got a hard head. Where's Anna?"

"With your father and daughter." When Grossman smiled, his wet, tea-darkened teeth were glossy as polished wood.

"When can I see them?"

"A visit would not be such a good idea. My advice is to wait until . . ." A click from the door. Grossman looked startled, fearful, but then he said, "On the other hand, medicine still has many things to learn."

★   ★   ★

She was wearing another one of Nina's blouses under her own denim jacket. Her jeans were tucked into the tops of her boots. They were out of scale next to her slender ankles. Lugged soles made for digging in, for gaining footholds, for persisting. Stubborn shoes.

She wore the wool skater's cap, her dark hair almost under it, but not quite. Tiny flashes of red, yellow, and gold light came from earring studs.

She had a violin case tucked under an arm.

"Anna."

She came and took his hand.

He looked at the case. His father's? "I hear you've been spending time with my father. You're brave."

"We're trying to put your house back together. The new windows go in today. The electric heat blew every fuse in the district."

He found this reliable, commonplace catastrophe cheering. "And Galena?"

"Making life impossible for the workmen. She should never have been allowed to read *Cosmopolitan*. Not at her age." She stopped, then said, "*Especially* at her age. How old is she?"

"It depends." He smiled. "How old are you?"

Her look faded back into itself.

"What?"

"I . . . I have to leave this afternoon. For the field. Back up to Tunguska."

He grabbed her hand tighter.

"They've been flying back and forth now for days getting Elgen cleaned out. But they wouldn't let me go. The camp . . ."

"It's gone? The Americans are all gone?"

Anna nodded. "Yuri told me what happened. How you pulled it out of the air. Americans! *I* can hardly believe it. How did you figure it out?"

"To be honest," he said, "it wasn't easy."

"But you did it. You made them say everything."

"Getting Kaznin to confess was easy. He was proud of what

he'd done. Believing that it was going someplace, someplace useful, that was a lot harder."

"Siberia is part of the world now."

"It seems that way," said Nowek. "I only hope the world is ready for us."

"I found out something, too," said Anna. "The man on the tape? The black man. Remember his sweatshirt? *CDC Pelican?* One of the Americans from Elgen was found out on the ice, dressed as a Russian. *CDC Pelican Bay* was tattooed on him. California Department of Corrections, Pelican Bay."

"Now he can go back there."

"No," said Anna. "He attacked Volsky's men when they came. They had to shoot him. He was killed."

Another life. Perhaps Dr. Grossman had been right when he said that life was suspended on the frailest of threads. The mystery was why his own thread had stretched so far, yet held.

She said, "Everything was right there on that tape. We were looking, but we weren't *seeing.*"

"The murders. The tape. AmerRus. This whole affair was a puzzle that stays hidden until the very last piece," said Nowek. "It's like a bridge. Until you slide the keystone into place it's just two piles of rocks. Then suddenly it isn't." He shook his head. "No one would have believed that Americans could get caught up in an old horror like Elgen. An old *Russian* horror." But then Nowek said, "What will they do with the prisoners now? Send them home?"

"Your friend Volsky's handling it."

Why didn't that leave Nowek with a confident feeling? "I'm not so sure he's a friend."

"Neither am I."

"What will they do about DeKalb?"

"He should be happy to be alive. It was all I could do to make them go pick him up. Volsky was against it."

"He doesn't like complications," said Nowek, "unless he's making them." He thought of the photograph in DeKalb's wallet. Wife, daughter. The crime. The weight of it. He wondered whether DeKalb was so happy to be alive. He'd run to

Tunguska, run away from a horror, and it hadn't been far enough. "Why are you going back to Tunguska?"

"The cubs. Lena's dead and so is one of her cubs. The little male. That leaves three alive. They can't survive without a mother to feed them. I'm going up to collect them."

"You don't just collect them like butterflies."

"I can. They'll have to be sent to live at a zoo." She looked out the window, then back down. "I'll have to stay with the cubs until they get settled in their new surroundings. To make sure." She watched his face, metering her words, and then said, "I may be gone awhile."

Just a week . . . I'll be back . . . Nina's last words to him as she boarded the plane. He let go of her hand and looked out the window at the steady drip of the icicle. The steady drip of liquid into his vein. The gurgle of wastes flowing out. He drew in a breath, too deep, because it reignited the pain.

"There's something else. Galena asked about going. I said I would speak with you."

"Go where?"

"The zoo that can take the cubs is in Denver."

Nowek turned to face her. "America?"

"I'll have to be there for several weeks. But I thought she'd like to see the Institute. It's in Idaho." She smiled. "She already knows someone there."

"The boy on the telephone. A real live American she can torment. What an opportunity."

"I'll look after her. Don't worry." She hesitated again, biting her lower lip.

"What is it now? You want to take my father, too? I warn you, he'll be after you the minute I'm out of sight."

She laughed, then placed the violin case down on the bed. "He sent you this."

He fingered the metal hasp and pushed the top open.

The violin was nestled in plush red cloth, almost a velvet. Not one of the homemade violins, but his father's concert instrument. The wood gleamed, a smell of lacquer and polish stung his nose with a delightful new scent. He took it from its case and tucked it under his chin. His beard rasped against the rich dark wood. He could smell something else, a hint of tobacco, of his father's cheek, his sweat. All the notes that ever flew from his fingers out into a darkened auditorium. The tube in his arm prevented much motion, but he took the bow and gave a small, experimental draw.

The sound filled the small room.

"Excellent voice," he said.

"Play something."

He gave her a mischievous look. "Something." He pushed himself more upright, feeling the protest from his belly. He drew the bow and began the slow, rich opening to Vivaldi's great F minor concerto, *L'Inverno.* Winter.

"It's beautiful," she said, "but sad."

"You're leaving."

The telephone burped. She reached for it.

"No," Nowek told her, "forget the phone." He tried the next few bars, feeling the notes emerge, then drop like leaves as they fell to the dark bottom of winter.

The telephone burped again. A toad swallowing a buzzing, nasty insect.

Nowek sighed. He put the violin back into the case and picked up the phone. *"Ya sluchayu."*

"Grisha! You sound better already! I heard you were receiving visitors."

Word traveled fast. "What is it, Arkasha?" he said to Volsky. "I'm thinking of having a relapse."

"Don't. I want to discuss your future."

What had Kaznin said? It would be short?

"I want to ask one question. How the devil did you figure out what AmerRus was doing? A tin of rations, a tape, a dead businessman. No one could have put those things together and come up with Americans behind the wire."

"I did."

"And putting it out over that camera. Making them admit what they were doing. It was magnificent. Frankly, I had no idea you had a talent for this kind of work."

"I'm drawn to the impossible. What's being done about Elgen?"

"The Americans are gone."

"They're in American jails?"

"What they do with them is their business. After the noise this has made, I mean the *United Nations* is opening an inquiry. Of course, it was the Chinese who insisted on—"

"Elgen is shut down? Entirely?"

"Don't worry," Volsky said quickly, and evasively. "They won't dump their garbage here again. That much I can promise you. But about you. Have you thought what you might do when your strength returns?"

"A mayor doesn't have time for speculation."

The silence reminded Nowek of the night he'd asked Volsky about the Ministry.

"Well? What is it now?"

"Listen, we had to make an arrangement with the governor."

"I thought we were going to bury him."

"It didn't work out exactly as planned. He said it was a matter of uncontrolled elements. He put it all on Prosecutor Gromov's head and then let us cut it off. Half a loaf is better than none, though. Don't you think?"

"No."

"Naturally, the arrest order against you has been dropped."

"Naturally."

"But the order removing you as mayor of Markovo will have to stand. Frankly, there's a lot of hard feelings around Markovo. AmerRus was paying many bills. It might be better if you spent some time away."

"How far were you thinking?"

"Don't worry. We'll try to find something that fits your skills. In Russia," said Volsky, "there's always work for a troublemaker. We'll talk later?"

"You know where to find me." Nowek hung the phone up, then, thinking about it, reached down and yanked the wire out.

"It seems my schedule has been cleared," he said. He looked at Anna and held his arms open. An incantation. An invitation.

"This is permitted?" she said.

"Medicine still has much to learn."

She pulled the skater's cap off and a lock of hair dangled down over her eye. She kissed his forehead, his cheeks, and, finally, his lips.

He pushed her away and said, "When?"

"When what?"

"When do you and Galena leave for America?"

"Not now." She put her finger to his lips. "Not now."

Later, she said, "Will you play something else? I don't want to go away with *Winter* in my head."

She was leaving, taking Galena with her on a voyage to the other side of the world, to another planet. What could be more appropriate than *Winter*? A fugue? A pavane?

Russians reach naturally for the dark, the minor keys; it's how they survive the impossible. Americans live surrounded by the bright, sunny majors. It was easy to dismiss them for it. Everyone did. But maybe they had a point. Look at Anna: she'd filled a bleak space inside him with hope, with light. One week ago, Nowek would have sworn that it would never happen.

And now?

"Will you play?"

"You know," he said, "I just realized something. I'm not like my father. He plays because it would be impossible for him not to."

"And you?"

"It sounds strange, but I play for the same reason I ran for mayor. The same reason I wanted to know who killed Andrei Ryzkhov and my two men." He drew the bow across a string and felt the vibration go through him. "It's a privilege."

"A privilege?"

"Mayor, troublemaker, musician. Piece by piece, note by

note, we try to make the world a little bit better each time we play."

She looked at him. "Even when it's impossible?"

"Especially. Like now. You're leaving and you want me to play something cheerful."

"Does that mean you will?"

"Open the window." He picked up the violin, tucked it under his chin, grasped the bow as she went to the glass.

Outside the last icicle of winter died, murdered by the new hot sun. "Winter's over," he said as she threw open the glass. "It's spring." Nowek drew his bow, took a breath, and brought forth the first note of the Concerto in E; *La Primavera.*

A warmer day yet. A clear, empty sky that matched the feeling in his heart. The ground was rising from the snow, the snow sinking back down to the layer of frost that lived five meters under his feet. A day for snowflowers if you were looking for them. Nowek was not.

He saw Galena. A face in a porthole, excited, her future opening up before her in a way she could not have dreamed.

The Air Alaska jet moved away from the dilapidated concrete terminal building at Irkutsk. Clean and brightly painted, it turned up its polished nose at the ranks of abandoned Aeroflot planes parked along the concrete.

He saw Yuri out there, working alongside his men as they assembled a whole new Antonov from pieces of three; gray fuselage met white tail and blue wing. Several engines sat nearby, black steel masses trailing wires and hoses and leaving a snail's trace of oil from the planes they'd been taken from.

Who owned the wrecks they were stripping? Nowek smiled at the innocence of his question. Forget ownership. This was the New Russia. Who controlled it was what counted, and looking from up here, who controlled it was Yuri and his partner, Plet.

A wing seemed to fly itself across the ramp as five men balanced it on top of their heads and walked it to the new *Annushka.* Ants, thought Nowek, at a picnic.

Antonovs, Illyushins, Tupolevs, engineless, some missing a wing, a tail, cannibalized for parts so that a few lucky stitched-together survivors might fly.

He was like that, too. Pieced together from parts, from different lives. Old and new, and where they joined the sutures still were raw, they still bled.

The jet carrying Anna and Galena taxied out to the single runway.

"So," he said to Chuchin. "Have you thought about it? Driving for the new mayor pays a salary."

"What?" Chuchin turned to put his good ear in the line of Nowek's mouth. The shattered eardrum, said the doctors, would never heal. It was why, Chuchin replied, he had two. He leaned in close.

"Driving for Mayor Nikitin. You know the job well enough. Why not accept it? It's not like you have a better offer."

Chuchin still wore a bandage over the spot where the steel had been embedded. His new sunglasses betrayed nothing, but Nowek could see in the subtle folds and twitches of his expression what he thought of the idea. "You want to be rid of me?"

"Of course not. But the new mayor needs a driver like you. Someone who can keep him out of trouble. Besides, someone has to do it."

"Then let someone else drive him. I'm busy." Chuchin drew on the filthy Yava, then spat out a long stream of foul smoke.

"Doing what?"

The jet's engines screamed. Black smoke rose at the end of the runway, a miniature thundercloud. The landing lights blinked on like two hot eyes. The air shimmered. The jet began to roll.

The plane roared by, drowning them in noise. It ramped up, its wheels disappeared. It started a long, gradual bank out over Lake Baikal, heading north by east.

"It seems to me," said Chuchin as the jet became a dot, flashed in the hot sun, then went dark, "that even if you don't need a driver, you still need someone to tell you which way to go."

"I'm not going anywhere." He watched the plane. "That's part of the problem."

"Today. What about tomorrow? Speaking frankly, you could use my help."

Speaking frankly, he could use a plane ticket. Nowek was following the jet as it merged, blue on blue with the sky above the lake. Aluminum, flesh, blood, and love of two very different kinds melted into the air above the Sacred Sea. Billowy white clouds massed over the mountains, thinking about thunder.

"So?" said Chuchin, "what do you say? Am I your driver or not?"

"Where I'm going, there may not be any roads."

"Who needs a road?" Chuchin spat out the Yava and mashed it into the filthy concrete. "We're Siberians, you and me. People like us, all we need is a direction."

Nowek noticed a piece of patterned stone. A spot among the drab chunks of concrete. He picked it up.

Schist, a metamorphic rock derived from the collision of sediment shale with the fiery blast of basalt. Old and new joined into something else, something different, a third way. Minor keys, major keys. Dark as graphite, bright as quartz, its minerals squeezed into parallel bands of black, white, and silver. A random piece of Siberia. And yet . . .

Stare at nothing long enough and it transforms itself into something. He put it in his pocket.

"Don't worry. I won't ask for a raise."

"In that case," said Nowek, "you're hired."

A direction. Forward. A direction, and a future.

He followed Chuchin to the idling car.